# Arrival

## Written By Marie Daley

Copyright © Marie Daley August 17, 2022
Cover by: germancreative
ISBN: 978-1733184823
LCCN:

# Dedication

To my gaming friends who are all so very dear to me!
GM's Bob, Timar, Lou, Mick, and Tom D.
And fellow Adventurers:  Dan, Seth, Tim, Mick, Tom H,
Jeanine, Alex, James, Paul, and from before, TJ, Marty,
Ryan, Keith, Lisa, Brian, Gwen, Heather, and Ellen.
We've been solving riddles and surviving mythic battles
for decades!

**Game On!**

## The Adventures of Ryes and Garth

Tayna's Dawn

Winterhaven

Winds of Change

Striding Forth

Rescue!

Arrival

# A Word About Space Travel

Yes, I am aware that you truly cannot travel between star systems by current knowledge and technology. I'm doing what SF writers have done for decades, treating space travel as if it were no more involved than a trip across our Earth's vast oceans.

In ages past, ocean travel was thought of as impossible, and now we regularly fly from one point on our planet to another on another continent with little thought. So, even if Fold Engines do not exist in our current reality, and I have no idea if they will be the answer to a form of travel we will take in the future, they are what I have settled upon for my books. They make far more sense than warp drives.

We've been told that space can bend. That our planetary masses do make gravity "pockets" in the "fabric" of space, and change the shape of space, itself. So, a Fold engine would "grasp" that fabric with a kind of gravity field and pull a large segment of space into an enormously large fold, the ship's engines would then "jump" the folded part of space to come out far from their starting point (after the engine lets go of the fold). So, the relative time to get from one point in space to another is very short compared to travelling in a conventional manner that would take generations for a simple voyage.

I'm offering my apologies to anyone who objects to the use of Fold engines in my stories, but it's currently my best working model of space travel that I can come up with, at this time. And at least we don't have the concerns expressed by other fictional characters from other SF books, where they use hyper drive engines.

# Table of Contents

# Whatever It Takes

## Prelude

"You do not need to constantly keep your eyes to the scan screens, when on duty.  You will develop a way to keep them in your sight peripherally, if you need to look away for a moment," Corsley of House Muratha gently chided Julie Larson, who was sitting at the main scanner board on Flutter-wing.  She'd started her duties here last week, but still appeared unsure of herself.  She looked up to him a little round-eyed, but gave him a nod in understanding.

"This is my first time being wholly responsible for a board.  I'll figure it out," she admitted as she blushed.  Corsley loved the blend of her features, knowing she was a starman-human cross from Booda.  Her blue eyes were alluring, and she appeared an artful balance between the two peoples.

"What did you do before coming here?" he asked, to draw her out and get her to relax; she seemed very young, not in years, but in life experiences.  He resisted using his Mind Voice to get answers directly.  Winterhaven practiced strict policies concerning Talent use, and he knew he wasn't ready to see the brutality she must've faced on that forsaken moon.  He knew so many of the Boodans suffered night terrors usually involving their former lives.

"In Winterhaven?  Or where I came from?" she asked, puzzled, as he was studying her face.  It was often the way others acted around the crosses, and she was past letting such behavior get to her by now.

"Both?" he asked as he took the empty second's chair beside her. "We are going to be working together and I am curious," he admitted as he smiled encouragement.  It was a slow day, so they had time.  She drew in a breath and gave him a nod.

"In Winterhaven, Max trained me to help in the control room and seemed very happy with my work, so supported my move up to Flutter-wing," she told him, smiling now, seeing in his eyes he was genuinely curious about her past.  He gave her a nod in understanding.  They were short on skilled people in Winterhaven, but this was an important post, too.

"If Max thinks you should be here, then that is a high recommendation.  And you have been doing a good job, from what I have seen," he assured her, as he smiled again.  She smiled in return, her blue eyes lighting up from within at his compliment. "And what did you do before that?" he pressed, wanting to be sure, loving the bright spirit awaking in her eyes.

"I was born on Booda, the third moon of Tyssen. When I was younger, I helped my parents with the gardens, then helped to care for the young crosses as I got older. It was heartbreaking at times, since not many lived long, but I was there to provide comfort and care as long, as possible. Not much, when compared to what I can do - all by myself - now," she finished, appearing more confident. "And you? You seem amazingly comfortable with this space station, as if you've lived here all your life." He chuckled in response, giving her a nod. It was a fair question.

"I was brought out of the fires of Hailys' destruction by Ryes and our strong Talent team, so am used to Tayna of old. I worked in Central Control for Hailys but had been at Nazaneen Starport to see my brother and his wife off to Kisteela for a family vacation. They never made it; I saw them crushed in an instant, right before my eyes," he related, his mind was immersed in the horror of that day for a few moments, the memories still horrific. Julie was saddened, unable to imagine it, and yet didn't want to see it for herself, knowing it would break her heart. She put a hand on his shoulder in comfort. He looked up and met her eyes, seeing her caring, and how she helped him back from his inner abyss.

"Corsley, we have an alert update from the Challenger, and they want to talk to you," Briel of House Jukoo stated flatly, not as curious about the new scan tech. She recalled he asked about her past too, when they were first brought up to the empty space station. She'd lived Hailys and was rescued at the time he was, too. She used to work in the business offices of the starport and knew only pure luck had saved her life the day of the attack. Corsley gave her a nod as he snapped back to the present and stood to return to his post, being he was the Station Chief for Space Station Flutter-wing. He put on the primitive headset, returned to his station, and tuned in. Maren had removed his neural net when they were processed at Winterhaven, after being pulled in from the past, and it frustrated him at times.

"Flutter-wing here, Corsley speaking," he commed.

"Hi Corsley, it's Axel. We have an update for you on those inbound Earth ships. It's confirmed they're due to arrive an hour before lunch today," he informed him on the vid.

"What are the standing orders?" he pressed, wanting to be sure. He used to work in the command center for Hailys as third officer, so this small station was in no way as complex. Usually, it was a completely boring duty. Still, he wasn't completely comfortable with so few defenses set up for the station; they were vulnerable. Phil assured him better defensive capabilities were in the plans for Flutter-wing's next expansion, but he was never given a date. He hoped it'd be soon.

"We'll invite them to dock there for a while, so be ready for company. We don't know how they'll behave, so keep an eye to protecting the secure areas, and our people. Shawn will be arriving shortly with some added staff to lend you a hand, food, and supplies you'll need for the larger population," he informed him. Corsley gave him a nod in relief, glad someone was on top of it.

"We will take care of it," he confidently assured him.

"Have their officers assist in policing their own people, too. That'll help give you a breather. See if you can come up with some good do's and don'ts to advise them about. We're leaving it up to you, if you want to lease any guest rooms for the crews to use, or not. Remember, it's our station, not theirs! And don't hesitate to call for help, or advice, if needed. We're all here for you," Axel offered.

"I will handle it, but appreciate the back-up," Corsley stated with confidence and a nod. A smile finally showed on his face. "After hosting a diplomatic party of Vastins, this will be easy," he bragged. Axel laughed and gave him a nod, with unvoiced questions in his eyes.

"It's why we thought you were the best one to head up this command," he replied. "Call us, or Winterhaven, if you need anything."

"Your confidence is very appreciated. We will be ready to receive our guests. Anything else we should know?" he pressed.

"Ryes is concerned that their Talents may not be very polite, so feel free to intervene, as needed," Axel added. Corsley nodded with another smile.

"My specialty! It will be fine. We will do whatever it takes!"

"Thanks! Anything you need from us right now?" He shook his head in response. Axel nodded. "Then over and out. Challenger on standby," he responded and cut the communication.

"What's a Vastin?" Julie asked with a frown, as she swiveled to face him. Corsley laughed, as did Briel, but it wasn't derisive laughter. Other people working in the command center appeared curious, too.

"They were a large, belligerent people, who smelled horrible and believe the whole universe owes them whatever they fancy, in any given moment. They were good warriors though, and a good people to have at your side in a fight," Briel explained with a merry light in her golden eyes.  Julie smiled in response and gave them a nod.

"Sounds like we could use a few with us now," she replied.

"Truly, we could," Corsley agreed.

"Incoming shuttle from Winterhaven," Julie chimed, seeing the tell-tale, turning back to her board, and recognizing it. "Shawn's almost here."

"Good man; good pilot," Corsley assured her.  She smiled and gave him a nod. "Now to get the station buttoned down for this friendly visit by potential allies.  We will all be on the alert and take nothing for granted," he ordered.  He turned for his own board and set to work.  The others here in the control center would handle the mundane tasks, for which he was grateful.  Still, he stole a glance at Julie, as she focused upon her console once again.  He smiled as he thought of getting to know her better during their next free time together.  She was a curiosity he wanted to explore.

# Flutter-Wing

## Chapter 1

Very early spring last year, seven Matlowe Villagers set out for the great ruins of Hailys because Sabin was banished for six months for killing a cub-killer; giving the elders time to collect evidence of the dead man's guilt – one way or the other – to affirm if justice had been served. It also allowed these villagers to escape Maren's father, Korman, who'd been known to kill others in challenges. Garth wasn't going to ever let Korman get his claws on Ryes, and she didn't want him to get his claws on Garth. During their journey they found the Temple of Doran and her evilness, but Ryes bested her in a Talent battle, which was partly a within contest of wills, as well as a physical assault. During the battle, Ryes' own Talents opened fully. Afterwards, they discovered Hailys and the treasures that could be gleaned from their people's technologically advanced past. Garth beat Korman in a challenge in Hailys, when Korman found them there. After leaving Hailys, they found a deserted, human research facility, which they named Winterhaven. Later, while Garth and Sabin were away to settle a peace treaty, Ryes called down a derelict, human, colony transport ship, the Star Quest, which was from Earth. She and Maren saved what few humans remained onboard in suspension tubes. Since then, the two peoples discovered they could meld; being of one heart in truth and later found they could actually interbreed; a first for both peoples. Now they wanted to build a secure future for them all. And it'd been foreseen they were destined to conquer the Snagospin, the dark enemy who destroyed Tayna's cities over three-hundred years ago. Being planet-bound, they only need a way to reach them! They had the Talents, determination, and heart to try.

"Hurry up, Ryes, this way," Mitt urged, climbing over a rocky outcropping between them and the area she was targeting, leading down into the vast bowl of sunken land.

"I don't go out as often as I used to," she returned in complaint, grinning to herself. She may work out at the gym three times a week, but the area around Winterhaven was level ground with no hills to constantly climb. It'd taken an unforeseen toll upon her body, apparently. She crested the outcropping shortly thereafter, getting a view of where Mitt was headed. She resisted the temptation to "fly" herself out to it ahead of her, feeling it'd be cheating herself, more than anyone else. So, she trotted down the hill, with Jim and Monty trailing her. They were her bodyguards today.

"Hey Mitt, slow up a little," Monty called out, panting, as he tried to keep up. He hadn't known how out of shape he was until now. It was embarrassing!

"Ah, you're just a bunch of slow pads," she teased in response, laughing merrily at the three of them and the way this little jaunt had them all huffing and puffing like Aric's bellows.

"I wish your aunt had come out with us. She wouldn't be doing this, if she were along," Jim commented, catching up to Ryes, as she'd slowed to a walk again. Ryes shook her head, her breathing finally returning to normal once more.

"I know she can outrun us all, but Hadu would easily outpace her," she agreed. "And Adina could probably pace her. Mitt just loves to torture me and unfortunately, you guys get to suffer too. Sorry."

"That's all right; I can use the exercise," Monty assured her, grinning as he walked on her other side. They finally caught up with Mitt, as she stood waiting.

"Now, let me check to make sure this is the spot," she said, looking to Ryes with a mischievous grin. Ryes chuckled as she nodded her head. She closed her eyes, calling up her full range of Talents. Mitt gripped her hand, then tapped Empath, delving below to see if this was where she saw, what she thought she saw, when they looked at this site from Winterhaven with the machine generated scans. Very quickly she had her answer.

"They're here, below us," Ryes breathed, opening her eyes with wonder playing in their emerald depths. Mitt still had hers closed, getting a better look at what lay in the pit, way below them.

"Are you sure you can do this?" Monty questioned, doubting her ability to deal with what they wanted to attempt, as he understood it.

"We're going to try and keep trying until we succeed. We need them desperately, especially to save the Earth," she replied, then closed her eyes to view things now through Mitt's Talent, too.

"Let's do it," Mitt urged in sending. Ryes gave her an affirmative.

"Let's start from up here and tunnel down," Ryes suggested, then focused both Earth Shaper and Manipulator fully, while keeping Empath up so they could "see" it all.

"I want to go up from below," Mitt insisted. They reached down into the pocket created by the tumble of the beams and other

13

debris, then started shoving the dirt and debris upwards from below. There was a lot of resistance, so Ryes pulled her Talents back, cutting Mitt off from them, seeing her determination to keep trying, using her idea.

"I told you, we need to clear it from the surface first, or we'll just bury them deeper in soil, trying from below," she scolded, with humor in her mental voice.

"Alright," Mitt gave in and calmed, ceding her point, then extended Ryes' Talents to the surface over the target area, causing the soil, plants, and debris to shower down on the far side of her intended hole, away from them and the two men guarding them. Ryes then started depositing the metal beams, plates, strange machines, and other interesting items in separate piles, knowing they could use them later. This amused Mitt as she kept up in her efforts to tunnel down, as quickly as possible. After what seemed an eternity, they finally broke through to the cavern below. Ryes was feeling excited, as she worked to widen the opening and preventing as much of the debris, as possible, from falling back into the cavern with Earth Shaper. She diverted it to the surface discard piles.

"There, that's it," she reported, opening her eyes. Mitt opened hers too and grinned merrily.

"Come on, let's go have a real look at `em," Mitt urged, letting go of Ryes and running toward the edge of the enormous, deep, dark hole they created. She stopped as she peered down into the seemingly endless darkness.

"Do you think any of that death dust might be down there?" Jim asked, following Ryes over and looking into the massive, gaping dark pit at their feet. Somehow, he imagined it as smelling of old death, like a dark, spooky grave of gigantic proportions.

"That's quite a pile of scrap metal. Kovin's going to appreciate it," Monty commented, grinning. The hole below looked scary to his eyes, and smelled of old, tainted air.

"He's not getting it all. I have other projects in mind and need some of it, too," Mitt returned, smiling as she looked to Ryes again. She then turned back to the pit, activating a small light she brought along. "And we'll check on that death dust."

"There was a reason you brought us out here in the Avenger, instead of a chopper, wasn't there?" Ryes questioned, shaking her head, as she realized the true reason Mitt wanted her out here for this effort today.

"Actually, there were a couple of reasons," she replied. "I wish my light could actually illuminate down there," she added, as she turned off her handheld lantern feeling slightly frustrated.

"You're not thinking of going down there?" Jim pressed, worried for them all in such a venture. He looked like he didn't want to go into that dark descent, at all.

"No, I'm going to be using Ryes' Talents, again," she assured him, smiling. "Ready Sis?" Ryes sighed as she gave her a nod of her head, knowing she was a resource. She smiled as she sat down in the tall grasses, and closed her eyes, relaxing more fully for this part, knowing it'd be a deeper pull on her Talents and energy. The sweet smell of the crushed grasses filled her senses, minding her of her younger days in Matlowe, even if those younger days hadn't been that long ago.

"Alright, Mitt, now I'm ready," she affirmed. Mitt sat down next to her, closing her eyes, and taking her hand.

First, Mitt fully opened her own Inner Sight, then melded with Ryes once more, tapping her Inner Sight, too. They reached down to the ancient space craft, which lay far below. First, Mitt checked the general designs, being well familiar with the Star Quest, the shuttles, and the human's fighter craft. These were quite different, but still rang "true" to her Talent. The ships, which were in the launch pit, were fighter craft, so they must've been trying to launch them to fight the Snagospin, at the very end. Many ships were crushed, or in pieces, having been blasted apart. This pit was far deeper than the rest of the starport, and both women wondered about it. Then Mitt started an examination of the engines. Alarms went off in their heads.

"They're WRONG!" Ryes declared, astounded. "How can they be so wrong, when Inner Sight is reputed to be an old Talent from Kahmarr? Why would they ever make them that way?"

"I've no idea, but we're not bringing those cursed things up out of that pit. The radiation will kill everyone who's near them. Let me use your Molecular and Manipulator Talents, then see if we can make this one, which I like, safe. It looks like a ship ready to do battle. They must've had a way to remove the engines for repairs, so once it's clean, I'm breaking it free from that power source and the engines, and it'll be lighter," she asserted, panic in her heart as she wondered if they were truly within a safe range to the radioactives, even now? There were quite a few spaceships down below, both intact and broken!

"Monty, check the area for radiation!" she sent him, as Ryes opened her full range of Talents for their use again. He was surprised by her order, but quickly grasped the situation.  He took the small scan unit from her belt and activated it.

"It's all right, but is a little higher than normal, background stuff.  We shouldn't stay here too much longer without donning suits from the shuttle to protect us," he reported, using his own Talent.  He looked to Jim and showed him what the scanner read.  He understood, nodding in response, having "heard" both Mitt and Monty, as they weren't narrowly focusing their conversation, and he was beside them.  It was a handy Talent at times, wishing he had it, too.  It was times like this he actually missed the neural net Maren removed.

"Let's hurry," Mitt urged.  She used Ryes' Molecular Talent and had the radioactive materials changed to inert molecules, as well as neutralized the death dust in the whole area of the pit and buildings around it, as well as the ships.  She reached over with her own Talent next, finding the connectors which secured the drive engines and reactor to the target ship.  She carefully opened them, using Ryes' Manipulator.  Once she had them released, she took a quick estimation of the remaining mass.  She realized between Ryes and the Avenger, they just might make it, and removing the engines had lightened the load a lot, but it was a big ship!

"What're you plotting?" Ryes demanded, wanting to know ahead of time, hating to guess, and she wasn't going to peek.

"We're lifting one of those ships out of here today.  My season starts in a few days, and I want one of these beauties secured, before I'm forced to stay home for a while," she told her, mentally smiling as she thought of having her own cub.  She didn't want to take the time from her work, but she wanted her own child, to pass her Talents onto.  Somehow, she knew she and Minn would make it work out.  Axel had faith in her, too.  Ryes opened her eyes, as she recalled what she went through last year, and was still trying to juggle her children, and the work she found she enjoyed in Winterhaven.  She also had faith in Mitt's abilities to work things out, and she let her know it.  Mitt returned with a merry feeling of thanks for her open-hearted support.

"Let's get back to the Avenger," Ryes told her, sighing as she dropped out of the meld.  She knew she'd need her Talents to get this buried ship out, once more.  Monty helped her to her feet as she smiled her thanks for him.  Mitt jumped up before Jim could give her a hand.  She was all smiles, too.

"Come on you slow pads, the day's wasting!"  With this, she trotted back the way they came, grinning as she glanced back to see the remaining three with humor on their faces, watching her.

"And the day's not over, yet," Ryes added, grinning as she started to trot, following her sister-in-law's path.  After a good forty

16

minutes of climbing and jogging, they reached the Avenger. Mitt already had her lifting rig out and ready, by the time they arrived.

"Took you long enough," she commented, smiling merrily.

"Now I know why you made the field ball team," Jim teased, panting as he tried to catch his breath. Mitt laughed and gave him a nod.

"Let's get aboard, before she makes us run back, again," Ryes suggested, laughing and grimacing. They boarded and Mitt took the pilot's seat, as Monty sealed the hatches.

"What's the plan?" Jim asked, wanting to know, even if he felt he could guess it already. He was only skeptical what he suspected she was planning could be pulled off.

"We're lifting out one of the old starships. I'm going to need Ryes to help with the lift. After she shoved Flutter-wing off from Booda, I know she can do it," she replied, already heading the Avenger toward the hole they created.

"Wait, I do have limits and that thing's huge, way bigger than Flutter-wing," Ryes reminded her, taking the copilot's seat and strapping in. The men strapped into the seats behind them.

"I know, but if you stretch out and try, I know you can do the impossible! Besides, the Avenger and Defender will be taking most of the weight. I put in a call to Axel, and he should be here any moment," she informed her, grinning with a mischievous light in her dark brown eyes. Ryes looked exasperated as she saw the telltale indicating the Defender approaching.

"I'm here," Axel told them, over the radio. "Getting into position."

"Roger that," Mitt told him, smiling, as she joined him.

"What about the radiation?" Jim pressed, not wanting the area around Winterhaven contaminated.

"We already have converted the radioactives to inert material for this ship. We tested Ryes' new Talent on the Star Quest and the current shuttles and fighters, and if there's anything left, Ryes can take care of it later today. Axel and I are planning on putting her down on the far side of the Quest for now, which is well away from our apartments. So, relax and enjoy the trip," she urged as she maneuvered into position. Axel set the Defender into the position she told him to take, the towing cables were dangling below them, all ready. "Ryes, as I direct," she ordered.

Ryes gave her a nod and closed her eyes, doing as Mitt instructed. She extended her Talents down, pulling what was left of the great ship up and away from its shut-down reactor and drive engines. Once she had it high enough, she pulled the dangling cables over to it and attached them to the hull, as she saw was set up on its original design, which was meant to accommodate being moved this way. Still, she saw the weight was too great for the tiny shuttles to bear, so clamped onto the ship with her Talents firmly, urging Mitt and Axel to get moving - FAST! After a few moments, she realized she couldn't fight Tayna anymore. Cold sweat was pouring down her body, as she strained to hold it aloft.

"You can let it go, but gently," Mitt told her, as she was about to do so, anyway. As well as she could, she released it to Tayna's keeping, hoping her action wouldn't pull the shuttles down out of the sky; not having realized they had released their cables already, and she was the only one keeping it now a few inches above the ground.

"Good job!" Axel said, over the radio. "It looks like we're starting our own spaceship junk yard," he added, as he laughed merrily. Both shuttle pilots returned the shuttles to their hangar landing pads.

"Well, I guess we have to start somewhere," Mitt told him, as she was going through her shutdown procedures. She got more of his laughter in response. Ryes looked to have fallen asleep. She hoped she was all right, knowing the strain it put upon her to do this operation.

"I'll get her over to Maren for a quick check," Jim volunteered, standing behind Ryes' seat, releasing her restraints, swiveled the seat, then picked her up.

"Wait. I'll go along to explain things, and even if our radiation exposure was minimal, I want Maren to check all of us out, first. I don't want any errors here," she replied, all business. Monty could clearly see Garth in her, when she acted this way. He smiled as he gave her a nod of agreement.

"Especially, with your season due soon," he quipped back, merrily. She laughed at this, then got up from her seat, leading them off the ship.

"Most especially because of that," she agreed, under her breath.

18

"That is why the dampening fields were so strong," Adina explained, as she and Hadu sat at the table with them for dinner, instead of eating at a table of their own, as they usually dined. Ryes had moved her into one of the larger spare bedroom downstairs, with Hadu sleeping outside her door, in the hall. This had distressed Ryes, but he wouldn't be dissuaded from sleeping on the floor in that spot, so she provided him with a simple sleeping mat, which he accepted and used, per her request.

"At least we removed the danger, since we converted the isotopes to inert matter for this ship, before we retrieved her yesterday. We'll work on the new power plant and engines soon," Mitt stated. Ryes was busy feeding her cubs, as she gave a nod of her head in agreement, glancing over to briefly meet her eyes, smiling, before wiping up Shyla's face. The cub loved to dribble out her food as a game now.

"Converted the radioactive isotopes? How?" Adina questioned, puzzled, wondering what equipment they might have used. This settlement was far from any true starports and the advanced decontamination equipment they'd have available to use in a real facility. Did they already retrieve that equipment from Hailys?

"Ryes' new fiftieth Talent, Molecular Manipulator," she replied, as if it were widely known already. She glanced over at Ryes, giving her a smile, and fully missed the startled shock on Adina's face, and the intent interest in Hadu's. No one else appeared surprised with her simple response.

"So, you think we'll be able to take the drive system from the Star Quest and install it into... What did you call it?" Ethan requested, wondering if they mentioned a name for the new ship yet, or not? He'd noted Adina's shock and was amused. There was light laughter around the table, as Ryes shook her head.

"We're still kicking that one around," she told him, smiling as she wiped Gareth's chin and neck. "The names gleaned so far are: the Last Defender, the Pit Viper, the Late to Launch, the Digger, the Mole, and the Half-pint Folly. We're just getting to know her; we'll come up with her name in time," she assured him.

"Since we already have the Sand Burrower, why not call her the Digger?" Maren piped in, chuckling as he did so.

"What was her original name, since she was a true ship before, and not a shuttle?" Adina questioned, pointedly.

"The Pike Forward," Mitt replied, still wondering what it meant.

19

"Ah, it is an ancient battle strategy.  To put the pikemen forward, to take the brunt of the first charge of the enemy calvary upon their great shields with long spears held between shields to damage all they could.  Usually, the archers stood behind them, to reduce the numbers of the attackers," she explained, delighted to see everyone paying her attention in this moment, "It was for ground-based battles from ancient times."

"Then maybe we should keep her name the same, only add it on in English, so everyone will be able to read it," Garth suggested, smiling at this simple decision.  It was a proper warship name after all.

"Who here cannot already read Dolbith?" Adina pressed in return, sounding exasperated.  She noted most things here were labeled in both languages, throughout the whole facility.  It was curious to her mind, and she needed to understand their reasons.

"The humans who'll be coming from Earth; if they can break through the blockade and reach us.  They may, or may not, want to learn Dolbith, and we might not want to teach all of them our language.  We've no idea what our enemy's numbers are in the vastness of space between us and Earth's Sol system," Ryes explained, meeting her eyes. "And we don't know what these new humans will be like, with having to live with this terrible war, and murderous aliens, for some years, already."

"Dr. Cruthers, do you know how this will affect our rank and assignment in the military?" Bitty suddenly questioned, appearing concerned.  She now sat across from Mitt and her family, feeling that as long as they allowed it, someone from their group off the Star Quest, which had been pulled out of the past by Ryes, should have firsthand knowledge of what was happening.  She found mealtimes were never boring with these people, and she rather enjoyed the warm banter.  She felt as if she'd found a new family in this mix of starmen and humans.

"Your contract with Earth forces has expired quite some years ago, and they will have you listed as dead, or missing.  It'll be up to you and your friends, Bitty, if you wish to make a new contract with them, or not.  The captains can reactivate you out of retirement, but then the length of that service is limited to one standard Earth year. You may still have family back on the worlds you originated, but until this matter with the Snagospin is settled, I wouldn't advise you trying to reach them.  You'll only cause yourself, and others, grief," he advised, seeing the hope, then understanding in her eyes.

"I can imagine we're so far out of date with the technology by now, that we'd be looked upon as colonial hicks," she returned, smiling tightly, as her stomach was now a lead lump.

"You think that's bad?  Amitell no longer exists, so we'll never see our last paychecks," Dotti teased, smiling, "At least with the Fleet, you still have a chance, even if you can't spend Terran credits here."

"Then I'll take mine in bags of coffee beans," she quipped back, grinning as she thought on it.

"Amen to that!" Justin agreed with a chuckle.  Their supply of coffee had dwindled down to the point where Chuck only served it at breakfast, two days a week.  It'd become a precious commodity in Winterhaven.

"We have a few coffee plants growing in our greenhouse, but they're growing slowly," Ethan sighed out in agreement. "The native tea mixes are all right, but not the same as my favorite beverage."

"At least we found a replacement for your tobacco, even if I think it's something you should quit," Ryes reminded him, smiling at the change in the look in his eyes.  She and Teris had altered the plants to be far less toxic, so wasn't sure if he truly like it, or not.  Ethan's eyes did brighten as he recalled this one, small blessing, giving her a nod in gratitude.

"So, once we get the Pike Forward ready for flight, we'll have some real firepower at our disposal," Maren commented, glad they had found the ship yesterday, after all. "How many usable ships are still out there?"  Mitt gave him a shrug of her shoulders and shook her head, appearing not to know.  "Yesterday's focus was to find one, not take a deeper survey," she minded him.

"We still need some weapons with greater power and range," Garth spoke up, thinking on an idea which came to his mind.  He'd have to ask his wife about it, later.  If they could retrieve this one ship, why not others?  And he wasn't thinking of the wrecks still resting in that pit in Hailys.  They only needed the time to do a proper search.

"You want me to go out and look for her?" she asked Garth, dumbfounded by his complete faith in her abilities.

"She existed, once.  Why not?  You know her," he assured her, confident she could do this task.  Ryes sighed as she sat down on the couch next to him.  The cubs were asleep, and since it was the weekend, Sayer and Raby were spending the night with Matissa, who was one of the Boodan girls, and Katas, over at Ardis and Sabin's.  Dotti had told them about the sleep-over parties she had, or went to,

21

when she was their age.  They took to it immediately.  Ardis commented that she doubted any of them would get any sleep.  But at least their younger cubs were sound asleep.

"And you want me to try it now?" she questioned, meeting his eyes.  He smiled down to her.

"Why not?  It's quiet tonight.  Your aunt and Hadu are visiting the Sleepers and all the cubs are either asleep, or gone," he pressed.  She finally smiled as she sighed her surrender, putting her book aside.

"Alright, but I don't feel safe extending beyond our solar system, still for you, I'll try," she assured him, "I can't get used to calling our sun Monrush.  Beda, as the humans called it, sounds so much better."

"For far too long, it was merely `the sun' to us.  But, if we want to expand out on a cosmic scale, we do need to start granting it a proper name and it was called Monrush, long before it was named Beda by the humans," he chided her.

"I don't know about that.  We'll have to delve back into Earth history, to be sure," she quipped back, smiling impishly.  He laughed at this, then nodded his head.

"But it's our sun, so our name," he teased in return.  She relaxed now, so it was time to try.  Ryes then closed her eyes, calling up her Talents.  Garth called up his Empath, then melded his consciousness with hers tapping her Mind Voice.

Ryes didn't waste any time as she opened her own Empath, pulled her husband along as she leapt up and outwards, streaking first to the remains of the colony upon Booda.  She saw there was little left now, as the salvage crews had already stripped out what was useful, leaving behind only what wasn't important enough to justify bringing back to Tayna, and the remote, computer-operated "listening" post.  It was another small link in their network for advance detection.  If necessary, it could also be used as a decoy, if the Snagospin took an interest in Tayna.

She then reached out to touch Beda, itself, as if to fix the feel of her home sun firmly within all her senses.  Now she turned out to face the stars, which beckoned beyond.

"Monrush," he teasingly reminded her. "Go to where that battle was being fought, which you showed us in the challenge you issued," Garth suggested, thinking it was a good starting point.

Ryes understood and extended her consciousness in that direction, feeling its location almost instinctively from within.  She wondered at what Doran had tried to do to her, so that what were only shadows of memories from the men Doran captured and consumed, still influenced her own senses and Talent so strongly?

"But, if it's helped us, why worry now? She has no power over you," her husband assured her, feeling her inner turmoil clearly.

"They were the essences of others," she replied, "Isn't it like stealing small pieces of those people?"

"Think of it as preserving the memory of who they were, what they did, and how they lived. You honor them, not deride them, as she was wont," he responded, feeling this was the right way to view it. She realized he was right, as she neared the place of the battle, noting the position of the stars around them.

There was a cold, alien presence nearby, but it hadn't noted them yet. She stayed well away from it, as she began a light, sweeping search for any of the ships which had participated in that ancient battle. She found small clumps of twisted metal and pieces of what might have been ships' hulls, drifting about the system.

"I don't think we're going to find any of the ships intact," she warned, expanding her search outwards, while keeping a sense of that cold presence, as well as where her own sun lay. It was so tiny and distant! Suddenly, almost as it was now attached, a slowly rotating asteroid swung past with the remains of a huge starship, almost wrapped around it.

"That's her! That's the Challenger!" Sabin clearly declared, letting Ryes know he'd joined them. She'd been so distracted with trying to keep an eye to everything else around her, she never felt him joining their commune, as Garth had.

"It's her," Garth agreed. "Let's get a closer look, inside," he suggested, wanting to know how extensive the damage truly was. Ryes got over her initial surprise and sent her agreement. She realized her Aunt Adina and Hadu were also a part of the group, too. She approached the ship, passing through the hull. She called up her Inner Sight, wishing hers was as strong as Mitt's.

"I will call her over," Adina told her, amused as she noted Ryes was surprised at the offer.

"Thank you," she replied, as she examined what she could of the ship. She realized the hull was still intact and that it was merely grappled to the chunk of planet debris, not crashed into it. The rock had a massive groove, which the ship fit into, very well. She didn't know if this was due to some effort to camouflage it, or further

23

protect it?  Maybe both?  Suddenly, Mitt joined her, calling up her own Inner Sight to get a look at the Challenger, herself.

"Clever," she commented, as she noted the deception involving the asteroid.  She delved into the systems, now familiar with their basic designs from the Pike.

"There's still power!" Sabin noted, seeing what Mitt discovered.  Ryes projected herself upon the bridge, striding over to the engineering post and using Manipulator Talent, at Mitt's direction. After several long minutes, she had the ship's systems powering up. Mitt then saw the damage to the drives and understood why she was secured as such.  It was serving as a temporary dry dock for the great craft.

"Program a course to bring her into orbit around Tayna.  Tell her to dock at Flutter-wing," Garth instructed, seeing what Mitt saw, that she was still capable of limited flight.  It might be slow, but it was better than nothing.  Ryes called up the star charts, noting where Beda lay.

"It's Monrush, remember?" Sabin teased her this time.

"Well, here it's a number, so I can still think of it as Beda," she returned, amused.  There was inner laughter from the others at her retort.  She set the coordinates as Mitt instructed, seeing more lights registering blue now.  Then, something within the machinery was responding to her Talent.  Could the computer detect Talent? How could a machine register its presence?

"The pilots and higher officers all were required to have Talent," Adina informed her. "Now I understand why.  Maybe the computer, as you call it, does require the presence of the right type of Talent to function?" she suggested, not quite sure on this matter.

"What do I do?" she returned, puzzled now.

"Use your Inner Sight and reassure it you're a starman," Garth told her, hoping.  She gave her acknowledgment to him, then turned to do so.

"I felt its affirmative.  If I hadn't done it, it would've self-destructed," she told them.  Mitt checked, seeing she was correct. The computer acknowledged her presence too, giving her a chill. "I guess it's to deter thieves," Ryes teased her. "Do you think I'm going to need a constant contact with it?"

"No, but you should probably check in with it several times a day, to let it know you're still around," Mitt suggested, feeling from her Talent that this was correct.  They saw the ship releasing herself

24

from the asteroid, her engines were now online and thrusting her on her course.

"Oh fine, chained to a machine again!" she retorted, smiling to herself as she realized it was something new to add to her schedule, for a few weeks at least. Even for being crippled, it travelled fast, as she called up her fold engine and jumped across to be far closer already.

"Garth, did you notice? This is our ship!" Sabin sent, trying to contain his excitement at his discovery – just like in his Vision!

"You're right! This is the ship! We're going to be piloting her out on her first voyage, as our own," he agreed, after having looked at the pilot's seat, as if viewing it for the first time.

"I thought the captain sat in his own chair," Ryes teased, "Or do you want to play crew and let me be her captain?"

"The captain had better know every bolt of his own ship and piloting her out on her maiden voyage, himself, is only making sure he can handle her, if he ever has to!" he retorted, humor in his mental tones, having learned it from human military traditions and stories on record here. "You only get to be her captain over my dead body."

"That means never," she quipped back, teasing him in return. "Time to return," she reminded them, pulling back from the Challenger, noting she wobbled a little in flight. "Maybe we should rename her The Flutter-wing II?"

"No! We'll get her back into shape. You'll see," Garth assured her, still excited over finally finding the ship from Sabin's Vision. Ryes didn't feel as happy, until she again touched Beda, then streaked on towards home.

"Let's go back and check on Flutter-wing," Mitt suggested, getting an idea. She pulled Ryes and the others over to the long shuttle which was now sitting in geosynchronous orbit over Winterhaven. "Now, let's get to work!"

"Doing what?" Sabin demanded, beating Ryes to the punch.

"Making her into a real space platform, of course," Mitt stated, pleased with her ideas now. "We have company coming and they'll need a place to park."

"You do not have much to work with," Adina observed cryptically. They felt her humor filling the commune and it sparked Mitt's own humor.

"Here's our materials," she assured the rest, pulling them over to the remains of the previous stardock, which was now grounded on Shaysa's bright, rocky surface. Through her Inner Sight everyone noted the stardock had been attacked and deliberately destroyed; probably by the Snags when they attacked Tayna and destroyed the cities. It looked like a sad ending.

"Let's give her new life," Ryes suggested, then opened her Talents fully and between her and Mitt pulled up all the wreckage from the moon's surface. They salvaged a lot of interesting items and some that Adina and Hadu felt were important to preserve, too. Suddenly Axel joined the meld, having been summoned by Adina.

"We sorely need that equipment you've saved down here," he agreed, surprising the women. Humor ran rampant through the link, again. Garth and Sabin merely hung back and watched – amazed at their determination and finesse.

Ryes encapsulated the salvage in a large, plastic bubble for now. Then she, Mitt and Axel used her Molecular Talent and broke down the rest and pulled it all over to Flutter-wing, which was first searched and salvaged for several things too, then melded the rest into their primordial ball of material. Slowly they formed the hub and power systems, the life support systems, and the main core systems that would be very necessary for any space station. They formed the frame, then enclosed the whole thing with the strongest metals they could form, copying the metals used for the support beams in Hailys, as they used for the station's framework, and now the outer, protective shell.

They filled the station with work areas, control areas, classrooms, and personnel and guest quarters. Ryes wanted to put in far more bathrooms than Axel and Mitt thought were proper, which caused even Adina to laugh merrily. Hadu, who had been peripheral to this all, added in some interesting structures within their construction, which some Ryes recognized as possible safe rooms, but some she didn't figure out.

"Armories," he advised, creating four of them and he instantly had Sabin and Garth's approval, as well as the others' understanding. The remaining two areas he finished, as Ryes realized they were auxiliary AI compartments. This got admiration from Axel, who agreed wholeheartedly.

"Excellent," he stated, as the women then added the finishing touches making it not just a station, but a home. Then Ryes involved their AI in the project and requested it shape and program the AI on the station. They felt its pleasure, which surprised everyone but Ryes. It instantly began to analyze the systems, then directed Ryes to make some minor adjustments for it, which she did, understanding its reasons.  Ryes then pulled over some ice from out-system and used it to form water for all the fluid systems, filtering it out correctly with the balance used to create breathable air.  She kicked on the heat exchangers set to low – to slowly remove the cold of space – knowing later it would be reversed to dump the excess heat, once it was occupied.

"Now we have a space station.  Flutter-wing has grown up!" Ryes pulled them back so they could all admire the work they'd done and suddenly Mitt found herself almost knocked out of the link, as she was laughing.  She held on, though.

"You gave her flutter-wings?" she finally got out, still astonished, never having noticed, when Ryes made them.

"And they're rainbow colored, too," Ryes bragged, feeling tired now. "I wanted her to be pretty and functional.  They add in solar energy to the spaceport's systems," she explained.

"You all did an amazing job!" Garth said, his pride for their skills and ingenuity was clear, emanating from his heart.  Ryes then gently pulled them all back home and Adina, who'd taken over the meld, dissolved it once they were truly back.

"How are you feeling, Ryes?" she demanded.  Ryes yawned, covering it with her hand and gave her a nod.

"I'm winded, but not floored," she reported, proudly. "But I don't think I should stay up too late tonight."

"Excellent," she replied, "you are learning!"  Hadu gave her a hand up, as well as Mitt, who didn't refuse his offered assistance. Everyone said their goodnights and left, with Adina and Hadu going off into her room for a bit of time together.  Garth put his arms around Ryes and kissed her soundly.

"I am so very proud of you," he said, speaking in a low voice. "You're the one who's given us a future."  She sighed and leaned her head against his chest.

"It was what I thought we needed," she said, then smiled as they damped down the lights and turned for their own room and welcoming bed.  She did a quick check on their cubs with her Talent and was truly content.

# Vision's Truth

## Chapter 2

"These are absolutely beautiful!" Tanns declared, grinning happily as she glanced over at Ryes. They were on their knees with Wynne, harvesting the little, purple-colored berries from these profuse allia bushes.

"Ah, they're all going to love us when Chuck puts these lovelies into his muffins," Wynne replied, laughing lightly at their great, chance discovery.

"And now we'll have plenty to try to grow our own, back home in the greenhouse," Ryes added, grinning as she tried to strip the ones she could reach, without getting too badly scratched-up in the process. The plants were armed with some nasty thorns! Teris trotted into view, having been picking fruits off a ridge tree. He smiled as he saw the allia berries.

"I don't believe our luck! Allia berries?" he stated, as he set down his carry sac, full of ridge fruit, to drop to his knees to help pick the berries, too, knowing their importance. His Talent turning the thorns away from his hands as he worked. "We'd better hurry. It looks like that storm is coming in fast," he added, meeting Wynne's eyes.

"We'll make it," she assured him, her belief clear in her voice.

"It doesn't look good; those clouds are moving in fast," Jim added, as he stood guard duty over Ryes. She grinned up at him, glad to see both he and Anders standing nearby, looking ready. She'd had the strangest prickling feeling on her neck all morning long and knew she was jumpier because of it, but their presence helped her relax a little. Was this a Talent warning? She had no idea.

"We're almost done, and I'd say we could call it a day," she assured him, then turned back to Wynne and her Aunt Tanns, "With all these flowers, we should have plenty more to pick later."

"That's the truth," Tanns replied, smiling merrily. She realized she'd finally come to the point where she could accept Ryes as herself. Maybe it was as Maren asserted, that because of Korman's intense focus upon her, she resented Ryes and shunned her for too many years. Ryes wasn't a bad person, nor hard to get along with, now that she, herself, was free of Korman and his influence. Ryes would sometimes seek out her advice for raising her cubs, which was pleasing and helped them both to relax with each other.

"Well, that looks to about do it," Wynne stated, putting the last few berries into her carry sac, and sealing it. She pulled out a cloth and began to wipe off her hands, noting the scratches. She already had sketched the plant, taken several samples, taken a few holograms of the plants and their pollinators, and made sure she KNEW where these beauties were located. She'd come back later to check them during the summer. They weren't too far from the road which ran between Matlowe and Winterhaven, so they were fairly accessible.

"I don't see any more which are ripe and ready," Tanns agreed with a nod of her head, as she stood up too, taking out her own cleaning cloth. Teris nodded his head and rose.

"I'm finished here," Ryes said, sealing her collection bag and looking up at the dark clouds, through the trees above them. "That does look nasty," she commented as she stood up. Rain suddenly began to pelt them, falling heavily, but oddly, as it was coming in horizontally now.

"Let's get back to the rover!" Jim ordered, pulling his collar up higher. The rain was ice cold, and it was picking up the pace, with heavier droplets being driven by the sudden winds.

"Time to go!" Wynne agreed as she, Teris and Tanns quickly grabbed the rest of their gear from nearby. Ryes retrieved Teris' carry sac and the group started trotting for the rover.

Suddenly, Ryes found herself slammed to the ground by a huge gust of wind. She got back up on her hands and knees to see a dark, swirling cloud, which sounded like a great machine lived within its core. It was emerging out of the clouds, touching down in the vast meadow near them.

"It's a twister!" Jim shouted over the noise. As the funnel cloud touched down, trees, brush, clumps of grasses, rocks, and everything it touched was immediately yanked into the air and hurtled about. "Let's run for it!" As a group, they got to their feet, and ran for the rover.

But Ryes suddenly stopped and walked back to stand in the cover of the trees, fascinated by this fierce storm. It called out to something within her. She realized it was her Storm Caller Talent, which she rarely used and ignored, so she carefully unleashed it and admired this "twister" from within. It was a deadly dance of beauty to her now-heightened senses, as it utterly entranced her.

"Ryes!  Come on, Run!" Tanns stopped to shout, seeing she wasn't keeping up with them.  She dropped her things and turned back to go fetch her only surviving niece.  Jim turned, seeing what she saw, and ran back beside her.

"Ryes!" he bellowed, as they ran.  She finally turned and saw them, then blinked as she realized both her own and their danger, with this terrible, whirling force so close to them all.  She turned back to the funnel cloud and reached into its matrix, trying to find a way to dissipate it, and eliminate the threat.  It responded to her touch, it turned in its path, now heading straight for her, as if she was calling it to her.  Storm Caller, indeed!

"What do you think you're doing?" Tanns demanded as they reached her side.

"I was studying it with my Talent," she shouted back.  She tried to urge it away, but it wouldn't obey. "I can't control it, so I'm trying to figure out how to stop it."

"Let's just get outta here!" Jim ordered, seeing it was almost on top of them.

"It's after me now!  I can't.  Go on and get back to the rover. I'll see if I can do something to get it to stop," she returned, her eyes now glued to the monstrous thing, feeling her panic rising up within, along with whatever tenuous control she thought she might have over it.

"Short of stealing its energy, or getting the wind to turn back on itself, I've no idea of how you're going to stop it," he advised, grabbing onto her arm to pull her back from the open area, at least.

"That's it!" Ryes replied, seeing a way through with his suggestions, and closed her eyes to concentrate.  She reached into the storm's heart and reversed the pattern of its wind force. Instantly, it died, the swirling ceased, and the remaining debris it collected fell heavily to the ground.  The rain continued to fall, but at a more normal pace.  Ryes opened her eyes, smiling her triumph, then saw her Aunt Tanns lying upon the ground with a piece of a tree's branch protruding from her abdomen.  She immediately dropped to her knees beside her, seeing the shock and surprise in her eyes.

"Calling Winterhaven," Jim said, talking into his headset. "Yeah, this is Jim Dawe, we've got a medical emergency out here.  We need Maren flown out to our position, stat," he ordered after a few moments' pause.  There was another pause, then, "No, it's not Ryes, it's Tanns.  We were caught out in the open by a twister.  So beware, the weather's pretty nasty," he warned, "I'll be standing by."  With this he shut off his mic, setting the com unit to standby.

"I've got her pain and bleeding handled, and in a holding sleep, but I'm not skilled enough to remove this by myself. Let's get her back over to the rover, at least," Ryes suggested, seeing Teris and Anders were back, ready to help. She had severed the tree limb and trimmed it back to a short stump on both ends, so it wasn't applying pressure at odd angles to the wounds and making it worse.

"How?" Teris questioned. Ryes removed her backpack and took out the blanket she usually used for the horde.

"We'll use this," she explained, handing it to Jim, as she stood up. It was a colorful, sturdy, thick blanket. She closed her eyes and extended Manipulator Talent, gently lifting Tanns into the air. She was reluctant to spend more of her Talent today than needed, still feeling unsettled, as if they were being watched. The men didn't question her, got the blanket unfolded, and each took a corner, with Wynne taking the last one. Ryes lowered her aunt onto the makeshift carrier and opened her eyes again. She tried to position her, so no additional pressure was being applied to the branch stump.

"You're sure handy to have around," Teris commented, smiling. Ryes laughed in return, nodding her head.

"Guess so, at times, but it's my fault she got hurt in the first place. That thing was calling to me from within. I guess my Storm Caller Talent's stronger than I thought. It kind of had me mesmerized for a few minutes," she explained, embarrassed.

"That's alright dear, at least you did what you could and did stop the twister," Wynne replied, trying to comfort her a little, unable to imagine having such a power.

"It was amazing the way you dissipated that twister, yourself," Jim commented, as they walked back toward the rover, Ryes was picking up Tanns' things as they went.

"You gave me the idea to turn the wind back on itself," she told him. He gave her a nod and blushed a bit.

"The medical team's on their way," he added as they reached the grassy knoll, above the road. Their rover sat below.

"Let's stop here and wait. The higher ground should make it easier for them to spot us. And you should take care of that nasty cut you have on your own leg, too, Ryes," Wynne suggested. They set the blanket with Tanns down, as Ryes saw she was bleeding from a deep cut upon her lower leg. She'd been so tied up in the storm, then in helping her aunt, that she never noticed her own injury. She smiled a lopsided smile as she nodded her head. First, she used Manipulator Talent to float the things she was carrying, down to set

31

next to the rover, then she sat down and closed her eyes, opening her Healing Talent, again. By the time she had her leg taken care of, she could hear the chopper hovering overhead.

"Ryes, Maren's asking if you could use your Talent to help him down from the chopper? Shadd's not too sure about setting it down here," Jim asked her, as she opened her eyes. She gave him a big smile as she nodded her head.

"Tell him, sure." She extended Manipulator Talent as she saw her cousin wave to her. He jumped out of the chopper, with three other people behind him. She caught them all and brought them gently to the ground nearby.

"The only way to fly!" Maren declared, as he rushed over to them. "Oh, my. What happened?" he asked, as he immediately knelt beside his mother. He could see why he'd been called out.

"A twister, a giant, swirling mass of wind and debris, caught us out in the open. This was my fault, as the storm was mesmerizing me, your mother ran back to snap me out of it," Ryes explained. She knelt beside her, ready to help if he needed it. He glanced at her, then smiled.

"At least she's finally decided you're a real person," he volleyed in return. He now had his Talent up and put a hand upon her stomach, near the wood. Ryes added her strength and Talents for him to tap, so he placed his other hand upon the branch and used her Manipulator to extract it more gently, than he could've alone, then called his own Talent to the fore, to deal with her injuries. After a few moments, he had her fully healed, but left her in a healing sleep, so she could recover more fully. He opened his eyes, relieved.

"Do you want to go back up to the chopper?" Ryes questioned, a merry light in her eyes.

"No, I'll ride back with you. But you can have Shadd take my mother on back now. That way Ted can put her into a recovery bed more quickly," he suggested. She nodded her head.

"Jim, tell Shadd to expect a passenger," she ordered, then lifted up her Aunt Tanns, until she was safely within the passenger area, in the back of the machine, and closed the door. Shadd gave them a wave of her hand and turned back for Winterhaven. "So, you like the rain?" she pressed, grinning.

"Ah, we don't get out that often, so even a little rain's sweet," Dotti told her, stepping over to them, grinning as she wrapped an arm around Maren's waist.

"Let's get the rover loaded up," Wynne suggested, glad for the extra hands. "It looks like it's letting up a little," she observed as she picked up the carry sac to her shoulder.

"Here, let's make this a little easier on all of us," Ryes suggested, extending her Talent, one more time. She lifted all the carry sacs, equipment boxes and supplies, quickly lowering them down the knoll, to rest beside the rover. "There, neat and sweet."

"You're just too handy, at times," Anders said, giving Teris a nod of his head. Wynne was laughing as she led the way down the rain-slicked hill, glad they weren't carrying the extra weight now.

Korman had been wandering in the woods for weeks, following game trails and streams. He realized he was truly lost but didn't care. He didn't have a reason to return to his old home, still that wasn't a reason to remain out here in the forest, either. He knew he could figure out how to get back home if he tried. It was that he didn't want to extend the effort. His oldest brother, Metta, was still away and there was no one left who would listen to him, or even try to understand. He was alone, as he'd never been before in his whole life, and he didn't know what to do about it.

Those cursed cubs! Sure, they set up a machine so they could talk with their friends in the village, but when he tried to use it to talk with his beautiful lady, it either didn't work, or he was told she wasn't available. He gave up in disgust. Even if he could talk with Tanns, she wouldn't let him talk with any of his cubs, nor even see his tiniest, newest daughter, whom she named Kassa, after his own mother. His arms ached to hold them all! His heart longed to hear their voices and laughter! How could she stay away from him so long?

The sudden windstorm surprised him, driving him deeper into the trees, seeking safety. Then, across the broad meadow, he spotted Her! She was standing there facing down a swirling demon of wind, which was tearing up everything in its path. Tanns ran to her and tried to pull her away, as did one of those almost hairless men, whom they were all so fond of, back where they now lived. He wondered if he could follow them back, so he could beg Tanns to come home with him? To have the life and happiness they had before... Then he saw Tanns badly injured, as She was facing off the wind demon, finally banishing it forever. At least She had the sense to try to help his wife, even enlisting the others there to help carry her away. He trailed after them, leaving a good distance between. He didn't want their machines to warn them he was close, as he still wore this cursed collar, which they bound around his neck.

As he caught up, he saw an air machine, like the one they frequently came to the village in, hovering overhead. He was shocked as four people boldly jumped out of it. Then it seemed as if they were caught by an invisible hand and were gently floated down to the ground. He was sure She had something to do with it. He saw his oldest living son was among those who'd come from the sky machine, and he immediately bent to heal his mother, while She placed Her hands upon his shoulders in support. After a few minutes, he pulled the branch stump out and cast it aside. There were smiles upon everyone's faces, as it looked as if he succeeded in saving Tanns' life. Relief flooded his system, as tears flowed from his eyes. She would live! He saw Her floating Tanns up to the machine, then it banked and flew off, vanishing into the rain clouds. They'd taken her away from him again! His anger was red hot. This time, he vowed, there would be an accounting!

As Wynne, Teris and Jim were loading their supplies into the rover, Ryes turned to look back to the woods, up atop the hill, the prickling sensation was back, and it was like fire along her nerves.

"What's wrong?" Maren asked, turning to survey the woods with her, not noting anything out of the ordinary.

"I have a feeling as if someone were watching us. Do you think any of those forest demons have journeyed this far southwest?" she asked, still uneasy. She closed her eyes, ready to call up her Talents, to verify what her senses were telling her. Could it be something with intelligence? That forest demon behaved as if it could reason. She didn't want something like that hunting them, so close to Winterhaven and Matlowe Village! She had to know for sure!

"What's that?" Dotti questioned, hearing what they were discussing. It gave her the creeps to know something had Ryes disturbed. She saw movement in the lower brush, on the hill above them. Maren turned to look where she was pointing.

"Yeah, what is that?" Anders questioned, his pistol now in his hand. He'd seen something move through the brush. Ryes reached out with Empath, resisting the urge to stop to see what they were trying to see, and touched pure fire and anger. She didn't know what it was, other than it could reason to some degree. There was danger here, deadly danger. She opened her eyes to see Wynne and Teris had stopped their loading, to see if they could spot what the others had seen. Anders was starting to move up the hill, back to where they'd been standing earlier.

34

"Anders, get back here!" Ryes shouted, "Wynne, get the rover loaded and powered up. We need to get out of here fast!"

"What is it?" Jim questioned, never having heard her shout like this before. There was panic in her voice. His pistol was out, and he activated his headset, ready to relay to Winterhaven.

"I have no idea, except I've never touched anything like it, ever before. It may be an enraged forest demon," she replied, unfastening the catch upon her own holster. "Everyone inside the rover!" she ordered, her blood running cold with panic.

She recalled the Vision, and this was the exact place! Maren turned to her with a surprised puzzlement in his eyes; the same realization having just occurred to him, too. As Anders turned and was descending the hill again, a horrible fury swept him up, crushing him in its iron embrace. Long, horrible claws dug into his flesh, tearing him open. He screamed out in horror, as his heart was ripped from his chest, as it still gripped him from behind. He saw his own beating heart for an instant, then died within the arms of the animal which claimed his life. Korman threw the human's body down, yowling out his challenge to his son and that creature he cherished.

"Anders!" Jim yelled, as he leveled his pistol at that thing which killed him so suddenly. It was gone from sight in an eye-blink, shocking him anew, unable to get off even one shot.

"It's Korman!" Maren yelled out. "His hair's matted, and he's covered with dirt, sticks and leaves. His clothing's torn and filthy; I barely recognize him! He wants me, let me get him away from you." Maren suddenly stepped away from Dotti and Ryes, issuing a real challenge cry of his own, for the first time in his whole life. Rage instantly ignited within him, and he knew the only remedy for it was to feel his father's blood flowing from his own hands.

"Maren, NO!" Ryes yelled, grabbing onto his arm. He pulled away from her, having never heard her, as his blood was now boiling.

"What do we do?" Jake demanded of Jim, not understanding these people at all, in this moment! He was rooted to the spot, shaking in his boots. Anders lay upon the side of the hill, bloody and torn to pieces!

"Calling Winterhaven. This is Jim Dawe. We're being attacked by a mad starman. Scramble a team, immediately! Anders is already dead!" Jim said into the microphone, nodding to Jake, seeing his fear. He suddenly realized he didn't have time to be afraid right now. He had these people to save! After a few seconds, he got a response.

"Jim, we already have a team scrambled. Torr heard what your open mic was transmitting and immediately got operations mobilized. They'll be to your location in about ten minutes," Bitty informed him, as calmly as she could. Dr. Cruthers stepped into the control room, seeing what the remote vid on the rover was transmitting. Anders torn and bloody body, lying on the side of the hill, was an alarming sight. They could see Ryes and Dotti practically hanging on Maren, trying to get him to stop.

"Thanks, Bitty. We'll get everyone under cover," he promised, leaving his mic open again, just in case. He saw Maren was heading up the hill, as Ryes and Dotti were trying to dissuade him. Teris and Wynne were now throwing everything inside the rover, as Jake had overcome his fear, run downhill, and jumped into the cab. He was now firing up the engine, getting it ready to move out. Ivan was following the others up the hill, having his pistol at the ready, and checking all around them, but still looking very nervous.

"This place has gone nuts!" Jim added in comment. "Ryes, Dotti, Ivan, get back down here. I'll bring Maren back," he ordered, trotting to catch up to the rest.

"Should we retrieve Anders?" Teris called out to him, a coldness settling deep within his stomach, knowing this didn't look good. He would've never known it was Korman! It was as if he'd evolved into a nightmare! And he'd attacked too quickly, vanishing in the blink of an eye!

"No! Wait here for the rescue team. We'll get him when things are secure," Jim shouted, turning back to do so. He saw a fast motion coming from the trees behind the rover and cursed as he realized the one he was hunting, had gotten in behind them! "TERIS, WYNNE, LOOK OUT!"

Teris just had time to turn, as he pulled Wynne out of harm's way. Korman missed her head by mere fractions of an inch! He threw her into the back of the rover, slamming the door closed. Korman stood for a few seconds, evaluating his opponent. He suddenly lunged, as Teris tried to dodge aside. He scored him across his ribs as he struck, just grazing him with his claws. Jim fired his pistol as he ran downhill, the pellets from the weapon striking the ground near him, and the back of their black-painted vehicle. He retreated, going back to the brush, glad to see Maren meant his response, in spite of the two women who were trying to get him to turn back. He had to get back up the hill. He had a score to settle with two of them. The other two would be only for his amusement.

36

"Sir, Torr says there's something you need to hear," Jett told Garth, as he was in a meeting with Sabin, Kovin and Phil. Garth looked up to her puzzled, then gave her a nod and opened the com unit build into his desk.

"That's a challenge cry!" Sabin declared, sitting up to listen more carefully. He could hear someone calling out to Anders, then someone else calling out the name Korman.

"Tell Torr we're on our way to the helipad," Garth told Jett. He'd heard enough. "Remember that Vision of Maren and Ryes'?" he questioned. Sabin suddenly understood, wondering how many people were out there with them right now?

"I thought they stopped going out together?" he replied, as they were on their feet, heading for the door.

"They did. Kovin, Phil, later. We have some people to rescue," Garth replied, giving them a nod of his head.

"Do you need some backup?" Phil questioned, on his feet and ready to help.

"Not from the Masterbuilders of Winterhaven," he scolded with a smile. "Let others, who're more expendable, come along." Then they were gone, running down the corridor.

"Sure, then why are the Base Commander and Exec going?" he returned, glancing to see the surprise upon Kovin's face, too.

"I don't know if I like this title, after all. I don't want to be coddled," Kovin told him, then bent to gather their blueprints, rolling them up with little care now.

"You've got that right!" Phil agreed, lending him a hand, wanting to know what was happening. "Anders is hurt? We should be there to help!" Kovin nodded, his face grim.

"Can we see the vid from the rover?" Garth asked into his headset, sitting in the copilot's seat, as the chopper was lifting off with Mitt at the controls.

"Yes, Sir," Bitty responded, relaying it to him now. He saw Anders' body lying on the side of a hill, Dotti and Ryes looked like they were trying to drag Maren back down the hill, as Ivan was trying to keep them covered, and Jim was running toward the rover, shouting something.

37

"What's happening out there?" Mitt questioned as she glanced at the screen.

"Korman," her brother told her, "That was about all we heard, and two challenge cries. I can guess who issued the second one," he said, pointing to Maren, as he finally shrugged the women off and gained the top of the hill. They were slow getting to their feet, but started running after him.

"Oh my, that Vision," she breathed out in shock, praying they'd reach them in time, as she turned back to her machine, pushing it to its top speed.

"Maren, let it go. You're not going to fight a challenge!" Ryes yelled at him, seeing the narrow focus of his eyes. He had only one thing on his mind now, and he didn't care about anyone, nor anything else. She couldn't even break through with Mind Voice.

"What's wrong with you? You're not going to fight your father. We need to get out of here before anyone else is killed!" Dotti yelled at him, seeing she couldn't reach him, either. What happened? He'd never been like this before! It was like a deep, dark fury's filled his being, and nothing else matters!

"Maren, I'm warning you!" Ryes threatened, ready to use her Talents against him, but suddenly her head was filled with a blinding headache, as both she and Dotti let him go, falling to the ground, clutching their heads. He bolted away from them, gaining the top of the taller rise at last. Ryes extended her Healing Talent, quickly freeing herself from the pain, then she helped Dotti to her feet, extending her Healing to her, too.

"He's NEVER done anything like that - ever!" Dotti cried, suddenly scared, as tears started up in her eyes.

"His hate for Korman runs too deep. I wanted to save him from it, and get him to let it go," Ryes replied, as Ivan caught up to them. "I have to go after him," she told him in apology, knowing he had to follow her into danger. Then she turned and ran up the hill, Dotti running with her. She feared for her safety but hoped. Ivan ran behind them. Ryes pulled out her pistol, Dotti copying her. Maren was searching further away from the edge of the small hill, looking for Korman. He vanished again and looked to be toying with Maren.

Suddenly, Ivan was tossed into the air away from her, as Ryes felt claws sinking deep into her back. She tried to bring her pistol to bear, but it was smacked out of her hand, then she found herself thrown against a tree. She screamed out her pain, realizing he'd released her, then saw Dotti was now in Korman's grasp, like a rag doll, all limp and looking wrong.

"Dotti's pregnant! She carries your granddaughter!" she screamed out to him, pulling herself back up and away from the trunk, not immediately seeing Ivan. Maren heard her too and turned to see his wife in his father's hands.

"She carries HIS child?" he demanded, stunned by this news.

"Yes. She'll be your granddaughter!" Ryes shouted as she charged him, ready to tear at him with her own claws. He tossed Dotti aside, as if she were no more than a doll. He was ready for Ryes, a cold delight in his eyes, which she noted at the last second. She struck him, but he took her claws readily, for she was now within his grasp. He broke her arm, then shook her and slammed her to the ground, as if she were no more than an old toy. Ryes lost consciousness as she felt herself flying through the air, cursing herself for being so stupid as to forget to use her Talents for defense, again.

Ryes came to, as in her and Maren's shared Vision, lying upon the side of the hill. The rain was coming down now as a gentle mist, as if nature was trying to comfort those injured, as it could. She saw Dotti lying nearby, so tried to move toward her. The intense pain in her leg caused her to scream out in pain. She almost passed out but determined that she had to save Dotti and her child, and she could endure her own pain. She wiggled across the distance between them, even with a broken arm, and straightened her out, as she called up her Healing Talent. She could hear Maren's absolute fury as he was obviously fighting now. Her heart prayed for him, as she bent to do what she had to do, for them all. She closed her eyes, trying to concentrate, as well as she possibly could, as she was inwardly crying for her cousin's soul. What could save him now?

"Ryes? Are you all right?" Jim questioned, having finally gained the side of the hill where they both lay.

"No, but let me take care of Dotti, first," she told him, sinking into her Talent fully. She saw Dotti was badly hurt and needed Maren's touch. Her own Talent was so weak, next to his. Then, she recalled Mitt teasing her about doing impossible things, like helping to hold aloft a whole starship. If she didn't try, then she realized she'd always fail. So, she dug into her stubborn streak and opened her Healing Talent, willing it to work on the level of Maren's, so she could heal her friend!  There was resistance, and she wondered if she could drive her Talent this way, then it was as if a dam broke within.  A flood of healing energy washed from her, into Dotti, setting her and her child to right once more.  After what seemed an eternity, she opened her eyes to look into Dotti's.

"Ryes, you're bleeding.  You'd better take care of yourself, too," she cautioned her.  Jim was nearby, checking on Ivan.  She sat up, hearing sounds of the battle nearby.  Ryes smiled as she turned her own Healing Talent upon herself, mending her broken leg, ribs, and arm, quickly.  She figured she could take care of the scratches later.  She needed to know what happened to the others right now!  She turned and saw Ivan.

"Is he still alive?" she questioned, as the sound of a helicopter approaching, came from the direction Winterhaven lay.

"Yes, but he needs help," Jim told her. "Teris is badly scratched up too, but he's locked in the rover with Wynne and Jake."

"Stay right here.  You don't want to get in the way," she cautioned him, seeing he looked as if he were about to check on things topside, since she looked better.  She crawled over to Ivan, seeing he'd been disemboweled.  She extended her Healing and Manipulator Talents to him, closing her eyes to concentrate.  She got his intestines cleaned off and back into place, as they should be, then finished healing him, until he was fully healthy again.  She left him in a deep sleep, seeing he needed rest after such a horrible ordeal.

"You're bleeding," Garth commented, coming up the hill toward his wife.  Sabin and Torr were seeing to the people in the rover.

"I'll take care of the scratches in a little bit, but I've got to see to Maren, first," she replied, overjoyed to see him.

"Let's get everyone here secure," Garth ordered the squad, which accompanied him.  Ryes saw he was carrying a rifle and had it at the ready.

"He's gone mad," she told him, not sure if she was talking about Korman, or Maren, or both.  He helped her to her feet, half-carrying her up the hill.  Dotti and Jim waited at the edge, at the top.  Dotti was crying, as Jim tried to comfort her.  This was like a knife twisting in Ryes' guts.  Her heart was hammering as she broke away from Garth's support, running the rest of the way to see it for herself.

# Taking Back

## Chapter 3

"If my wife dies, I'll tear you to pieces!" Maren threatened, after he and his father had gone a few rounds of strike and retreat with each other. He heard Ryes' scream of rage and pain, and knew she was awake and determined to help Dotti. That sound was hope and comfort right now, the first he allowed himself to feel.

"You fathered an abomination upon her! You should be happy I killed her and ended your shame!" Korman returned, with a low growl in his throat, baiting him to get him to drop his guard. His face was a mask of hate.

"That's your granddaughter she carries! She'll live and will never know you ever existed!"

"I want my wife and cubs back!" he fiercely returned, the deep pain in his heart goading him to action once again. Not waiting for Maren's attack, he charged him, trying to wrap his arms around him. Maren dodged, trying to claw at him in return, as he passed. They both missed.

"They don't belong to you! Rowis has forgotten all about you. I told her that you left Matlowe and went away to live by yourself in the forest. She hasn't even mentioned you in weeks!" he taunted his father, knowing little Rowis was his favorite, and truth always hurts more than any lie. Korman bellowed and charged him. He twisted aside and kicked out, tripping him, then fell upon him and they scuffled on the ground, rolling around and trying to get at each other with their claws, or teeth.

"As long as that green-eyed demon is dead, it'll all be worth it," Korman hissed out, almost nose to nose with his son. He saw the added fury in his eyes and knew he'd struck another nerve. "You don't have the courage to finish this fight, the way it's supposed to be finished," he added, trying to get at his face with his claws. Maren blocked him, catching his wrists in his hands, then tried for his side, as Korman managed to twist out of his grip, breaking free.

"It's not a question of courage, father. It's one of opportunity," he yelled in answer. Korman laughed out, spitting at this cub, who still dared to call him his father.

41

"A Healer can't kill. Everyone knows that! You're soft, you're weak, and you'll never kill me!" he taunted in return, knowing in this, he was right. He suddenly wondered when Maren had grown taller? He was almost as tall as himself. He looked smaller through the chest but seemed more wiry. At least he had the strength to put up a descent fight! He'd enjoy this dance a little more, before finishing him off.

"Anyone can kill, father. Isn't that what you've taught me through the years? Don't you think I've learned a few things watching what you did to the others in Matlowe? Your time is over, old man. Best say your prayers!" Maren returned, then charged him, trying to get a good, solid kick in if he could. Korman dodged, twisting aside, then came rapidly up at him from behind, pinning his arms, as he held him tight. He was going to squeeze the life out of him now. It'd gone on long enough.

Maren realized he was well caught, and knew it was one of Korman's old tactics. He was being crushed to death. He couldn't move, nor breathe! He wanted to use his Talent to inflict some true pain upon his father in return, but through the narrow-trunked trees saw Ryes cresting the hill; she looked deeply upset. Dotti was crying, as Jim was trying to comfort her. He knew he couldn't win this fight with his Talent. He had to do it the right way and be there to deliver his daughter, just as his cousin said she saw in her Vision.

So, he used his Healing on himself to grow, strengthen and extend his claws as much as he could, then tore at Korman's sides and leg, as best possible, before he passed out. Korman yowled out his anger and pain, as he released Maren, and stepped back. Maren turned, his anger again coming to the fore. He realized he couldn't let Korman live to continue using, hurting, and killing others, just because he felt like it, as he'd just did to Anders. He had to stop him now, for all time, or die himself in the effort! He charged him, throwing the both of them to the ground, tearing at him with his claws, as he'd never imagined doing ever before, in his whole life. Korman finally managed to throw Maren off himself and rolled, gaining his feet quickly.

"So, the fury does live in you, after all," he gasped out, the blood seeping into his eyes, as he faced his son. "But you don't have the strength, nor the courage to finish it."

Maren didn't bother with a response. He tackled him again, throwing them both to the ground, once more. He knew his vulnerable spots, from his medical training, and was doing his best to end his reign of terror, once and for all time. Korman again managed to throw him off, twisting away from his grasping, bloody claws. He backed away, then realized he was on the edge of a seventy-foot drop and had nowhere else to go. He stood his ground, as Maren stood to face him.  Blood was blinding him also, as he swiped at it, taking a measure of his father.

Korman suddenly charged him, throwing him back to the ground.  He punched him hard in the chest, then tried to claw at him, but Maren had rolled out of his grasp, yet pulled him down, as he grabbed his leg and yanked Korman off his feet.  They struggled for a time, Maren managed to twist out of Korman's grip again, gaining his feet.  Korman stood, facing him.  Maren gave him a small nod of his head, then suddenly lunged at him.  He struck quickly, hearing the crack of bone he'd been striving to hear.  Suddenly, Korman's body slumped, and dropped backwards, tumbling down the steep drop.  He seemed to fall forever.

Maren stood there for several long heartbeats, looking down upon his father's body, as it lay twisted and broken in the shallow rill at the bottom, still twitching.  He felt so empty and hollow inside, he didn't know what to do now.  He almost wished he had the courage to throw himself off the cliff, too.  He shed his lengthened claws, not wanting them as a part of himself, and regrew his normally again, but still feeling aimless; unable to think.

"Maren?" Ryes said in a low voice, as she stepped closer to her cousin.  He turned to meet her eyes, pain and self-incrimination shouting out to her from within their dark-brown depths.  She opened herself up to him from within with her Talent, understanding what he'd done, better than anyone else could.  He stepped away from the edge and started crying as he threw his arms about her, holding her tight. "Come on, let's go home," she urged after a few moments, sending out her love and support to him from her heart.  They stood that way for what seemed a long time, then he released her, pulling back as he wiped at his eyes.

"How can I ever face Dotti, or my mother, again?" he asked in a hoarse voice.  Ryes smiled sadly as she gave him a nod of her head.

"I think Dotti understands this, far better than you're willing to give her credit.  If she had Talent, she'd be the one standing here right now.  Garth thought since I have Mind Voice, I should be the one to check on you.  Don't belittle Dotti by doubting her heart, Maren. You're her life, as much as she's yours," she scolded, "As for your mother... You'll both need time to let this heal between you.  But I think it'll be all right when you get over it.  So, you'd better start getting over it already, as you'll drive the rest of us crazy, otherwise," she finished, grinning as she tried to encourage him.  He didn't smile, merely gave her a sad nod of his head.  She sighed.  This might take a lot of time.

"Let's go home," he replied, as this was the simplest thing that lay in his heart right now, then turned to walk back through the trees, letting her go.

Ryes took a step, meaning to follow, then collapsed upon the ground. She realized her body felt cold and couldn't understand why. Maren was quickly by her side, extending his Talent, just noticing she'd been injured. At some time, Korman had sunk his claws deep into her back, perforating her liver. He returned to the others shortly, carrying her in his arms.

"Are you all right?" Garth asked, not sure if he meant his wife, or her cousin, or the both of them. She smiled for him, as Maren merely nodded his head.

"I lost more blood than I thought," she admitted, chagrined, "those weren't just scratches on my back." Garth took her from Maren's arms, smiling as he shook his head.

"At least the two of you are still alive," he stated, as Dotti tearfully threw herself into Maren's arms. He held onto her tightly, his own tears threatening to return, neither one minding his shredded, bloody clothing, nor her own bloodied clothes.

"Now you can take back your life," Dotti whispered to Maren as they held onto each other. He gave her a nod, relieved it was over; a new freedom he now felt for the first time in his whole life.

"Let's go home," Sabin suggested, seeing things were finally settled here. "We'll have a team collect Korman's body later today." But he'd never seen Maren look the way he did now. He hoped, with time, his heart would heal, and he'd get over this nightmare of a day.

"Look, it's a rainbow," Ryes sighed, as she saw the rain had stopped and the sun was finally peeking out, lightening some of the dark clouds.

"A rebirth omen of good blessings," Garth said with a chuckle as he gave Sabin a nod of his head in agreement. The group turned and began to descend the hill. They'd recover Korman's body after the rest were home and safe. Anders' body was already secured.

"Ryes?" Ethan questioned, seeing her entering the dining hall. It was the middle of the morning and she had two ceramic mugs in hand, obviously making a tea run. She stopped and turned to face him and her grandfather, as they sat quietly talking at one of the

44

tables. "Why haven't we seen you at mealtimes, the last few days?" he asked. His bright eyes were demanding an answer. She smiled sadly, then sighed as she stepped over to them.

"Do you want the Truth?" she questioned, to be sure.

"Always," Rowan replied, puzzled over her hesitation.

"I don't want Maren to avoid coming out to eat dinner with everyone, just because I'm here," she told them, looking sad, barely keeping her tears back as she sat at Rowan's urging.

"Why would he do that? What happened?" Ethan pressed, frowning with worry. This didn't sound like either of them, at all!

"I was talking with him a few days ago and healed a few of those deep scars on his face, while I was distracting him with our conversation. He was furious when he realized it and said he didn't want to see me ever again. That night he walked out of the dining hall, as soon as I came in, leaving his partly eaten dinner on the table. I know he meant it and he won't even answer the messages I send, except when it's something official dealing with his department. He still carries those scars all over his body from that fight, as if he's afraid to let himself heal, especially in his heart," she explained, as a few tears trickled down her cheeks now. She wiped at her face, turning her back upon the elders, as she tried to compose herself. Rowan leaned forward and gripped her shoulder in comfort.

"Give him a little time; he'll get over it," he told her, trying to assure her it would pass. If he had anything to do with it, he'd make sure Maren would quit treating her this way. She sighed, relaxing her shoulders, turning back to face them with a brave smile upon her lips.

"At least he didn't try to re-inflict the scars," she added, "and the horde and I get to eat our meals in quieter surroundings."

"Ah, but we miss all the activity," Ethan stressed.

"I'll have Garth bring them in with him tonight, so you can be reminded what it's like to be able to eat in peace," she teased, smiling more genuinely.

"But it's not the same without you," Rowan stressed. "I'll go talk with Maren," he offered, outright.

"No. This is my fault. We'll settle it eventually. I'll be helping Axel and his crew work on the Challenger, as soon as she arrives anyway, so it won't be an issue for a long time, since I'll be living up in space," she told him. She already had plans to take her smaller cubs up with her, even if she hadn't told Garth about it, yet.

45

"Well, since you're here right now, could you look at this pain I've been getting off and on in my shoulder?" Ethan requested. She looked surprised at this but gave him a nod of her head as she stood up and moved closer to sit down beside him. She put her empty mugs down upon the table, and reached over to Ethan, calling up her Healing Talent.

"But won't the little ones miss you while you're up, working on the starship?" Rowan asked, sitting down next to her, on the other side, so she was between them.

"I'm taking them along," she informed him, as she closed her eyes. "I just haven't told Garth about it, yet." She extended herself into the task before her, quickly repairing the stressed muscles. An impulse ticked at her senses, so she opened herself up more fully, doing a more complete restoration of Dr. Cruthers' body tissues, as she felt should be done. She opened her eyes, still having her Talent called up and ready.

"Grandfather, may I check on you, too?" she requested. He gave her a smile and nod of his head in agreement, realizing he was overdue for his next check, anyway. Ryes did a restoration for him also, feeling this was a more proper healing for an aging body, bringing back his vitality. She opened her eyes, sighing in relief.

"I feel better than I have in some months," Ethan told her, chuckling merrily.

"So do I!" Rowan agreed. "What did you do?" he questioned.

"Something my Healing sense said you both needed," she replied, grabbing her mugs as she then got to her feet. "I'd better go. I've got some work to get finished on my desk. See you later," she said.

"Yes, at dinner tonight! I want to see my great-grandchildren," Rowan scolded, smiling at way he could move with new freedom. Ryes sighed at this, then nodded her head. She'd make sure Garth and the girls brought the cubs, at least.

"Later," she replied, then went to fill the two mugs she had in her hands. As she went out into the corridor, she almost ran into Maren. She stopped, panic gripping her heart as she froze, not knowing what to do.

"It's a little too far to run for the forest," he teased without a smile, in a low voice. "I'm sorry, I didn't realize what I was doing to you," he added. "You don't have to take your little ones and hide out in space, just to make me happy."

46

"I have to go up there anyway and would be very lonely if I don't take the cubs. If it means letting you win and have some peace, I don't mind. We'll manage."

"Have I gotten to be such an ogre, as the humans say?" he asked. He'd followed her, wanting to talk with her alone, but took advantage of the opportunity to listen in on their conversation.

"You don't smile anymore, and I can't recall when I last heard you laugh," she told him. "I realize I don't feel much like it, myself, either, but I don't want Korman to hold the ultimate victory over you. Even from the grave, he's stealing your love and happiness, leaving you to live in the same misery he lived each day," she pressed, then sighed, "I'm sorry, I'd better go," she suddenly apologized as she took a step back, intending to go around him. She realized she was pushing things and had been almost singing to hear his voice again. He put out an arm to block her, stepping over so they faced each other again.

"Could you please, cousin, Heal me?" he requested. He knew she was right, that he couldn't heal within, if he couldn't first remove the scars on the outside. Ryes stood looking at him for several long moments, barely daring to breathe. He stood, looking into her emerald-colored eyes steadily for several long seconds. "I was impolite in not letting you finish what you'd begun."

She smiled hesitantly, then closed her eyes and wrapped her arms about him, almost forgetting the mugs of hot tea in her hands. He wrapped his arms about her, too. Tears sprang to her eyes as she extended her Healing Talent to him. After a few moments, she was finished. She opened her eyes with a sigh of relief.

"That's about as good as I can do it," she teased gently, "and you truly should be eating a more balanced diet," she scolded, smiling as she let him go, splashing some of the tea on her own hands. He opened his eyes and wiped at the tears in hers, but still not smiling, as he would've before, she mentally noted.

"When's the ship due?" he asked. He realized her Healing Talent had grown a lot stronger, not quite up to his level, but not far! She only lacked the real training to hone her skills now.

"At around three in the morning, the morning after tomorrow. We're going to be there to meet her and reassure their equivalent of a computer that we're truly her rightful owners now. It might get interesting," she informed him.

"And you're taking the cubs with you, into that?" he questioned. It didn't sound like something she'd do with the cubs.

"Sabin said he saw us having no problems with handling the computer," she returned. "And I'm having the cubs brought up, after we get things settled down."

"How long will you be up there?" he pressed, concerned now.

"Last I heard, it could take a few months. It depends upon how hard it'll take to convert her over to the new drive system and AI we want to install, and whatever other repairs she needs," she admitted. "I've done what I can from afar."

"So, what'll I do when I'm bored? I could go sit in your office, but you won't be there to talk with," he stated, feeling as if he was going to be cut off from something very precious.

"Since Mitt's down here, wrestling with the Pike, you could always tap her Talent, if there's something you want to pass along. And if you're truly bored, you could come on up to visit us for a couple of days. We'll need regular supply runs, and give the crews a break off and on," she offered.

"I think I might," he breathed out, realizing now he'd miss her terribly. "See you at lunch," he reminded her. She smiled and gave him a nod of her head. He stepped aside, letting her go. She walked down the corridor back to her office, fighting the tears which were threatening to flow again. Her heart was singing and breaking at the same time.

"At least you patched things up, before she leaves," Rowan commented, nodding to his grandson. He'd come up behind them and both he and Ethan heard it all. Maren nodded his head to this, then turned back for his office, feeling even more burdened.

"You are going up to meet the ship tomorrow morning?" Adina asked, her brows knitted with concern, as she returned to the dining hall for some fresh tea, having eaten her meal early. There was a note of consternation in her voice. "Can you not use a subordinate in your place?" she pressed. Ryes sighed but gave her a nod and smile.

"Mitt and I are the only two here with Inner Sight, and right now, I'm the one who'll meet the ship. Later, Mitt can spell me for a break, so I can come home to visit," she responded, knowing it wasn't what she'd want to hear.  Her cubs were now settled with teething biscuits in their hands.

"And your children?  Are they to be raised by strangers?" she pressed concerned, as Ryes was presently putting them into her "stroller" to take them to daycare. "I heard the repairs can take a good deal of time."  She stood back up and faced Adina.

"As soon as we have the computer settled, I'm having my cubs sent up to me.  Garth finally agreed.  And yes, I could end up working on the ship for some months.  With my range of Talents, I'm the best choice to get repairs done quickly and in good order," she assured her great aunt. "If you'd like to see the ship, and our operation, you could take a shuttle up and visit for a day," she added in offer.  Hadu gave her a nod while Adina still appeared undecided.  Axel stepped over, seeing she had her cubs all set to go.

"Do we meet in your office, mine, or one of the conference rooms?" he asked, as she didn't specify yesterday.  She gave him a warm smile.

"How about a conference room?  It should be more comfortable than my office, or yours," she suggested.  He gave her a nod.  She then used her Talent to search for an available room and to reserve it. "Give me another half hour to get things settled and it looks like meeting room Ko will be available for us.  Please let Mitt know?"

"I will.  We'll be there," he promised, giving her a smile, and left to go deposit his tray and get things moving.

"Is there something I can do to help?" Adina asked, wanting to spend as much time as possible with her before her departure.  She felt they'd barely been introduced!

"If you'd like, you could hold our base meld while we go up and do an assessment of the ship and make sure things like heat, air and water are available for early tomorrow morning?" she requested with a smile.  Adina seemed to relax at this point and gave her a small nod of agreement.

"I would be delighted," she replied.  With that she left, but Hadu paused and gave her a nod too, before departing.  She smiled, a merry light in her eyes.  After having almost no true family around her most of her life, she was now having to learn to deal with her own relatives!  And she realized Hadu had fast become a very dear "uncle," too.

Ryes, having kept track of the Challenger with Empath, had already informed the shipboard computer that she would be arriving by shuttle as soon as it shut down its drives, after maneuvering to park next to Flutter-wing Space Station. Axel piloted the Defender while Ryes kept Empath and Inner Sight up the whole time, riding in the copilot's seat. Everything was going smooth as they pulled into one of the shuttle bays, as close to the ship's bridge as possible. The airlock cycled and he double-checked on the oxygen readout, as well as the ambient temperature and gravity outside the shuttle.

"Looks good, let's go," he said, after shunting everything over to standby, rather than shutting down all the systems. He wanted them to have options. She smiled and gave him a nod, still staying in contact with the ship to check on things her own way.

"The internal shuttle system's down right now, so we're going to have to walk," she advised.

"We'll be fine," Setta stated with a laugh. "I can use a walk now, anyway." Ryes gave her a smile and nod, realizing she'd been sitting too much recently too. Shawn stepped up and took the pilot's seat.

"I'll keep the seat warmed – just in case," he assured them with a cocky grin. Ryes gave him a nod.

"I disabled the bots in this bay and locked it down so no others will be coming in from any other area of the ship. They used them for maintenance and defense. We have to get it to recognize us as her new owners still, so don't let anything into the shuttle, unless it's us," she advised. His grin faded as he gave her a serious nod, understanding her fully.

"Aye, Ma'am," he responded, then turned about to keep a sharp eye to his screens. She smiled as they headed below to exit the shuttle's main hatch, sealing it behind them. It was a party of six, who headed out of enormous bay. Ryes and Axel were in the lead with Setta and Logan behind them, and Ivan and Leon bringing up the rear, as security for the mission.

"The main bridge is about twenty minutes away," Ryes let them know, as she led them now across a spacious lounge, as a short-cut.

"Couches and chairs? And they look plush!" Setta commented as she looked about the room they were walking through. She was amazed and grinned merrily at seeing this luxury on a star-spanning warship. Ryes laughed as she pointed upwards, and Setta noted the

50

huge screens overhead which currently displayed Flutter-wing and Tayna behind her. "Wow!" was all she added, as she then had to hurry to catch up to the rest, who were now laughing.

"It looks in good shape in here," Ivan said, then they headed off into a wide corridor with a lot of sealed doors leading off of it.

"I've been slowly fixing the inside of her the last few weeks," Ryes admitted with a laugh. "It was practice, and Mitt thought the lounge was pretty extravagant, too."

"It could be useful," Axel supplied grinning, having liked it a lot. "It's something you only see on a luxury cruiser but could be a good place to gather the crew for briefings." Ryes just nodded her head, leaving it to his experience to know.

She was concentrating upon keeping their path ahead and back clear of any defense bots. The presence of the humans with her seemed to alarm it, which in a way could understand, but in a way was totally uncalled for, in her mind. They were a new people to it, but with her presence, it should not have been an issue.

"Are these meeting rooms, or what?" Leon asked, wondering.

"Yes, and offices. The crews' quarters are the next two decks below us, and there's a small galley and kitchen near the lounge we went through, but a full one also two decks below," Axel explained.

"Until she actually gets underway, I'm going to adapt some of the conference rooms as temporary quarters," Ryes let them know, as they arrived at the bridge. She stopped, signaling Axel to stop too.

"Chief Exec onboard!" she called out to the computer in Dolbith. It did not respond so she stepped forward, expecting the defense bots that zipped towards her. She deactivated them on the instant, as well as the defensive killing rays which were about to fire. She stood there with her hands upon her hips, appearing disgusted.

The main control room for the ship was huge. There was a gallery of raised seats immediately to her right side with wide stairs going up to them. The captain's seat, which was raised, was plainly the center of the room, with a commanding presence and various screens at hand for the captain to use to get information immediately about a situation. Across from that seat was an expanse of floor and then two main stations set right before the actual window, which looked outside the ship. She knew these were the helm and navigation stations with two chairs for each of them. Along the sides of the room were stations for shipboard operations, weapons, communication, scans, tactical operations, and a few other stations. Some stations were displaying blue lights, with the rest showing green, yellow and red lights. All reflections of the current state of the ship, itself.

"I am Ryes of House Li and am one of the now rightful owners of this ship, formerly known as The Challenger. This ship will now consider itself to be owned by Winterhaven upon Tayna, and the Command staff of Winterhaven will be instantly obeyed in all the directions issued. I am the current Chief Executive Officer in Winterhaven and will be obeyed," she stated, then strode over to the main systems board and placed her hand on the activation screen. It took a reading of her and since she had her Inner Sight already active, it noted her Talent, too. That part still gave her a chill, but she held steady.

"Acknowledged ownership and rank of Officer Ryes of House Li," it finally responded in Dolbith.

"You will know the people who accompany me today are from a race of people named Human. These people here have our full trust and same privileges granted to them here as in Winterhaven. They are a race equal to the Starmen people, and have variances of appearances, as starmen, in skin coloration, hair coloration, height and weight. You will recognize these ones now. Axel of House Reguild who is our Chief Engineer," she motioned him forward, he gave her a nod in understanding, stepped over, and put his hand to the same plate she used for the identification scan. The system "tasted" him and the light below the plate went blue. He pulled it off and stood near her, ready. She gave him a grateful smile.

"Poinsettia of House Swan, who is a technician, and will assist with restoration of this ship." She too stepped forward and placed her hand on the scan plate and removed it as soon as it turned blue, which was the starman version of the human green light. Ryes smiled for her as she stepped over next to Axel.

"Logan of House Lewis, who is a starship technician and who will also assist with restoration of this ship," Ryes stated, the whole while keeping a constant contact with the computer with her Inner Sight. The ship processed Logan next.

"Ivan of House Resnick, who will assist with staff security," she instructed as he stepped over, doing as the others before him.

"Leon of House Rhona, who will also assist with staff security," Ryes said, then he, stepped over to the console.

"And finally, I have Shawn of House Winter, who is a pilot of my shuttlecraft, The Defender, and still aboard it, awaiting further instructions.  I will have him provide you with his hand soon.  Right now, I need you to tune into this signal from out of Winterhaven, so you and our computer there can get acquainted and learn to understand and work together," she ordered, as she stepped over to the communications station and typed in the broadcast channel she set aside for this virtual meeting of the electronic minds.  She was ready to step in, if needed.

"That's a good start," Axel said as a few more of the lights on some of the boards around them went blue, but there were still many green, yellow, and red ones.  All the systems' boards still showed there was great damage to the ship.  He stepped over to the main ship's status board, his quick eyes trying to take it in.

"Is it safe?" Setta asked, to be sure.  Ryes smiled and gave her a nod.  The rest started to relax now. "So, should we get to know the ship layout first, or unpack our things, or get something to eat?" The others laughed, having succeeded in taking the ship as their own, so now the real work could begin.

# Practice and Plans

## Chapter 4

"Are you sure you're rested enough for this?" Axel questioned as Ryes took a seat on the bridge's gallery. The seats swiveled, so they could use them to form up their work circle in some comfort. She looked up at him and gave him a nod.

She'd brought Shawn to the bridge and introduced him to the ship's computer. She'd then been busy helping to move their supplies and equipment off the Defender, actually using a cart instead of her Talent. After that, she helped set up the kitchen so they could all have a good breakfast. After Shawn left to bring up more supplies and crew to help, she spent some time catching up on her work from down in Winterhaven. using the portable computer, as their home AI and the numerator on the Challenger were still trying to figure each other out. She added in the program files from Prince Callas to the ship's computer, as an added measure; knowing her own AI had already added them into its system and was now running better.

"I'm fine. I haven't been using many of my Talents today and I'm planning a nap after this session, so I'll be ready for when Garth and Sabin bring up the cubs and check out the ship later this evening," she assured him, grinning merrily.

"We don't have a Healer with us, so keep track of your body temperature," he minded her, as Setta and Logan each took seats next to them.

"What do I do?" Logan asked, then saw the others joining hands and closing their eyes, so he copied them and tried to relax, as he recalled Setta warned him about beforehand. Ryes was chuckling then relaxed herself, extending her Mind Voice gathering the others in her keeping into a comfortable mind meld.

"Now, let's take care of that power plant and the drive engines, since we're going to be here living aboard her for a while," Axel suggested. Ryes readily agreed and opened the full range of her Talents, all ready to do as he directed, which by now, Axel could use them directly, too.

For the first time in their lives, Setta and Logan got to see a starship through Inner Sight. It was an amazing journey for them, and it seemed Axel and Ryes were old hands at the high energy conversion process, enabling the bridge to remain at full power through the whole process.  The remaining inert material was dumped into four empty hangar bays for later use, as base materials for other projects on the ship.  Now they were all safe from the wild energies of the old drives and all radioactive contaminated structures were "scrubbed" and free of all danger.

"That wasn't too bad," Axel commented and got agreement from the others. "Let's get her pulse, now," he invited.  Ryes had been striving for some time now to fully open her Inner Sight to function as well as Mitt's, and it was now working on a similar level.  Axel had been amazed and took full advantage of her Talents.

They swept the whole ship, now seeing fully that it'd been a miracle she'd reached them at all!  It appeared the attack was concentrated upon this ship, perhaps to buy other ships time to get free?  They noted the missiles still in one of the bays, which had been damaged and unable to release them, were of a far different manufacture than the ones designed by the humans.

Ryes shared the brief memory Dr. Cruthers had shown her of the attack upon the Star Quest, and how some missiles from an out-system planet had fired upon the Snag hunter ship, and actually got through its shields, damaging it.  This was the first time any of the three had seen an attack upon a real starship, and while it scared Setta, it brought new wisdom to both Axel and Logan, as it had herself.

"We'll have to see if that fire base still exits," Axel stated, wondering if she'd shown this memory to Garth, or Sabin, yet.  She returned with some humor in her thoughts.

"I haven't shown it to them, yet.  I'd forgotten I had that, but I'll show them tonight," she promised.

"Wow!  The Quest didn't stand a chance against that ship, and it was just one," Logan stated, still amazed, but loving this inner exchange and sharing.

"We've seen the result, but it seems those missiles did buy her enough time to get some survivors off on the escape pods and shuttles," Ryes added.

"So, if they work against the Snag shields, we'll keep these ones, and make our own missiles like them, and update them if they've changed their shields in the years since," Axel assured them all, pleased.  All the other missile bays were fully empty.

They then turned to doing some minor repairs and helping the ship to operate more normally.  Logan and Axel's knowledge of starships helped provide a solid anchor for their efforts.  Setta's understanding of the electrical systems also gave them direction for checking out how badly damaged they were, too. Ryes included an upgrade to the computer, while they were at it. It still wasn't quite right, but would do for now, and it was operating more smoothly. Logan and Setta, once they'd gotten a feel for how to use Ryes' Talents, did enjoy tapping them, too. Ryes was happy to lend them out to the others with her, so she could learn how to use them better, herself.

"Let's take a break, get lunch and let you take a good, long nap," Axel ordered, feeling she was reaching her limits, even with that vast pool to still draw upon. He knew she was the only real resource they had to actually get this ship fully functional, as quickly as possible. Still, with the size and scope of the ship and her systems, it'll take time to understand how they operated, and set them right, once more, or adapt them to work better.

"That's a good idea," Setta agreed with joy igniting her senses. It was hard to let go of Ryes' Talents, and she wished, with all her heart, that she'd been born with some of her own. Ryes felt her truth and agreed, then gently released them, adding in a touch of Healing to both relieve their headaches, which she knew would come next, and bring her body back up to its normal temperature range. They opened their eyes; smiles being shared all around.

"The lights didn't even flicker once," Leon told them, as he stood nearby. There were still a lot of red, yellow, and green lights displayed on the boards around them, but overall, more were blue now.

"There's still so much to get done," Setta declared, but also proud of having a hand in this project all the same.

"We'll get there," Ryes assured her, smiling. Axel added in a nod.

"Since the main galley hasn't been repaired, let's go over to the little one on this deck. It should serve as our main, for now," Axel suggested.

"Ivan and Minn are over there now, setting up our lunch," Leon told them which got the others to laugh.

"We're going to end up with everyone in Winterhaven wanting to come up and look at her, now," Logan warned with a laugh. They had a starship, a real starship, he thought, so entirely pleased, excited, and proud.

"As long as they lend a hand, I won't mind," Ryes returned, laughing as they stood and started heading off the bridge. She couldn't wait to show it off to Garth this evening. And even if they'd only been separated for a few hours, she couldn't wait to hold him and her cubs!

After two months, they had at least gone through half of the Winterhaven population as either visitors, or helpers, in their efforts to fully make this grand battle platform their own. Ryes was surprised to find out her Aunt Adina was amazed by the ship. She would've thought they'd been more common with the Kahmarran starmen. Hadu had been highly approving of Challenger and her capabilities; having Ryes give him and Adina an intense tour with her Inner Sight. He utilized her Talents to make a few small changes, which she'd come somehow to fully expect. Still, these seemed to make the ship function better, even more than before. In her heart, she wondered at his training as a Sword of Demia, that he knew of ships and their systems so intimately. He was far more than just a bodyguard.

The Sleepers had also highly approved of the ship, especially the central lounge, which they seemed to view as required on any ship of large size. This amused the humans and Ryes, herself, as they thought of it as extravagant on a warship. And after Setta and Logan were telling others of the attack on the Star Quest, Ryes found herself asked again and again to show that snippet of memory. Finally, she asked if Ethan would mind sharing it with the rest of the Winterhaveners, who still felt they needed to see it. He was highly amused and asked Adina to assist him. Many now came away from that sharing with a better understanding of what they might be up against. Garth highly approved as it did give them some perspective.

And the surprising thing ended up that Ryes and Garth's younger cubs all loved being in a weightless environment! They frequently had to turn off the gravity initiators during different phases of repairs and all her cubs seemed to relish this new environment. When they had to turn on the gravity, it'd take a few minutes, at least, to get them to stop crying. And when she went to visit home, they again took some time to adapt back to Tayna. She discovered if she "connected" them to Tayna with Empath, they settled down quickly and were more themselves.

Ryes ended up spending time on her visits home in either training her Talents with the Sleepers or being the trainer. The Sleepers, and her aunt, finally decided they needed to direct her Talents more, or give her ideas of how to use them, than expose her to the limitations they were placed under when training their own, when they were younger. They felt she had good instincts, which only needed to be honed.  Ossa finally approached Ryes, deciding to see where she was with her Storm Caller Talent.

"Truthfully, I've been so wrapped up with the ship, I'd forgotten to actually take the time for my Storm Caller," she admitted guiltily, not having used it since that fateful day when Korman died. Ossa smiled grandly.

"Let's go over to the Yuri and get in some practice," she suggested. "You've spent enough time catching up for the last few days and should get some time outside," she mildly scolded.  Ryes smiled at this, giving her a nod of her head.

"Instead of the Yuri, I've another place in mind," she replied, getting an idea for an outing.  It was just past breakfast and there wasn't a lot to be done this morning, so the idea of getting out and away from Winterhaven seemed a good one.  So, Ryes put in a message for Torr to supply a guard and reserved rover seven, as it was still her favorite.

"Give me a few minutes to change and I'll be ready.  I want to put on an outdoors outfit."  Ossa nodded, as she was already dressed for outside.  She found she felt more alive outside than cooped up inside all the time. "We're taking rover seven, so meet you there," Ryes added with a smile.

"Where are we going?" Ossa asked, wondering.

"A place I haven't been in a while, Hailys," she said, watching her face closely.  She frowned slightly but gave her a nod.

"I can say it's been centuries," she replied, not sure to be happy with her choice, or not.  But it'd be getting away, and far from any possible harm to others.

"Great, then it's an overdue visit for us both!  Meet you in a few minutes, then," she replied as she shut down her system. "Larissa?" she asked but saw her nod through the open door and smiled.  She already knew.


"Lake Ever," Ossa breathed, finally recognizing something of Hailys as Ryes pulled the shuttle to a halt.  They arrived at Lake Ever, a place where she'd played as a child.  It brought happy memories to her heart once again, even if it was wildly overgrown now.  A warm smile now graced Ossa's lips, which Ryes noted and gave her a smile of happiness in return.  She was shutting down the rover.

"You were here before?" she asked.

"Yes, long ago, when I was very young. I had forgotten," she admitted, blushing. "I was born in Fettin, in the Southern Isles, but my mother often came to Hailys on business," she explained. Ryes nodded her head in response and got out of the shuttle. Ossa scrambled to get her door open and then rushed to the edge of the lake, looking about her.

"I think she looks happy," Jim commented, as he emerged from the vehicle and closed his door, released his two drones, then came around and closed Ossa's door. He stood by Ryes as she kept back to give Ossa some space to enjoy her memories of this place for a moment.

"She does," Ryes agreed, smiling herself; glad she picked this place for her practice spot today. She felt they'd have more privacy here than by the Yuri, where the bridge construction was underway.

After a few moments, Ossa seemed to come back to herself and turned to see them granting her some peace. Instead of immediately schooling her face into her normal neutral mask, she kept a wistful smile, as she gave them a nod of appreciation.

"I'm ready, whenever you're willing to proceed," she told her. Ryes gave her a nod, then stepped closer.

"I'm ready now, too," she replied, smiling happily with the light in her eyes showing her own inner joy. "We once camped here for a few weeks," she admitted, pointing to the old firepit and oven they'd built, which seemed so primitive to her eyes now. "This place is special for me, too." Ossa noted the remains of their camp and nodded, understanding her choice, too.

"Come, let's form our meld," she urged. Ryes stepped closer, extending her hand.

"There aren't any clouds about to work with," Ryes stated, once they established their inner bond. They both had their eyes open for the work ahead. Ossa was one of the few Talents she knew who usually worked with her eyes open all the time.

"You're going to start by making your own clouds using some of the water of the lake," Ossa advised, amusement in her mental tones. "Practicing this now when there're no storms, so you'll learn the ways of the wind and clouds, that way, when there are storms, you'll be able to deal with them with better ease," she explained. "Now open up your Storm Caller Talent."

Ryes wasn't quite sure how to recognize this specific Talent, since the only time she'd used it was when a tornado struck near the road on a very fateful day. With Ossa's guidance, she found it and purposefully opened it up. She directed her attention upon drawing water from the lake, finding herself concentrating upon forming clouds. Great puffy white clouds began to form in the air above the lake. A great mass of them. A loud gasp pulled her out of her concentration, and realized she'd closed her eyes.

She opened them and saw she'd dropped the level of the water in the lake by at least halfway! Her mouth formed an `Oh!" as her Empath Talent awoke, and she was now feeling hundreds of fish and other aquatic animals dying. Fighting her nausea with Healing, and without thinking, she reversed her earlier draw of water, and a great cascade of it fall from the sky back into the lake, restoring its level and churning up the whole lake. Then she kicked up her Healing, using her Booster, and did her best to save as many of the fish and other marine animal lives as she could. Finding those fish who were already gone, she brought up Manipulator Talent and pulled them free of the water. Being practical, she gutted the fish, letting their entrails fall back into the water, creating a feast for the survivors. She floated those fish over toward them, scaling them with Manipulator on the way.

"Jim, could you please get some of the big plastic containers out of the back. I usually use them for plants, but this is an overriding need," she finally voiced. Jim chuckled, having witnessed, and recorded everything with his drones from the outside, and understood. He brought over two of the largest plastic containers and had them open and ready to receive her catch. She cleaned the containers, then gently deposited the fish, filling them both to the top. He put on the lids, then she lifted them over to the shuttle, closing the back hatch as soon as they were loaded. He had followed the plastic bins over and activated the temperature control for the back compartment to keep the fish from spoiling.

"I think we have lunch," he commented, chuckling, as he returned, "for all of Winterhaven. Chuck's going to love this surprise!" Ryes laughed in agreement. "I hope they don't mind the change in the menu," he added.

"I think I need to practice control," she returned as she grinned, then noted Ossa was very quiet.

The lone cloud Ryes'd left for practice was staying exactly in place. Their meld was still strong and in place too, yet it appeared Ossa was trying to grapple with all she'd seen and experienced through it. And she realized it'd taken her years to get a cloud to stay in one place! She'd seen Ryes using her multiple Talents in concert from within and was awed, still she was the teacher today.

"Let us begin, then," she said, finding her mental voice once again. She pushed the rest of the experience to the back of her mind to muse upon later. "This one is just the right size for our exercises."


"What is wrong, Ossa?" Prias asked when she saw her friend appearing unsettled, as she sat in their meditation room after lunch. Raya entered the room behind her and noted Ossa's mental disarray too; it practically shouted across her senses.

"I finally know what it's like to die, even if in a small way," she replied, still grasping the events of the morning's lesson with Ryes.

"Please show us and let us help you find a way through this," Prias requested, kneeling next to her. Raya sat down beside her, wondering if she'd be invited too. When Prias established the link, she was readily included, which pleased her greatly to be allowed. She felt welcomed.

Ossa showed them both the whole experience, as it was still very fresh in her mind. Her wonder over the enormous cloud Ryes was shaping using pure instinct, then the realization that the fish were dying because of her theft of the water they needed to live. The way she suddenly released the water back, and the rest she did to recover as many as she could to health, then the salvaging of those, who were beyond help, as food. Prias was amazed while Raya was amused.

"Ryes is very Talented," she empathized. "I've lived with her longer than you, and while all this seems remarkable to you, it isn't to her. It's as natural as breathing. She only needs a deeper understanding of her Talents and how to use them best. Her instincts can only guide her so far," Raya explained.

"Saree told us Tyra was a Talent of One, remember? Why would not Ryes, her daughter, be one, too? Adina of House Li has hinted so, and Denas has remained very quiet about Ryes' Talents, and she is a Catalyst, but they are close by family relations and friendship," Prias minded the others.

"It's never happened before," Ossa began, then paused, uncertain, "but it truly explains it all."

"It does," Raya agreed, knowing the truth, herself, but more than easily skilled in keeping it locked up where they were unable to glean it from her, even here in this close sharing. She had learned many new ways of using her Mind Voice from Ryes' Aunt Adina, for which she was very grateful.

"You seemed surprised she could will that one working cloud to remain still, while she took care of the fish," Prias noted from Ossa's memory, "why was that so remarkable?"

"It took me years to learn to do it!  It took her moments!" she exclaimed, exasperated and frustrated with the whole situation.

"That's Ryes," Raya assured her with light humor, as if that small statement explained everything. "You were teaching her, but did you learn anything more about your own Talent in the process?" she asked curious now. Ossa seemed to be thinking upon it for a moment, trying to see through her charged emotions.

"Actually yes. I found a way to refine my cloud-forming skills! I didn't realize it was happening at the time. I showed her and she taught me," she finally stated, calming down and seeing the whole truth.

"And that is how you teach Ryes," Adina assured them, having been eavesdropping on their conversation.  They felt her humor clearly. "You gain valuable nuggets of your own to cherish, too." Raya agreed, having known Adina was around at the beginning.  She knew Adina liked to keep tabs on the Sleepers, not wholly trusting them.

"You're leaving again, tomorrow," Garth said in a low, halting voice.  There was a deep sadness as he spoke, and Ryes turned from feeding the cubs to look at their father.  Her heart went out to him, as her own was also reluctant to leave him again.  With each visit home, it was harder and harder to go back to space.

"It'll be finished soon, and I'll be with you from then on, once again," she assured him, also in a low voice.  Maren heard their exchange and gave her a nod in understanding.

"It's a huge ship with a lot to get done," Maren offered. "I've heard Mitt complain that it's too much."  Ryes nodded her agreement, smiling for him.  He still hadn't found his full healing within, and she missed his laughter and teasing.

"We're tackling it a bit at a time, so we're not overwhelmed.  Once we're finished working on the Challenger, herself, then we'll move on to the ships in her bays.  I've already converted their drives and power systems to make them safer, at least," she said with a sigh, still thinking on all they still had to do. "We should be winding things up before the Great Fall Gather."

"Those shuttles, how good do you think they're going to be?" Sabin asked, wondering, now. She grinned merrily at him, understanding him wanting something more to pilot now. Some of the men were like cubs with new, shiny toys when it came to the huge machines, they'd never even dreamed existed last year. Now they wanted more.

"Better than the current Avenger and Defender," she assured him. "Think of the Pike Forward with more teeth and never having been buried for centuries. They are armed and armored."

"So, we could have two of them renamed to replace our current Avenger and Defender, if they're going to be bigger and better?" Jim asked, curious. Brenda looked up, eager to hear this news. Ryes smiled and nodded her head.

"They only appeared to have been numbered, with no given names, so we could name them, if everyone else thinks so, too," she offered. Garth appeared to consider it for a few seconds then nodded his head, as he looked to Sabin. Sabin nodded his agreement.

"Then we will have the Avenger II and Defender II. While we're at it, let's name the Challenger, the Challenger II, since you, Mitt, Axel, and the others are remaking her to be different from her original build," Garth suggested.

"That sounds great," Dotti added in, with Tars nodding her head. "And will keep the original fighting spirit of the ship, at the same time."

"How many of these fighting shuttles are still left on the ship?" Sabin thought to ask, wondering.

"Only fifteen out of what appeared to be two hundred fifty. Six were heavily damaged while nine were fully untouched. I don't know if they were being held in reserve for a last escape of the remaining crew members, who never reached them, or," she ended with a shrug, leaving it to the others to draw their own conclusions.

"They might not have had enough crew left to man them," Bitty put in, as she frowned. "Did you find any bodies on the ship?" she added, wondering. Rye gave her a nod.

"One of the first things we had to do was remove the remains of what was left of her crew. The bodies were mostly skeletons, or dust. I used Empath and Manipulator to gather what was left, and then we held a ceremony of parting for them. After that we sent them off to the fires of Monrush, as a pyre of purification. It was what we felt the best we could do for her brave defenders," Ryes explained, her eyes somber, as Raby took over the cubs' care for her, while listening to the discussion. "We have yet to go through the crews' quarters to see to their personal belongings."

"That was a good spaceman's way of parting," Bitty breathed out, smiling now at hearing it. Garth nodded, understanding it now. They had shown proper respect for the ship's previous crewmembers.

"And we'll honor their spirits by doing our best to take out the Snagospin," he promised with all his heart. Ryes nodded her agreement.

"Which is why it's so important for us to get this one massive ship repaired – and do it correctly - so she'll be ready for battle, once again. At times, when I'm in a deep meld with the ship itself, I can almost hear her spirit calling out to hurry and get her back into action. She wants to take them on again, too, and I also get the impression that she feels we're doing the redesign right," she sighed. Most of the others at their long table laughed at this, but Bitty gave her a nod, meeting Ryes' eyes with a knowing in her own.

"The best ones are like that," she assured her, then she smiled and blushed and returned her attention to her plate.

"Thanks, Bitty," Ryes said, smiling at her surprise when she looked back up. "You should come up and see her. We can use your expertise to refine the safety measures we've taken so far," she invited. Bitty gave her a nod and smile.

"I'd like the chance," she replied, her eyes showing her inner joy at being asked.

"Would you be packed and ready by tomorrow morning?" Ryes asked, thinking it was a great idea, after all. "We lift at eight in the morning."

"I'll be ready," she assured her, wondering if she'd be able to sleep tonight? She was going back to space and couldn't wait!

# Once Upon a Time Walker

## Chapter 5

"Alright, that one's good," Ryes said, speaking into her headset. She was under the maintenance console on the Challenger's bridge, her head halfway inside a panel, on the level of the floor, looking at the thick stretch of cabling, which lay beneath her in a deep channel below the floor level, using Inner Sight. They were just getting the new drive engines properly wired in, so they could obey the parameters they were establishing for the new system, and the ship's computer, and helm station would have regular full access, as they should.

The computer stopped having fits over everything they did, as it and their AI in Winterhaven had finally found a true meeting of the electronic minds. Winterhaven's AI was now directing the numerator, or computer, on the Challenger to function more in line with what they were used to back home. And she knew both systems were in the process of recreating themselves. She wondered what the end result of that would be? At first Neil was worried it might be due to an influence of a digi-sona, a human that had been translated to pure data, that someone might've survived from the Star Quest, or left behind in Winterhaven, and only awakened. But, after intense studies, this didn't seem to be the case, so he left it entirely in her hands. Neil, too, was curious about the conclusion of the project. The changes had to be the files from Prince Callas, at the heart of it. Normally Ryes wouldn't be so free about it, but somehow trusted this gift from him.

The rest of the vast bridge was empty, with only her five cubs napping at the end of their tethers, which were secured to a rail, at the front of the observer's gallery, behind the captain's chair. It was the only place she could put them, where they were out of reach of everything, in case they woke up before she finished the task before her. They took to maneuvering around in weightlessness far more quickly than she would've ever believed! She kept a keen eye to their health, doing adjustments on them, and all the crew, as needed for the weightless environment. And she even had plenty of toys tethered near them so they wouldn't get bored too quickly, while she was working.

"Great. How about this one?" Cassie Reddin asked, activating another circuit. Ryes could do this with her Talents, but they both needed a slow day break after the last few weeks of major, manic work on the ship's refit.

"Nope. That one's dead," she replied, concentrating. "It looks like another one which ran through that blown compartment. That makes eleven dead, so far."

"Eleven out of twenty. It doesn't sound too good to me. Guess the Snags knew where her vulnerable points were. I still think it's a miracle she made it to us," she responded with a sigh. "Let's get the rest of this bundle finished, then call a break," she suggested, disgusted with the extent of the damage.

"Then we won't be so predictable with our wiring. We'll have to avoid using both the human and starman techniques," Ryes responded, grinning to herself as she did. "Setta and I have a plan and I might give it a try after our break, and repair that blown compartment, if you're up to it. And it looks like they didn't have many redundant systems, so we'll make sure to add in a few important ones. They couldn't have been so hard up for building materials! Why such damming lapses?"

"No, they probably didn't lack resources," Cassie laughed in response, "but Axel could tell you larger projects are usually built by the lowest bidder, back in the Earth Fleet. So, you get corners cut to help make it look more affordable."

"That's terrible! It should be done right, or not at all," she replied, disgusted by such a concept. "Now that one's good," she added, sensing the signal along the cable.

"Ahhhh, blessed by the `Tron God Sparky," she merrily returned as she tagged it. Ryes was laughing now. "I'd love to see what you and Setta have planned, so after our break, let's tackle it?"

Suddenly, Ryes felt the tugging of the presence of another mind nearby. It felt very different from any she ever encountered before. She closed her eyes, reaching out with Mind Voice to determine who, or what, it was. She knew it wasn't a Snagospin by the "feel" of it, but it avoided her deeper contact, as if it didn't want her to understand its true nature.

"What do you want?" she sent out to it, hoping it would understand her question.

"Who are you?" it demanded in return, still not giving her any clues.

"Ryes of House Li," she replied, unsure if she should give it so much right away.

66

"The Ryes?  One of the lion people?" was the unexpected, surprised response.

"Only a human would refer to me in such a manner, but yes, I am of the Star People," she answered, nervous as she realized it didn't feel like a human! "Who are you?" she asked in return.

"I'm Lieutenant Alec Scott.  Where are you?" it pressed.

"Let me find you, then you'll see," she offered in return.  She reached out with Empath, stretching along the path where she felt this presence originated, all the while remaining in contact with it, letting it see she could easily find it.  She zeroed in on a motley collection of three starships of various builds.  She delved within, seeing they were filled with humans.  Joy ignited along her senses, relieved.  But why didn't it feel like a human's mind, she wondered?

"Because I'm not human alone," it informed her.  She finally found it, seeing it was an animal and a human man, joined in an inner bond.

"So, I see," she returned, humor in her mental tones.  "I'm on the Challenger, helping to effect repairs," she told them, seeing the man opening his eyes, as if he could see her presence in the room with them.  It looked as if he were sitting in a seat upon their bridge.  "Would it be better if I made myself visible to everyone, or not?" she questioned, unsure.  She didn't want to panic anyone.

"Yes, if you can.  That way they can see you, as you truly are," they responded.  She willed herself to be seen, standing near Alec and his animal.  She realized it looked something like a cat, from the pictures she'd seen.  There was an instant reaction to her appearance, but another man next to the one talking with her stepped between her, and the security men approaching.

"She's not really here.  It's a projection of herself," he explained to the ship's commander, speaking up hastily; having been filled in on the circumstances by Storme just as she was about to appear.

"I'm Ryes of House Li," she told an officer, who'd run over to access the situation; the commander remained in his chair, but had it swiveled around so he could see her easily.  "You're only a few hours outside of the Beda system.  I was merely curious as to who it was, who was trying to contact me."

"How're you here?" he questioned, surprised to be so directly addressed.

"I'm not physically here. I'm using my Empath Talent to both find you and project an image of myself for you. I find it more comforting than having you talk with the empty air," she explained, smiling merrily. The man who'd stepped over to defend her, smiled in return.

"Is Montigue Elbridge all right?" he asked, appearing hopeful.

"Most definitely," she assured him, nodding her head. "It's almost lunch time, so I'm sure Monty's heading for the dining hall right now, down in Winterhaven."

"And you're not in Winterhaven, now?" the officer questioned.

"No, I'm on the Challenger. We managed to retrieve her from a nearby system and have finished replacing her drive engines, so now am revamping her control and computer systems," she told him, smiling.

"Then you have a working starport?" he pressed, hoping. She laughed at this, shaking her head no.

"We have a very simple space platform for now. But we have two Talents with Inner Sight and two with Manipulator, and a few with Fire Shaper, so we've been managing to get things done, even so. Mitt would have more accomplished with the starport, but she's been busy trying to restore the Pike Forward."

"We're in need of repairs," he told her, a sinking feeling in his stomach, which was reflected on his face, giving Ryes pause.

"We'll handle them," she assured him. "You should've seen the damage to the Challenger when she first arrived. A mixture of Talents can do more than you imagine," she warned, hoping he wouldn't give up hope, "You'll see."

"How far out are we?" he pressed, wondering at her ability to measure time and distance.

"Looks like about just after lunch tomorrow, at the speed you're traveling," she replied, smiling. "My energy's running out. See you all soon!" With this she faded, flying back to her own self, settling once more.

"Ryes? Are you all right?" Cassie demanded, with panic coloring her voice.

"They'll be here tomorrow!" she told her, over the headset. "And I'm a little winded, Cass. We'll have to finish this later today. I need to rest," she added, feeling the full measure of her labors. They started the work before breakfast this morning.

"Who'll be here?" she returned, wondering what she was talking about? They were working on this control cable bundle.

"Three ships from out of Sol system! I was just in contact with one of them," she replied. "I've got to relay this below, take a break now and I'll tell you about it after I call it in," she said, cutting off the mic. She wiggled back out, rolled out from under the console, and kicked off. She floated across the cabin, heading for the communications station.

"Challenger calling Winterhaven," she said, as she activated the console, seating herself before the board. "Come in Winterhaven."

"Winterhaven here, how're you doing, Ryes?" Neil asked, smiling to himself as he heard her voice. He missed her presence.

"I'm doing great! Get ready to expect some company tomorrow. I just spoke mind-to-mind to a human, who was using his cat to boost his Talent. It struck me as odd, but they seemed friendly. He's on a ship called the Aurora," she told him. "But I guess I should report to Garth first, before we get to chatting about it."

"That's the truth," he returned with a chuckle. "I've never heard of a fleet ship named the Aurora, but I'm sure I'm out of date," he added as he piped in a quick message directly to Garth's console, to see if he was in his office.

"That's the impression of the name I got, as I was talking with her officers," she replied. "But she's not the lead ship in their small group. That came through very clearly, too."

"I've got Garth standing by, and ready to transfer. Take care up there, we miss you!" he told her, then patched her call through to her husband. He sat back in the chair with a sigh, as Max glanced over to him, smiling.

"They're here, at last! I only hope there're more ships out there to tap, or we're not going to be very effective against those Snags," he offered, in opinion. Neil shook his head at this, knowing it was a knotty issue.

"We'll manage. Once we've got a real, operational warship, we'll be able to check to see what's left of Kahmarr's other old colonies and allies. There must be some forces left, somewhere!" Neil insisted, knowing there was still so much to get done, and so little time left for Earth.

"I hope so," Max returned, then turned his eyes back to his screens. "We could sure use a planet-full of Demmias right now." Everything looked all quiet down here, at least. He heard Neil chuckling behind him, as he smiled.  He wondered what Hadu's homeworld was like?

"And you're sure it was only three ships?" Sabin asked as he and Garth were now standing on the bridge of the Challenger.  Ryes had turned back on the gravity, so while their cubs were fussing, it made the others more comfortable with getting around the ship. Raby and Sayer were with them in their room while their parents had to take care of important matters.

"Yes, there were only three, but they seemed to be the advance ships and two appeared to be heavily damaged," she explained. "They're seeking repairs, at the very least.  I let them know we'll handle it."

"After all the work you've done on the Challenger, you should be able to handle their ships," Jim said, looking about the bridge, amazed by this huge ship each time he was aboard her.

"She was truly in sad shape when we found her," Sabin admitted with a chuckle.

"It's taken time and a lot of effort to learn her, and how to repair her, so she can't be easily disabled again," Axel added, shaking his head. "It hasn't been easy, but we've all learned new things, doing it," he admitted.  Ryes nodded her head in agreement.

"Just how big are those ships?" Garth suddenly pressed, wondering how much work they still had ahead for his team?  Ryes gave him a nod of understanding, then pointed toward the gallery seats in the back of the room.

"Let's get comfortable and I'll show all of you," she invited.

"Can you do it without alerting their Talents?" Garth pressed, unsure now.  Her smile brightened as she gave him an assured nod. Their eyes met and he realized he should have more faith in her abilities, as he gave her a nod back.  She had put in far more practice than he had with his own.  The five of them started moving towards the seats, then Ryes noted Cassie paused, looking unsure, so she motioned her over in invitation with a smile upon her lips.

"I wasn't sure," Cassie breathed out as she sat down between her and Sabin.  Ryes laughed, nodding her head.

"I'd like your opinion of the shape they're in," she invited. She extended one hand to Garth and one to Cassie, who got the idea as she saw Axel joining hands with Garth and Jim, so extended her other hand to Sabin, with a smile lighting up her face and blue eyes, as her quivering within quieted.

Ryes and Sabin established the meld, then once they got everyone settled, Minn and Setta joined in, brining mental humor back into the mix once more. Finally, Ryes opened her Empath Talent and took them all out along the path to the three Earth ships. She realized they'd picked up their pace a bit, but two of the ships appeared heavily damaged and were just limping along. Ryes kept her contact with the ships to minimal, staying away and keeping to Empath only, so as not to alert the crews who might have Talent. She and Sabin had previously cautioned the others in the meld to save any comments until after they were back.

The largest of the three, The Aries' Wrath, by her hull designation looked to have taken the brunt of their blockade run. The second one, the Orit's Tablet, was also heavily damaged, but the third, the Aurora, which was the lead ship, appeared only lightly damaged. Ryes was sorely tempted to pull up her Inner Sight to do a quick check on the extent of the damage the ships sustained, but Garth cautioned against it for now. He'd seen enough, so she pulled them all back. They gently dropped the meld, and everyone opened their eyes, some with smiles, some thoughtful.

"They're new designs, but you could tell they were military craft," Jim commented. Ryes chuckled at this, nodding her head.

"So's the Challenger," she teased, smiling broadly with the light shining in her eyes. Axel and the others were laughing. He nodded his head as he blushed and laughed too.

"They have more obvious guns and weaponry. Ours are tucked away until needed," Setta bragged, "but if we don't have time, they can still fire through, without the covers being drawn back."

"That sounds handy," Sabin stated, pleased with that idea. "You never know the situations we'll be facing." Axel nodded his agreement.

"That's why we did it that way," he assured him. "It's too important to leave it all to chance; to have something impact the hull nearby and seal the hatches, if they know where the weaponry is located."

"That's solid," Garth replied as a compliment, smiling at his team with pride. "I want to think about these ships, and we'll discuss them more tomorrow. Now I've got to go collect the cubs and get them settled again back on Tayna." He didn't look happy with this one special chore, which was still ahead of him. He stood and moved out of the gallery for the exit.  Ryes quickly caught up to him, catching his arm and giving him a smile, as he turned to look into her eyes.

"Use your Empath to reconnect them to Tayna, then they'll be fine," she assured him. He huffed, having forgotten his Talents might be handy in this situation, once again.  He gave her a big smile and nod as he wrapped his arm around her shoulders, as they continued towards their suite of rooms to get their children.

"It's going to be too quiet up here," Cassie commented in a low voice to Setta, while she and Minn nodded their heads in agreement.  The little ones were an active, fun distraction at times.

Ryes sighed as she sat in her rooms staring at the computer screen, trying to concentrate upon doing something that would take her mind off the slowly dragging clock.  The humans were never going to arrive!  And not having the cubs around to take care of, made their departure more of an acute ache within.  Finally, she stood and moved away from her desk, having done all her work again, and didn't want to sink into one of the computer games right now.  One of the screens above her desk was set to view different scenes outside the ship, while another had scenes from various places from inside the ship.  Flutter-wing displayed on the one for a few minutes and she considered going over to it for to check who was there today.  It was still early evening, just before dinner, but after their work hours.  They'd buttoned up the ship, so it'd be ready for any visitors; invited or uninvited.  She wanted something to do that wouldn't just be a waste of time.  Then she got an idea.

Ryes pushed her chair back in against the desk so it would lock in place, not sure she could do this out here, but now that she had the idea, she wanted to see if she could.  And while she didn't have anyone to help, she felt this wouldn't be extended, nor too out of her league to deal with, as she planned it.  She felt tonight would be her one chance to do something daring and still have plenty of energy for the work ahead tomorrow.  She lay down upon her bed, then built up her inner body heat with Healing until she was sweating heavily, finally she closed her eyes and called up Time Walking.

She drifted back to when the former starport existed, and there was starcraft traffic coming in and out of the system.  The intense wrenching was fully expected, and when she opened her eyes, after the gold and green mist cleared, she was drifting high in space. She saw the starport in what appeared a geosynchronous orbit over Hailys.  Excited, she remained where she was for a moment just admiring its original form.  She drifted closer, itching to pull up her Inner Sight to truly see it, but with no oxygen around her, she didn't dare!  So, she sought out a nearby space craft.

The Margiiti was running by her, so she willed herself to be unseen and drifted through the hull to stand in a cabin inside. The shock next came as she saw her own mother in this cabin, changing her clothes.  She felt like an intruder but didn't dare move in any manner, as she feared to attract her attention.  Of all the people she knew, she felt with Tyra's Talents and training, she could discover her, if she felt her presence.  And she didn't want to intrude, seeing she was about Raby's age and still had so much before her to live through. She left the cabin, and being curious, Ryes followed, but not too close.

"Good news," a man, who looked of a close relationship to her announced, as Tyra and a youth joined him in a spacious lounge, a smaller version of the Challenger's lounge.  He smiled grandly for his children.  Ryes noted the family resemblance among them was easily seen.

"What news, Da?" she and her brother asked at the same time, then grinned at each other, teasingly poking each other in jest. He cleared his throat, so they turned their attention back to him.

"Elofin of House Aletin, you are going to lose your house affiliation, I am happy to report.  You have been accepted into the ranks of the Foresters," he told his young son, who was all of twelve years old now.  They both started to talk, but he held up his hand to stall them a moment.  He took out a beautiful gold chain with a pendent hanging upon it out of his pocket, then stepped forward to put it about his neck.

"Father, I am going to have to give this up," he minded him while admiring its beauty.  There was his house symbol upon it and his eyes shone with pride.

"I know, but keep it if you can, as a keepsake and remembrance," he advised, as he kissed the top of his head. "You can at least enjoy your family seal for now."  Elofin nodded his head, smiling as tears were in his eyes.  He wrapped his arms around his father, giving him a hug and kiss.

"I am going to miss you, Da," he told him from the heart. Tyra stood patiently to the side, waiting for her turn to give her brother a hug, too.  Ryes realized, in this moment, that this was her own other grandfather!  And she so wanted to meet them all but knew this couldn't be the time for it.  She didn't have the chance she was given to waste, right now.

"And for you, Tyra of House Li, I have this, as is befitting your station and Talents," he said, turning to her. He now pulled out the silvery opal and diamond chain with the House Li seal depending upon it, as Ryes now well recognized! She blushed and her eyes shone as he put it over her head. He gave her a kiss too, then she threw her arms about him and hugged him with tears in her eyes.

"Thank you so very much, Father," she told him, once she could. He let her go and looked her in the eyes.

"I have arranged for us to meet with a handmaiden of Doran of House Forental in Hailys. She will evaluate whether, or not, they may be able to shelter you. I requested only for a few years, until I can rally my family to help protect you from this ill-arranged marriage," he informed her. Ryes noted the fear and hope that warred within his eyes, seeing this was something he didn't want to do at all. Her heart went out to him; to lose both his children to a future he had no control over must have been wrenching! She wondered if she would ever have the courage to do, as she now saw her own grandfather doing today.

The three then gathered close again to share their love for each other and tears; knowing they were approaching the starport and would soon be parting company. Ryes left them and headed forward to the ship control room, realizing her one purpose in coming here was to see the starport for herself.

She found the broad viewport in the front and then opened her Inner Sight, pulling herself into the past, once again. She kicked in Empath and Booster and willed Inner Sight to function at a higher level, as her other Talents. Then she just stood there for several long heartbeats, taking in the grand beauty before her.

It was a stacked disc, which towered with lots of levels for ships to dock at, even one as large as the Challenger. There were repair facilities for ailing ships, and as Hadu had added into Flutter-wing, there were safe rooms to use in case of an emergency, armories that were well stocked, and independent AI areas, all of which could be used in a time of need. The top-notch defense systems were impressive and gave her ideas. There were shops, crafting areas, living areas for the people who lived and worked here, as well as guest quarters for visitors, some appeared quite elaborate and posh. Schools were here and lots of children, too. She stood admiring it, as they approached, then heard a noise behind her and turned, surprised as she let go of Inner Sight.

"You are not my sister, but appear like her," he commented, shock in his eyes.

74

"You will be my uncle someday," she replied, smiling as she'd been caught. "Uncle Elofin, it's so nice to see you!" They both laughed at this with him giving her a nod of his head. He didn't think this was a game, nor a waking dream, as she did appear to be standing in the family ship.

"How?" he asked, wonder in his eyes. She was physically here! And appeared older than either himself, or his sister.

"Time Walking and I should be getting back before I get into trouble," she told him. Then, still feeling daring, stepped forward and gave him a quick hug and kiss before pulling herself back to her own time. He stood rooted in shock as she disappeared.

Ryes pulled herself back, fighting her way through time, and as the protective mist dissolved, she opened her eyes, feeling exhausted within. She noted her body had still dropped in temperature, so pulled up Healing to restore it. Still, she hadn't passed out this time, so it must've helped. And now she had a lot to relay to Mitt, Axel and their AI about the ancient space station. She wanted to use some of the things she learned to incorporate into Flutter-wing's next expansion. She felt she could improve on both designs, since the original Hailys space station had still been destroyed by the Snagospin, and it had had good defensive systems.

"Are you about ready for dinner?" Axel asked, as he stood in her doorway, as it appeared she was waking up from a nap, when she didn't usually take naps. He had some suspicions now. "So how are the ships progressing?" he added with a smile. Ryes climbed out of the bed, securing the mesh once again, before turning to face him.

"I've no idea," she admitted, but then beamed a proud smile, "but I now know what the original space station here was like!" His eyebrows shot up in surprise, not having expected such a thing.

"You were Time Walking?" he pressed. She gave him a nod now, understanding his concern.

"It was a one-time thing, and the space station was amazing. I'll show you all the memory after dinner. I'm starving!" she assured him, as she joined him at the door. He gave her a nod, knowing if she told him it was a one-time adventure, it would be, that much he'd come to know about her. He gave her a warm smile and nod.

"I'm looking forward to seeing it," he replied. She gave him a nod, as they turned for the smaller dining room. She realized Elofin's perfume was still clinging to her clothing, which got her to smile. She'd discovered she had an uncle, and actually met him! She had to tell Aunt Adina all about it!

# Arrival

## Chapter 6

Axel, Ryes, Cassie, Bitty, Ivan, Minn and Setta stood on the bridge of the Challenger, as the three Earth ships finally came into range of her instrumentation. A sigh of relief went up from the group as a whole. They were finally here! Suddenly, the lighting within the room shifted from a soft white to a red color, startling everyone. Alarm claxons started sounding, as Ryes saw the weapons systems were trying to come online.

"What's happening?" Bitty demanded, putting her hands over her ears, not sure what she should do to help.

"The main computer's decided the ships are unknowns and is preparing for action," Axel shouted, rushing, as well as he could in the weightlessness and without having anything to push-off of, or grab, to get to the main computer board. Ryes held onto Minn's shoulder as she closed her eyes. She tried to reach out to it from within, to cut off its control over the weapons, but didn't have enough time to trace it down! She opened her eyes, then released Minn's shoulder, pushing herself over to the main computer console, swimming through the air.

"Shut the thing down before it fires!" Ivan urged, panic starting to rise within at the thought of the nightmare this was turning out to be now.  The horror on everyone's faces was plain to see.

"Computer, if you don't shut down the weapons and return to standby mode, I'll blast you to bits and rebuild you the way I think you should be built, from the scrap that's left over," Ryes threatened the ship's AI in Dolbith. She felt it take a reading of her, and as suddenly as it had gone to red alert, it began shutting the systems down in strict obedience. "You will classify these ships, and all ships which look of the same basic manufacture as allies and you will not EVER take hostile action against any of them, unless directly ordered to do so by one of the Winterhaven Command staff," she ordered. It still gave her the chills that it responded to her because of her Talent and instantly obeyed, because of the strength of her Talent. It fully believed her, it seemed.

"Good going, girl," Axel told her, floating at her side. She sighed and smiled as she turned to him.

"The darned thing thinks too much," she commented, relieved. "I'm taking those weapon systems offline, until we're ready to go to full operation. I don't want something like this to happen again."

"You might want to wait, to make sure they weren't followed, first," he countered, as he thought the weapons might help buy them a little time, if an attack ever came, even if they were only on auto. He thought he'd feel better if they had a real gunner onboard but wasn't sure if anyone in Winterhaven was trained for the task. He'd have to check into it, since it seemed he was now crew chief for this ship at this time. New jobs were kind of created that way, and usually he didn't mind it overall. He still didn't want to be on her when they went to war, even if he was the most skilled for the work. He wanted to be home, supporting their efforts here, and home for Kerry and their coming baby.

"You're right! I should've already checked their backtrail yesterday, to make sure," she agreed, instantly alarmed.

"Yeah, we don't want to be welcoming any Snags just yet," Cassie said, floating over to the console and gripping the edge to steady herself.

"How were you going to protect us, if you had to blast the ship to bits?" Poinsettia questioned in English, worried that it sounded as if Ryes meant what she threatened.

"Merely seal off the bridge and direct the force of the blast away from us and our platform," she told her, speaking in Dolbith, to make sure the computer understood she was serious about what she said, knowing it was still listening in. "With the range of Talents and power I have, it would've been easy." She smiled assurance for her, knowing Setta didn't like having to help out up here, since she was due to deliver her son in less than two months. She was going to be sent back down later this week, for which she seemed very glad. While Setta loved working in the Library in Matlowe Village, she'd be staying in Winterhaven to be near the Healers, per Maren's orders. And Ryes thought it was a good thing Garth took the cubs back to Winterhaven, until things settled down again. She was sure Raby and Sayer had missed them, anyway.

"At least things look like they're back to normal," Axel added, giving her a nod of his head. He knew why she did things the way she had to. They'd had their share of headaches from the ship's computer already. "Better grab a seat and start checking their backtrail," he advised, worried about such a possibility.

"Right," she agreed as she pulled herself into a chair before the computer and activated the seat's restraints. They secured her in as she closed her eyes, ready to call up her Empath Talent. She suddenly felt Alec's inquiry, as she cast free.

"Why were the weapons powering up for a few moments?" he asked in a very concerned tone, as she called up Mind Voice to speak with him more clearly.

"The stupid computer didn't recognize your ships. I told it I'd blast it into a million pieces, if it didn't stand down. It believed me and obeyed, but Axel won't let me take the weapon systems offline, until I've made sure you weren't followed. So, I'm going to do a thorough check now, just to be sure," she replied.

"Give me a moment to report this, first," he urged. She gave him her agreement, amused he wanted to help. So, she waited for Alec, feeling centered once more. "Alright, let's go check things out," he advised to let her know he was back.

"Hang on," she warned, as she fully unleashed Empath and touched Monrush's spirit, briefly. She then extended herself back along their flight path, reaching well beyond her home system. She went to the point where she first found them, finding the area here and between empty. Then she extended her search, doing slow sweeps, as if she were looking for another derelict ship again.

"Amazing!" he told her, enjoying being so free. He'd never experienced anything like this before! "Wait, what's that?" he asked, having the faintest impression of something artificial nearby. Storme noted it too.

"Let's see," she offered, zooming over for a closer look. It was a derelict ship. A human, derelict ship! She reached for the bridge, noting that one side if the rear hull had been blasted out, but something within this ship called out to her Talents! "Is this one of the ones accompanying you?" she asked Alec, wanting to know if he recognized it.

"No, but I think I know whose ship it is," he returned. "I believe it's a free trader named the Quicksilver, belonging to the Elbridge family from a colony world named Trinity. She was lost long ago, with a special stone to guide her, at the time."

"The Windrose Stone!" she returned excited, feeling its presence aboard the ship, but the pull from it was far weaker than their own. Instinctively, she kept the knowledge of their own stone from him, not wanting to give out such important information, when she barely knew him, and knew nothing of his culture. She pulled them before the ship's main computer board to check the extent of the damage. It looked far worse than it actually was. "This was done on purpose!" she protested.

"I heard the story went they were being boarded by pirates," he explained, seeing the tales were true. "The captain was trying to blow the boarding ship away, to destroy it if possible, and make it look as if they were beyond repair, and not worth taking. He did take out the pirate ship. What was left barely managed to limp into Velomax Starport, with the last crewman dying as he docked. He did a better job than he intended, it seems. I don't think they escaped harm, themselves."

"Well, I'm heading her toward Monrush and our little platform. We can repair her at least. I wonder what happened to the rest of her crew?" She activated the engines and gave the ship her new course.

"We'll work on that mystery later. Let's finish our sweep, first," he pressed, humor in his mental voice. She smiled to herself, recalling they did have a special reason to be out here right now.

She extended out once more, searching for signs of any other ships, doing her slow sweeps again. Then, she spotted it. It wasn't that she saw the ship right off, but that she felt the presence of a Snagospin Talent nearby. She instantly zoomed in, grasping his awareness, holding onto his mind tightly. She recognized him from his light brush with Sabin, through those memories Doran had stolen, and she borrowed for that challenge. Sabin's Talent with hers had merely taken them out to touch another presence in space, in their own time, and here he was before them.

As Ryes held him, his hate and panic were strong, and he started attacking her in retaliation, to free himself from her mental grapple. After facing off Doran and the Southern Talents, it didn't surprise her, as they struggled. He was trying to kill her with mental strikes filled with spikes and terror. Alec managed to distract him for a moment, to give her the freedom to press the advantage and attack the Snag with the huge mental hammer she recalled being used on herself, before. It did the trick and stunned him, in a manner, to prevent further retaliation for a few moments. Thankfully, there were no other Snag Talents around to know anything of their fight, and her initial strike had blocked him from calling for help, in any fashion.

She mentally girded herself, then reached within him, burning out his Talent. Next, she took his memories as she recalled the way Doran used to do to the men, leaving him unconsciousness upon his cabin floor. At least there was no one around to witness the attack, either. Then she searched for the ship's engines, looking for their vulnerable points with her Inner Sight. She ripped out some of the fail-safe components using Manipulator. Very quickly, the systems went into overload and the ship's drive unit exploded, just as they were radioing in about the severe malfunction. She withdrew, noting there were no other ships nearby.

"I can't believe it was so easy," Alec commented, once she was through. He'd been practically holding his breath through the whole thing, not wanting to distract her at a critical moment. Storme was fascinated with her abilities. She was drawn to Ryes as much as he was, as if he was a moth to an open flame.

"I'm not proud of what I did, but I'm not letting them follow you here to destroy us again. We're going to have to go through what he knew, to see how much they're aware of your operation, and if they even suspect we exist," she explained. "With destroying the ship this way, it could be merely chance, and they shouldn't suspect my involvement."

"Definitely, a really bad day for them," he agreed, understanding more of what was at stake here. He didn't know if he had the courage to do, as she'd just done. While her attack was quick, it didn't have the vicious edge the Darken's attack in return held. It was as she said, what she had to do.

"At least a few escaped in pods, so I'll have to keep an eye here for a while, just in case. No one made sure to see if their Talent was among those evacuating the ship. They must not care for each other, as we do. We'll see what develops," she warned, hoping this would stop it for a time.

"Storme's reaching her limit. We'll be seeing you soon, anyway," he told her, feeling exhausted himself. She returned him and Storme to themselves, making sure they were settled, then returned to her own self, sitting strapped into the chair once more. She opened her eyes, realizing she was practically shivering from the chill she now felt.

"What's to report?" Axel questioned her. Minn and the others were gathered near to hear it, too.

"First, we found another derelict which I have heading toward us," she told him. "She's a trader ship, which used to belong to Monty's family."

"We? We who?" he pressed, surprised and alarmed.

"Lieutenant Alec Scott and Storme, his cat, from off the Aurora," she explained, smiling. "We found a Snag ship following, a long way back along their trail. I attacked it and it's been blown to pieces. Some of the crew survived, escaping in life pods, so I'll keep an eye that way for a while," she informed him.

"His cat? A hemi-cat?" Cassie asked her, frowning, "Then, he's a psi, of some kind?"

"Yes, he is," Ryes agreed, smiling as she was rubbing her arms. Minn noted it, then pushed away.

"You'd better call down and report this all to Garth," Axel suggested, as Minn quickly returned with a blanket for Ryes. He released her restraints and wrapped it around her.

"Yes, I'd better," she agreed, smiling her thanks to Minn with a grateful nod. The others went back to watching for the starships, as she turned for the communicator to call below. She knew she had to show him what happened, but wanted a quick nap, first. At least it'd be several more hours before the human ships could join them in orbit around Tayna.

"You're sure she destroyed the Darken ship?" Captain Yun sharply questioned the young lieutenant closely, needing to be exact on this item of news. They were in his office, as he didn't want any of it out among the crew, with the situation the way it was. That ship powering up her weapons so quickly had put a good scare into them all! He didn't need any more surprises!

"Yes Sir. She removed several fail-safe devices from their engines, and it blew. There were a handful of survivors, but she thought this made it look more as an accident, than an attack," he explained. He sat holding Storme in his arms, as she purred her encouragement to him. There were other psi's aboard the other two ships, and he knew they'd be called in now to try to verify his story. For now, he'd leave the Quicksilver out of it.

"How big a ship was it?" he pressed in return, serious questions starting to come to light within his mind. Could this have been all a fabrication created for the lieutenant to gain his trust? How strong a psi is she?

"It was frigate-sized with almost four hundred hands aboard. I think we estimated maybe sixty to sixty-five got off before she blew. They were fighting each other for the life pods," he told him. He saw his mind was awhirl, with trying to estimate the amount of threat they were under from this one, alien woman. He wanted to reassure him that they were not being threatened at all, that he knew of the pure joy she felt, that they finally arrived, but understood this wasn't the time. He'd only hear, what he wanted to hear, in this moment.

"Let me show you," he offered, holding out his hand. Yun hesitated only a moment, then took it and closed his eyes. Alec first opened up his first contact with Ryes, so that he could see how she thought and acted. Then he showed the whole time from the first discovery of the Darken ship to when she brought them back to themselves. Yun was instantly relieved. They both let go within and

81

opened their eyes. Yun took in a deep breath, then let it out slowly, feeling more centered, again.

"Good job. You're dismissed, lieutenant. You may return to your quarters to rest for now," he finally ordered, noting the neutral look upon his youthful face. He was never sure of what a psi was thinking, or if he, or she, was spying upon his own thoughts at any given time, so was usually wary, but his sharing the experiences had greatly allied his inner worries. He knew he held his own counsel most times, only speaking openly with his First, Commander Ashton Briggs. He'd have to brief Briggs later, after he had time to pass it down to the captains. Now, he had to get this information to Captains Walker and McMurray to help put their fears to rest.

"What did you tell the captain? He's practically shaking in his boots," Ash asked, as he caught up with his friend in the officer's mess.

"I showed him that we found a Darken ship and Ryes took it out," he replied, keeping his voice low so it wouldn't carry.

"Ryes? THE Ryes?" he questioned in return, in a low voice too, as they each grabbed a tray and headed for the line.

"Yes, it's really her. And she's strong! I've never felt anyone like her, in my entire life," he told him, stopping to meet his eyes. They started making their selections then went over to a vacant table, away from the other diners.

"So, what's she like? Would she try to blow us up, too?" he asked, suddenly understanding Yun's concerns. Alec smiled for him, shaking his head no.

"Never! She's not that kind of person to begin with. She's a very normal person with a husband, kids, and family to worry over. She's helping to repair the Challenger, one of their own ships which they recovered from a nearby system. There was something about needing it not to protect their own world as such, but to help break the Snagospin, or Snags, as they call the Darkens, away from Sol system, and drive them back to their own home system," he explained with a smile, knowing it would go straight back to Yun soon.

"So, what's to keep them from trying to conquer us, too?"

"With only one ship?" he returned, chuckling at the thought. "No. They're trying to figure out strategies for attacking the Snags,

82

and it looks like all their stronger `Talents,' their psi's, are going to have to play a part in it. After seeing the way Ryes destroyed the Snag ship, I can see how and why." Ash didn't look comforted as he turned his attention to his food.  Presently, Connor appeared, and they started talking about what they thought they might find on this Tayna.  Ash was paged, as they were talking.

"Got to run. See you, later," he told his friends with a smile and nod of his head.  Alec gave him a small wave.

"Sure," Connor added, grinning.  Ash left his tray off at the cleaning station and disappeared. "So, what did you see while you were out with Ryes?" he asked, turning back to Alec.

"A wonderful surprise," he teased, knowing he'd find out before much longer. "You'll see."

"I can't wait," he agreed, nodding his head as they stood to leave, too.

"I've got to catch a nap.  Make sure to be on the bridge for our landing," he invited, knowing Ash would allow it.

"You'd better believe it!" he returned, as he turned for the lounge.  He wanted another look at this large, blue, and green world.

"Alec," a voice intruded, just as he was getting comfortable in his bunk.  Alec sighed as he turned over to lie upon his back.

"Yes, Mona?" he returned, having hoped she wouldn't bother him until after his nap.

"Show me what you saw her do," she urged.  He could "feel" the others were now joining them in this link, wanting to experience all he knew about Ryes, so far.

He focused in; it being easy with Storme lying beside him. Keeping all other thoughts away, he started from Ryes detecting an alien's mind presence out in space.  He showed them the whole sequence, until she returned him to himself and let them go.

"My god, what power!" Ken declared, amazed.

"She could do anything she felt like doing," Mona agreed.

"But she's not like that!  Power isn't what drives her!" Alec returned, with Storme in full agreement. "Look at her deeper thoughts. She's worried about whether or not we'll be able to respond in time to save the Earth, not plotting how to take us all out."

"Your hemi-cat trusts her, so I'll trust her. It's hard to fool a hemi-cat, no matter how powerful a psi is," Ken finally sent, after a few awkward moments of silence. Storme's delight and agreement came immediately, clearly through, causing all seven of them to mentally laugh in response.

"Be careful, Alec. It's apparent she likes you and seems to trust you, but still, keep on the alert. None of us, individually, could take her on. And the way she burned out that Darken's psi abilities makes me shiver. I didn't know such a thing was possible until now," Flann stated.

"They've been breeding their psi Talents for generations untold. I saw the report and Doctor Cruthers said they have fourteen distinct Talents, but he'd only witnessed a very few of those by the time he sent off the probe. Could you imagine where the human race would be, if we'd been doing the same? I'm sure it's why those Darkens are so strong too, and why we're having such a tough time trying to beat them off. Give these people a chance. We'll see what happens and what they're really like, once we land," Alec urged, trying to bring out some understanding.

"Yeah, but they were defeated once too, so, it might not be as easy as you think," Ken added. Then the group dissolved the link, and Alec and Storme were once again alone, themselves.

"Storme, don't ever let out all the things we suspect Ryes can do. And I'm betting she could take on the lot of us, without raising a sweat, but I'm letting them believe what they want, as long as they leave us alone," Alec told her. She rubbed against his side, purring loudly as he smiled and scratched her head. He finally relaxed and dropped off, Storme curled up at his side, resting and keeping watch.

"We'd merely like to meet you and get a quick look at your warship, perhaps we can suggest improvements to help," Captain Walker pressed, speaking to the image they finally had transmitted out to them from off the huge warship they were slowly approaching. Ryes didn't trust this man. His smile seemed pasted on, but she saw Garth's approval flash on her communications board, from out of Winterhaven. He and the rest of the Command staff were monitoring this communication. She put on a more genuine smile for him, as she gave the image before her more attention.

84

"Our base commander has approved it, so a small party may come aboard for a guided tour. The only request I have is Lieutenant Alec Scott and any other of your Talents, who wish to come along, be included in the party," she told him. He looked uncomfortable with this request, but finally nodded his head in approval.

"It will be so. You may expect us within the hour," he replied, then the screen blanked.

"What were you doing with that request?" Sabin questioned her in Dolbith, their link still open and operating. They decided to stick to Dolbith in their transmissions, until they could feel comfortable with these newcomers. Even their humans understood this attitude and agreed. They were sure their communications would be tapped.

"I'd like to meet Alec. He seems young, but wise in some ways. And if they're suspicious of us, after my destroying the Snag ship, this is a good way to get introductions off to a good start," Ryes explained, as she saw Ethan nod his head in agreement.

"Just don't take any chances. Just because it's impolite for us to `spy' on each other with Mind Voice, don't make it so there. You and Axel get everyone prepared for the visit and seal off the ship from any attempts of intrusion they might make," Garth advised, wishing he could be up there with her right now. That ship's captain had appeared too controlled and false.

"Be on the alert, in case they try to use any kind of sleep gasses, stunners, or drugs," Maren advised. "You're a Healer too, after all," he reminded her. She smiled merrily at this, giving him a nod of her head. His once putting her to sleep with his Talent, reminded her that she was vulnerable and too trusting most times.

"I will," she promised, thinking it'd be wise to have all her Talents up and available for this "friendly" visit.

"What if they want us to accompany them down, when they land on Tayna?" Axel questioned, feeling it needed to be addressed. "Hostages were not uncommon throughout human history."

"Ryes and another to help guard her, may accompany them down. The rest of you will stay up there for the time being. Keep the weapons online in case any other Snag ships come snooping about. From the report we had originally, there were twelve ships in the task force. Only three have made it, and they've not told us how many actually made it through the blockade yet. I wonder if their own Command never told them what information they already disclosed to us?" Garth responded, making his decision on the matter, and seeing the reasons for the rest of his orders come to light in the eyes of both his staff around him, and the rest up on the Challenger.

"Hmmm, a good point," Ethan stated, nodding his head. "We shall see what kind of people we'll be dealing with soon enough. Be careful Ryes, not all humans can be trusted," he added in warning, knowing her tendency to extend her trust too readily.

"I will," she assured him, smiling as she cut the signal. "How long will it be before they figure out our language base?" she questioned Axel, turning to face him. He chuckled in response.

"It may take them a while. After all, you and the Snags are the only intelligent, speaking peoples we've encountered, as far as I know. First, they have to figure out the basics, like the names for the physical things around us, then extrapolate from there. Since none of us picked up a rock and called it that, it'll have them in fits for a few months at least," he assured her, still grinning. She smiled in return, looking relieved.

"I didn't have that hard a time with it, when I was Time Walking into the past. And really, I picked up the language fast once Neil started teaching me," she protested, then sighed. "If Garth wants us to stick to Dolbith, unless we need to address them directly, then we shall, until we can call them our friends."

"That's the best advice I've heard in a long time, but remember, you're exceptional," he agreed with a grin, then turned to take care of securing the ship the rest of the way for their visitors, glad they had locked down most things yesterday. She laughed and blushed, helping to get ready for this visit too.

# Tour

## Chapter 7

As the airlock began to cycle, Ryes realized her excitement was growing. Even if these people weren't her friends, she still looked forward to meeting the new humans. She'd turned on the gravity field in the areas they were going to entertain them. As the pressure equalized and the door opened, six heavily armed and armored men strode out into the wide corridor immediately outside the bay, stepping three to each open access, cutting them off from the rest of the ship and effectively surrounding them. This immediately turned the smile upon her lips to a tense line, glad they were transmitting everything down to Winterhaven. What did they think they were pulling aboard her ship? Axle and Minn stepped closer to each of her sides, putting their bodies between her and the soldiers. Ryes stood patiently, as the rest of the men stepped forward into the bright hallway, looking about curiously. She noted they were all dressed in military uniforms and while they moved with ease, they seemed on edge.

The hangar was cavernous, and they could've easily parked four of the Earth shuttles in it, without worrying about spacing, eight shuttles, if needed. There was bright light illuminating everything. The walls were an immaculate white, as if fresh out of the factory. The support equipment for the shuttlecraft was neatly tucked into the walls, or otherwise well out of the way of anyone walking in the room, with many modules mounted in the ceilings and walls. The access-way hatch was again large enough to support a sizable number of people, or large equipment modules for ease of passage to the spacious corridor outside the room. And they'd seen there were numerous such outer hatches along the sides of this massive ship. It was meant for war, as a carrier and battlestation in its own right! The humans tried not to look impressed, but it was very evident on their faces.

"You rather take harsh liberties when visiting a ship, which belongs to one of your allies," Ryes told the lead officer, as he stepped up, leaving two paces open between them. He had light brown hair, which was neatly clipped, with every hair in place. His rich brown eyes bespoke intelligence and alertness. He smiled, uncomfortable at her kind reprimand, knowing it was deserved, but orders were orders.

"Commander James Kaminski, First Officer of the Aries' Wrath, at your service, M'lady," he stated, giving her a small bow, then quickly straightened. "There was some concern, considering the Snagospin were reported to be nearby," he told her, as the official excuse. She sighed, realizing he already knew the name their ancestors used, when referring to those they usually called "the Darkens." But his knowledge of the ship incident was no surprise to her, at all.

"You may be at ease Commander. There're no Darkens in this solar system," she told him, smiling once more. "I'm the Chief Executive Officer of Winterhaven, Ryes of House Li," she introduced herself, using starmen naming traditions, then indicated the people around her. "And may I present, Axel of House Reguild, Minn, and Poinsettia of House Swanilde, who're some members of my crew." The First stepped forward and shook hands with everyone, smiling more genuinely.

"And may I introduce Commander Gene Corliss, First Officer of the Orit's Tablet, Commander Ashton Briggs, First Officer the Aurora, Lt. Mona West from the Wrath, Lt. Alec Scott from the Aurora, Lt. Blair Nesbit from the Orit's Tablet, and Ensign Yaell Ingolla, who'll be serving as our recorder," he introduced his party, leaving out the armed men around them and the remaining four, standing behind them. She noted he hadn't ordered the soldiers to stand down yet, and two drones were over their heads. Handshakes were exchanged all around, with Ryes ending up between Alec and Mr. Kaminski.

"So pleased to finally meet you, Alec," she told him, smiling. "You didn't bring your cat? We've all been teased about resembling cats, and I wanted to see what one was actually like." There was laughter at this, finally breaking the formality.

"You'll get to meet her soon," he assured her, still chuckling with his light brown eyes appearing merry. "She was still tired and needed some rest, but I promise to even let you pet her, when you do see her." From the way he said it, she guessed it wasn't a privilege he let happen very often.

"Then, I'll look forward to it. Let me show you all to one of the nearby lounges. We have some refreshments prepared," she invited, gesturing the way they needed to go, making three of the soldiers move aside for her and the others to pass. Having all her Talents up and active, she already knew Mona and Blair held Talents, too. She wondered if they were here only at her request, or to keep an eye, so to speak, on her and Alec? She decided to push it, as they walked. "Are you all right, Alec? You don't look too happy to be here. If I'd known this would be a burden for you, I would've never extended the invitation," she openly sent to him. She immediately saw the interest in Mona's blue eyes.

"No.  I just didn't get enough time for a proper nap, after all we did earlier," he assured her, still feeling sleepy.

"I know what you mean. I'm still a little winded, myself," she confided in him, knowing Mona clearly heard them.

"How long have you been working on this ship?  It looks in good repair on the inside," Mr. Kaminski commented, as they walked, noting the many section seals secured.  He was sure it was because of their visit.  Scans had read oxygen levels and temperature constants were stable throughout the entire ship.  All the figures he came up with on energy use for just maintenance on this ship were staggering.

"We only got her in a few months ago. We were vexed with getting her computer to synch in with our AI in Winterhaven for a while, but we think we finally have that problem solved, and got the new drive system finished, before we complete the other, smaller repairs.  Overall, she was in pretty good shape when we found her," she told him, leaving the details of finding the ship out of her surface thoughts.  She had already blocked attempts of the two Talent women, to spy on the thoughts of the people with her.  Minn had his own Talent up and now linked with her to help monitor the situation for her, freeing her to concentrate upon other matters.  She was so glad they practiced such teamwork with their Talents regularly.

"She's a huge ship, it must take a large crew to do all the work, but why did you replace the drive system?  Wasn't the one already on her operational?" Kaminski questioned, walking beside her as she shook her head no.  The massive corridors narrowed down to smaller, more regular corridors, making him feel more comfortable.

"The drives were barely working, and were so dangerous, we decided to rip the whole system out and reconfigure them to a newer, safer system.  It's now getting all the sensors and wiring between finished, then testing them," she told him, leaving how many people were aboard, unspoken.  It was none of his business, after all. "For the most part, the work's completed on the Challenger."

"You tore out and reconfigured a new drive system on a ship this size in only a few months?" Mr. Corliss demanded, astounded.  There were no real repair facilities here at this platform of theirs!

"It truly didn't take long.  You'd be surprised what a combination of Talents can accomplish," she retorted, blushing as she heard the consternation in his voice. "We broke down the dangerous radioactives and reused the resulting substances for other things in the process.  We have direct control of the process, so it does make things easier."

"Amazing," Ash commented, in a low voice. Axel smiled at him as it echoed louder than he intended in the long corridor.

"Yes, it was," Axel agreed, nodding his head to him. They entered the lounge area, noting the table set up for their welcome. Bitty, Cassie and Ivan stood ready to help, if needed. The armed soldiers appeared to instantly disturb their humans, with the whole situation.

"But how can you know to repair, or use, this technology, if by Doctor Cruthers' report, so little of your own machinery even existed?" Mr. Kaminski asked with a frown, as he struggled with this concept. "I need to understand how you can blithely change out a starship's drive system and install a new one, when you can't possibly know what you're really doing?"

"Let me show you," Ryes urged, her smile melted as she stood solemnly contemplating him. If she couldn't convince him that Talents actually existed, and they were eminently useful, it was all for naught. Every instinct screamed she had to gain this man's trust! After several long moments, as he considered her offer, while everyone else seemed afraid to breathe, he finally gave her a small bow and a smile.

"Please, show me," he requested. She smiled at this, giving him a nod of her head in response. Ryes stepped up to him, extending her hand. He placed his in hers, meeting her eyes, waiting. Gene steeped over and placed his hand over theirs, noting she didn't object.

"Close your eyes," she instructed, as she closed her own and forged a meld, getting them quickly comfortable. She opened her eyes then stepped closer to one of the armed men in his party and touched his weapon, as he held it nervously with their closeness, but remained still. The others had moved with her. Ryes opened her Inner Sight, as she closed her eyes. She then showed them what she saw, when using her Talent. They examined the rifle with her, seeing its flaws immediately.

"This is wrong," Kaminski told her, unnecessarily, astounded at what she could perceive. No wonder they could serendipitously rip out and install new engines, even their balancing would be no problem with this kind of ability! Ryes allowed Blair, Mona, and Alec into the contact, so they could all see it with them. Minn stayed peripheral to them, remaining on the alert.

"Yes, there are flaws and they do scream out to my senses, when our eyes would see nothing wrong," she agreed, then using Manipulator, she lifted over one of the weapons they found on the ship. She let Mr. Kaminski hold it, as they all looked at it through her

90

Talent.  Ash had watched the plasma rifle come hurtling out of nowhere to rest in Kaminski's arms and gave one of the nervous soldiers a nod of assurance; he didn't want this to spark anything and was glad Ryes chose to put the weapon into the arms of the one person it was safe to hold it in this unknown situation.

"Now this one's made right," Mr. Kaminski told her, knowing she knew it, too.  He felt her warm humor at his statement.

"Amazing!" Mr. Corliss added, trying to grasp this unique psi. Their own psi corp members were equally stunned; having never seen such an ability before.

"We know they must've had people blessed with Inner Sight in on the design of these weapons, but conversely we're totally mystified over how they could've ever used drive engines so poorly conceived. Axel and Cassie thought it must be something like a lowest bid on a construction contract, or a political ploy to keep an older design. We have no idea and my great aunt never paid attention to such things. They used force fields to keep the crew and rest on the ships safe from the wild, destructive energies," she explained, giving them a small glimpse of the old engines, using a memory of it with her Inner Sight's view. Then they stepped back as she dissolved the link, opening her eyes to meet his.

"Now I understand many things," he told her, smiling with more warmth as he could now, clearly, see the way her mind and heart worked. "Let's get something to eat, sit down, get comfortable and get to know each other, better," he suggested.  He glanced down at the foreign weapon in his hands, then passed it over to one of the men standing next to his hostess.  Minn slung it over his shoulder until Ryes could put it away.

"Are these baby things?" Mr. Corliss questioned as they stepped over to the table, indicating the toys and tethers setting nearby. There was laughter from the Winterhaveners.

"My children are down with my husband this week. We take turns caring for them," Ryes explained. "It's too quiet up here when they're gone, as they're very active and love to explore, with or without the gravity turned on.  They're little spacemen already."

"How many do you have?" Ash asked, as they sat down at the table, seeing there was plenty of room and food sitting on the serving tables nearby. The smells were intoxicating, and his mouth started watering.

"Five little ones and two older daughters," she replied. "They all keep us pretty busy most times. And the little ones love it best when we have to turn off the gravity field, having figured out how to get around when the fields are off."

"All this and raising a pack of kids, too," Blair commented under her breath to Mona. She laughed lightly at this, nodding her head. It sure sounded like a lot for anyone to take on.

"Ah, fresh food!" Gene declared with delight, as they started passing the bowls and platters around. Laughter sounded from others at the table.

"We do tend to forget what it was like with the ol', stale preserved shipboard foods, when we have this here," Cassie said, as she set down the bubblenut cups by each person. They had enough food to easily feed everyone twice over, having this sent up by Chuck and Raya this morning. All but the soldiers dug into the fresh vegetables and fruits first and the bubblenuts were eaten with relish.

"You don't get fresh foods too often, Mr. Kaminski?" Ryes asked as she was eating her food, enjoying it, too. Cassie, Bitty and Ivan had sat down to eat. Since he never introduced the four others in their party, Ryes didn't introduce the others in hers. The officer gave her a nod of his head, while trying to clear his mouth to speak. He'd been delighted with the rich flavors.

"Not since we left Earth," he admitted, "And please extend my compliments to your chef," he added. She smiled, her eyes lighting up with humor.

"I'll let both Chuck and Raya know," she assured him.

"This is great, I'm afraid to ask what it is," Ash asked, enjoying a fish dish.

"Silversides is a fish, and truly good eating. They sent up a variety, so you could each try what you wanted. Mine's bounder steak, which I love the new marinade Raya came up with for it," she replied, holding up her fork.

"I never had fresh fish. This is so good," he assured her, then turned back to his plate. There was scattered light laughter while they ate, and agreements sounded around the table.

"Are your solders allowed to eat?" Ryes asked, concerned. Mr. Kaminski nodded. "We have plenty for everyone."

"We'll let them get their share in shifts soon," Mr. Corliss replied. She gave him a nod and started nibbling her bubblenuts.

"We'll have to set up a trade or something to make sure you get some fresh foods while your ships are here, at least," she assured them.

"That sounds wonderful," Blair commented in a low voice, as Alec gave her a smile and nod in agreement.

"We wouldn't want to put a strain upon your own food supplies," Mr. Corliss stated, hoping, but understanding limits after all. The Winterhaveners laughed at this, most shaking their heads.

"We have some farms growing our grains in fields, caged birds producing eggs and meat, vegetable and fruit gardens that produce quantities of produce, trees we can collect plenty of fruits and nuts from, we now have bounder pits, where we have a captive population to breed from, and korom in pens to provide meat, hides and more. Our fruit and nut trees may still be young, but we have access to plenty of food," Ryes assured the first officers with a smile. "We'll manage it," she promised. Her confidence impressed Mr. Kaminski and Mr. Corliss, while Ash nodded, expecting it.

"We'll all be looking forward to it," Mr. Corliss assured her, grinning happily.

"Now that you have her, what are you intending to do with so big a starship?" Mr. Kaminski pressed, as he sipped some interestingly flavored beverage, they called tea. All the Winterhaveners were eating and drinking the same foods, so felt they weren't being poisoned, but he still wanted to understand more of these people. Ryes smiled as she gave him a nod.

"First and foremost, free Earth from the Snagospin," she assured him. The clear look in her green eyes showed that she spoke the truth. "We hope we can drive them back to the worlds they came from and keep them there – away from all others they would try to harm."

"That's a noble ambition," he noted before setting his cup back down. She gave him a nod of her head in agreement.

"I know it's not going to be easy, but it's what we're going to be trying to do," she replied, "I have a feeling it's going to be a lot of work, so we're going to have to find some friends out here, somewhere, and hope we're there in time to make a difference."

"Can you explore out there and check how things are on Earth now?" Alec asked before he thought on it, then blushed as the others all turned to look at him with questions in their eyes. Ryes smiled, lighting up her green eyes from within with humor, which put him at ease once more.

93

"I keep my explorations small and far closer to Monrush," she admitted, shaking her head. "I'd be afraid of losing my way home." He gave her a nod of understanding.

"Space is vast," Ash commented, trying to understand what Alec had tried to tell him earlier. "But you do have amazing gifts," he added. She smiled at him and gave him a nod.

"Thank you," she said, seeing the way Alec seemed to keep close to his side, rather than near the other Talents, and realizing they had to be friends.

After a half hour of light chatter exchanged, they finished their meal. Everyone seemed to get his or her fill and as they moved over to the couches to continue to get to know each other better, Kaminski signaled the watch officer to allow his men and women to take turns at the feast still sitting to be enjoyed. He was impressed that they'd taken pains to keep cold foods cold and warm ones still gently heated. They knew food serving tolerances for everyone's health. From the reports Dr. Cruthers sent, they knew only one chef survived. One person couldn't teach them this alone, they had to have had such knowledge from before. Such simple things were important in Kaminski's mind. These were not primitive people.

"Are we going to get a chance to check this baby out?" Mr. Corliss asked, seeing the huge screens overhead displaying the area around here, the moons, and their space station. Flutter-wing turned out to be amazingly new and well equipped, but they'd been surprised to find it was manned with a skeleton crew.

"We'll let your people finish their lunch, then show you a little bit. We only have the one internal shuttle finished so far, so can't easily get to the engineering compartment yet, but we do have plenty of other areas to show you," Axel informed them while Ryes went to show a few people to the nearby bathrooms. Minn had gone to put away the plasma rifle, which left Axel, Ivan, Bitty, Cassie and Setta who all appeared to be at home in this cavernous room.

"Have you had any problems adjusting to your new lives?" Mr. Kaminski asked them with a sweep of his arm in the direction Ryes went, curious as there were no outward displays of being uncomfortable in the presence of the cat people. Axel's eyes took on an interested glint while Cassie and Setta both laughed at this, as if it were the oddest question he could've asked. Bitty was thoughtful.

"Actually, it hasn't been any problem at all," Ivan supplied with a huff of a laugh. "They treat all of us as if we'd grown up together and are part of their families. Even if I could have a safe ride home tomorrow, I think I'd rather stay, as this place is more home than the world of my birth."

"They don't treat us like outsiders, and they'll give you the clothes off their backs, so to speak, if you were in need – without asking," Bitty said, speaking up too. Axel nodded his agreement.

"Don't mistreat our friends. They're decent people," Axel added, suspecting why he was asking now.

"I'm looking forward to having my son here and raising him in Winterhaven. He'll have a decent life and grow up among friends," Setta asserted, a hand to her budging stomach. Her eyes held an unspoken challenge as they met the First of the Wrath's. He smiled for her in acknowledgement.

"We only wanted to be sure," Mr. Corliss said, speaking up as he saw the passion in these people around them.

"None of you have a wire anymore," Ash began, as he formed his question. "We've tried to send you messages directly and to verify you are, who you say you are..." It was met with mirth.

"I know we are raised to think they're wonderful and we need them every day in our lives, but when Maren was checking us over in Medical after saving our lives, he removed them. He felt they were unnecessary and a source of possible infections. I haven't missed mine at all, and never realized before how intrusive it'd been in my life," Setta assured him with the others giving a nod of agreement.

"I like only having my own thoughts running around inside my head," Ivan added with a laugh. "I wouldn't ever want it back again."

"Then please verify for me who you really are? Some of you match who we have on file as survivors and two of you don't," Mr. Kaminski stated as if in challenge.

"I'm Babette Louise Parleer, from the Star Quest. I was a Fire Control and Safety officer before and am now so, on the Challenger," Bitty said, speaking up first.

"And I'm Cassandra Anne Reddin, also from the Star Quest, but I was just a shipboard maintenance tech before," Cassie told him.

"Noted and comparisons will be made," he assured the women. "Do any of you have anything you wish to report?" Mr. Kaminski added, wanting to be sure.

"Life here has been good for us," Axel replied, meeting his eyes steadily. He understood the timing of these questions and it galled him a bit, but he held his peace. They made sure the starmen were away and not able to intrude right now.

"It has," Bitty added with a smile.

Mr. Kaminski noted that each of them seemed relaxed with the only tension coming from their line of questioning.

"They're telling the truth about all of it," Alec verified for Mr. Kaminski, speaking directly to his mind, as previously arranged.

"Thank you," he formed in thought in response, feeling better.

"Ensign Ingolla, you and Ensign Snyder seem to have infections in your heads," Ryes began cautiously, as they waited for the rest to finish in the bathrooms. "I have Healing and can at least remove the infections," she offered. David Snyder considered her offer while Yaell awaited his decision.

"The headaches have been getting pretty intense," he finally stated, having gotten a wired response from Mr. Kaminski to allow her to help. "And we have limited anti-biotics onboard now."

She gave David a nod and smile, then opened her Healing. She put a hand gently upon his arm and cleared his infection out quickly, then altered his wire, which had been harboring the intrusive organisms, updating it to be something between what her Aunt Adina had in her head, and refused to let her or Maren remove, and what these humans had now. She also cleaned out other problems he had. All in all, it only took her a few moments. She opened her eyes and gave him a nod. Walker's aide had a look of pure and utter relief on his face.

"Thank you," he told her with a smile, "I never realized how bad the headaches actually were, until now," he added.

"You're very welcome," she replied, smiling merrily as she gave him a nod. Ensign Ingolla immediately stepped to her side, offering her his arm. She gave him a smile and nod as she placed her hand on it and closed her eyes, repeating the process even more quickly this time.

"Thank you," Yaell told her, "I appreciate it." She gave him a nod, too. She resisted telling them she upgraded their wires, as she figured they'd figure it out for themselves soon enough. And the recording drone which hovered over them was something she could easily ignore, as they now used them in Winterhaven, at need, and understood. They were gathering data, most probably everything they could gather on them and the ship. She had their drones restricted to only fly where their humans were present. She didn't need them wandering the ship wildly, as they initially tried.

96

"Appreciate what?" one of the other aides questioned, as she stepped over to join them.  She was Ash's aide and was curious.

"They had infections linked in with their wires," Ryes explained, "and I do have Healing and removed them. They're now free of headaches."

"I had a really bad one last year that took forever to clean out," Mr. Corliss' aide commented.  She offered her hand to him.

"I can make sure no remnants remain," she invited.  He instantly got an okay from Gene, so gave her a smile as he placed his hand in hers, realizing the others would've gotten their authorizations from Kaminski, first.  She went to work very quickly, once again.

"Do you feel it?" Yaell wired to David, "it's much faster!"

"I feel like I was driving a jalopy and now have a race car under my hands," he returned. "Wait until we're back on the ship to see what she changed."

"Yes, Sir," he replied, "But, I'm just going to enjoy this for now."

"And you're sure there seem to be no ill effects from this upgrade?" Mr. Kaminski wired his aide, concerned.  They were on a short tour of the ship, but with a ship as large as The Challenger was, it was taking some time, still he enjoyed the spacious compartments and rooms this ship had in comparison to their own.

"None, Sir," he replied. "You know the functionality they promised would be happening soon for our wires?  I have it now," he informed him, "and probably a few steps beyond it."

"We'll take scans when we get back to the ship but let me know if you have any problems with it," he wired.

"Yes, Sir," he wired back.  They finally reached the bridge and all of them were alert and curious about it.

"Amazing," Mr. Corliss breathed out as they stood at the back for a few moments taking it in.  There were blue lights across most of the boards with a few displaying green and an occasional yellow. Helm and navigation were up front with two seats to each station, as well as the captain's chair being obvious, too.

"We still have some work to do, but we're almost there," Ryes stated, her arm then raised and took in a sweep out the grand view of space before them. "And I have to admit, space is simply beautiful!" This got smiles and laughter in agreement.

"I never tire of it either," Blair admitted, smiling too. She'd been trying all day to break through Ryes' inner defenses, but never even got near. It was frustrating, never having this much trouble before! And it was like a solid wall protecting the whole party, both humans and starmen.

"May we take a closer look?" Mr. Kaminski asked, noting that their drones couldn't seem to fly past where they stood, either. How did she restrain them, he wondered, sure she was the one doing it.

"Not today. We have a diagnostics program running and are staying clear of the boards ourselves," she returned with seeming regret in her fascinating green eyes. She led them up into the gallery area and from there they did get a good view of the very large chamber. From here it was evident there was a program running with the way the lights were flashing on and off on the different boards. "As you can see, it's busy now and when it's back to normal operations, I'd be happy to let you see more of it," Ryes added. As soon as their shuttle had been enroute, she'd started the diagnostics program for the entire ship. It was due, and she could've delayed it a few days, but it just provided a nice opportunity, and was just as she'd Dreamed it last night.

She began to point out some of the boards and described the basic functions for their visitors, while reining in the drones, so they didn't wander all over the room gathering more data than she thought appropriate for them to know right now. The future was still unwritten, and she wasn't sure if she wanted to see what kinds of interactions she would have with these people in the future, right now. Shortly thereafter, she escorted them from the bridge and into a nearby conference room for some small refreshments.

"That's about all I have to show you right now," Ryes offered as she sipped her mug of Raya's tea. It was Dancing on the Tongue and still one of her favorites.

"We're going to be landing the Aurora first, tomorrow morning," Mr. Briggs spoke up, meeting her eyes. "And I would like to extend an invitation to you to accompany us down for the landing," he invited. Something in Ryes told her this was a man she could trust. It wasn't his youth; there was a feeling about him which had won her trust early on.

"Thank you so much, Ash, for the invitation. I believe I will accept your offer and look forward to the landing," she replied with a smile.  It was what Garth had decided already, after all.  He gave her a nod, noting this was the general response among the Winterhaveners, after spending most of today in their company.

"We'll be by to pick you up about oh-eight hundred hours, Winterhaven time," he replied, smiling.

"I'll be waiting for your shuttle," she assured him, giving him a nod in return.

# Aurora's Landing

## Chapter 8

The Aurora was chosen to land, as she was still the best of the three ships available, but did need repairs, which were best accomplished under gravity conditions. The captains of the other two ships transferred over, as they were invited to begin negotiations concerning the formation of the new alliance between Tayna and Earth. Ryes was invited to accompany them down, because she was a mystery the Terrans were still trying to solve. Ivan came with her, to serve as her bodyguard, as Garth ordered.

"Where should I be for this landing?" Ryes asked as they were leaving the reception lounge on the ship where they had a snack, and now everyone headed for the bridge. She'd been briefly introduced to the captains and some of the key ship personnel. She noted they saw her youth and didn't seem to take her rank seriously. Truly, she didn't care what they thought of her, only that they were here to work on an alliance of worlds for the future benefit of both peoples. Ash gave her a smile.

"I'll show you. Sorry but our ship doesn't have the space for guest seating," he apologized as he showed her to the bridge, playing host. She gave him a nod.

"I need to remain with my Chief Exec," Ivan stated firmly, in a low voice. He smiled for him, too.

"Here, you can both stand and observe everything," he invited, having shown them to a spot behind the captain's chair and near to his own station. She gave him a smile and nod and stayed where he directed.

"Hello, my name's Connor Elbridge. I'm from Trinity," a tall, blonde man walked over and introduced himself to her in a low voice, as she stood behind Captain Yun's seat. She saw he looked a lot like Monty and had caught the Elbridge surname. She smiled for him, giving him a nod of her head. He was dressed in a plain blue jumpsuit, which bore no insignia denoting rank. All his outfit had was the decorative patch which stood for the Aurora.

"My name's Ryes of House Li. Are you related to Monty? You do look something like him," she replied, keeping her voice low too, and noting his surprise at her question. He smiled broadly and she saw him resembling her good friend, even more so.

"He's my great uncle," he informed her, as Alec sat at his station near them, Storme in his lap now. He smiled at their conversation as he checked his board. Everything looked ready for landing. Captain Walker looked down his nose at the two of them, while Captain McMurray was quietly chuckling, as they stood next to Captain Yun's chair, away from the visitors. Yun ignored the circus as he had a ship to run.

"He'll be so surprised," she returned, grinning as she imagined their meeting. "I'll introduce you personally, but for now, it looks like things are ready for us to land." He gave her a nod, understanding the need for them to be quiet and allow the ship's personnel to do their work. He stepped closer to her, as if he was afraid of becoming separated from her, so she was now crowded between him and Ivan. She smiled to herself, realizing she was probably far more deadly than either of the men trying to protect her.

"Ready for descent," Commander Briggs reported to Yun, having gotten the all-clear from each of the ship's stations.

"Commander Briggs, land the Aurora," Yun ordered, settling back into his seat. Everything was running smoothly, and they'd be setting down near this Winterhaven shortly. The ship did a gyro turn to put a view of the huge bulk of the Challenger at one side of the platform, opposite the much smaller Wrath and Tablet, on the other. Each of the smaller ships could be carried like sucker fish to a shark's mass by the Challenger, once she's fully operational. It gave him a chill of excitement at seeing the great ship. She would've made their own largest ships look like shuttles, sitting next to her. He'd give anything to command her. It was a wonder that the Darkens ever defeated such a ship! It had to be by numbers alone!

"Aye Sir," Ash replied sharply, then turned to the officers before him, "Helm, navigation, take her down to Tayna," he ordered.

"The beacon is clear and locked in. Our course is set, and all systems report ready, Sir," the navigator replied, smiling as he glanced up.

"Helm is responding, Sir," the helmsmen replied, having cast off from the platform, before swinging them into position, ready to take the ship down. She was uncomfortable with this landing, as there were too many systems which were still marginal for her liking. Still, the ship began her descent, gently dipping down into the atmosphere normally.

"Are you all right? You look nervous," Ryes whispered to Connor, seeing that he was practically shaking.

"This is my first landing, and I had a kind of daydream earlier. It's got me a little jumpy, is all," he whispered in return, afraid of letting such a thing out. Ryes looked at him, surprised, and then not so in reflection. His great uncle had Talent, after all. Maybe it did run in the family, too?

"We'll be fine," she breathed in assurance, in response, smiling for him, "You'll see, we'll be there soon." Suddenly, as she just finished speaking, and they started to hit the heavier air mass, the alarms started up, sounding from one of the boards near them. Heads snapped up with shock in the people's eyes, as the bridge crew realized what kind of alarm was sounding.

"What's the matter?" Ivan questioned Captain McMurray, shouting over the noise.

"The stabilizers and half the main thrusters just gave out, we're going to have a very bad day," he returned, then rushed over to Yun's other side. He and Walker were talking about something, their heads were bent close.

"Cut the audibles," Ash ordered, needing some sanity to reign on the bridge, at least. "Sir, do we abandon ship?" he asked, turning to face the three captains.

"No, we don't have time to get everyone to the life pods," he stated. "Engineering, is there something you can do?"

"We're too high up for the landing thrusters to do us any good," a man's voice stated, coming over the speaker near the captain's chair. "The main circuits and stabilizers are smoked. We're seeing what we can do down here."

"All right, Mosley, we're all counting on you," Yun reminded him. He had to find some quick answers. The other two ships were too far away, and they didn't have any thrusters to break free of the planet again.

"I can help," Ryes offered, stepping around to them. Yun's eyes met hers, seeing she meant it.

"How?" he demanded, seeing the panic on the faces of the rest of the crew around him, yet she seemed totally calm.

"With my Talents. At least let me try," she requested. "You have nothing to lose right now."

"How can something like a psi ability help us here?" Walker demanded, upset over this whole situation, "Are you going to wave a magic wand and make the ship fly right?"

"I'll show you," she snapped back with ire, then turned to see if there was a place where she could sit. There was a seat empty, as the crewman was trying to help another at one of the stations. She sat down, smiling as she tried to relax, so she could concentrate. She had everyone's interest now; the hope in their eyes was painful. Connor and Ivan stepped closer to her, once more.

"Do what you can," Ash urged her as he stepped over, knowing it was a lot to ask of her, but their lives were at stake.

"If I'd known I'd have to work for it," Ryes teased, smiling as she closed her eyes. Captain Yun had doubts playing in his eyes, but hoped he was wrong. What could she really do to help them now, he wondered? Captain Walker stood next to him, nervous, but helpless to be able to do anything else. All their ships had sustained heavy damage to some degree, and they were beyond everyone's reach. Connor hoped she could do something, or this landing would be their last. Alec looked like he believed in her, at least.

"Do what you can," Ivan breathed, echoing Ash, his prayers playing within his own mind. Some of the crew had their heads bent with their eyes closed, as they prayed their last prayers.

Ryes fully unleashed all her Talents, extending out. First, she checked the engines and saw they needed more than she could accomplish in a few moments, then using Manipulator she pushed back against Tayna, herself. She didn't have the finer control she'd normally have, being it was taking every shred of power she had to help slow the ship's rapid descent. She could imagine the crazy dance the Aurora was doing as she descended, then recalled Sabin's Vision, knowing what it looked like from below.

"She's doing it!" Ash shouted, letting out a whoop in shear relief. There were relieved shouts, laughter and smiles all around the bridge as Ryes sat, clutching the arm rests of the chair, with her claws digging in and sweat beading her forehead as she concentrated. Everyone's eyes were turned toward her now in utter disbelief and gratitude. The movement of the ship leveled out and seemed to glide smoothly in now.

"She'll need immediate care as soon as we land. Could you please radio down and tell them to have Maren on the alert, after we touch down?" Ivan requested of Ash.

"Why?" Alec questioned, not understanding.

"Her body goes into a kind of hypothermia, as she exerts herself this heavily, and she needs her cousin to bring her back up to normal," he replied, unsure if this was information Garth would want known, but feeling he had little choice right now. He saw the communications officer was already relaying the request at Captain's Yun's direction. Ivan realized he felt a little out of place with these people. Sure, they were humans from the Sol system, but they were strict military, too. He'd been born and raised on outer colony worlds, so had managed to keep himself far from the concerns of the military. And here on Tayna, the ones who'd been in the service had discarded their uniforms, as they were years beyond their service time and were now colonials, and real people.

"Prepare for landing," the captain ordered. The landing gear was extended, and the landing engines came to life, aiding Ryes in her efforts. The ship gently set down, settling upon this new world as if nothing had ever been wrong. Ryes' body instantly went limp, spilling out of the chair. Connor quickly picked her up, being just a few seconds faster than Ivan.

"Is she still breathing?" Connor demanded, not sure if she was, now. Her skin was ice cold!

"I'm not sure. Let's get her to Maren, fast!" he urged as Ash led the way to the closest hatch, now trotting ahead of them. Ivan wished he had Talent and could warn him where they were emerging, to not delay her getting to him. The door opened and a ramp extended, seemingly taking forever, but they ran down it as soon as it touched down. Alec caught up to them at the hatch, wanting to help too.

"Here, let me have her," Maren called, running up to the ship, as a hatch opened, revealing the four men and Ryes. They quickly ran down the ramp, to meet him at the bottom.

"She kept us from crashing," Ivan explained, meeting Maren's eyes, as Connor handed Ryes over to his keeping. "The engines gave out." Maren gave him a nod, then quickly closed his eyes, extending his Talent to his cousin. After a few moments, he relaxed as he opened them again.

"She'll be all right. It just took a lot out of her," he explained, seeing the worry in the faces of the strange men around them.

"She's not waking up," Ash commented, still concerned, even if the cat-man looked happy with her condition. He didn't dare reach for her hand to double check, unsure of their welcome yet.

"She's tapped out and probably won't awake for a few hours, at least," he informed him, realizing he didn't know any of these uniformed people. "I'll take her home and put her to bed."

He noted Garth, Sabin, Ethan, Rowan, Torr and Metta were now behind him, ready to greet their new visitors. The officers and their escorts stepped down off the ship, behind the men who brought Ryes out. They were looking around at their environs. The new construction, the fields on the far side, away from the central tower and the grasslands nearby with the pens holding the small horses. The blackened, scarred bulk of the Star Quest rose up beside them; a reminder that this planet had felt the touch of the Darkens, too.

"She'll be all right?" Garth questioned, sure Maren wouldn't be this calm, otherwise. He gave him a nod of his head in response.

"Yes, she will. Mitt's going to have to go back up for a while, to take her place. She can always take some motion sickness pills, if she must," he urged, an almost smile quirking at a corner of his lips. She'd been having morning sickness with her pregnancy, and she avoided weightlessness now because of it. Garth smiled in relief as he gave him a nod of his head in agreement. He didn't want to think of his sister suffering but wanted his wife back home with him again.

"Ivan, could you please take her home? There may be others who'll need Maren's Healing touch," he ordered. Maren looked rebellious for a few seconds, then sighed as he entrusted his cousin to Ivan's keeping. He stepped back as Ivan gave him a nod and a smile, then left, bearing Ryes in his arms, with Alec and Connor trailing him. Their desertion was noticed, but no one said anything to stop them. Ash saw Captain Yun deliberately turned around to look at the Star Quest, for a few moments. Captain Walker stepped before Garth and the others, noting there seemed an easy equality about this mixed, welcoming group.

"I'm the leader of Winterhaven. My name is Garth of House Ladearis," he said, as Ethan advised, when introducing himself, in perfect English.

"I'm Captain Lindell Walker, commander of this task force," he replied, extending his hand. Garth grasped it readily, giving him a warm handshake and smile in response. "This is Captain Wing Yun of the Aurora, and Captain Devin McMurray of the Orit's Tablet," he introduced the other officers with him.

"This is Sabin, my Executive Officer, you've met my wife Ryes, who's our Chief Exec, next to Sabin is Doctor Ethan Cruthers, who's still our Head of Research, Torr, our Head of Security, Elder Rowan, one of our advisors, Elder Metta, who is visiting us from Matlowe Village, and Maren, our Chief Medical Officer," Garth offered, introducing the others, letting everyone shake hands and exchange greetings, in turn.

"We cannot thank you enough for the bravery and skill your wife displayed, in bringing the Aurora safely down to land. I've never seen anyone, in my whole life, who could do such a thing," Captain

Yun said, wanting to know more about her. It was why he didn't object to Connor and Alec's departure. Every scrap of information about these people could prove vital.

"Ryes is a Talent of One and it's said they're only born once every twenty thousand years," Rowan explained with pride. Torr rolled his eyes, as Metta heard him quite clearly. He was practically swallowing his tongue at this news! Garth caught it too and sighed. They'd have to have a talk with him about it later. Captains Walker and McMurray noted all their reactions, wondering what was going on? Obviously, this was something they hadn't let out too commonly from the way the visiting elder was reacting.

"Are there any wounded aboard your ship? I can Heal," Maren pressed, wanting to be away from this group, seeing it looked to be a lot of shifting for advantage with their imagined power, as they would soon begin their negotiations. Everyone seemed too much on edge for his tastes, and he didn't think it'd all be due to a stress-filled landing.

"Yes, there are," Captain Yun replied, "Commander Briggs can take you to our medical area, but our people have already done all they can," he warned him. But this cat-man, who wore a lab coat with a medical insignia, gave him a nod of his head and followed, as Ashton Briggs led him up the ramp and into the ship.

"Maren's very gifted, too. He's an excellent Healer," Ethan assured him, smiling jovially. "It's because of him and Ryes that any of we humans are here now."

"Yes, we saw a copy of your report, Doctor," Captain Walker stated, agreeing with him, as he coldly met his eyes. He still didn't quite know what these "Talents" were, and more importantly, the extent of the doctor's desertion, to side with these strange people. Ethan noted the look and returned it with one of quiet evaluation.

"Since it's almost lunch time, let's retire to our main facility and have something to eat, as we get to know each other better," Garth invited, smiling. He hadn't liked the tone Walker took with Ethan but withheld his judgment for now. It'd been a very harrowing landing and he was sure everyone wasn't quite settled yet. Luckily, he'd listened to Ethan and had one of the large conference rooms ready for them to have their lunch in today. It'd keep the curious looks from the other Winterhaveners away and afford him a chance to get to know these alien men better.

"That sounds marvelous," Yun agreed, smiling. He could use a good, stiff drink after that landing, hoping they'd have something suitable!

"Will she really be all right?" Alec questioned, as he trailed Ivan into a spacious apartment. A young girl ran into the living room, from around a corner, shock in her eyes at seeing them all in her home.

"MOM!" she yelled, as she ran over to Ivan. "What happened?" she demanded, as she looked at Ryes' face, pulling a lock of red hair back away from her closed eyes. She'd missed her so much!

"Overextended herself, again. Not that I'm objecting, as we would've all died, if she hadn't," Ivan told Sayer, smiling, "your dad told me to put her to bed."

"Alright, this way," she replied, turning to lead them, as Raby appeared at the base of the stairs, surprise in her eyes, too. She was holding a squirming Rhin in her arms.

"Nice place," Connor commented, looking around him, as Alec still followed Ivan into the hall. He stayed in the main room.

"We just moved in a few months ago," Raby told him. He stopped before her, as she reached to bottom of the stairs, letting the other two continue following the other girl. "We like it, too. Who're you? And where did you come from?" Both unknown men wore strange outfits, which looked a little alike. One was plain while the other was more decorative.

"We just arrived on the Aurora and your mother prevented our ship from crashing," he explained, "My name's Connor Elbridge. I came along to meet Montague Elbridge, my great uncle."

"Monty?" she replied, grinning merrily, now, "yes, you do look something like him," she agreed. "Let me get a message out for you," she offered, walking across the living room, as he followed her. She set Rhin down on the floor beside her, then accessed the message system and typed in a quick message for Monty.

"How's he doing?" he asked, watching the small cat child get to his feet, as he clutched the base of the console. He started tottering toward him with one hand on the base making happy baby sounds as he went. Connor was unsure if he should encourage him, like he would for his little nephew, Ronnie.

"He's doing all right, but he's not responding right now. I guess he's outside, watching what's happening," she reported, then grabbed for Rhin, as he was about to clutch at this man's pant leg.

107

"He should be over, pretty soon, though." Ivan and Alec reappeared from out of the hallway.

"I just told Sayer for the two of you girls to keep an eye on her. Let one of us know if there's something wrong - immediately," Ivan ordered. Raby nodded her head in understanding.

"I will," she promised. "Will she be all right?" she questioned, "and why isn't Maren here with her, now?" she pressed, worried. It had to be the big ship they watched land through their upstairs bedroom window. It had looked like a very odd landing, compared to their much smaller ships.

"Maren took care of her already. She'll be fine," he assured her, smiling now, "and your father wanted him to help the people on the ship which landed, first. Would you two gentlemen like some lunch? I'm sure Raya and Chuck prepared something special today, in honor of your landing," he offered, not wanting to leave them here with only the girls to protect Ryes.

"Lunch sounds like a good idea," Alec replied with a smile, "We skipped ours today."

"I'm staying here. I'm waiting to meet my great uncle, Monty Elbridge," Connor told them.

"Then, I'll have someone deliver lunches here for you and the girls," he replied, still not happy with this arrangement.

"We'll keep an eye on things," Sayer volunteered, smiling as she now watched them from the head of the hallway. "Thanks for getting us lunch," she added, as Raby nodded her head in agreement. Ivan then recalled Sayer had Mind Voice and could instantly tell her father if something were wrong, directly.

"See ya later, munchkins," he said, as he and Alec turned for the door.

"I'll be back later," Alec promised smiling, before he exited. "I promised Ryes that she could pet my hemi-cat."

"You have a cat?" Sayer questioned, surprised, and instantly interested.

"Not a cat, a hemi-cat. She's a genetic cross and is only part cat. I left her sitting on my chair, as we rushed your mother out to Maren. She's probably heading back for our quarters by now, miffed that she's been left out of things again," he responded with a chuckle, then closed the door behind him.

108

"Is it all right if I sit down?" Connor asked, "By the way, my name's Connor Elbridge and my great uncle is Monty," he told Sayer.

"Sure, make yourself comfortable. I'll tell him you're here," she replied. She called up her Mind Voice, closing her eyes and reached out for Monty. She opened her eyes and gave him a brief look at his great nephew, telling him he was waiting to meet him, here in their home, as she closed them again.

"I'll be right there," he promised, then let her go. Sayer opened her eyes, her smile beaming.

"He's on the way," she assured him. Then went to get them all drinks, as Raby went to get the horde's indoor play area. There was a knock on the door just as Sayer was handing Connor a drink, and Raby put the last cub into the enclosure.

"It's either Shams, Maren, Monty, or our lunch," Raby said as Sayer dashed for the door, laughing.

"Come on in," she invited as both Shams and Monty stood there waiting. "Two out of four, not too bad," she teased Raby.

"Is your mother all right?" Shams demanded, stepping into the room, noting the strange human at once.

"Yes. Maren said she needs rest," she explained as she closed the door. "Ivan said she overextended herself, is all."

"Great Uncle Monty?" Connor asked, as he stood up with a big smile upon his face. He couldn't mistake him, ever! He looked just as he did on that vid image! And still so young!

"Well, I'm Montague Daniel Elbridge, from Earth colony Trinity," he replied, grinning in return. "Who are you?"

"I'm Connor Alan Elbridge from Trinity, son of James Stanton Elbridge, who's the son of Earl Benton Elbridge, your younger brother," he explained their relationship. "I took my one and only chance to break free of Trinity, for what may be the only time this decade, and since I get to meet you, that makes it all the better," he finished. Shams headed down the hallway, to check on Ryes, himself.

"I recall that I couldn't stand being on Trinity one minute more than I had to, myself," he told him with a chuckle, stepping forward to grip his hand in a handshake, questions still dancing in his bright, blue eyes. "But you don't look much older than me," he scolded, "Ah, wait until Ryes wakes up!"

"You two do look a lot alike," Sayer said, seeing the strong family resemblance. There was another knock at the door, this time

109

Raby went to go see who it was, laughing merrily.  It looked to turn into a fun family gathering today.

# Home Again

## Chapter 9

"You're really Maren?" Ash turned back briefly, as they were walking down the main corridor on the lower, living quarter's area. They were getting a lot of stares from the other crewmen they met in the passageways. Maren's appearance was very distinctive and alien. There were questions in his eyes, but he gave him a nod in response. "Extraordinary," he added, grinning as he turned to lead him again.

"How would you know of me?" Maren questioned, wondering. These people were supposed to have come from Earth, herself! How could anyone on Earth know of any of them?

"From Dr. Cruthers' report," he replied, as they arrived at main medical. He turned back to him, before they went inside. "I was utterly amazed at how both you and Ryes were reported to bring everyone out of stasis and back to full health, by just your will. But, after seeing how Ryes prevented us from crashing upon your world, I believe I'm now living in an age of miracles." Maren huffed at this, shaking his head in wonder and denial.

"I'm not a miracle worker but do try to do my best to help others, as my cousin, Ryes," he explained, doubting if he understood Talent, at all. "Will isn't the whole answer. You have to be born with the specific ability, and training helps focus, too."

"Here we are," Ash told him, smiling grandly as he indicated the doorway before them. As they entered, Maren got many strange looks from the crew within, as he had out in the main corridors.

"How can I help you?" one of the physicians asked, stepping forward, from around the front counter.

"I'm here to help you," Maren replied, meeting his eyes.

"Dr. Keel, may I introduce Maren. He's a starman and a Healer among the people here, and Chief Medical Officer for Winterhaven. Captain Yun accepted his offer of aid, so we're here to see what he can do for our wounded."

"We're swamped but should be able to take care of everyone just fine, without your help," he stated, not wanting some voodoo, alien witchdoctor in his medical treatment facility!

"Why is that woman wearing a bloody bandage over her eye?" he asked, as he neatly stepped around him to get closer to her, as she sat upon a chair in the hallway, looking unhappy and in pain.

"Her eye was cut accidently. We're getting her into surgery, as soon as Dr. Monroe finishes with the amputation he's working on," Dr. Keel explained.

"Amputation?" Maren demanded astounded, then looked for where this surgery's door was, knowing there was something he could do about that, right away!

"In there," Ash said, pointing out the door for him, down the inner hallway. Maren rushed in, then after a few seconds there were shouts from within the room, as Ash and Dr. Keel rushed inside, too. Maren was facing off the surgeon, who was shouting something at him.

"Get this animal out of my surgery!" Dr. Monroe shouted, seeing the Aurora's First Officer entering the room.

"Maren's not an animal and I'm ordering you to back off and let him handle it," he ordered in return. Monroe stood in absolute shock, utterly speechless, as Maren stepped over to the patient and closed his eyes.

"What's this all about, Sir?" he demanded, recovering a little. "What do you think you're doing, letting that creature in here like this?"

"Just watch a true healer at work," he invited, gesturing for him to see for himself. He could already see the patient's vital signs were elevating back to something more normal, up on the monitoring screen. The nurse pointed it out to the rest of the staff in the room. All eyes were now riveted upon that screen, most appeared astounded.

"Look at THAT," she breathed out, as the doctors saw what it was reading. After a few minutes, Maren opened his eyes with a sigh.

"It'll take another session tomorrow, but he should be all right," he reported, glad he could save this man's leg. His eyes locked upon Monroe's. "I am not an animal and I do know more of what I'm doing than you, apparently. How could you even think of operating upon this man when his vitals were so low?"

"The poisons from the gangrene were killing him," he returned, in defense, his anger now evaporated.

"A good schedule of antibiotics for a few days, would've pulled him back up to where there wouldn't have been as great a danger of losing him," he fiercely retorted, surprising the surgeon.

"We've run out of our better antibiotics," he admitted. Maren saw the pain in his eyes and knew this was something he couldn't fight. He gave him a nod of understanding now.

"Who else's critical, besides the woman with the cut eye?" he questioned.

"We have most of them in stasis," Dr. Keel told him, "Until we could find a major starport, or treatment facility."

"We'll have them transferred over to our facility," Maren replied, "Then, once Ryes has recovered, she can assist myself and my staff, to make sure everyone's properly Healed," he ordered, "Let me go ahead and take care of those I can, now."

With this, he turned and left the room, heading back to the woman with the bandage over her eye. The attitude of these people was almost unbearable! It was a good thing this officer of theirs knew something about him, and the way he worked, after all. He took in a deep breath and tried to release it slowly, to shed the deep ire he felt, so it wouldn't interfere with his bedside manner, if he wanted to truly help these people.

"Lilly, get him to a bed and run some labs to check, please," Monroe ordered after doing a cursory exam, then turned to Ash, "I've gotta see this! How does he do it?"

"It's one of the psi abilities his people possess, simply called Healing," he told them with a smile, seeing understanding now on the faces around them. "He and his cousin Ryes brought all the surviving humans out of an eighty-year stasis each in minutes with this Talent, as they call it. It still took them several days to get it all done, but they've saved their lives!"

"Frankly, we could use these Healers on all our ships," Keels stated. He nodded his head and went out to find that not only had he fully restored the cut eye but had moved on to the next patient. The injured crewwoman's joy was easily understood now.

"Dr. Keels? What is this cat man doing to me?" an injured fighter pilot asked, as Maren was working on him next. Keels smiled at him and gestured for him to remain calm.

"Putting you back together, son," he told him, "just relax and let him do his work." He gave him a nod, not appearing to fully trust this alien, but saw the doctors, corpsmen and nurses were watching him closely with approval.  And he was wearing a lab coat with the medical insignia upon it and the name Maren over the pocket.  It was a puzzle, but he realized the pain was now fully gone.

When Ryes awoke, she realized from the nearby sounds, that her home was filled again.  Shams was sitting at the foot of her bed, waiting for her to awaken.  She shooed him off, so she could grab a quick shower.  It felt so good to be home, after all!  As she was dressing, Maren came in, looking for her.  She saw he was haggard and worn.  She realized she hadn't seen him in almost a month and was shocked at the change.

"What's happening?" she demanded, as she pulled on her T-shirt and turned to face him.  He sighed as he sat heavily down upon a chair next to the window.

"I was on the Aurora, trying to help take care of some of the wounded men and women on the ship, at her captain's request.  First, the doctors were shouting at me, accusing me of being an animal, but their First was with me and ordered them to stand down.  Then, there were far more wounded than I would've ever believed.  I could only take care of the lighter injuries - there were so many!  I ordered the remaining people transferred over to our facility, with the severe ones remaining in stasis until you can help me with them," he informed her, sighing heavily at the last.

"I'm still tapped out by having to help support that ship, almost all the way down," she admitted.  He nodded his head as she sat in the chair in front of him.

"I thought so.  That's why I ordered they be left in stasis.  The only thing I'm worrying about is there are two other ships up there and heaven only knows how many wounded they have for us to treat," he replied.  Now she understood what had him so upset.  It wasn't that he couldn't finish what he saw still needed to be done, but that he had no idea how many they could lose, before they'd have the others either transported down, or them get up there to deal with it.

"We'll pray for Aletagga and Korenda to help, then do what we can," she assured him. "Just look at this as a chance to further my medical training," she teased, still trying to get him to smile.  He looked at her with an eyebrow raised, then gave her a nod of his head. "I thought you were planning on a trip back to the Valley later this week?" she added, hoping to distract him.

"I was, but with all of this... I don't know if I can spare the time, or energy," he admitted. She shook her head.

"The next two days, we'll take care of those we can. Don't you dare forget those women. You made them a promise! And I refuse to let you back out of this one," she stated, meeting his eyes as he looked at her in surprise.

"Now I know you've been working too long in Command. You're too tied up in schedules," he teased in response. She laughed lightly at this, shaking her head.

"No, I think it'll do the both of us some good to get away from this place for a couple of days. We want to make sure the temple is safely secured for the coming winter, too. I don't want us to run into any nasty surprises when Dr. Cruthers' evaluation team starts working on checking the site in the spring. Those denizens were pretty nasty, and I don't want them using any of the temple rooms, or underground areas to hibernate, or nest, in," she explained.

"You could always use your Empath to drive them off," he volleyed in return, frowning as he felt her uncertainty.

"I don't know," she replied, suddenly looking uncertain. "I've been having some strange dreams again and I don't know if I'm even going to be on Tayna in the spring." He suddenly sat up straighter in the chair, concern etching his face.

"You know you're not allowed to have any Visions without me," he scolded, extending his hand. "Let me see them, too," he urged, closing his eyes. She sighed as she grasped his hand and closed her eyes, too. They sat that way for quite a few minutes then they opened their eyes, again. "You may be right, but it also looks like I'll be there with you."

"At least you're smiling, again," she told him, wishing with all her heart that he could find the ability within himself once more!

"It's overrated," he quipped back, a corner of his mouth twitching just a tiny bit. "I'll find myself, again. I think I'm still mourning for Anders, my father and myself, inside. When I can let that go, then I'll see who I am." It was the best he could do to explain it, knowing she knew part of it already. Then an infant quickly crawled up to them, snatching onto the chair Ryes sat upon and pulled himself up to cry at her, as if he were scolding her.

"It looks like Gareth's unhappy over something," she commented, as she snatched him up into her lap, hugging him to comfort him.

115

"It looks like the girls are giving mom a hint," he returned. Ryes sighed, looking at the clock.

"I didn't realize I spent almost the whole afternoon in bed!  No wonder I'm so hungry," she stated, standing up. "And I imagine the cubs are well past their nap time, too."  She saw Gareth looked tired and his crying was his tired cry.

"There was quite a crowd out there, when I came in," he warned her, standing too. "Why don't you put the cubs down for their nap and then see about having something light to eat delivered here? That way you don't have to answer every question they throw your way, cause you're busy eating, he suggested.

"And dinner will be in about two to three hours, instead of in an hour and a half, since I'm sure Chuck and Raya are cooking up something special for our guests," she returned, smiling. "That's still too much time for them to drive me crazy with questions I don't know how to answer."

"We will help," Adina assured her, standing in the doorway, glad to see her awake once more.

"Thanks, Aunt Adina.  I truly appreciate it," she replied, smiling as she, with Maren following, stepped over to her.  She gave her a warm smile in return and a one-armed hug, nodding her head after they parted.

"It is no effort, my child," she said, a warm smile alighting her face, then she turned and lead them down the hallway.  With these new humans, things would be in an uproar again.  It was exciting and entertaining.

Commander James Kaminski watched the bridge vids of the event during the Aurora's almost tragic descent to Tayna.  It was clear that Ryes had been the one to keep the ship from crashing, and enabled it to land gently, as normally as possible.  He remembered, when they were touring her grand ship, Ryes would occasionally bring objects from elsewhere at will.  He recalled the weight of the very real plasma rifle he'd held briefly in his arms.  It hadn't been an illusion, as they'd closely examined it through her "Talents," as she called them. This wasn't smoke and mirrors!

"Sir?" Mona West asked, as she stood in his open doorway, as per his summons to his office.  He looked up to her from his inner contemplations and motioned her to enter.  It was little more than a

116

closet, but it did afford the look of an office.  It had a desk, three chairs and locked storage cabinets along the wall behind him.  Her small cabin was more spacious!

"Lieutenant, close the door and come take a seat," he instructed, as he briefly met her eyes.  She did as he bid and resisted the urge to peek within his head, until he gave her reason.

"How can I assist you today, Commander?" she asked, as he'd turned back to look at his screen display, as if puzzling something out.  He looked up to her again and smiled.  His smile had melted her heart, when he first stepped onto this ship, and even now, she found those emotions hard to wrestle back down again.

"I need your expertise and honest opinion," he requested.  He then called up the display monitor on the far end of his desk, which was placed for visitors to view what he wanted to share.  It was more of a projection only, and not as high quality as the real one on the other side of the desk, which was still turned so only he could see it, but it'd do for his purposes, as it had many times in the past.  He picked up its wand and activated it.  She shifted so to see it clearly.  James played the bridge vid but stopped it before it showed Ryes going unconscious and slumping out of the chair.

"What kind of psi ability is that?  It seems far more than simple telekinesis," he stated.  Her mouth was hanging open for a moment, as her brows knit in thought.

"May I see it again?  With the volume turned up?" she requested.  He nodded and did so, honestly watching her reactions and wanting her opinion.  After seeing it a second time, she sat thinking on the event for a few moments, noting his patience and understanding.

"I've never heard of anyone, in all human history, who could do such a thing using a psi ability," he stated, once she turned her eyes back to him.  She nodded her head in agreement.

"I haven't either," she admitted. "Should we see if we might have cause to fear these people?" she asked, unsure.  He shook his head no, understanding the root of her discomfort.  The unknown was still a primal instinct he himself had managed to wrestle and put aside already.

"I think this woman alone could be key to Earth's salvation.  We saw, when we were in mind-link on that tour of her ship, the way she thought, her passions.  She's not after control, nor power, only setting everything to right, and in balance again.  I only want to know if your people can find a way to make friends with her and their other more powerful psi's.  I'd like to see if this could be a skill honed and learned by our people?" She smiled and nodded her head, clearly seeing the advantage here, too.

"Ken has telekinesis and Alec seems to have a friendship started already with Ryes. I'll get him to play it up and see where it goes. He and his hemi-cat might be a useful in this matter," Mona suggested.

"Good," he replied, smiling once more. "Thank you, Mona. I do appreciate your help.

"Perhaps he can stay as a houseguest with one of the families there, in consideration of Storme's needs?" she suggested, slyly. He chuckled, nodding his head, loving the idea.

"I'll suggest it to Briggs and let him take it from there," he agreed, feeling they might have an important key in their hands now.

When Ryes entered the great room, she found it was filled with people; many well-known and several unknown. She put on a grand smile as she walked out with Gareth in her arms. She was surprised, and yet not so, to see that Alec and his hemi-cat, Storme, were the center of attraction in the room. He was managing to keep everyone back from her, which she instantly understood as a way to keep from stressing her out, with so many strangers. Still, it was clear this small furry being had captured the hearts of all the starmen in the room.

"Mom!" Raby called out, as she saw her now in the room. She and Sayer rushed over to her and wrapped their arms around her, with tears in their eyes. Gareth and Jann were now in the middle of the press and expressing their opinion with their crying, as Ryes was lightly laughing and distributing kissing all around, feeling so complete in this moment.

"Please get the little ones down for their nap, my dear," Aunt Adina suggested, seeing she was now the center of attention in the room. "And I am sure your lunch will have arrived by the time you finish." Ryes' eyes met hers and she gave her a nod. Rhin had crawled over and had a death-grip upon her jeans leg now, so she stooped down and picked him up too, while Raby went to retrieve Shaysa and Shyla from Denas.

"I'll be right back," Ryes announced to the rest. Ardis followed them up the stairs with a very tired Adris and Dale. Ryes turned and gave her a welcoming smile and nod of agreement. She kept six extra portable cribs in one of their guest rooms ready for little ones, for times like this.

"So, you were the one that brought them down to land safely," Ardis pressed with an expression halfway between pride and amazement. She shook her head and since she'd cut her hair short again, her brown curls bounced about on their own. For the first time, Ryes was tempted to cut her own hair short! It looked fun.

"Well, I didn't want to die, nor did the others on the ship, so I had to do something," she replied, having finally gotten the last cub, Rhin, settled down for his nap. "I did what I could, and we landed safely." She stepped back from the crib and stood a moment admiring her brood with joy in her heart. They were the ones she'd always fight to protect!

"Mom, you're so heroic," Raby commented with a look of happiness in her eyes too. Ryes laughed merrily, shaking her head no at this silly notion, as she met her eyes for a moment.

"Heroic was taking their offer of a ride down in the first place. I only did what I had to do," she told her girls, meeting their eyes. "But I don't back down from a challenge, unless it's for a very good reason."

"Like someone getting hurt?" Sayer supplied, and she nodded in answer.

"Let's go back downstairs and let the little ones sleep in peace," Ardis suggested, understanding what Ryes meant. And she didn't want their voices to waken the cubs too soon.

"I'm truly late for lunch and need something to eat," she agreed as she nodded to her friend. The others left and she closed the door quietly behind them. They went around Hadu, who stationed himself at the top of the stairs, keeping a sharp eye on everything below without being noted. Ryes paused beside him for a moment, giving him a brief hug and light kiss.

"Thank you, dear Uncle Hadu," she whispered. He smiled and gave her a small nod. She smiled in return, her happiness lighting up her eyes from within, as she returned his nod, then went down the stairs. She knew her children and all of them were very safe with him keeping watch!

As Ryes reached the base of the stairs, there was a knock on the door and Raby ran to see who it was, while Ryes was wondering where she could find a place to sit. Every inch of her two couches was taken, as well as all the chairs. She was thinking of sitting on the floor, when Maren saw her dilemma and gestured her to a seat next to Alec and Storme, which appeared to be the last empty one in the room. It was a chair they had placed between the two couches.

"Thanks, Maren," she said as she took it, grateful to sit in a chair after all. He gave her a nod and turned as Raby appeared with a tray in her hands.

"And here's your very late lunch," he said, his eyes merry at least. "And per your doctor's orders, you need to eat now," he added. She smiled and nodded in agreement as she accepted the tray. Maren removed the light covers and gave them to Raby, who took them off to their kitchenette for the time being. Ryes realized her mouth was instantly watering. She picked up her fork and dug in, having missed the cooking from home so very much, in this moment. She completely forgot she was surrounded by others, who'd been here to see her.

Light laughter and small conversations continued around her, as she tried to not scarf everything on her tray too quickly. She realized within the first few moments how much she missed being home. Ryes missed working in her office, with her little ones sometimes spending the day with her, then loading them into the stroller and bringing them home. She concentrated upon the flavor of the new tea for a moment to give herself time to let go the building emotions.

Finally, she picked up her bubble-nut custard and her spoon and looked up. Ryes found herself sitting between Denas and Alec. She didn't know if they had shifted closer to her just to be near, when she was ready to socialize again, or just wanting to be closer to her. She smiled.

"May I please get a saucer of something tasty to drink?" a voice softly intruded into her mind. Ryes turned and realized, as she met Storme's eyes, knew the request had come directly from her. Alec was busy talking to Ash and never noticed.

"Of course, please give me a moment," Ryes responded with a smile for this very intelligent little one. "Sayer?" she then sent, quickly getting her attention, "Could you please get a small, shallow bowl of cold milk and bring it to me?" she requested, having felt that was the base of her guest's request.

"Sure, Mom," she sent in return, with humor in her tones. Ryes shifted her empty dishes to leave plenty of room on Storme's side of the tray.  Sayer was quickly there with the bowl and curiosity bright in her eyes.

"Thank you," Ryes told her, as she accepted it and then placed it upon the tray.  She quickly did a health check upon it, in tune with Storme's body balances and needs.  She saw there were some things that needed to be Healed within her small body, and showed it to her, immediately getting her agreement.  But in so doing, she felt her thirst more intently, so invited her to drink her fill.

"There's more if you need it," she let her know.  Sayer had been party to it all and now knelt down to watch her with adoring eyes, now understanding looming over her did not make her feel comfortable.

"She's beautiful and looks exotic with the pointy ears," she sent to her mother.  Ryes lightly laughed, nodding her head as she was now spooning her bubble-nut custard into her mouth, enjoying the flavors once again.

"She is wonderful," Denas agreed, as Monty was talking with Connor and not paying any of them attention.  Alec turned and noted that Storme had garnered a snack all on her own and appeared surprised.

"That might not be good for her," he sent, with a small edge of panic he couldn't quite suppress in his mental tone.

"I balanced the proteins in the milk to be fully digestible for her and nourishing," Ryes assured him, showing him fully what she discovered with her Healing Talent.  It stunned him, as he never suspected that she might still need more care.  Then he felt her gentle humor. "I'd rather Maren do this Healing when he's rested, for his is the stronger Talent and more skilled approach," she informed him.  She felt his deep appreciation for her offer.  She knew in a flash how deep the bond between them actually was and felt the love they felt for each other flow.  She opened her heart to them to let them know she'd never betray them to anyone else.

"With the crowded conditions on the ship, perhaps we should let Alec and Storme stay in one of our guest rooms," Denas offered, speaking aloud to Ryes, in a low voice. "Connor was telling us about his shipboard life," she explained.  Ryes turned back to her and nodded her head.  Alec appeared doubtful with questions in his eyes.  Ryes could imagine that the offer was very tempting, but his First Officer and Captain needed to approve it, first too.  But, before she could finish forming up her question for him, Ash beamed.

"That would be a great idea, actually," he agreed. "They were two years living on a destroyed space station, and a little time off the

121

ship might do them both some good." The relief in Alec's eyes was almost heart-breaking!

"It was that bad?" Ryes asked, her brows knit as he gave her a nod.

"It was living through a seemingly never-ending nightmare," he told the ladies, also in a low voice. "I'll tell you the whole story when things settle down a little," he assured them, while he was petting Storme. She finished her milk, appearing very satisfied.

"But what about Shimmer?" Sayer asked, looking worried.

"Shimmer?" Alec asked, wondering if it was a pet of some kind?

"A scion of a servant, whom I freed from his evil mistress," Ryes related, smiling, and giving Sayer a nod. "Let's do an introduction, first, then see how it goes. If it's not a comfortable situation, you and Storme can stay here in my home, in a guest room, but it's gets noisy and very busy with all the cubs, family and friends around," she told him and Ash with an arm sweeping the room about them. They both laughed and appeared to understand.

"Monty, could you please get Shimmer? We'd like to do an introduction for your possible houseguests, first. We wouldn't want any disagreements, or misunderstandings to break out," she suggested, knowing Denas would've cleared it with him before making her offer. He grinned and gave her a nod.

"Be right back," he promised, then stood and was quickly out the door.

"Shimmer?" Ash asked, "what is Shimmer?"

"A snake," Denas supplied, smiling with warmth in her eyes. "A beautiful young lady, whom we're raising to be a good scaly daughter." Sayer chuckled at this, while Ryes smiled and nodded her head.

"Her father was highly intelligent and possibly had his life extended for hundreds of years. Shimmer's proved to be highly intelligent and has Mind Voice, like him. Still, she's a baby, who's learning about the world and loving her people, who pamper her and pet her and admire her. We're still trying to gauge how much schooling she'll need when she's old enough for it. She might not be able to speak, but we're not discounting her intelligence," Ryes explained. Denas chuckled as she saw this seemed to shock the two men. Ryes nodded and tried not to laugh.

122

"This is a joke?" Ash asked, wondering as they seemed highly amused by their reactions.

"Never," Ryes assured him with a shake of her head. Denas likewise shook her head no, too. "This is too important, but somehow it appears you don't know how to accept an intelligent snake. We know her and know better."

"Mom, that vid with her father coming to help you against that jungle marl," Sayer started, but then the door opened again before Alec could ask about it, and Monty returned with Shimmer draped across his shoulders. Her presence was welcomed by the other Winterhaveners in the room with praise and petting by all who could get near. This seemed to stop the new humans in the room, as they'd never seen such a sight before. Storme sat up peering intently in Shimmer's direction, and Ryes could swear there was delight in her bearing.

Monty stepped over to their side of the room and extended his arm, inviting her to side down it to get a better view. She seemed equally interested in Storme, too. Alec was uncomfortable but held himself steady.

"Shimmer, I would like you to meet Storme and Storme, I would like you to meet Shimmer," Ryes and Denas invited, using Mind Voice helping to form the bridge between them to make it more a controlled environment. Sayer, Monty and Alec all watched from the "sidelines." They met with caution, but both were filled with open curiosity for the other, pleasing the others watching over them.

# The Valley of Death

## Chapter 10

"His time had come, Maren. There wasn't anything, any of us could've done for him. I saw it. I was there, too," Ryes scolded, seeing he was still upset over being unable to save one of the men, who'd been critically injured when they were breaking out of the blockade of the Sol system.

The Aurora's doctors had him in a suspension chamber, until he could receive proper trauma surgery. Of the fifteen held in suspension, he was the only one they lost. The Auroran doctors, who attended the Healing sessions, were highly praising Maren and his staff for all the lives they saved in what seemed a miraculous way. They hadn't been upset that one man hadn't made it, at all.

"If I'd waited to rest up a little, first," he countered, still not believing the way his life trickled away from him as he watched, unable to stop it. He'd never felt so helpless in his whole life!

"You weren't that tired, and I was Boosting you, remember? He didn't want to stay to face whatever new trials life would hold for him. He wanted to be released. He was ready for it, and nothing either of us could've done, would've prevented his journeying onward. Now, will you let it go and worry about what you're going to say to the remaining sleeping ladies? We'll be there in a few minutes," she informed him.

She'd borrowed the Sand Burrower, as she was larger, able to seat thirty passengers with plenty of room for cargo, and due for some test runs anyway. She flew just as well as their other two shuttles, so far. She'd flown up to the Challenger, circling it a few times, teasing Mitt. Then she flew down to hover over Kyma's stronghold, waving happily when he stepped out to see them, as he laughed merrily. She then practiced several rolls as they flew over Matlowe Village, and was now bound for the Valley, since they did have a mission after all. There were fifteen shuttles of varying sizes aboard the Challenger, but Mitt and Axel hadn't had time to repair them, so they remained in their docks for now. She now wanted to see how well one of them would perform, compared to the human's shuttles.

"Maren, please let this one failure go. If you raise barriers within yourself, you will not be able to reach the rest of us. It was your openness, which surprised us, and enabled us to trust you,"

Lissel urged, from her seat. He swiveled his around to look at the two Valley women, who chose to accompany them on this trip. He saw in her eyes that she meant it.

"Lissel speaks the truth, Maren. I finally decided to try at life again, because of the love in your heart, and the openness of your thoughts," Poli assured him, smiling. "I had given up on all men, and life itself, until your courage bid me to make the attempt. You cared for us. Have you lost that, too?" she pressed. They all knew his heart was deeply troubled since he fought and won a challenge against his own father. She wept for him within her own. He was too gentle a person to bear such burdens!

"I do still care for all of you," he told her, "I just don't want to lose anyone else, again. There's been so much death around me, lately."

"Then what about all those beautiful babies you have delivered, the last few weeks? Are not these new lives even more important to you, because you brought them into this exciting world?" Lissel questioned, smiling for him.

"I only hope they'll live good lives," he sighed, as he half swiveled his chair to look at Ryes' profile.

"They'll live the lives they're meant to live and take a life path they choose to follow. At least you gave them a joyful beginning," she chided him, smiling a crooked smile. "You can't take away all the world's pain. It's meant to hone each of us, to help us learn life's lessons and become stronger. But, if you're there to provide a shoulder to seek comfort upon, I'll always be most grateful," she told him, hoping to reach through his pain. She swept in over the valley, noting the way the plants looked wilder and more unkempt. She was recording everything outside for Dr. Cruthers and Sabin to review later.

"It has changed so much!" Poli exclaimed. Sadie let out a sigh as she nodded her head in agreement, glad to see it becoming more natural. She wondered how many of the animal guardians Doran had before were still alive? She recalled that huge one, trying leap up to grab the chopper right out of the air.

"I wonder what it'll look like in another five years?" Sadie speculated aloud, feeling this question would be "safe." She didn't want to set off the two Sleepers with them. Ryes chuckled at this, shaking her head.

"We'll see, when the time comes," she offered, as she swung about and set the shuttle down near the main entrance of the temple. "Let me check things out my way, first," she ordered, as she shunted the systems to standby. She wasn't going to completely shut the Burrower down, in case they needed to lift off quickly. She closed her eyes and opened Empath fully. Taking a measure of what lay about them in the garden, and inside the temple.

"I keep thinking back to our last trip here," Maren commented to Sadie. She let out a huff, as she nodded her head. She recalled it all too clearly, still, as she rubbed her cheek, which had been torn open during the battle. Ryes had fully erased it, but it was still there at times within her own mind. Gleds was beside her, giving her a nod in understanding. Raya had showed him the battle, when he asked it of her, so he could better understand Sadie's inner wounds. He hoped this trip would ease them for her. Shams unbuckled and stood up, to get a better view out the window.

"It's beautiful," he commented. "It's too bad it's so far out here. No one can truly appreciate such a wonder, if they can't get here to see it."

"It was even more wondrous, so long ago, with many colorful banners decorating the entrance," Poli told him, her eyes looking back to what was. "In a way, we now have what we originally sought. A society which lets us have the choice of whom to mate, or to put it off for a while, so we can find a man whom we can accept. It is too bad Doran never saw the chances for change, which lay within Ryes, when she sought to kill her, before."

"It wasn't Ryes alone. All we women decided it, and enforced it," Ardis told her with a smile, seeing the temple for the first time. It was beautiful! Too bad it also held such evil. She remembered Sabin's nightmares and the stories about it later.

"There's something wrong," Ryes told them, opening her eyes. "I'm not getting anything from Doran, herself. Could she have escaped?" she asked the two Sleepers. Poli looked shocked, as Lissel shook her head no, still there were doubts in her eyes.

"There was no way for us to either break into her crypt, nor for her to emerge. The mechanism would have triggered and instantly killed her, slicing her to tiny pieces. You are not mistaken?" Lissel questioned, her brown eyes mirroring her inner turmoil. "Could Doran have succeeded at last in escaping her ancient sentence?"

"No, I'm not mistaken," she replied, shut down the ship, then unfastened her restraints. "I've driven out the animals, which were nesting inside and secured all the other entrances, so it's safe to go in. Let's see if we can solve this riddle," she invited, standing up. They went down to the craft's lower level, then opened the hatch. Shams was the first one out, so helped Sadie, Ardis, Poli and Ryes. Lissel paused in the opening, then allowed him to put his hands upon her, to help her down.  There was shock in her eyes as she felt the strength of the Talent which resided within him.

"What is your Talent?" she asked Shams in a low voice, as they all followed Ryes and Maren up the grand marble stairs toward the front entrance.

"I have two.  Mind Voice is my stronger one and Ryes discovered I have Dreamer, using her Catalyst Talent.  I never suspected I carried two Talents," he admitted with a smile.

"I never thought to ask Ryes to check if I carried a second one.  Perhaps I should?" she replied.  He didn't look too bad, to her eyes, and her season would be upon her in a couple of months' time.  She didn't want to ask Maren to delay it, as she realized she did want children, which would remain her own.  Her one and only son had been taken from her by her husband's family shortly after his birth, due to a feud between their two families.  She had time to make her decision, but the fact that Shams carried two Talents recommended him to her mind.  And she knew Ryes and Garth wouldn't let anyone take her cubs from her!

"Before, I would've never given it a thought, but now I recommend it," he assured her, glancing down to see the humor in her lively brown eyes.

"Then, if you recommend it," she started, as they reached the entrance itself, then stopped as she saw the dirt and leaf litter on the marble around her, for the first time.  She stood, looking about this place, shocked anew.

"There are signs of neglect," Poli whispered, her face had gone pale, too.  There had always been women to help upkeep the temple!

"We'll have to address this," Maren told them, noting it disturbed those who'd lived here before. "Even for all this place stood for, it shouldn't be allowed to deteriorate.  It's a masterpiece, which we should preserve for our children to see, and their children as well," he said, looking to see agreement in Ryes' eyes.  She nodded her head in response.

"We'll have a party out here to help with the upkeep, maybe every month, if we can," Ryes replied, then sighed as she turned for the great hallway before her. "I know where the switches for the doors lie, so I'll make sure to seal them, when we leave.  I thought I had locked them before we left last time, but some auto-system opened the doors later, on some programmed schedule.  I just disabled the program, so that should help, but anyone can unlock them and open them manually now.  We'll set up some surveillance and alarm systems."

"In all honesty, we should be the ones to care for the temple. It was our home for so many long years," Poli insisted, comforted to see they cared, even when they had every reason not to. "We will add this to our list of duties and will see to its preservation." Lissel nodded her head to this, glad Rhodi wasn't here to view this mess, too. She so loved this temple, even if she'd come to hate Doran long ago.

"We'll make it a full crew, anyway," Ardis insisted, smiling at Poli. "I'll add it into the schedule for my crews to see to it, and it'll give some of our pilots in training some practice." Poli gave her a small bow and nod of her head at this, smiling. Everyone KNEW the way Ardis was a stickler for cleanliness and how exacting she was over the way her people worked. They'd have no worries, if she oversaw the project!

"Thank you, Lady Ardis," Poli responded, "we will meet with you later to set up a schedule, so we can work together on this project." Ardis chuckled at this, as Sadie laughed lightly.

"You don't have to call me a Lady, but I thank you for doing so," she returned. "It's no problem to create a new schedule, let me assure you." She then turned her eyes to look at the strange hooks along the walls in the passageway before them. It looked as if they once held something. She wondered what? She pointed at them with questions in her eyes.

"Our hall of weapons," Lissel explained, smiling as she recalled the battle. "Doran had hurled them at the group Ryes was protecting, but to no avail. Most of them were so primitive, to begin with."

"We'll put them back, even so," Ryes told her, glancing back to see her surprise. "They belonged here. I left a crossbow at the far end of the valley and should go retrieve it too. But the sword I used; my mother took with her. I forgot to ask her why."

"If she was a spirit, how could she have taken it with her?" Shams questioned, not understanding. Neither of them saw the utter shock upon the Sleepers' faces at this revelation. Then Ryes rounded the last bend, to stand before the great statue of Doran, herself, the rest close behind her. The morning sunlight slanting in through the dome made the whole room seem too bright, reflecting off the light-colored marble.

"I've no idea, Shams. I'll ask her the next time I see her," Ryes replied, smiling to herself, noting the damage to the statue for the first time. "My goodness, this'll need restoration, too."

"We will have to tell the others about the sword," Poli tightly sent to Lissel directly, mind-to-mind. "How could Tyra do such a thing?" She felt her agreement, but knew she was distracted by the scene of destruction before them.

"But Doran did it, herself!" Sadie protested, uncomfortable with seeing this room again. "She was trying to kill you and the others and damaged it. I saw the whole thing, remember?"

"Yes," Ryes agreed, smiling as she turned back to her friend, seeing how she was rubbing the same spot on her face, which was cut open during the battle. It must've truly frightened her. Gleds stood beside her, granting her his support. "But we'll still do what we can to restore it. Everyone on Tayna should be able to appreciate this temple the way it was, even if few would agree with Doran's methods, or principles." Maren huffed at this but nodded his head as he walked around the statue, toward the crypt beyond. He stopped, waiting for the rest to catch up.

"Look," he prompted, unnecessarily. They could all see the front of the crypt was breached. The doors, which they couldn't even distinguish before, stood wide open. They all ran to it, looking within. Doran's stasis chamber was open, and her body was gone. There were the tracks of animals, nesting debris and remains of what looked like her bones. Ryes stooped down to pick one up, noting it was a starman's arm bone. She stood, displaying it for the others.

"Could this have been programmed to open, if she ever died?" she questioned the two Sleepers. They were utterly shocked and looked dismayed at such a thought. "This is a starman's lower arm bone and if her sleep chamber's open, I can only think this might happen if she passed away. At least she wasn't shredded by a machine while trying to escape."

"We were never able to open it, so I have no idea if it might have been a part of the mechanism's programming, or not," Poli replied, her eyes shadowed to think of her passing away unnoticed. It was a sad ending for an unhappy soul.

"We'll bury her out in front of the temple in a few days, after we've gathered together a proper funeral party. For now, let's collect what we can find and lay her remains back in her chamber, so, they won't be disturbed. As a once-living being, she deserves some honor," Ryes assured them, seeing their sadness and shock.

They all began to search about, finding this bone and that one, leaving it up to Ryes, Maren, Ardis, Gleds, and Shams to identify if it was one of Doran's, or not. In the process, they cleaned out some of the debris. After an hour's work, they thought they'd collected what was left. Ryes closed the chamber's door, leaving the device inactive. She sadly noted it was a pitiful-looking collection of bones.

"Now, let's take care of what we came to do, it's almost lunch time," she offered, smiling as she turned back to the group. They walked over to the center of the great chamber, the Talents taking each other's hands, as they formed their circle.

"Poli! Lissel!" a mental voice greeted them, as they made contact with the sleeping women once more. "You have returned! Have you come back to stay with us?"

"Never," Lissel replied. "There're too many things to learn and do out here. There is no way I am coming back into the darkness! The light's far more exciting."

"What can be there, which you cannot have here?" another one demanded, disgusted with her joy.

"Cubs, for one thing. Denas and Saree have found men they approve of and are bearing their own cubs!" she returned, her excitement plain in her thoughts. "I'll have my next season soon and I know Ryes, Garth, and the others, will never let anyone take my children from me. I cannot wait!" Shams suddenly caught a side wisp from her, that she was thinking of mating to him. It surprised him, but he kept still, not wanting to attract the attention of these women, now. There were far more important things to discuss, in this moment, and discussing a mating needed to be private.

"If I do come out, I do not want to have cubs so soon," a third protested, as the others were still in shock over what Lissel revealed to them. A few even saw what Shams saw, surprised that she was actively choosing her own mate already.

"You don't have to," Maren sent to comfort her and a few of the others, who were in firm agreement with her. "I can delay your seasons, until you've found men you find acceptable. But I want you to understand I will not stop them entirely, as it'll be very unhealthy for you, for me to do so. We don't want women just to breed with and have babies. We've plenty of newborns in Winterhaven, as it is," he told them. In his mind he projected the several births he attended, the last few weeks. "What we do want is for each of you to have the chance to live as you choose to live. You don't have to stay with us in Winterhaven, but we'll welcome you, if you so choose."

"We have what we dreamed of. We choose whom we mate with and when we mate," Poli added, feeling better about coming out here, even if it meant opening too many pain-filled memories of darkness, torture, and cold. Doran had been a cruel keeper, most times.

"Why is it only you two? And Maren, you have changed. I feel no joy in your heart, even as you have been the one to bring new lives into the world," the first voiced within their minds, alarm in her mental tones.

"We didn't want to overwhelm you with all the others, at once," Ryes replied, before anyone else could. "And, as for my cousin, he was forced into a challenge, killing his own father. My heart weeps for him. I know he'll recover from this, but it's going to take time," she explained, feeling Maren's embarrassment at her revelation. The love between them was still there, as was his deeper love for Dotti, but he felt as if all he could do was fumble about with it, having forgotten how to express it somehow.

"Who is this other man with you? We have not felt him, before," another woman stated, scorn in her thoughts at his presence.

"I am Shams. I'm a caravaner, who's come to live in Winterhaven. I need to be near Ryes, but know she's married and happy with Garth. So, I do what I can for her and her family anyway, until I find a woman whom I can love, and will accept me. I've never known of such a beautiful place, with such a sad story behind it, as your temple here," he admitted. He could feel Ryes' embarrassment, but felt that she cared for his welfare, too. He saw in her mind that she equated him with her cousin, Maren. This was something he could accept, feeling relieved for some unknown reason.

"What has happened to Doran?" the second one demanded, having gained some sense of something not quite right with the temple, from the edges of Shams' thoughts.

"She's died," Ryes admitted, "We found her crypt open and her remains ravaged. We collected what of her we could find, but I'll have to use my Talent to find the rest. We're going to bury her out in front of the temple in a few days. She may have been my enemy, but I could never see anyone treated with anything less than honor at the time of passing."

"Doran is dead? How can she be dead unless you did it?" one voiced, as the rest were silent in utter shock at hearing this news. Ryes realized she needed some advice and to tell Rhodi and the others of this situation, too. She reached back out to Winterhaven, quickly finding Rhodi, as she just finished teaching a class.

"Rhodi, we're in the temple, talking with the rest of your friends, but you should know that we found Doran gone, as just a few scattered bones lying about. Now, they're afraid we killed her. What should I tell them?" she requested, seeking her advice.

"Let me speak to them, through you," she returned, sitting down, and closing her eyes. She felt Dunn, Mitt, Raya, Adina, Nesa and Sayer's interest, as they linked up with them, but they held back and were merely "watching."

"Ryes and the people with her had nothing to do with Doran's death. I feel that it may have been her being cut off from all of you and her inability to tap power from the Stone of Power, which drove her into her final despair. She might have willed herself to death, since all she had left was cold and darkness, in an endless, lone existence," Rhodi sent to the remaining Sleepers. "I now am well familiar with Ryes and the other people here. They would never have caused her death, intentionally. I fell that Ryes sees this was a pitiful way to find her, as scattered bones to be recovered from the ravages of the animals she bred and enslaved to perform at her whims. I fully agree with her. It was a pitiful way to end."

With this, Dunn brought in the other Sleepers in Winterhaven, quickly catching them up on the events, back in the Valley. Raya helped her tie them all together, adding in her own Talent to boost her efforts. They clearly felt the shock of the remaining Temple residents at Ryes' ability to reach with her Mind Voice far across the land to bridge them all together. The Winterhaveners realized this small thing didn't surprise them at all. They were now well used to Ryes' Talents.

"I saw this months ago, but never thought it would ever actually come to be," Renes told them, revealing her very clear Dream about Doran's final end, and the funeral upon the lawn in front of the temple, where she and the others who had previously passed, were laid to rest.

"You can Dream again, Renes?" one of the remaining Sleepers questioned, astounded.

"Now that we are free, we can do many things, again," Saree teased them. She let them feel the sensations she now felt, of her cub moving inside her. Her joy was clear in her mind and heart.

"We are safe here, as we have never been before in our lives," Almas assured them. "I can sleep peacefully at night as the nightmares are gone. And Maren put my season back for me until next year. It is a blessing I do not know how to repay. It gives me time to decide whom to mate, and when to mate. We never had that in the Valley!"

"And you are truly happy in this Winterhaven of theirs?" one of the women questioned, still not believing it.

"Ryes, could you please allow me to fully open up to them?" Rhodi requested. She felt her reluctant concurrence then she opened their contact more fully, more strongly, at the same time opening from within herself, as Ryes knew she had to, for this to work.

Rhodi paused for the barest moment in shock, as she saw Ryes' inner wrestling with Maren's withdrawal from the joy of life he used to know, with the Challenger's computer and its need for contact with her and Mitt's Inner Sight, and her cautious dealings with these new humans, and their coming aboard the Challenger with soldiers, still had her upset. But Rhodi couldn't afford the distractions right now, so immediately opened up to all of them from within, knowing this was the only way to reassure the women what life was like in this new home of theirs; both from Ryes' view and her own. How originally, she and Poli wanted to overthrow the current leadership of Winterhaven, but realized, as they were drawn into the community, their plans were dust on the wind, and how they found themselves fitting into their new home. How their lives were changed by the new challenges yet were secure in being able to make their own choices in facing them, yet still having plenty of loving support.

"We see your truths in full," the first one replied, as they saw all that these two women held in their minds and hearts. "You are right, Rhodi. It is time for us to come out into the sunlight. After all, we should help bury our Lady, in all due respect for what she did give us in answer to our original needs."

"Please release us," another added, as Rhodi and Ryes returned to a more normal level of contact.

"Life is never simple, but together we can manage things," Raya urged them. "I was coming to the valley, at the urging of Doran's call, but found my home here after Ryes fought her the first time and ended the luring call. I know you'll find a good life here, too."

"We will try," the first one assured her, then withdrew. Rhodi let go of Ryes, then the others, leaving only her, Mitt, Adina and Raya still in contact.

"Is there any way to save Maren?" she questioned.

"Ryes had a Dream," Mitt returned, then showed them the small glimpse she gave her of it. "So, we'll have him back, but we don't know if it'll be next year, or later. But he will be himself again."

"I hope so. I can't imagine Dotti putting up with him like this much longer," Raya returned, teasing. "We'll all try our best. But this may have to come from him, and him alone," she warned. "And you'd better be careful up there, Mitt! If Ryes doesn't trust that computer, don't you trust it, either."

"I knew the military always required their officers to have Talent. I just did not understand why, until now. It is frightening that

133

the computer can connect into a Talent like that!" Rhodi commented, still disturbed.

"I heard of it, also. I had no idea it was so intense a contact," Adina added, utterly shocked at some of the things she saw within Ryes, when she opened herself up to them all. Hadu, who had been shadowing her as usual, had seen it, too. He didn't react before the others, as to keep his presence a secret, but deep down she knew he was unhappy with it all.

"I'll be careful. I promise. The only thing I can think of is that it's the one and only way to be sure that the people trying to operate it are of the right people. Did any of Kahmarr's allies of old possess Inner Sight?" Mitt asked, wondering.

"No. It was supposed to be a Kahmarr-only Talent. I now think some of the military had to be on Tayna for it to be passed down to you, Mitt. Perhaps, Ryes' father carried it as a recessive, too?"

"I have no idea. But I've got to get this board finished, so I can get my three days break down there, tomorrow," she urged, "See you all tomorrow!" Then withdrew, still surprised at some of the small background thoughts Ryes had about these new humans from Earth. If she was concerned about them, there was reason to be concerned. She hadn't known about the soldiers being brought aboard their ship! She'd talk with Axel about it, as soon as she was finished, and dig out any video of that "friendly" visit. She wanted to be fully aware – in case they tried to take any actions against them!

# New Awakenings

## Chapter 11

"What I don't get is a looker like you and Him," one of the ship's officers asked Dotti, as she sat down to lunch at her usual place. She looked over at him, puzzled by his question.

"I don't understand. What do you mean? Him, who?" she returned, as she frowned. She had a sudden suspicion of where he was going, from the look on his face.

"I mean, I even heard you're having HIS kid," he replied, scoffing at her innocence. Then he saw her anger ignite and his eyes grew wide in surprise.

"JUST WHO DO YOU THINK YOU ARE?" she demanded yelling, startling Bethy, as she was coming over to the table to join her. Dotti stood up as she faced this rude man down, her face red with intense anger. "What I do, or don't do, is NONE of YOUR business! You can just take your tray and go sit elsewhere, if you're that stupid to begin with!" She was pointing down the room to where the rest of his shipmates sat, utterly disgusted with his attitude. "I don't care where you think you come from; manners are still manners where I come from. And prejudices are NOT tolerated here!" She yelled it out at the top of her lungs, as he stood up, blushing in embarrassment at her unexpected outburst. There was scattered laughter from around the room at his display, as he gathered his tray and went in the direction she clearly indicated. He started out at a rush, then slowed down when almost across the room and started to saunter, as he approached his shipmates. Dotti sat back down as Bethy and Brenda joined her, trays in their hands.

"Well, I think they learned that one real quick," Bethy commented in Dolbith. "What do you think? Should we stick to Dolbith, while they're around?"

"Sure, it'll drive them nuts!" Jim answered with a big smile, as he stepped over, too. "I think everyone in Winterhaven heard what you just told him."

"Well, it serves him right. I can't believe such an attitude," she returned, still flustered. Brenda looked at her and chuckled.

"My grandmother told me about the way they used to treat her great-great grandmother when she was a kid, back on Earth, just because her parents were from another country than the one they settled in. They spoke with a strange accent, sometimes conversed among themselves in their home language, and held some different beliefs. It's been going on for centuries untold. Remember the way most of the inner colonists were treated, up until the last hundred years, or so. Then they had to outer colonies to pick upon. Do you remember the way the slurs used to go?" she questioned, as Dotti gave her a nod of her head.

"It still doesn't mean they need to bring all that here," she returned, still mad. Garth and Sabin emerged from the kitchen, trays in their hands, as they came to sit across from the group. He chuckled as he gave her a nod of his head.

"I'm getting a little tired of it," he admitted. "They try to behave with such discipline, but it still comes through very clear at times." Sabin grunted and nodded his head.

"And if we say anything to each other in Dolbith, they almost go ballistic, as if English is the ONLY language anyone's allowed to speak," he added, as Jim laughed at this, nodding his agreement.

"I say go ahead and speak in Dolbith when you need it. It's their problem if they haven't figured out to ask us for lessons. We could always start up Spanish classes and see if they could conduct the meetings in Castilian, which is another common Earth language," Jim encouraged, smiling. Ethan, Rowan, and Metta came over, sitting down at the table. Garth chuckled merrily at Jim's suggestion.

"My feelings exactly," Ethan agreed, laughing at the image it brought to mind. "If they can't accept that there are other, older cultures out among the stars, they deserve to stew in their own frustrations." Neil and Jake joined them.

"Did you just do all that shouting, Dotti?" Neil questioned, grinning. She nodded her head, with a smile of pride upon her face.

"Had to. He was questioning me about Maren being the father of my baby. It's none of his business to begin with, and I've never been so insulted in my whole life! Maren's a far better man than he could ever hope to be!" she declared with an angry glint in her eyes.

"Maybe we need to protect both the mothers carrying crosses, and our Boodan crosses?" Sabin suggested, suddenly concerned that the man was focused upon Dotti because of whose child she carried. There was sudden alarm in Dotti's eyes, as she realized what he was suggesting. She never would've believed her life could be endangered for such a stupid reason! Not here... Not in their own home...

"They wouldn't go that far," Jake denied, then paused as he realized he honestly didn't know. "They're still military and would be up on charges, and military courts are usually harsh," he finished, his doubts plain in his eyes.

"IF THEY WERE CAUGHT," Ethan finished for him, suddenly agreeing with Sabin's good sense. "We have many mixed couples now. It might be a good idea to increase security, to ensure everyone's safety," he suggested. Garth met his eyes for several long moments, getting no relief from the sudden fear in his heart for his people. Ethan looked like he didn't trust this situation, either!

"Monty, could you call Torr over to our table, please?" he requested, seeing he was talking with his nephew, translating what they were saying for him. Connor had already told everyone he was staying, but hadn't taken Dolbith lessons, yet. The newcomers from Trinity were just starting to get settled in. Monty looked over and gave Garth a small bow, then closed his eyes.

"He's coming," he informed him, a moment later, as he rejoined them. Connor looked puzzled by all this.

"You're psi?" he questioned him, surprised.

"Yes. I have Mind Voice Talent. It's not as strong as some, but it's getting stronger as I practice it more. Maybe we should have you checked? You could carry Talent, too," he suggested.

"It does run in the Elbridge family," Connor agreed, then blushed. "I saw something while I was on the Aurora, with Alec and Ash. Could Ash carry this Talent, too?"

"You saw something? What did you see?" Sabin sharply questioned, looking at this human with new curiosity in his eyes. Could he have Visionary Talent, as Monty carried Mind Voice?

"It was the Quicksilver, drifting through space. Something told me that she would be found," he related, not sure if telling them this was a good thing now. Then Garth smiled as he chuckled at this, nodding his head.

"Ryes found her a few days ago, before she helped the Aurora land. She set up her computer to bring her in to our little space platform. Given a few weeks, we'll get to check her out, ourselves. Since she belongs to your family, she's still yours to do with as the two of you see fit," he informed them, just recalling he hadn't had the time to tell them about her earlier.

"Thanks, Garth!" Monty replied, his eyes filled with wonder at the thought of the Quicksilver on her way here! "We'll have to fix her up and see if we can use her to check out Tayna's old allies. There must be someone left! Maybe Hadu's people? He's bad enough, I shiver at the thought of anyone going up against a whole planet full of Demmias."

"Now, there's some real allies to go hunting for!" Jim agreed, chuckling as he nodded his head.

"But what about the Darkens? They're still out there," Connor countered, wondering if they could actually do anything without real military cover. He knew what happened to Trinity with the attack. The few military ships that had been there trying to defend it had been quickly destroyed.

"Let's see what she's like, first," Monty replied. He recalled the stories of what she was capable of because she had the Windrose Stone to guide her. And now he had his own Talent; it had to be fated.

"Monty, you truly mean to fix her up and take her out?" Denas asked, alarmed. "You are not going without me," she added. He looked into her eyes steadily and shook his head in denial.

"I want you and our children safe at home, while I go out to face whatever lies out there," he said, speaking in a low voice. She looked unhappy about it. "It'd tear me apart to ever put you into such danger," he admitted.

"That's how I feel about taking Ryes out," Garth added, in support. "But I won't have a choice with her. We need her Talents, too much. If the Challenger was taken out before, she could be our only edge in defeating the Snags."

"If we could train more of our Empaths to stretch out, the way she does," Torr suggested as he sat down with them.

"But they still won't have the ability to burn out the Snag's Talents, as she can, nor find the flaws in their engines and blow their ships to bits," Alec countered, sitting on the other side of Denas. He usually learned more if he let everyone forget he was still sitting among them. But for this, he'd been there and saw it was her unique combination of Talents, which quickly overcame the enemy.

"Since when did you learn Dolbith?" Monty asked him, questions in his eyes. Alec laughed at this, nodding his head. It was a fair question.

"Ryes advised me to ask Raya about it. And since Ryes had been the one to send me to her, she granted my request. It seems Raya doesn't quite trust we newer humans," he explained. "I wanted to learn more about the Star people, since you've been developing your psi abilities for countless generations. Frankly, with our two peoples being able to breed, it jumps the human race ahead a little with that problem. We have some established `Talents,' but none of them are as clearly defined as yours. Once my term of military service has ended, I intend to return to Winterhaven to join the Alliance," he assured them, seeing he had the whole table's attention.

"You sound as if the Alliance is already established," Sabin commented, chuckling as he did so.

"It will be, and soon. I've seen it," he returned, confidence in his voice.

"Exactly what Talents do you have?" Garth asked, frowning as he considered the lanky young man sitting nearby.

"As you would say it, Mind Voice, Visionary and something we call Psi-shield and Sword," he answered, still smiling. These people were his people, and he knew he had nothing to fear from them. Storme agreed, as she sat at his side.

"Then you might want Ryes to check you, to see if you have any other Talents, too," Torr suggested. "Since you already have three, it's best to be sure."

"Why does everyone keep forgetting I have Catalyst, too?" Denas demanded, smiling as she saw the surprise in Torr's eyes. He had forgotten!

"Our apologies, Lady Denas," Garth told her, giving her a small bow as he did so. "With Ryes around, we do tend to forget others have such Talents, also. It's not on purpose," he admitted. She smiled, accepting his apology with a return bow. Then he turned to Torr. "We should see to some added security for our crosses and the women who're bearing crosses. We might even increase our security in general, considering all the mixed couples we now have. There's some concern," he told him. Torr nodded his head in agreement, grimness touched his face for a moment.

"I've heard the comments. I don't know why the humans from the ships think only a very few of us can actually understand and speak English around here, but they seem to. It's proven handy when I want to listen in on their offhand comments," he told them, smiling at his cleverness. Garth laughed at this outright.

"Great idea! Pass the word around for everyone to stick to Dolbith, if possible. Let them suffer from their own ignorance, for now," he ordered, as the rest gathered around the table, saw what he meant and smiled their agreements with this idea. "And Connor, you need to see Raya about learning Dolbith, too," he added in English, getting an embarrassed grin and nod from the young man.

"I would've never believed they could think in such a way," Jake commented. "It makes me ashamed to be human."

"Don't worry, they'll get over it with time," Neil assured him, seeing how the seven individuals they rescued off the Star Quest in their little time experiment, had come to fit in with the rest of them already. They didn't think of Jake any differently than their other human residents.

"Well, Dotti, may I escort you back to your lab, or wherever you're going today? I had watch early this morning and am free to be at your service," Jake offered her, smiling. She sighed as she returned his smile, hating the necessity. Torr gave him a nod of his head in affirmation and agreement.

"Yes, thank you. But after we finish our lunches," she returned.

Denas had her eyes closed and was already working with Alec, fully intending to check him and Monty's nephew. She'd never seen a Shield and Sword Talent before and was thrilled to get the chance to examine a new Talent, again.


They began to cycle the remaining eighteen chambers, three at a time, as Ryes, Shams and Sadie began to check out the rest of the rooms, to see what still lay about and what was now badly damaged. Gleds, Maren and Ardis were seeing about setting up the shelter they brought, so they could prepare a late lunch. Ryes had planned on everyone sleeping inside the Burrower, tonight. Poli and Lissel were keeping a close eye on the chambers wanting to be sure they were still functioning properly.

"Ugh, a nest of some kind," Sadie commented, finding it in the middle of a pile of colorful silk-like gowns, in a corner. She loved the dresses and filmy scarves she found in this chamber, which Ryes thought might belong to whomever was left to care for the temple. Since she had killed the last caretaker and silenced Doran's call, there was no one to use this room anymore. Ryes stepped over to look at it. She wrinkled up her nose at the intense smell, too.

"What a stench! I'll put it outside," she offered, as she lifted it up with Manipulator, until only the eggs and the scarves which were part of the nest itself, were included. She and Shams escorted it outside, opening a nearby rear door. Sadie looked about the room, finding the wardrobe. She opened it and saw a very lovely, dark green and gold wrap made of a thin see-through material hanging in the front. There were many others, of varying colors hanging behind it, but this one caught her eye. She pulled it out and stepped over to a nearby mirror, smiling mischievously.

"Now that'll look nice on you. It goes with your green eyes and the color of your hair," Shams commented as he returned to the room to see her looking at herself in a mirror, with a filmy dress draped about her shoulders.

"But it's not truly mine," she returned a little sadly, taking it off.

"Nonsense!" Poli assured her, stepping in to join them. "You may have it. It originally came from my sister's things, and I give you, my permission. It does look nice on you." Sadie's eyes shone with happiness, as they met hers.

"Thank you," she breathed, giving her a small bow. "Pardon me, I'd better find Ryes as I'm supposed to be here to watch over her." With this she carefully folded the filmy wrap and headed out the door with it in her hands.

"Did Lissel mean what was on her mind, earlier?" Shams questioned in a low voice. "That she's considering mating with me in a few weeks?"

"I believe so, but it is best if you ask her, yourself," she replied, smiling to see his discomfort. "Do you not like the prospect?" she added, needing to be sure of him and his way of thinking, herself.

"I have three cubs, by two different women, already. My father and mother wanted to `breed' me, to keep my Talent strong in our bloodlines. I know Ryes doesn't want me in her life that way, but I haven't felt any strong attraction for any other woman, including Lissel. Do you think she'll mind that I'm not in love with her, if she decides to choose me? I guess my parents are right, and it's important to breed Talent to Talent, so I won't refuse her. But, if a breeding is all she wants, I think she'll be shorting her children. I can't be there to help raise the cubs I was already forced to create, but would she want to let me be a part of the lives of the ones of mine she may carry?" Poli looked at him for a long moment, fully understanding what he was asking of her and surprised at his candid sharing. She sat down, gesturing for him to join her. He sat near her; his troubled heart clearly reflected in his eyes.

"Breeding by family will has been a long tradition on Kahmarr. It is what led to Doran's imprisonment here. Her mate was chosen for her, and she killed him, because he physically and emotionally abused her; she utterly despised him. There are at least two months until Lissel will have to mate. Take the time to get to know her. I believe she will understand your concern about any children the two of you may have. But do not father any cubs because you feel you must. Wait until it comes of the heart, and then you will be free," she advised, smiling. She realized she was probably only a couple of years older than Shams but felt so much older in other ways. The time spent in the stasis chamber would've been considered wasted, except for the rich reward they all found at this end of time. He gave her a nod of his head, determined to know Lissel and if such a mating would be the best for them both, or not.

"You remind me of my older sister," he replied, smiling as he gave her a small bow. "Thank you. I'll talk with her, and we'll see where this goes." She smiled as he got up and left the room, heading for Lissel, to open up his heart to her to see where hers truly lay.

"And you of my younger brother," she whispered, now that he was gone. Even his eyes were the same golden-yellow color. And she realized she truly missed him so much, now that she was free.

"Well, we finally got those underground chambers swept out," Ryes told Maren, as she, Ardis and Gleds came up the stairs to join him and the others in the main chamber.

"Poli had me hauling some boxes out to the Burrower. There were some things here which used to belong to her and the others. Look what they did to the altar," he suggested, his voice suddenly dropping at the end, and he was speaking in English, not wanting to attract too much attention to himself, now that they had another nine Sleepers awakened. They were busy cleaning the main temple hall and collecting what other pieces of bone they found, for him and Shams to examine.

"Oh my," Ardis commented, looking over to see it was now shattered, well beyond restoration. "That stone was dense. How'd they do it?"

"Talent. Lady Callio is a strong Manipulator," he replied. "I don't think they want it restored."

"We could always put up a holo for anyone to look at, from when Dotti did the scans the last time we were here," Ryes suggested, "if anyone's truly THAT curious." Ardis gave her a nod in agreement, the concern showing in her eyes. "There's one more thing I want to do, before we go to dinner," Ryes stated.  Maren saw the determination in her eyes and was curious.

"What?" he finally asked when she didn't supply the follow-up right away.

"A restoration of all but the alter," she finally stated, meeting his eyes.  "It'd be a gift to all our Sleepers, in remembrance."

"Can I see you work, from inside?" Ardis asked, hoping.  Ryes turned and met her eyes, laughing and giving her a nod.

"Of course, you can," she invited.  She sat down on the floor next to a hibernation chamber.  Ardis sat next to her.

"Can I see it, too?" Sadie asked, as she sat down next to them. "I need to practice my Booster."  Ryes laughed and nodded, then held out her hands.  Even if they could link up without the physical touch, she felt this was still the best way, a joining of hands and a joining of hearts.

"I'll keep an eye on things here, while you're busy," Maren supplied.  The others had closed their eyes, while Ryes had her open.  She gave him a nod as she established the commune.  Once she got the others calmed down, she let Sadie feed in her Booster, as she opened her own pool of power and other Talents.  Ryes recalled what it appeared like when she first stepped into this chamber, when she felt she was so young, even if she was only a year older now.  First, she sought out and found the final remains of Doran's body and moved them into her crypt, once again closing the door, so it could still be opened easily.

Like an artist with a set of fine tools at her command, she first repaired Doran's green marble statue.  Then she swept the room, repairing and restoring the rest of the room, the benches, small tables and other items all repaired and returned.  The hall of weapons was next, as she pulled them all carefully over to their places on the walls, even brining the crossbow from across the far end of the valley.  To replace the spot where the one sword had been, she pulled some sand from beside the stream and formed a replica from the resulting glass after she heated it and purified it with her Talents.  She strengthened it and put it up on the brackets where the original belonged.

Ardis then urged Ryes to check the rest of the Temple, to be sure.  She was thrilled to be a part of it, even if she'd never been here, before.  The skill the craftswomen used to create this great place amazed her and gave her ideas, not the subjects, but the techniques.  Sadie was almost drunk on the amount of power in Ryes' pool, but still practiced Boosting her, anyway.  Seeing how she used her ability, gave her ideas in directing her own. After a very few moments they were done, and the inner link was gently released.

"Enough for today," Ryes stated, standing up, knowing she still had plenty of power left in reserve – just in case. The other two got to their feet, too, while Maren chuckled.

"Nice job," he commented with a nod. Ryes smiled and gave him a nod back. Shams appeared shocked, as he turned about, trying to look at everything. Lissel and four other new Sleepers, who'd been in other chambers sorting and cleaning, had stepped out to look about the room in surprise now. Poli just smiled and gave Ryes a small bow in gratitude.

"It's beautiful, but let's go get cleaned up," Gleds suggested. "It's past time for dinner," he pressed, "I want to get something to eat before taking watch."

"Hey, that's MY line," Maren countered, causing Gleds to laugh as he nodded his head. He remembered what Maren was like, before Dotti became his wife.

"Not since Dotti, it isn't," Ryes teased him, grinning. "You seemed to slow down a little, when she came into your life." They started to walk towards the exit.

"Yeah, the only thing that slows you down is all those cubs of yours," he quipped back, the corners of his mouth quirking again.

"You should've brought them along," Sadie commented, joining them, as they were headed for the shuttle. "I bet some of these women would've loved to hold them. They've noted my pregnancy and have been asking all kinds of questions. It's too bad you're not properly the father, Gleds," she added, giving her husband a wink.

"The next one," he promised, smiling, "if you want another one."

"A lone child is a spoiled child. I should know as my father was one, and while I loved him dearly, he sometimes acted like an overgrown, spoiled brat, even if he was an adult. You'd better believe I want another baby. This small son of ours will need a little sister, or brother, to look out for. Past that point, we'll think on it," she told him as they started walking down the temple steps to the first landing. The sun was just touching the horizon, turning the clouds a reddish gold. Gleds was blushing as the rest of the group were laughing, understanding her sentiments too well.

144

"The sunset is absolutely lovely," one of the new Sleepers commented, as they joined her and another on the steps. Ryes stopped to meet her new charges.

"Yes, it is," Ryes agreed, smiling.

"It's been too many years, since I last saw one," her companion added, joy upon her face. "I want to see the moons, stars and the sunrise," she added. Ardis and Ryes were merrily chuckling at this, giving her a nod, as the rest of their group began descending toward the shuttle. There were only two showers and could wait their turns, anyway.

"It's too bad the summer's almost over now. It snows in Winterhaven in the winter, but if you want to get away from the snow, you could always go visiting in Matlowe Village. They're much further south than we are. It gets cold, but very rarely snows," Ryes told her. "My new favorite time is the early spring and watching the new plants and flowers springing up through the snow in Winterhaven."

"Flowers! I have not seen, nor smelled a flower in too long a time now!" the first one replied, seeing the questions in second one's eyes. "My name is Macca of House Tamik," she added, in introduction. Ryes smiled, nodding her head.

"And I'm Ryes of House Li. My friend is Ardis, partly of House Ledearis." Ardis blushed as she waved a hand at Ryes.

"We've no idea how close any of us are to Prince Callas, except for Maren, who looks like his twin," she denied, grinning.

"What do you mean?" Macca questioned, "I am related to House Ledearis, on my father's side."

"Prince Callas founded the Caravaners and the Laws here on Tayna, after the Snagospin attack. He lived and executed his office from Matlowe Village. Since Ardis, myself and many of our close friends come from Matlowe, we now have to trace our family histories back, to see to what degree we're all related to him. But he did name my husband Garth, as his heir in the message he left for him. His wife was a Forester and a strong Visionary," Ryes explained, as much as they knew upon the matter, since Macca was of House Ledearis, too.

"Oh my," Macca declared as she put a hand up, over her lips in surprise. "That makes your husband the Crown Prince and a cousin to me in some degree."

"Yup. And Ryes teases Garth about being the crown prince from time-to-time," Ardis added, chuckling.

145

"We wouldn't want him to forget it, nor let something like that to go to his head!" she quipped, laughing now.

"I'm from Matlowe, too," the second woman stated, speaking up now. "We used to live down near the river and I loved the sound of the Yuri, as I went to sleep at night," she told them.

"My grandfather, Rowan, says he misses the Yuri's voice the most at night. We go down to the Yuri to fish, or swim, sometimes," Ryes told her.

"Rowan? Son of Tian? He was my friend's newborn cub when I left Matlowe at Doran's call. My name's Raffa," she told them, smiling. "He's still alive?"

"Yes, he is. Tian was my great-grandmother. Rowan is my father's father, who was Ronn, who was true mate to Tyra Li, my mother. You came from Matlowe! Did you know Jana, as well? She was my grandmother," Ryes told her, smiling as tears formed in the corners of her eyes. She couldn't believe it that one of the villagers knew her grandfather as a cub!

"Jana was my youngest sister!" she declared, throwing her arms about Ryes as she started laughing and crying. "You're my great niece!" Ryes was laughing and crying, too.

"Then Maren's your great nephew, too. My father and his mother are siblings," she told her, as Raffa started to cover her face with kisses. Ryes laughed at this, pulling back a little to look her in the eyes. "If I'd known before," she started, but Raffa shook her head merrily.

"I'd mostly withdrawn from everyone else then. But it's good to know I still have family in the world."

"Dinner should be almost ready. Why don't we talk about all this over dinner?" Ardis suggested. "But Ryes and I have to wash up a bit, first. It was pretty dirty in the lower chambers."

"We should all wash up. That time in the sleep chamber has left me feeling dirty, too. Would you have something more appropriate for me to wear?" Macca questioned, hoping.

"Yes. We brought some warmer clothing along, as we knew you weren't used to weather. With the summer closing, the nights have been getting cooler," Ryes assured her, still smiling.

"Your turn!" Maren yelled up to her, seeing she and Ardis were still standing on the stairs.

146

"Thanks!  Maren, come and meet our Great Aunt Raffa.  Jana was her little sister," she called back, then laughed at the surprise on his face.

"Let us all go down to greet him there," Raffa suggested, as she took a step down the great staircase.  The other three women agreed, following her down.

"Rowan's going to be so surprised," Lissel commented, as she and Shams had heard the last of what they discussed, having stepped out of the temple behind them.  Shams chuckled as he nodded his head.

"I wonder what stories of the village she knows?  I'm sure Rowan could learn lots of new old ones from her," he said, as they went down the stairs together.  Maren was now being fussed over by Raffa.

"Had you ever been to Matlowe?" she asked, knowing he had travelled about in his profession before.

"A couple of times when I was a cub, but not in a very long time," he admitted.  "I don't even remember Ryes truly, as she was just another cub to me then.  Will it bother you to be sleeping here, this close to the temple tonight?" he asked, changing the subject, not wanting to think of what he lost out on by staying away from Matlowe.  "I don't think Ryes would mind flying you and Poli home, if you want," he offered, fairly sure on this score.

"I will be fine," she assured him, smiling as she noted the clumsy way he tried to shift the topic.  "But I am hungry, and it does smell good.  Let's go clean-up for dinner, then return to check on the last three we have going, tonight.  Poli might appreciate the break."

"I'm going to relieve her now, as I've already had my dinner," Gleds told them, coming up the stairs.  "You two take your time.  Sadie said she'll be joining me as soon as she's eaten."  Lissel and Shams laughed at this, Shams giving him a nod of his head.

"Thanks," he told him, as the two of them started down the stairs to join the others.  Four of the newer Sleepers came out of the temple, trailing them down.  Gleds chuckled as he stepped into the hallway, knowing the smell of the food must be very tempting after uncounted years of going without.

147

# Wary

## Chapter 12

"Shams?" he heard, as a hand lightly touched his shoulder. He opened his eyes, still a little groggy. There were no lights on and no voices calling out, so he knew it wasn't an emergency.

"Yes Lissel?" he questioned, realizing it was a familiar female voice.

"You were right. I'm having trouble sleeping so close to the Temple. Do you mind if I sleep next to you?" she requested, hoping. He chuckled in a low voice in response.

"Yes, you may," he invited. He was sleeping down on the floor, instead of using one of the seats, as most of the others. He found he preferred the air-mattresses. "Do you want me to get you an air-mattress?"

"I already have one," she informed him, pulling it closer, so it was now against his. He helped her get it set, then took her hand into his, after she lay down and got comfortable.

"Goodnight, Lissel," he said, as he got settled.

"Goodnight, Shams," she replied with a sigh, then closed her eyes. Yes, she thought, he felt very right. Shams caught this as he was dropping off, a smile upon his lips. Would he truly have a choice, he wondered? Somehow, he found he didn't mind it now.

"Dad, it's way past your bedtime!" Sayer scolded, standing at the stairs' landing, seeing Garth was still up talking with Sabin in the living room. Both men chuckled at hearing her admonishment.

"It's an old habit of ours, well before we became husbands and fathers," he replied, giving her a nod of his head. "I promise to be to bed soon."

"Is Mom truly going to be all right, out in that wicked Valley all alone?" she pressed, voicing what had been keeping her awake tonight.

"She's not alone," Garth reminded her, smiling. He missed her, too.

"Why don't you try to check on her, yourself?" Sabin invited.

"I'm not that strong," she returned, with a heavy sigh. "Mom can easily reach us. She had to have Rhodi show the other women that not only didn't she kill Doran, but that she felt sorry for the way they found her. Rhodi and Mom convinced the rest of those women that life here in Winterhaven wasn't so bad," she told him.

"Doran's dead?" Garth questioned sharply, sitting up at this news. Sabin looked disturbed too, as they exchanged glances.

"Yeah. Mom showed us that all they found were a few scattered bones. The crypt was open, and it looked like some animals had gotten to what was left of her," she explained.

"Show us, Sweetling," Garth urged, motioning for her to come closer. She smiled, nodded her head, and ran down the stairs, then walking over to the couch. She sat down next to him and closed her eyes, reaching for his hand, as she brought up her Talent. Sabin placed his hand over theirs, as he joined them. Sayer brought up the whole experience, even when Ryes had to open further from within, so she and Rhodi could truly set their worries to rest. When she finished, she opened her eyes to see the shadow in her father's eyes.

"Then they kind of dismissed me. Guess they had some other things to talk about, but I think Rhodi and Mom got through to them," she said.

"Thanks, Sayer," Garth replied, giving her a kiss on her forehead. "If you truly need to check up on your mother, just go in and say goodnight to the cubs, again," he suggested. She looked mystified for a moment, then her eyes brightened as she smiled and gave him a kiss on his cheek, then kissed Uncle Sabin.

"I will!" she agreed, "Thanks, Dad! And don't forget to get to bed, so you'll be rested enough for tomorrow's meetings." With this, she jumped up and ran upstairs for the cubs' room, realizing to be careful and not wake Hadu.

"That intrusion of the soldiers onto the Challenger truly had her upset. And we both know that Ryes likes humans, and usually grants them more leeway, than she'd grant any other people, so far," Sabin stated.

"She's been having Dreams but has been keeping them mostly to herself. There was one on the Challenger and it did have the feel of her being underway. Our proposed trip to Kahmarr, do you think?" Garth questioned.

"Must be," his friend replied, smiling as he'd seen the Challenger a few times in his Visions, too.

"Alright, we're on the Challenger, then who's going to be left to watch over things back here? I don't trust those ship humans that much. It needs to be someone smart and strong."

"Why not see if we can get a couple of their ships to join us on our first journey? We could use this as a training exercise for working together. Once we have the Challenger cleared for duty, we'd better have our protocols established, or there could be all kinds of problems, as we go up against the Snags to break the blockade. That should help, a little," Sabin suggested.

"That's a good idea," Garth agreed, thinking on it a moment. "Let's take up Monty's idea of finding Demia and her colonies. Who knows who else's left out there, still able to take the fight back to the Snags?" Then a tall lanky form approaching them. "Sorry, we didn't mean to keep you up, Hadu," he apologized, truly meaning it.

"I sleep lightly," he told them, sitting down on a chair. "I will go with Monty to find Demia. Otherwise, his voyage could prove a tragedy," he asserted. Garth found he still got shivers from listening to his voice, no matter that they'd been living with them for a while now.

"Are you sure this is what you need to do? Couldn't you record a message for Monty to broadcast for them?" Sabin asked, knowing he'd have a problem leaving Adina's side.

"Yes, I must go. They would never believe a recorded message," he assured them. "I have been gone for almost three hundred years... Would you believe such a message?" Garth shook his head no, understanding now showing clear in his eyes.

"Then as soon as the Quicksilver's ready, you and Monty may go to see about Demia and of any other of Kahmarr's allies of old. We'll need everyone we can get to drive the Snags back to their home system and keep them there," Garth said. "Thank you, Hadu. I appreciate your assistance." Hadu gave him a nod of his head, then stood to return to his pallet.

"I'd best get home to get some rest for tomorrow," Sabin told Garth, standing up.

"And I'd better go to bed before Sayer starts yelling at me, again," he added in response, grinning. "Later," he said, as he saw his blood-brother out the door. Sabin waved as he walked to his own door. He then closed his door and shut off the lights, but the night light which they'd grown into using lately. He went upstairs to check on the cubs one last time, sending Sayer off to bed as he did so. He could "feel" Ryes about him, as he reached his own room. When he got into bed, he called up his Talent. She extended herself to him and they exchanged a little news and their deep love for each other.

"She's gone off site to work on a special project, which was planned out months ago," Larissa explained to Commander Kaminski, as he stopped by Ryes' office to see her in the morning. He appeared puzzled by this news.

"But she was gone all day yesterday," he pressed. She gave him a nod of agreement. "I thought she was only out to test one of your reclaimed shuttles." She smiled for him as she nodded again.

"She combined the missions," she brightly informed him, "and won't be back home until late this evening."

"It must be something important," he commented, wanting to find out more, but seeing he wasn't going to get anything further. He sighed. "Could I please get an appointment set up for tomorrow morning, then? I have a few important matters to discuss with her." She shook her head at this.

"She has tomorrow set to take a shuttle up to the Aires' Wrath in the afternoon. Do you still want to see her in the morning?" she asked. Kaminski called up his calendar briefly and saw it was already there, so shook his head no.

"I can wait for her on the ship," he finally told Ryes' office assistant. She nodded as he quickly left her office, somehow feeling she'd dismissed him, which was unsettling. He was Fleet, after all, and they were only colonials.

"Here we are, back in Winterhaven," Ryes told her newer passengers, after settling the shuttle down upon its landing pad near the hangars. It was just past dinner time now. She typed in a quick message, requesting someone to take the Burrower on into the hangar properly. She didn't feel like leaving her charges yet, to do it herself. She promptly got an affirmative.

151

"Ryes? Garth wants everyone to stick to speaking and writing in Dolbith, until things settle down," Raya sent to her, knowing she was back. This shocked her, as she turned to look to Maren and Ardis, seeing they must've gotten the same message, too.

"What's that all about?" Gleds questioned, puzzled.

"There have been some comments made and I would think for security reasons, too," she replied, shrugging her shoulders at the same time. "Other than that, I've no idea," she added. "We'll find out, as soon as we get inside," she invited, as she unbuckled and stood up.

"Alright, but is Raya holding some dinner for us?" Ardis teased, grinning, "I'm starving!" Ryes and the others laughed at this, except Maren, who merely nodded his head.

"I swear, it must take you some serious effort to keep such a straight face at times, Maren," Sadie scolded, smiling teasingly as she did it. He shrugged in response.

"It's hard to explain, but honestly I'm not trying not to laugh, or smile," he told her. Then Ryes grabbed his arm, grinning as she pulled him below, toward the main hatch.

"Later," she warned them, not wanting anyone harassing him about it, other than herself. "You're mine and Dotti's to torture, after all," she whispered to him, as they jumped out of the shuttle ahead of the rest. He sighed at this.

"Don't I know it! Tanns took Rowis and Karis back, but Tars refuses to leave Dotti and I. I don't know if Mom will ever talk to me, again," he told her, looking very unhappy.

"She will. She only needs time, just like you," she assured him, as he stepped back over to help their new inhabitants down to the ground.

"What is the problem with the visiting humans?" Lissel asked Ryes directly, concerned for all their welfares.

"Nothing, yet. I get the feeling Garth's trying to prevent a problem from arising. I'll talk to him about it later," she promised, smiling assurance, while she worried within at what set it off?

"No need to worry. There he is, coming to meet us," Shams stated, pointing to Garth, Ethan and Rhodi, as they approached.

"This is the one you fought Doran over, the first time you came to the valley?" Prias questioned Ryes, having stepped over to hear what they were discussing.

"Yes. That's Garth, my true-mate," she assured her, smiling in relief.

"He does look like one worthy of such an effort," she returned, smiling in response. True-mate? In truth, she'd never known of anyone before to have taken the vows!

"He was and is," she replied, then trotted out to him, throwing herself into his arms, as he opened them to wrap them around her, kissing her soundly.

"Oh my, I had forgotten that people will do such things, at times," Macca said, putting a hand to her lips as she imagined what that kiss must feel like. Shams chuckled at this, nodding his head.

"Her heart's set upon him, so I have to look elsewhere," he replied, looking down to Lissel. She looked up to him and smiled. There was still much they needed to talk about, first. She could understand his reluctance to merely breed – too well – it echoed what lay in her own heart. At least they had a little time.

"You will find plenty of men here. Some seem a little rough at first, but almost all of them seem to be of good heart," Poli encouraged the women, seeing them standing near Lissel and Shams, as if they were afraid to venture any further.

"And some of them are human men?" Tieva questioned. She laughed lightly in return.

"Yes, it seems we are compatible. A first, I must say," Poli's eyes straying to Gleds and Sadie, who were standing near them, arms about each other, as they waited. Rhodi strode up to them, smiling her welcome. Ethan was at her side.

"Harvest and hearth, welcome my friends," she greeted them, spreading out her arms. Ethan chuckled merrily, enjoying their surprise at seeing him. Maren and Ardis stepped up to the front, having sealed the hatch behind them. The women were suddenly laughing and crying, all at once. They each greeted Rhodi, exchanging hugs for the first time in countless years. For some, they were finally putting a face to a name, as if greeting old friends for the first time in ages. The Winterhaveners stood back, letting them get to know each other again. Ryes had an arm around Garth and another around Maren, while Ardis had hers around Garth too, as she sighed at their display. Finally, Garth let the women go, so he could address their newcomers, once they calmed down again.

"Welcome to Winterhaven. I am Garth, leader of this place. We have a special dinner prepared for you in our dining hall. Rhodi, Poli, and Dunn will be helping you become acquainted with our facilities and how we generally conduct ourselves here. If you have any questions at all, merely ask anyone who has a red Phoenix symbol upon their shoulder, like this one," he urged, showing them the badge upon his shoulder. Ryes had seen it and suddenly had a suspicion as to why he now wore it. Had things gotten that bad with the negotiations, she wondered? She saw the questions in Maren's eyes, too. Ardis didn't look surprised, which interested her anew. "And I'd like to introduce to you, Doctor Ethan Cruthers, who is our head of Research and one of our own Elders. He is also a human as you might have already noted." This got polite laughs from the women as Dr. Cruthers stepped over next to him to address them.

"Welcome to Winterhaven, indeed. Our small home is graced by your beauty. We presently have two human starships up at our space platform and one down here for repairs, and their request for allies. We're planning an attack upon the enemy which destroyed Kahmarr and currently holds Earth in its grasp. These strange, new men and women are somewhat without manners. If any of them ever bothers you, let any of us know immediately, and we'll handle the situation. We don't allow challenges here in Winterhaven, as I'm sure Ryes has already told you, nor do we tolerate rude treatment of our citizens. Your guides will further inform you of what to expect. Please give everyone here a little time to get used to you and we'll be sure to do the same," he told them, smiling jovially at all the uncertainty around him. Rhodi bowed to him, as due an elder, then turned to her charges,

"Come along, ladies. The hour is already late," Rhodi invited as she and Poli stepped forward, heading for the new nearby entrance below. Garth and the others brought up the rear, as he and Ethan were quietly filling them in on the day's happenings. Maren was upset, as he thought of his precious wife endangered now.

"We'll weather this," Ryes assured him, seeing the anger in his eyes. "I'm surprised she didn't pop him in the mouth for his insolence." He looked at her surprised and then nodded his head as he had an eyebrow raised, as he imagined the scene again. He realized she would've if she felt herself truly in danger.

"Has that been it, so far?" Lissel questioned, concerned.

"That and some whispered comments, spoken out of turn. In our official meetings, you can sense the strain they're under, trying to treat us as equals and not pets to order around," Garth returned, grimacing as he thought of the next round, starting up in the morning.

"It sounds like the situation's building," Sadie observed, a hand to her stomach. Her son may be pure human, but Gleds was still her husband by choice, and she could guess they'd think she was carrying his son instead.

154

"There has to be some way to get through this, there's too much at stake! We have the Snags too close to our system and Earth's surrounded. What do they think they're doing, being so petty?" Ardis demanded, disgusted with the whole situation.

"I'm bringing it up tomorrow, but maybe I should let you address them for me, Ardis?" Garth teased, smiling, as Ethan chuckled and nodded his head.

"It's pointless and I thought something we left behind, long ago," he commented, sighing as he considered the problem before them. "It must be some kind of reaction to the threat of the Snagospin. Perhaps some fear of the unknown?" he offered, in question. This had the rest thinking, as they entered the long passageway, heading inwards toward the dining hall.

"It could be, but it'd better stop being conducted against us," Ryes intoned, wondering what she could truly do about it?

"So, you're sure that tension's starting to develop between the cat people and humans?" Ash questioned his friend, not believing what he was saying.

"No. Not between the starmen and humans, just between the ships' crews and the starmen. Our people are starting it. The humans who've lived here are fine and are united with the starmen. They don't even think of them as different. It's the ships' crews who're posing the problem. Something's going to have to happen, or the whole thing's going to blow," Alec warned, meeting his eyes.

"I'll pass it along to the captain," he replied with a sigh. "So, where've you been staying?"

"Monty and his wife have allowed Connor and I to stay in their guest bedrooms. It's far too comfortable to refuse. Storme's over there now, cozy on the bed, waiting for me. I heard they have some new women they rescued from some valley, arriving tonight. They're friends of Denas and Saree's. I'm heading over to the cafeteria to quickly check them out before I join Storme. Want to meet them, at least?" he pressed, knowing Ash needed this jaunt out tonight. It'd give him the chance to talk with Garth, without anyone pressuring anyone.

"Alright. I could use a late snack, anyway. I missed my dinner," he replied with a chuckle, as he stood up. They walked out into the cool night air, the last of the summer was starting to fade. It

155

was strange to experience seasons again, Ash realized. He'd lived under a dome most of his life and this open air sometimes drove him to distraction. The light rainfall the other day had him running for shelter in panic! They finally entered the comforting passages below ground, heading for the cafeteria. As they entered the room, they saw several tables were already filled.

"Alec, Ash, grab some food and come on over," Ryes invited, calling out to the two men. Alec waved, then they went to grab a tray and see what was left. There was a feast for the asking, surprising both men, as they each heaped their plates. They grabbed their mugs of tea, as they were starting to get accustomed, then headed for the head table. They usually sat at it, most times now, anyway. It was full with several new faces, women he didn't know.

"So, what's up?" Ryes asked with a smile, as they sat down and got comfortable.

"Storme proved she's more cat than I thought. She caught a ` squeaker' today, leaving me its body, after she was finished with it," he told her. The others were laughing heartily at his tale.

"My mom always told me that cats left their kills for their favorite humans, because they think we're such lousy hunters, that they feel sorry for us," Sadie countered, "So, tell her thank you, very much and quietly dispose of it, when she's not looking." Alec laughed as he nodded his head, feeling she might have the right of it.

"I'll take your advice," he replied, grinning, "I didn't know what to do with the thing."

"How're things going on the Aurora?" Garth asked, hoping to find a way to get a handle on her captain. The man still puzzled him; he seemed warm and friendly, yet sometimes aloof and strict with others.

"It's been busy. We can't thank you enough, Maren for all you did to save the crew. Everyone's been so amazed and in such high spirits, that it's a true relief. Our repairs are progressing well, thanks to your people again, Garth. Yun was even singing today, as he inspected the repairs. I can't recall the last time I heard that from him!" Ash told him, his happiness plain on his face. Garth chuckled, giving him a nod of his head.

"You're more than welcome," he replied, giving his wife a wink.

"I don't think your problems lie with the Aurora and her crew," Alec suddenly spoke up in Dolbith, smiling. "It may stem from the crew on the Wrath, but a few words to Mr. Kaminski should get things

156

straightened out. He's pretty savvy and will handle things, without involving Walker," he advised. He got a raised eyebrow from Ryes, so he gave her a small bow of his head. "I follow the rules here, but Command has never given me such a set of rules to follow, because they want me to spy for them. So, what's to prevent me from doing the return favor?" he prompted, getting chuckles from most of the others, who knew of the situation already.

"You're going to get yourself in trouble, Alec," Ryes scolded in English.

"I didn't understand anything!" Ash stated, glancing to Alec, "I haven't tried to learn your language yet, so I can't be held accountable; unlike some people who cut things too close, at times," he warned. Yes, he felt like this would be a good place to call home, but he wasn't going to throw in with them until his term of duty was up. Still, he'd grant Alec this one, because of their long friendship and he knew he had overall good sense. "Anyway, I'm busy eating now. The food here's heavenly! My compliments to your kitchen staff!"

"I'm glad you enjoy it, Ash," Ardis returned, smiling, "I'll let Chuck and Raya know."

"I'll see if I can get a few moments alone with Mr. Kaminski," Ryes offered. "Maren, I and some of our Healers are scheduled to go up tomorrow afternoon, to see what we can do to help with the injured on the other two ships." Garth gave her a nod of agreement at this, liking her approach. It'd be less stressful than a direct confrontation with Captain Walker.

"Are we allowed to speak with these two? They do not carry this firebird symbol even if one knows Dolbith," Callio questioned, as she considered the two strange humans sitting among them, at Ryes' invitation.

"These two should be fine, but for now, only Alec can speak Dolbith. Dunn should be able to help you understand English, the human's language, soon," Ryes advised them, seeing the interest in the men from their new Sleepers. She wondered, for a very brief moment, if she should warn the men of Winterhaven to be on their guard? "But they don't know Winterhaven as well as we do."

"We're new here, too," Alec volunteered, smiling as one woman couldn't keep her eyes from him, from the moment they sat down.

"You are human, yet you both carry Talent. Yours is strong, next to your friend's," Tessi told Alec, seeing he noted her interest. He smiled as he gave her a small bow and translated what she said for Ash.

"No, I don't have Talent. I leave the smoke and mirrors up to Alec," Ash denied. He was wondering about these strangely dressed women. Ryes closed her eyes, extending a hand to him, too.

"Yes, you do, Ash," she stated, smiling as she opened her eyes. "But it sleeps for now. I could awaken it for you."

"You are a Catalyst, too?" Tessi questioned Ryes, having felt her using her Talent, briefly.

"Yes, I am," she replied, switching back to Dolbith.

"It is getting late, ladies. Let us retire and plan our departed one's funeral in the morning," Rhodi prompted, seeing their interest in Ryes, and wanting to head it off for now. They got to their feet at her urging, then filed out of the dining hall following in Poli's wake.

"They've been in stasis for centuries," Ryes explained, with a heavy sigh. "And we found their former leader dead."

"Oh," Alec responded, seeing Ash's eyes still glued to the doorway, curiosity in them. "Time for bed for us, too," he urged his friend, as they had both eaten their fill, and getting to his feet. "Goodnight, everyone." They put their trays on the cleaning belt and turned for the exit.

"Goodnight," he heard called in return by more than one voice, as he got Ash out the door. He felt their warmth in that simple wish.

"Where are they from, that they could survive so well being in stasis for centuries?" Ash quietly asked Alec as they headed down the corridor to the stairs up, once more. Alec shook his head, not knowing how to answer him. He smiled ruefully.

"I was afraid to peek," he admitted with a sigh. "It felt like a dangerous thing to do around them, somehow." Ash appeared puzzled for a moment, then nodded his head.

"I had a feeling of danger from them, too. I'm sure we'll hear more about it soon, anyways," he agreed, then smiled, "and that was a great late supper!" Both men were laughing as they reached the main floor and the doors outside.

# Aries' Wrath

## Chapter 13

"The quiet one, who did not know Dolbith, was very nice," Rinth commented, as she and Tessi were preparing for bed. They were sharing a spare bedroom in Minya's home. Dunn had given them each a quick "lesson" in the human's tongue, English. It was interesting but seemed to lack some of the more definitive descriptions they could use in Dolbith.

"Just out and the first thing you want to do is hop into his bed?" Tessi teased, astounded with her friend's comment.

"You had your eyes on the other one," Rinth returned, grinning, "It is interesting to know we could bear their cubs, if it was something both we and they chose." Her friend sighed as she started brushing her hair out.

"Yes, he has a nice smile," she agreed, "This place is an interesting conglomeration. It should prove entertaining for a while, at least."

"Deny to me that you are even considering going back to those cold chambers," Rinth demanded, upset with such a notion being voiced. There was no way for any of them to run back to that place of empty darkness and despair! Tessi smiled, shaking her head in denial.

"I meant, what about Kahmarr, or any of our other colonies, which might still exist out there?" she asked her, laughing lightly as Rinth blushed at being so caught.

"We will see. I would rather help them fight these dark monsters, who destroyed the world I knew and loved best. Once that is done, I might be tempted to seek out a new world, where we might fit in better," she said, feeling this place felt right to her senses, but realized she was still exploring herself anew. She didn't think she would find a better place, if Kahmarr had truly been destroyed, still she had boundless possibilities.

"I wish I had Visionary, or Dreamer, so I would know where to find the man I truly want. I thought Lissel was going to tear Igula and Lelas' hair out this morning, when she found them sleeping next to her chosen man, too. It was very funny," Tessi commented, wanting to change the subject.  She didn't want to be stuck on Tayna for the rest of her life, she craved more.

"I did not see it but heard about it later.  I was still in my chamber at the time," Rinth confessed, grinning as she could imagine it. "Little shy Lissel has greatly changed."

"She, Saree and Denas.  Yes, they have all changed, but I rather like the changes I saw.  Saree and Denas both looked so radiant with their pregnancies, as if this was what they awaited, for too many years.  It makes me wonder what it is truly like to be with a man, if they are so happy," Tessi sighed out, closing her eyes as she recalled seeing Garth and Ryes' joy at seeing each other again and kissing, as if they meant the world to each other.  Could she find someone like that, herself?

"We will find out for ourselves, soon enough," Rinth chided her. "Time to turn off the lights.  We have a busy morning ahead of us," she reminded her. "It is so strange to actually have a schedule and things to see and do, once more."

"Yes, it is," her friend agreed.  She got into the bed, under the light covers and relished the sensations anew.  A real bed... a real home... real sleep...  She thought she had to still be dreaming. "Goodnight," she wished Rinth, as she switched off the lights.

"Goodnight," Rinth returned as the light went out.  She got into bed and relaxed.  She was relishing the sensations as much as her friend.  She hoped it would be enough to keep her nightmares at bay; they were Doran's parting gift to them all.  She mentally reviewed the suggestions to get through them Minya gave them earlier.

"Aunt Adina?  May I come in for a few moments?" Ryes requested as she respectfully stood outside her door.

"Yes, of course you may," she replied, as she opened it for her, a smile upon her lips, so glad to see her return, once more.

"You've already seen all this?" Ryes questioned, wondering if she had Visionary, too.  Adina laughed lightly, shaking her head, as she stepped back to let Ryes into the room.

"No, my dear, your grandmother is the Dreamer in our family," she denied. "What is it you have on your mind?" she asked as she closed the door behind her and gestured for her to sit upon one of the chairs nearby. Ryes sat down, her eyes shadowed, as if weighed down by uncertainty.

"I felt you were there and saw everything. I want to apologize for not being able to warn you, beforehand. Some of my troubles are of my own making and I'd never want you to feel obligated to help cover for my mistakes," she told her.

"It is not me you should worry about, but Sayer. She is only going on to thirteen years of age and should never have to carry the burdens you choose to bear," she chided her in return. "Your problems are not always easy to address, but it looks to me that you are fairly competent in finding viable solutions most of the time."

"Sometimes it seems like I stumble along a lot," Ryes returned, smiling relief. "I had a Vision the other day. It was of you. I haven't had the time to talk with Garth yet, but if this one is true, then I think you're going to be left here to manage Winterhaven in our stead, for a while. I thought you might want to see it, if nothing else," she offered, extending her hand for her great aunt. Adina appeared surprised for a moment, then reached out and grasped it lightly, closing her eyes as she did. Ryes opened what she saw for her, showing her the whole Vision. After a few moments, they both opened their eyes and dropped their hands, looking to each other.

"It would appear so," she agreed. "I am glad your staff is already well trained to take directions and respects me."

"I don't know if I should share this with Garth, or not. I don't want him to choose you because of my Vision," she confided in her, smiling impishly.

"Then do not, until he comes to ask me whether, or not, I would be interested in performing the duty. This way, it will, or will not, come to fruition upon its own merits. But I do thank you for the warning," she replied, smiling warmly.

"But where was Hadu? He's always with you," Ryes voiced her worry aloud.

"For the answer to that, I have to tell you that he has already volunteered to accompany Monty on his quest for Demia and any other, remaining Kahmarr Alliance allies. He knows that if he is not with him, the ship will be destroyed out of hand, no matter what kind of recorded message he might have onboard. Of all the allies Kahmarr used to have, Demia would be the one most likely untouched by the Snagospin. They are strong Talents and deadly fighters when provoked. If they wish to join our fight, they will be the best allies we could ever know," she assured her. Ryes nodded her head, well understanding how this could fully be the truth.

"That explains the mystery. Then we'll await Garth's decision and see what he says after we tell him we already knew," she replied, standing up. "I'd best get to bed. Thanks, Aunt Adina," she told her. Adina stood and enfolded her into her arms, hugging her tightly.

"You be careful up in those human ships. At least you have Talents, and have the Challenger close by," she warned, then released her, kissing her cheek, like her own daughter.

"I'll be careful. Maren taught me that lesson, once," she related. "I'm not going to let all my power be depleted to the point where I can't defend myself, nor the others with me," she promised.

"That is wonderful wisdom! Have a good night, dear," she wished her, seeing her back out her door.

"You too, Aunt Adina," she said, giving her a kiss then left quickly. She had Garth awaiting her in their own bed. Adina chuckled to herself as she signed her goodnight to Hadu, who was standing nearby, then closed her door. It was a curious Vision, after all. She would share it with him in the morning. He needed his meditation time right now; it was the only time of the day when it was quiet in this household.

"Aunt Raffa, you don't have to come with us," Ryes scolded, as she and Macca followed Maren aboard the Avenger. "I would imagine you'd want to get used to your surroundings here first."

"I'm a Healer and there's need," she replied, looking like she was ready to do battle with her over her right to be included.

"I tried to dissuade her, too. Save yourself the trouble and let's get going," her cousin told her, taking the copilot's seat. Minya, Tennan, Bitty, Jake and Leon were already in their seats, the women saw there wasn't going to be a contest over their presence, so quickly took seats, too. Tennan smiled triumphantly, nodding her head to Aunt Raffa in approval. Bitty and Leon helped them with the restraints, so Ryes took her seat, after securing the hatches. They were as ready as they could be for the work ahead.

"Why don't you take her up, today?" she asked Maren, as he watched her preflight routine.

"Oh no. You're bad enough. I don't want to hear people screaming in terror over my piloting," he teased her. She saw the twinkle in his eyes, but his lips seemed unable to find the way they should operate - still.  She laughed merrily for them both, giving him a nod of her head.

"The trick is to act confident, even if you just did something you didn't mean to do.  If the passengers believe you know what you're doing, everything works out fine," she advised him, giving him a wink.

"If that's the way it works, let me take the stick," Leon volunteered, laughing, and grinning broadly.

"No.  Don't do that!  I want to see my next birthday!" Jake protested, playing along, and laughing, too.

"The offer was only open for Maren, today," Ryes teased, smiling as she looked back over her shoulder.  She turned her attention back front, finishing her remaining procedures. "All is ready, Winterhaven.  Avenger lifting off," she advised.

"All clear, Avenger.  Have a good flight," Shawn wished them.

"I intend to," Ryes replied, then lifted upwards over the landing pad, just a little.  Once she had a feel for the stick, she turned her nose skyward and hit the thrusters, pushing everyone back into their seats.

"You fly, like you drive on land, cousin," Tennan commented dryly once she could find her voice again.  Ryes laughed lightly at this, nodding her head.

"You should've heard the officers on the Earth ships, the day before yesterday," Maren told her, swiveling his seat so he could see his littermate. "They used words that I had to ask Sadie to translate for me.  I don't think they think too much of her piloting skills."

"I always get us there quickly and in one piece," she quipped back, smiling to herself. "It's not my fault they have no faith in my abilities."

"They just don't know you yet," Leon assured her, grinning. "Give `em time."

"Nah, they're stick-in-the-mud military.  Protocol is all they care about," Jake denied.  Ryes then banked, bringing them up towards the Challenger.

"What're you doing?" Maren asked, wondering.

"Just checking her out, first.  Mitt's taking a few days off and I want to make sure there's no major problems happening.  The darned thing almost demands the constant presence of a person gifted with

163

Inner Sight," she explained, having her Talent extended, so she could get a reading of the ship's computer, as she was flying by.

"Tieva has Inner Sight, as does Prias, but hers is not as strong. Perhaps they could help with the ship, too?" Macca suggested, as Raffa nodded her head in agreement.

"Great. I'll ask them if they could. Mitt and I would truly appreciate it, believe me," Ryes replied, satisfied with things on the Challenger for the moment. "I'll have to make a quick stop there, once we finish on the Aries' Wrath," she added.

"Axel hasn't put in any calls for assistance," Maren prompted.

"Well remember, it's Axel you're talking about. He wouldn't call unless it was building up to a major catastrophe," she quipped in return, smiling. "This is the Avenger, requesting docking instructions for the Aries' Wrath," she said, activating her mic.

"This is the Aries' Wrath. You may dock at port four. Surrender control on my mark," the operator replied.

"You only have machines to work with. I have Inner Sight. I'll be just fine," she replied, ducking toward the designated port, opening on the side of the ship, dumping her velocity suddenly.

"Negative, negative. This is a military ship and it's done by strict procedure," was the panicked response, but she was already nosing into the bay, perfectly aligned and at a pace which would make a slimer envious. She ignored his protests as she gently touched down, perfectly centered on the landing pad. The hatch cycled behind, sealing them in, as air was pumped into the chamber.

"They're not going to like that," Bitty warned, as they all unbuckled. Ryes finished her shutdown procedures, then turned to face her.

"No, they won't, but we're not military and we're not under their command. I don't care what they think on the matter. We're here under an invitation, and I will not bow and scrape before their boots. I have Talents and know how to use them," she stated. Tennan and Leon were grinning and nodding their heads to this. Jake was taking it in quietly, in contemplation of their stand.

"Still, watch yourself. They're tight about their standing orders," he finally warned her, giving her a nod of his head. She met his eyes and saw his inner concerns clearly within them.

"I will. I'm facing this place as I faced Doran's temple, when she'd taken Garth's soul captive to feed upon. I'm not going to back

164

down and I'm not going to lose," she assured him. Minya smiled, giving her a nod in full understanding, while Raffa and Macca merely looked shocked. Ryes went over to the hatches, opening them one at a time as soon as it read the oxygen was properly equalized.

"Lady Ryes," Mr. Kaminski greeted her, as she stepped out of the shuttle. "You do have a way of keeping people on their toes," he gently scolded her, as she smiled, giving him a small bow.

"What's the use of having abilities, if you never use them?" she returned. "Have you fared well Mr. Kaminski, since I last saw you?" she questioned merrily, as the rest of her group got out behind her. Jake and Maren now positioned themselves at each of her shoulders, protectively. This brought the hint of a smile to James' lips as he thought such measures were so unnecessary on his ship.

"Yes, I have fared well, Lady Ryes," he replied.

"Please, just call me Ryes," she begged, feeling a title made things far more complicated, when she'd rather keep them simple.

"Then you may call me James," he returned. "Please come this way. I thought a short tour of the ship would be due, before making your team labor in our medical section. I spoke with Ash, and he couldn't say enough about the miracles your people performed for his crew," he told her as they exited the shuttle bay and entered the corridor. There was a half dozen men and women awaiting them, none of them were bearing arms.

"It would be better..." Maren started but relented as Ryes used one of their old hunting hand signals to bid him be quiet for now. He understood. There were protocols to attend, before they could get done what they knew needed to do. Mr. Kaminski pretended not to hear his protest, seeing that Ryes had already dealt with the matter.

"Let me introduce you to Mr. Daniels, our head of Engineering, Commander Pachtman, our Chief Medical Officer, Mr. Lucas, our head of Security, Lt. Rocklin, our head of Communications, Lt. Watters, our Sciences Officer, and Lt. JG Fox, who will be serving as our recorder, today," Mr. Kaminski said, introducing Ryes and her group to some of his key personnel. Ryes smiled grandly as she shook hands with everyone named, surprising Lt. JG Fox, who's never supposed to be officially recognized. Ryes then stepped back, smiling.

"May I introduce you to Maren, our Chief Medical Officer, Lady Tennan, one of our Medical staff, Lady Minya, another from our Medical staff, Lady Macca and Lady Raffa, who're assisting us with Healing today, as well as Babette Parleer, Jake Tuppins and Leon Rhona, who're assisting us with Security," she told them, giving everyone who wanted to, the chance to greet the ship personnel. She noted that Mr. Kaminski hadn't asked to take the weapons from their Security staff, yet. She thought he saw this as a way to repay her for not physically removing the weapons from his own, more numerous, armed guard earlier.

"You do realize that you've now been introduced to more of this ship's staff, than your husband?" Maren commented to her in Dolbith, as he stepped back beside her. She smiled at this, nodding her head, but didn't respond. She saw he was prodding them a little with his speaking to her in their own language, to gauge their reactions. They noted the only one who looked truly annoyed was Fox.

Then, as she had done on the Challenger, James took her, her people, and his department heads on a short tour of the ship. They finally ended in an Officer's lounge. Maren was starting to get a little edgy by now, for he had deliberately skipped their medical facility. He was here for a "purpose," not for a neighborly visit. Ryes gave him a look, to let him know she would handle it.

"Our chef has prepared some treats, if you would like to stop and rest for a few moments to refresh yourselves, before continuing on," Mr. Kaminski invited, as he stopped near one of the tables in the lounge area.

"In truth, we came to help. We do appreciate your hospitality, but would rather take a break, after we've seen to your injured people," she asserted. Behind her Tennan, Minya and Raffa were nodding their heads in full agreement. Mr. Kaminski stood and weighed the situation for a few moments, then nodded his head in response.

"Amelia, would you be so kind as to escort us to Main Medical?" he requested, smiling. She looked surprised for a few seconds, not having believed they actually meant to take these strange people into her medical wards to treat people. But she saw the look in the First's eyes and knew she wasn't being given a choice. She thought, the best thing to do would be control the amount of damage, at least.

"Yes Sir," she replied, then turned and lead the party back out into the corridors, heading toward Medical, with Lt. JG Fox trailing them. James stalled a few moments to dismiss the rest of the department heads, for now.

"About time. But they're a nice bunch of kitties, at least," Mr. Daniels commented, as he turned to leave.

"Tom, these are our allies. These people are what's going to save Earth. If you haven't done it yet, take a look at what the

Darkens did to their own world, once. They mean business," he suggested. Daniels stopped, seeing the rest were waiting for his response.

"Beg pardon Sir, but I don't see much more than one, big ol' beat up warship. I don't see how they're going to save the Earth with just that ol' wreck," he returned.

"Then come with me to Medical and you'll get an idea. These people have special abilities already hardwired into their genetic code. Ryes could touch a rifle and see if it was built right, or not. She knew if it would function, how it functioned, or could break down. I know, because she showed me what she saw, when she did it. Can you imagine being able to look at a ship and tell its vulnerable points, without even touching it? She can," he told him, trying to get him to look at these people in a different light.

"There was a story that some of the human women are bearing babies fathered by those cat-men," Lt. Rocklin added, her voice low, so as to not be overheard.

"Yes, and they're even some starwomen who are bearing babies fathered by human men. We're genetically compatible enough to breed," he replied, his eyes ice by now. "And your point is?" he demanded. She blushed and took a half step back, away from him. "These are not pets! These are people. The humans off the Star Quest have come to see them as nothing more than people, and it wasn't because they had to, it was because they could look beyond the outside to what lies within. They're not perfect, and they're really no different from us."

"So, what do you want us to do, Sir?" Mr. Lucas asked, seeing no one else was speaking up. It wasn't like James to get so set about something like this.

"Quash any signs of prejudice you see starting up. These people were settling other worlds when we were just discovering fire. They may have kicked the rock first, but their homeworld was totally destroyed because of it. We kicked the rock next and it's getting damned close for the Sol system, now. Currently, we have no idea how many other colonies survived, beyond Trinity. We need their knowledge and skills to save our worlds. Ryes is a special Talent; one they call a Talent of One. She was born with all fourteen of their distinct psi skills, an occurrence which only happens maybe once in twenty thousand years for them. She's the key to finally breaking the blockade. She took out a Darken ship that was trailing us, with her will alone! She burned out their Darken psi, first. It's one of her abilities. It's felt that because they didn't have a Talent of One to draw upon, the starmen lost to the Darkens before. We have her and we're going to win this time. So, we have an official duty to watch

167

over and protect Ryes. And just for humanitarian's sake, to treat all her people as People. This is to be kept confidential and I will personally handle any situation where any of our people put her life in jeopardy," he warned them, at the end. He got acknowledgments from his staff, then they stood there, still in shock, as he turned to leave. Daniels hesitated for a few moments, then followed. After all, he'd been invited to come along to see.


"Now wait a minute, just what do you think you're doing?" Dr. Cathleen Reyes protested as Maren donned a lab coat and started to scrub his hands. The rest of his staff copied him, ready now to treat these people. They ignored her as Ryes stood back, ready to play Booster for them today.

"We're officially invited by Captain Walker to help care for and Heal your wounded," Ryes explained, as she saw the anger building in Doctor Pachtman's eyes.

"What are you going to do? Practice some kind of voodoo?" Cathy demanded, following as Maren ignored her and walked past her into the trauma treatment area.

"We don't use witchcraft," Ryes chuckled, smiling merrily at her and her leader's growing anger. "We're all gifted with special abilities, we call them Talents, you call them psi skills. All I ask is that you don't interrupt Maren or the others, as they work. Don't touch them, nor distract them," she requested, noting the way Amelia Pachtman suddenly gave her a curious, evaluating look. A man suddenly pushed his way out of the ward doors to confront the two doctors with Ryes. He was dressed in a lab coat, as they were.

"Who let the cats loose in here?" he demanded, "I thought we don't allow pets aboard!" He stopped to look appraisingly at Ryes, a sneer upon his face. "Go home, kitty. We don't need any furry pussies here."

"Ensign, you are officially on report," James ordered in a clear, ringing voice, having come in to hear what he said and how he said it to Ryes. She was still grappling with a come-back, recognizing his insulting phrasing. Both doctors still were standing there in complete shock at Tomkins personal outburst toward a perfect stranger, even if she was an alien. "You will report to my office tomorrow morning at zero six hundred hours. For now, you are confined to quarters, and you're not allowed to communicate with anyone," he added, seeing the man immediately standing at attention, saluting him. Jake nodded his head in approval, doing his best not to smile.

"Yes, Sir," he responded. Kaminski returned the salute, dismissing him. He quickly left the area, knowing he'd done it to himself this time. Mr. Daniels resisted chuckling, as he passed him on his way out. He'd stepped in from the corridor just in time to take in the whole thing. He saw several others nearby who were suddenly engaged in looking busy with their own duties, not wanting to be noticed.

"Sir, it might've been the surprise at seeing these alien people," Amelia said, in Tomkins' defense.

"That was NOT a reaction to alien people, that was a far more deeply-seated response. I'll deal with it, one way or another," he assured her, then turned to see Ryes blushing a dark gold, anger in her eyes, too. She was too smart to not understand all he implied with his insult.

"Enlighten me. I don't understand the problem with us looking a little different from you? We're truly not so different - genetically," she said. He smiled, nodding his head. He'd seen anger and surprise when aboard her ship, but only because of the presence of his troops, never derision, nor disgust. Her people seemed far more civilized, in many ways.

"You are the first, starfaring, non-human people we've encountered, other than the Darkens," he explained. "Some amount of fear would be considered a normal reaction, but anything beyond that is uncalled for, considering your people are our allies in this war against the Darkens," he explained.

"In all the worlds and systems you've visited, you've never once ran across another creative, intelligent race of people? That's absolutely incredible," she returned, astounded. "From what I saw, of Kahmarr of old, there were dozens of different peoples, who were part of their alliance. Either we were farther traveled, or had the luck of finding more peoples, than you have." She suddenly didn't know if she felt sorry for them, or not. "Considering the way I was just treated, I'd hope that you have time to get things settled on an emotional level, before you find any other, new people. I wouldn't want to see the welcome you'd get from the Demmias, if you accidently wandered into their territory!"

"I have not heard of these Demmias. What're they like?" Mr. Daniels questioned, wondering from the way she spoke of them. Were they to be feared that much? Ryes grinned merrily, nodding her head.

"I've only met Hadu, myself. And he's enough, by himself," she assured him. Jake huffed a laugh at this, nodding his head, as he smiled broadly. He couldn't image what a whole planet full of them would be like! "And we call the Snagospin that because it's the name they call themselves. But I do think `Darkens' does describe them better."

"You've seen them?" Amelia demanded, frowning as she wondered if Captain Walker was aware of this too?

"Not personally, nose to nose, so to speak," she told her, giving her a nod of her head, as she recognized her paranoia, having seen it in the other Earth humans. "But I first saw one from an ancient recording left for all of us, then later when I reached out and destroyed the "Paws' Scrape," which was following your ships. They truly don't think any differently than either of us, but they don't want to recognize there may be some kinship between any of our peoples. They're extreme xenophobes and don't want anyone becoming more powerful than they. I believe they fear what we intend to do to them. Break their forces and drive them back to their own home system, for all time. I only feel they've brought the whole thing down upon themselves and deserve it."

"Ryes, Tennan says she needs your help," Bitty advised, poking her head out the ward door. She heard what she was telling them, wondering if she should say so much to these common officers? But it wasn't her concern just now. There were so many people in here who needed their help. It was shocking, and she never thought she could feel such inner helplessness from seeing it all.

"I'm coming," she assured her, then followed as Bitty turned back for the smaller hall behind her. Jake followed Ryes, as the others did too. Bitty led her over to Tennan, in a large room with the beds curtained off from one another.

"Maren's busy," Tennan apologized, as her cousin was suddenly at her side. "I can't take care of her the way she needs to be taken care of," she added, pain in her eyes.

"I may have the power and ability, but you've had more training, so you'll have to direct me," Ryes replied, smiling for her as she called her Healing and other Talents up, ready to use them. Tennan smiled, nodding her head, relieved Ryes was here with her.

"Not a problem," she answered, as she closed her eyes and took one of Ryes' hands. Ryes put her other hand on their patient, as Tennan guided her Talent, Healing the stricken woman on the bed. Tom shifted over to see what they were doing, as did Amelia. Both were amazed to see her body being repaired, right before their eyes.

# A Day Off

## Chapter 14

"There are still so many left to attend to," Raffa protested, as she and the others were sitting down to a late lunch, provided by the ship's personnel. "I never knew all that war could mean."

"We'll come back tomorrow to finish what we can," Maren vowed, as James sat across from them, glad for what they had done for his people. Ash was right. They were amazing!

"We appreciate all your efforts. I can't thank you enough for what you've done, already," he told them, noting the exhaustion in the eyes of most of them. Ryes' were still sharp and clear, as if she were holding a little of her power back in reserve, in case she needed it. Before today, he would've been insulted, but after witnessing several small incidents, as well as the one belligerent ensign, he couldn't blame her. It was only sanity, after all. How had it devolved down to where they didn't feel safe, even on his ship? He usually ran a tight ship, but this was new territory, and they were far from home. It still didn't excuse the behaviors.

"It's no problem," Ryes replied, smiling. "But perhaps you could help us resolve a small problem of our own?" she asked in return, hoping this wasn't too poor a time to approach him about their own problem with his people.

"How can I be of service?" he questioned, wondering what they needed?

"There's been a feeling of being under siege, here in our own home. The people from off your ship, and the Tablet, have been openly aggressive towards us. We've mostly dropped from using our regular mix of English and Dolbith, to using straight Dolbith. Even our own humans have done this. We've had to increase our Security, to protect our people, our expectant mothers, and the natural crosses, which we rescued from off of Booda, a moon of the third world of Monrush's system. We found that long ago some one of our ships had crashed upon it, as well as several of the Star Quest's shuttles and escape pods, later. The people were not living as peacefully as we, but when we brought them back to Tayna, we made sure they understood that their previous behaviors were not tolerated here. It was a little difficult at first, but they've learned to adjust and are starting to fit in with the rest of us. Now, we find we're having problems with your people," she informed him, noting it was no surprise to him, or the rest of his people, who were eating with them now.

"I never knew it, until I saw it displayed today. It could be a reaction to being under threat from the Snagospin for so long," he acknowledged.

"We've come to the point of just calling them `Snags,' for short," Ryes advised, grinning merrily. He smiled at this, nodding his head. "I believe you could be correct, but is there anything we should, or should not, be doing? I'm not comfortable in letting this continue. We have many children among us now, and it's not the kind of thing we want happening around them. These are things they don't need to learn from any of us."

"You might loosen up a little and return to speaking your blend of the two languages. We're still trying to understand your language and have been amazed at the grasp you've had of ours," he admitted to her. Maren huffed, his eyes merry.

"Ryes was Time Walking back to learn about humans and the way the machinery of the installation operated, so we wouldn't hurt ourselves, when we first moved in. Garth ordered her to learn English, so she could interface with the AI. He appointed her the `Keeper of the Computer,'" he told them, getting laughter from the others at their table.

"Time Walking? You can walk through time?" James questioned, as Ryes blushed, nodding her head.

"Yes, I can. If you ever get the chance, I'll take you back to watch the Star Quest when she lifted off Tayna, the last time she could still leave," she offered, smiling.

"From what I saw, it was a miracle she survived to land, again," Tom Daniels stated, grinning as he nodded his head at her. "Are you planning on keeping her as a trophy?"

"No. The AI already has the remaining metal listed as scrap. She's going to become our new hangar, and a few other things. We're metal poor and every piece is precious. I intend to take out one of the shuttles, after we've seen to the health of the rest of your two ships' crews and seeing what scrap I can pick up in system. It's a way to put a shuttle through its paces, while finding some useful metals, too."

"Those engines on your big ship, who designed them? They're different than I've ever seen before," he pressed, wanting to see if she knew anything about their design. She laughed lightly, blushing again.

"It was a composite project with Axel, Mitt, Selena, me, and our AI all having a part in their design. They're really something special and should be ready to begin a battery of tests about when the Great Fall Gather is happening. I think Garth intends to invite some of the elders aboard for the final round of tests. I'm sure you, Mr. Kaminski and Captain Walker would be welcome, too," she invited him, smiling.

"We might take you up on that," James answered for Tom, before he could say anything in response. "I'll talk with Captain Walker, later."

"That brings up another matter. Are any of your people going to attend the Great Fall Gather with us? We would want to make sure everyone was minding his, or her manners, while there. While Winterhaven is prominent, we still haven't taken the whole planet, yet," Maren said, teasing his cousin.

"Do you think our teams are ready for the competition? We've only played Matlowe, Wicker and the Moon Dance Tribe," Jake put in, wondering.

"You play some kind of team sports?" Mr. Lucas questioned, appearing curious and interested.

"Yes. We have three Field Ball teams, now. We mostly play each other but have expanded our games to include Matlowe and Wicker Villages, even if Wicker is a good distance away. The Moon Dance Tribe just became involved the last month or so. There's some kind of big competition among the teams during the Great Fall Gather," Ryes explained.

"Who's on your three teams?" Tom pressed, interested in this too. He loved sports and wanted to know.

"We have one composed of both sexes and a mix of the humans and starmen from Booda, the second one is a mix of human and starman women, and the third one is a mix of human and starmen men. So far, the Boodans are the champions. Matlowe badly beat our first try at a team. Since then, we've come up in the rankings, but could still use some polish," Jake replied, grinning. "My money's still on the Moon Dusters."

"That's what we need; an outlet for some of our stress and boredom. We could form a team from each ship and compete, too," Mick Lucas suggested, looking to Mr. Kaminski for approval. He smiled, liking the idea.

"Could you please send me a copy of the complete rules and requirements of your game, and any video you might have?" James

173

requested, turning back to Ryes. She was grinning and nodding her head at this wonderful inspiration.

"I'll have them sent, immediately," she promised, then turned to face the ceiling in the room. "Computer, please relay Mr. Kaminski's request to Winterhaven, with my authorization. Please inform my own computer that it has my permission to send the requested information, as well as a copy of its archived video files from the last four games to his queue, immediately," she ordered.

"Affirmative," it replied, then complied, since there was no objection voiced from its ranking, present officers. There was utter shock in the First Officer's eyes at Ryes' casual display of skill. The other officers at the table had halted in mid-motion too, stunned.

"People often forget how ever invasive their computer systems are," she told him, meeting his eyes. "I'm sure the information has been sent to you, by now."

"I'm sure it has. Keeper of the Computer, for certain," he replied, finally finding his own voice. "Why would you think our own computer would respond to you?" he pressed, needing to understand this whole situation.

"First off, I'm officially listed as the Chief Executive Officer of Winterhaven, formally Amitell research station ten thirty-three. Secondly, I'm listed in the systems as a possible ally of yours. What I requested was of no hostile intent and didn't involve your operations in any way, shape, or form. Since you didn't object to the request, it complied, seeing there was no reason not to obey. I've spent a lot of time learning normal computer operations, and all about our own AI, specifically. It's interesting to note what things they will allow, and what things they won't, when you get right down to it."

"I'll have to keep that in mind," he assured her, looking at her in a totally new light. She was intelligent and highly skilled.

"I can't begin to express how wonderfully logical your computers are, compared to the super numerator that's on the Challenger. The only reason I can think which lies behind its design is that our people interacted with many other peoples in the past. It must be to prevent anyone from casually doing what I just did. It's more limited in its abilities than your computers, and took forever for Mitt, Axel and I to get it `talking' with our AI in Winterhaven. Our AI has taken some of the numerator's designs to heart and is presently redesigning itself and the Challenger's machine, all by itself," she told them.

"That's crazy. You're not supposed to let an AI redesign itself," Tom declared, worried about these people now.

174

"Mitt and I are keeping a close eye upon them both.  Actually, what it's come up with is right and will save us a lot of time and effort, later.  Did I tell you that our AI's decided what Winterhaven will be like, already?  It's decided to start building a bridge across the Yuri River next year. Part of it will come from the metal we can still safely retrieve from Hailys, and part from the Star Quest.  It's going to be interesting, to say the least," she teased.

"And you're just letting it do what it feels like?" Tom asked, astounded.  She laughed at this, shaking her head no.

"Never.  But this was one project Phil and Kovin already had in mind.  They're still arguing and settling the final design with the machine now," she assured him, her eyes merry. "In all reality, a bridge across the Yuri makes perfect sense.  It'll allow the caravaners to cross safely and grants us easier access to hunting and the plants growing across the river."

"You hunt?" Amelia pressed, surprised, changing the subject deliberately.

"I can't anymore, myself.  I've become too sensitive to the animals' deaths.  But yes, we do hunt to keep fresh meat upon our tables.  I was thinking, if any of your people would like to go out on our next big hunt, you're more than welcome.  Most times it's fun, but we do have each team closely supervised, so as to keep accidents to a minimum.  And with the Healers with us, we can usually take care of any problems which do occur," she offered, wondering if any of the Earthmen knew how to hunt?

"Now there's a real sport," Lt. Ara Rocklin stated, wondering if she could duplicate in real life, what she could do with the computer simulations? "May I be included?" she added, in request.

"Yes, you may," Maren assured her, humor in his eyes.

"I'll have the computer make sure it notifies you when the next hunts are scheduled.  We have one scheduled right before the Gather," Ryes told her.

"What is this Gather of yours?" James questioned, sharply interested in everything they were telling them.

"The Great Gathers are held twice a year.  One in the spring, after all the smaller gathers are held individually by the tribes and villages across this continents, then one in the fall, before the smaller, fall gathers are held.  It's a time when all the peoples of Tayna are invited to come meet each other.  There are sporting events, musical and entertainment events, trading, peace treaties formed, exchanges of information, classes conducted, dancing, drinking, mating... most anything that people can do, as they come together as a group, happens. This'll be our first Fall Gather, but we know a little of what to expect. We have six booths planned this time, we have a group of musicians ready to perform, our teams are still trying to come up to snuff, but they're willing to try, we have some performers who're interested in putting on a new play they wrote, some of our home brewers are ready to enter their wares, and we plan on pushing the Laws through, so all of Tayna can be in agreement on something," she explained. "Your people may attend with us, but we'll need to know how many at one time, and that they will be on their best manners. We'll have shelters available for their use, since we just finished the apartment expansion, so all the Boodans now have homes of their own."

"I'll speak with the captain about it. Who do I talk with, in arranging for our participation?" Mr. Kaminski asked.

"Me," Ryes answered with a big smile. "Since the negotiations are still ongoing about the new Alliance, I'm left with planning the Gather."

"Then, I'll be speaking with you about this, later," he promised, smiling in return. A chance to get his people off the ships and busy with sports, hunting and a gathering, which sounded like a country fair! She was the answer to many of their problems. And he knew this would help alleviate the problems with prejudice. As the people got to know them better, they'd understand them, too. The other officers in the room with them were all happy to hear this news, too.

"Want to go fishing, Mitt?" Ryes asked, as she found her at a terminal, in her and Axel's office. She looked up at her, frowning. Fishing would be great, but she still had all this work to finish. She'd be heading back up to the Challenger tomorrow morning.

"I can't," she protested, pouting, as their eyes met.

"Look. You can just as easily do that up there, as you can down here. Leave it for tomorrow. It's the kids' weekend and I thought it'd be a great way for all of us to unwind," she pressed. Mitt sat for a few seconds undecided, glancing from Ryes' face to her screen. "Sernn and Minn have missed you. It's a chance to spend some time with them, too," she prodded. Mitt finally grinned as she saved her files, then shut down her terminal.

176

"Alright, you talked me into it," she said, giving in. Ryes smiled happily, giving her a nod of her head.

"Let's gather our gear, then go shake Garth and the others out of that meeting. It's too nice a day to worry about negotiations, anyway," she replied. Mitt laughed merrily at this, nodding her head.

"It'll do them all some good. Let's get Ardis to help, too," she suggested, as she joined her at the door.

"That's a good idea. Let's go change first and grab everyone's swimsuits. Then, tackle the men." Both women were laughing as they headed for their homes.


"Is there something you need?" Garth asked, as Ryes opened the door to the meeting room, looking in.

"You. Sabin. Ethan. Rowan, and everyone else can come along, too," she replied, grinning merrily. "We have our lunches packed, and the rovers loaded. We're adjourning this meeting to indulge in some free time down at the Yuri, to go fishing."

"Not now," he told her, chuckling at her boldness.

"We're not giving you guys a choice," she assured him, stepping aside to let Ardis and the others into the room with her. The ship people were amazed and amused.

"You're coming right now, husband," Ardis ordered, stepping across to put Dale onto his lap. "We all need a little time off, together." Dale immediately squealed with delight, reaching for the papers on the table in front of Sabin. He managed to push them out of his reach, laughing.

"We're not being given a choice, Garth," he stated, chuckling as his son redoubled his efforts.

"I see," he agreed as Sayer and Raby were now playfully grabbing at his arms, to pull him to his feet. Ethan was laughing as Bethy put her infant son in his arms, too.

"I'd say we adjourn for now and resume where we left off, tomorrow," Rowan said, as Tennan was pulling him to his feet.

"Agreed," Captain Yun replied, laughing as Ryes put a silly hat upon his head.

"This is to shade your eyes," she told him, grinning. She had one for each of the captains, in her hands. Mr. Kaminski appeared in the open doorway, amazed to see the pandemonium inside. He grinned as he saw the hat Ryes put upon Lindell's head. And he didn't appear to object!

"Ah, James. I'll have to go get a hat for you. We're going fishing down at the Yuri," she told him, as she led them to the door. "We're bringing along plenty of extra poles," she added, as he nodded his head to her.

"It sounds like fun," he agreed, then handed his captain the packet he requested. Lindell took it and then tossed it onto the table. He put an arm over his First's shoulder and laughed.

"Let's go fishing. I haven't fished in too many years," he told him. James nodded his agreement, allowing himself to be swept up in this merry crowd. Ryes locked the door of the conference room her way, by removing the opening in the wall entirely, so no one could sneak in and create any mischief. Their escorts fell in, as the group passed them, Ryes already taking their presence into account. It was the other reason they were using three large rovers for this trip. They loaded everyone up, with Ryes taking the wheel of the lead machine.

"Hey, they're not used to your driving," Maren teased. Sayer turned back to stick her tongue out at him, as he shook his head.

"This is a good time, then," she replied, as she started the engine, smiling.

"I've seen the way you pilot," James warned her, laughing as he sat behind her.

"Then, it's no surprise," she quipped back, pulling out of the garage. The other two vehicles fell in behind her.

"She's still a better driver than I am," Garth admitted, "even if I occasionally feel as if we're leaving my stomach behind."

"The crew's finished the road all the way up to Matlowe. We're only going to the Yuri, not to Hailys," she scolded, blushing. There was laughter from behind her, which she ignored as she turned for the main road. She drove at her normal pace, quickly getting them to their favorite, sheltered fishing spot. The coolness of the breeze coming in off the great river instantly caught their interest, as the newer humans stepped out of the vehicles.

"Now this is a beautiful spot," Lindell Walker stated, as he stood there with a big grin upon his face. Ryes had made all the officers change into plain polo shirts and shorts before leaving, making only their escort as the only ones left in uniforms. He forgot what it was like to be outdoors in a beautiful place like this. There were mature trees, a small meadow nearby and gentle hills on the other side of where they parked the large vans, in a wide, paved parking area. It even looked like a large, rest-stop like building was there with available toilets and showers to use. And there was a covered area with picnic tables beyond that. But the sparkling, flowing water of the great river drew all eyes towards it, with its inviting relaxation.

"I've never seen anything like it," Ash said, low under his voice, so only Alec and Captain Yun caught it.

"You lived under a dome, too long," Yun cheerfully scolded, smiling to see such beauty.

Ryes walked down to the beach, where they usually set out their chairs. She extended out, retrieving all the old fishhooks and other things they lost in the water and sand, cleaning it up again. She put everything in a plastic container she brought, as she returned to the others, as they were taking out their chairs and poles from the back of the vehicles.

"Now, this has been here since early spring. I don't want you to go about losing any more stuff, here," she playfully scolded. Torr stepped over, looking into her box.

"Hey, that's my favorite hook. How'd it end up here?" he teased, retrieving one out of the box. "Thanks for finding it," he added, as the others were laughing. She handed him the box with a laugh and went to go help with her cubs.

"Mom, you should just float them out," Raby suggested, grinning.

"Not in front of the captains," she returned, shaking her head with regret. "I'm trying to keep things low key for now," she explained.

"Come on, Sayer. I'll race you to the water!" Sernn shouted, seeing she was still taking off her T-shirt and sandals. He was all ready for swimming.

"I'll race you, too," Casta teased, grinning as he joined them. Chris Tobias, his father, was working as Security today and Ryes told him he could come too.

"You go ahead. I'll manage," Ryes assured her as she paused. She threw her a grin, then threw her T-shirt into the rover and ran, racing the two boys.

"Thanks Mom," she called back to her, as she ran. Ryes laughed as Garth came over to help her.

"You go ahead too, Raby," he told her, seeing Katas and one of their Boodan girls waiting for her.

"Thanks Dad," she replied, giving him a quick hug, then ran off too.

"You do know they're only supposed to help us out every now and then, not stuck managing the horde all the time," Ryes scolded, smiling. Adina stepped around to the door, realizing they might need some help with their younger children. She loved these happy little ones, missing her own, now that they're grown and gone, and Adina wondered what her grandchildren had turned out like. Hadu followed, keeping an eye to everything around them.

"I know," he assured her as he took Gareth and Jann up into his arms. "They're getting heavy," he protested. Ryes laughed merrily at this, nodding her agreement.

"You haven't been paying attention. They're starting to figure out walking. They latch onto anything they can to stand up. I figure, give them another month, or two, then we'll have to make sure we don't leave anything down low enough in their new, higher reach."

"Wait a couple of years and see how manic it gets," Adina warned, smiling. "I recall what I went through with my two little ones, and you have five to deal with." Hadu chuckled at this, nodding his head. Ryes was just getting used to his chuckle now. It was different...but still spine-chilling.

"I think I'd better start planning ahead," she replied. "So, they don't overwhelm me by then." The three of them managed to get them into their outside enclosure in a shady spot, near the water. Ryes then took them out into the water, one by one, while Garth, Sabin, Torr and Maren went fishing, her way. Mitt and Minn joined them out at the rock, making it crowded.

"We're going to have to build a dive platform, now," Ardis suggested, as she had her cubs out in the water, too. Dodi joined them, appearing as if she wasn't sure if Tobin was old enough for this, or not.

"It's never too early to teach the cubs to get used to the water, and some rudimentary swimming lessons," Rowan advised her, noting her nervousness. He and most of the others were setting up their chairs to fish, some out in the sunlight, some sitting in the shady spots. Dodi nodded her head to this, still not sure.

"The river's different from our swimming pool," Ryes said. "If we can teach them to survive in both, then that only helps them if anything ever happens later," she stated, noting what Rowan already saw in her friend.

"But, if he learns to fly a chopper, how would swimming here help him?" she pressed, smiling timidly.

"What if his chopper ever went down in the water? Or if he had to rescue someone in the water? You never know what life will put before you. You can only hope you're up to facing the challenges. My grandmother drowned before I was born, so Rowan taught me to swim, to be sure I could handle myself around the river."

"It makes sense," Raffa agreed, joining them. She had Shaysa in her arms as she did. Tars ran up, splashing them as she jumped into the water. "And especially with feisty nieces around," she added, grinning. Shaysa was now splashing the water with her little hands too, having quickly picked up the idea.

"Ethan, how could you have kept this place a secret from us, for so long?" Wing demanded as he stepped up to stand next to him and Rowan, smiling grandly. Ethan chuckled at this, nodding his head as he was lighting his pipe.

"We've got to have somewhere to escape and unwind," he teased in return as Rowan was laughing in a low voice, nodding his head in agreement. "Are you going to come out to the Fall Gather?" he asked, having forgotten to ask it before.

"I was thinking of it," he stated, watching as Garth and the others were catching the fish with their own claws. He suddenly wished he could fish like that, too. Then he got an idea and kicked off the sandals Ryes gave him. He pulled off his polo shirt and snatched up a net from the ground near his feet. "Talk with you, later," he promised, as he trotted off toward the rock. He heard Ethan and Rowan laughing in response, in his wake. He found the water cool and invigorating, as he swam out to the rock, net still in hand.

"So, you decided this was the better way to go fishing?" Sabin asked, pulling Wing up on the rock with him.

"It looks far more fun," he agreed.

"We'll be filling our bins long before the others, for sure," Mitt stated, then dove into the water, having spotted a big one.

"Just watch for their shadows in the water, as the fish swim by, then remember the way water distorts things," Sabin instructed, pointing down to show him the several fish slipping by below. Wing gave him a nod of his head, spotting his young First starting to swim out to the rock to join him, then dove into the water, having spotted a big, spotted fish below. It was difficult at first with the net, but he quickly got the idea and deployed it better against his second target, now accounting for the net's drag.

"Ryes, I didn't realize you really had so many children," James told her, having come out into the water to talk with her. There were several people around her, and as a tall, dark, and white-haired man turned to look at him, he stopped, utterly stunned as he met his eyes. Those silver eyes were closely evaluating him, as if he was deciding if he would allow him any closer to this small group of women and children. Ryes laughed merrily, noting his shock.

"Commander James Kaminski, I'd like you to meet Hadu-Ramashan from Kesper," she said, stepping over to his side, seeing he was still absorbed in studying her Aunt Adina's guardian and lifelong companion. Gareth reached out to James, trying to grab at the colorful plastic tags, which were suspended from his neck. He finally turned to meet her eyes, an understanding of what she commented to him earlier, lay into their blue depths. He could not imagine a whole planet full of such beings! He then turned back to Hadu and smiled bravely.

"An honor to meet you, Sir Ramashan," he told him. Hadu smiled at this, giving him a small dip of his head in return.

"The honor is mine," he replied, then turned his attention back to Adina, realizing she was addressing him in a low voice.

"He's relaxed somewhat now. The first time I saw Hadu smile, I practically had a heart seizure," Ryes merrily teased him, seeing James turn his attention back to her. He sighed as he looked into her emerald-green eyes.

"You're right. We have a long way to go, still," he told her, glad his drone was catching everything. Then reached out his hands in an offer to hold her son. She paused for a moment, surprise in her eyes, then handed him over with a gentle smile.

"They're getting bigger and heavier, already. I think all of them take after their father and are going to be far taller than me, when they're grown," she related, as she gave in and floated Rhin over from the enclosure. Now, all her cubs were in the water. She saw James' quick interest, but also his restraint. "Let me introduce you to my family," she offered. He laughed as Gareth was trying to chew on his dog tags, giving her a nod of his head, having found it the best way to communicate with the starmen.

"I'd love to meet them all," he assured her, realizing he meant it.

"First off, you're holding Gareth, my firstborn. This is Rhin, my last," she started. "My Great Aunt Adina is holding Jann, my Great Aunt Raffa has Shaysa, and my friend Dotti has Shyla in her arms. They're not even a year old and are quite a handful. And we usually just refer to them collectively as `the horde,'" she explained.

"All this and Chief Exec, too," he commented, now understanding why she was so straightforward in almost everything she did. She didn't have the luxury of time to beat around the bush in any other aspect of her life!

"Ryes, even on a day of relaxation you're working," Connor teased as he splashed into the water, deciding upon a swim instead of fishing.

"I'm a mother. I never get a day off," she returned, laughing as she splashed water at him. "Alec just followed Ash over to the dive rock. Ardis thinks we might need to install a diving platform. Our dive rock is too little, now." He laughed and nodded his head, resisting the urge to splash her back, since she had a kid in her arms. Rhin was splashing about, getting her anyway.

"I'll let Kovin know, tomorrow," he replied, then turned to join his friends.

"Ryes, did you do a check of the area?" Minn asked, swimming over to the women. She appeared puzzled at this, nodding her head.

"Of course, I did. Why?" she returned, knowing he'd have a reason.

"I just spotted a large animal on the other shore and didn't know what it was," he told her. She sighed, nodding her head.

"I merely checked to see if the fishers were in their den, away from the rock. I forgot to look for anything larger, or more dangerous. I should know better, by now," she admitted. Minn took Rhin from her as she closed her eyes, calling up Empath again. "It's a bear-like animal. I'm driving him off now. He was merely curious as to why all this noise was down near where he likes to fish too," she informed him, her eyes still closed as she made a second sweep, making well sure the entire area was free of dangers on either shore, and in the water. Minn reached out a hand to steady her, seeing her face go pale as she made her passes. He suddenly saw why. She was feeling the deaths of all the fish they were catching, and it nauseated him, too. She opened her eyes, having quickly let go, once more.

183

"Thanks, but I apologize to you for that," she told him, as he let her go and handed Rhin back to her.

"Now, I don't feel like fishing, anymore," he replied, then smiled for her, seeing how it pained her to have exposed him to it.

"What? Why?" James questioned, not understanding what happened at all.

"I was doing a better sweep of the area and the impact of the fish dying accidently was sent through to Minn, as he tried to steady me. It's hard for me, at times," she explained. "Usually, when I fully open my Empath Talent, I pull up and away from the cycle of life and death around me. I'd rather see the dance of life in its entirety, than in such microscopic detail."

"Could you show me, some time?" he requested, wanting to see this `dance of life,' as she saw it.

"I've already promised to take you Time Walking, now this? You're going to become a sensation junkie, like Mitt and Maren already are," she teased, smiling. Minn laughed at this, nodding his head.

"It's scary with the power you have and the recklessness the three of you possess in such great quantities, when you're off together and up to things," he teased her. "I'm going back to the rock to catch some sun," he added, then turned and left, glad she handled the original problem quickly.

"You know us too well," she called at his back, grinning to herself. Raffa looked at her, curiosity in her eyes.

"What kinds of trouble do you, Mitt and Maren get into?" she questioned before anyone else could ask. Ardis and Dotti started laughing at this, nodding their heads.

"Whatever they happen to think up, in the moment," Ardis replied for Ryes, as she was blushing a dark gold.

"We've settled down a bit," she said in their defense. This only got the two women laughing louder, so she gave up and turned her attention back to Rhin and Gareth. Mr. Kaminski wondered about this, but saw it was all in good-hearted fun.

# A Visit Home

## Chapter 15

"Ryes, we need you here in Matlowe," Ellen Fortney told her, having been forwarded to her queue by Larisa. "There's a secret vault we discovered, which we can't even begin to open."

"Alright, I'll grab a chopper and be there in another couple of hours," she promised, glad she'd already gotten most of her desk work finished for the day. "What're you having for lunch?" she added, teasing her as she smiled. Ellen looked surprised, then grinned mischievously in return.

"Just some ol' nuts and berries, today," she replied. Ryes laughed at this, nodding her head.

"And I'm the one who has to go out and bring them in, too," she returned. Her friend laughed with her, nodding her head.

"Of course. And you'd better hurry as we're starving!" she quipped back. "We'll be waiting for you," she added, then signed off. Ryes sat back in her chair, still smiling. She wondered what they found? Garth and the rest of their group were on the Wrath, today. She bet herself it was to keep the women from dragging everyone out of their meeting to another, local adventure. But Mitt was back, getting some of her backlogged work done, now that Tieva was helping this week on the Challenger.

"Larisa, I'm going to be out for the rest of the day. If things stay quiet, go ahead and take off, too," Ryes told her, as she stepped out of her office.

"That sounds like a great idea," she replied, all smiles. It was why she loved working for Ryes. Yes, they sometimes had some impossible challenges, but many times they could take off early, when they were caught up. Ryes gave her a nod of her head, closed her office door, and headed out to see what Mitt and Maren were up to, and if they had the time for a trip to Matlowe this morning.

"Prias, Selena, Callio, Willas and I are working on the Pike. I don't have time, today," Mitt unhappily protested, as Ryes stopped her out in the hallway. "Just be really careful. Remember the last time?" she reminded her.

185

"But that was before I knew I had Inner Sight. I'll be able to manage it this time," she promised, sure of her abilities, "If it's nothing more than records, do you want my help later?"

"No, we'll manage things. You don't forget all those cubs, who need their mother to abuse from time-to-time," she teased, smiling to take the edge off her mild scold. Ryes smiled and nodded in return, thinking it was a wonderful idea. She wanted to take them out for some play time outside, after all.

"I think I will. Thanks for the reminder, Sis," she returned, then gave her a nod of her head, as Mitt turned for the hangar, a smile upon her lips.

"I'll go with you, since our Vision's already past," Maren offered, stepping up behind her. "Why do you need to go to Matlowe, in the first place?" he added, frowning.

"Ellen said they found a secret vault, which they can't open. I'm the handy-dandy can-opener," she replied, turning to look into his brown eyes. "So, once I get the vault open, I'm heading straight back and am taking the cubs out in a rover to that little creek we crossed on our way here, out from Hailys. I want to give them a little fresh air and see what's out there now." He nodded his head to this, thinking it'd make a nice outing.

"Count me in. It seems like a nice day to get out, anyway," he agreed. "It's too bad Dotti's tied up in finishing that study for Ethan. Although, I can see why she's had to compile the report."

"What's it about?" Ryes asked, as they turned, heading down the main corridor. She wanted to ask a favor of Chuck first, then change for the outing. It was cooler here now, than in Matlowe.

"A study of these new humans. He feels they need to address the cultural attitudes and changes which have occurred in the last eighty years, or so. I think, so they can get an idea of how these people think, as they try to work through those negotiations. There seems to be some kind of problem, which has popped up the last few days," he told her. She nodded her head to this, knowing of it already.

"Garth won't tell me what it is. I wonder if he even knows. If he'd treat me as if I was his second in command, rather than Sabin, then I'd be more effective in helping him. I'd hoped the day out fishing would've helped relax things," she said, sighing.

"We'll know, when they decide to tell us," Maren quipped back. "Let's go change for the outing. At least it's being away from here for a little bit. I'll be by to get you soon," he promised.

"I want to stop by the dining hall, first. I'd like to bring out a little surprise for the excavation team, while we're at it," she told him. He nodded his head, so she trotted off, ignoring all the other problems weighing her mind now. She had a perfectly legitimate escape.

"Larisa said you're going out somewhere?" James Kaminski questioned as he caught up to Ryes, as she and Maren stepped out of her home. "I had hoped to have a few moments with you, today."

"If you've got the time, why not come out to Matlowe Village with us?" Maren invited when Ryes didn't speak up right away, wondering if he'd take him up on it? It might be a way for them to find out what's going on, after all. Ryes' eyes briefly met his, curiosity in their depths, then returned to Mr. Kaminski's.

"You're more than welcome to come along, but if you don't have the time, I'll make sure to accommodate you tomorrow morning," she promised, smiling affability. He stood for a few seconds, considering it. This would be a chance to see how the more "normal," indigenous people lived.

"Let me check my schedule, first," he requested, as Ryes gave him a nod in response. She well understood schedules by now. He stepped away from them as he activated his personal com unit. After a few minutes, he turned back, giving them a nod of his head. "I have the time, after all."

"Great. The more, the merrier," Ryes replied, smiling, "as they say on your world." He laughed and nodded. She led them to the waiting chopper, throwing her tote bag into the back storage compartment. Seena emerged with a large bundle in her hands, stepping over to hand it to Ryes, with a big grin upon her face.

"Your order. I hope they don't come to expect such service all the time," she commented. Ryes laughed, shaking her head.

"They can't possibly come up with enough reasons to keep me running over there, too often," she assured her. She put the bundle in the back, securing it with a small cargo net. Seena threw her arms about her, hugging her tightly, when she turned back, noting she was still waiting. Ryes laughed, as Seena gave her a kiss.

"Be careful. There're many new Easterners living there, now," she warned her, as she let her go. "You watch her," she scolded Leon, Sadie, and Maren.

"We will," Sadie promised, smiling as she had a hand atop her bulging stomach.

"We're going to have to reassign you to something other than escort Security," Ryes scolded her friend.

"I've still got the best eye of the team and can hold my own," she retorted, daring her to refute her. Ryes nodded her head, understanding her far more than anyone else. She'd been highly restricted from doing anything by Garth, during her own pregnancy.

"Alright, then let's load up and get to Matlowe," she replied, gesturing for the three of them, plus the two men guarding James, into the back. "James, you may ride up front with me, if you like," she offered. He paused for a moment, then nodded his head. Maren gave her a nod in understanding, jumping up into the back with no protests. Ryes got in, making sure everyone was secure, then began her preflight procedures. They were soon on their way to Matlowe.

"You're sure she should be here any minute?" Sonta asked Ellen, doubts in his eyes. She turned and smiled merrily for him, nodding her head.

"Whenever she says a couple of hours, she means in about an hour and a half. It only takes an hour to fly out here from Winterhaven," she assured him. "And it usually takes her the other half hour to change and get things organized."

As she was talking, the helicopter came into view overhead, circling the Village. They had a landing pad laid out near their new apartments, on the far side of the village square. Ryes set down upon the designated spot, glad to see the Village still looked peaceful from above. It'd been a long time since she'd been here. They unloaded from the chopper, Maren now carrying the bundle they brought out with them.

"Well, here we are. Seems I can't do anything without a mobile crowd, anymore," she teased Ellen, who was laughing and nodding her head to this. "We even brought lunch along," she finished.

"Great! If I'd known you'd do this, I'd have ordered take-out long before," she quipped back, happily accepting the large package Maren handed over to her. It was a rare treat from the one place she now considered home.

"Commander James Kaminski, I'd like you to meet Matlowe Village's Head Elder, Sonta. He's the oldest living son of Metta," Ryes said, introducing them first in English, then in Dolbith. Sonta nodded his head to this human, who was dressed strangely from the rest. He noted there were two others with him, who also dressed in a different manner, as if it denoted something special.

"Pleased to make your acquaintance, Sonta," he replied, Ryes translating it for him. Ellen stood back, closely observing the uniformed men. She wasn't sure if she liked the idea of Earth's military having a presence upon Tayna. And their drones appeared different from their own, and didn't trust them, either.

"We've come here to check on that new vault," Ryes told Sonta, bowing to him slightly. He grinned, throwing an arm about her and Maren's shoulders, hugging them both to his sides as he laughed.

"I don't want you to ever be so formal unless it's something involving the whole council. You're from Matlowe! I want you two to feel like you've come home," he urged. Ryes laughed, while Maren nodded his head. "How's my father truly doing? When's he coming home?" he added, as he released both cubs. Sadie now took up the role of translator, for the Aries' Wrath's First Officer, seeing Ryes was giving Sonta her full attention in this moment.

"Uncle Metta's doing well. I think he was planning on coming back before the winter snows hit Winterhaven. Right now, he's helping Garth, Rowan, Ethan, and Sabin form a treaty with the Terran Federation. He man's the Elder Office and looks information up they need for the meetings and communicates it to the team. He seems to love working with the computer and learning new things. The computer makes sure the signal is clear and not blocked. We're formally starting our own Alliance of Worlds," Maren told him, his eyes merry, as Sonta looked like he was trying hard to believe it.

"We have starships, now," Ryes added, grinning at his shocked expression. "They need a little repair, but we have them."

"Are you sure he intends to return?" he questioned, smiling as he tried to picture his father as a trendsetter in stellar politics.

"He wants to make sure Matlowe's a part of things, too. He's going to return to reshape Matlowe to what he thinks it should strive to become," Maren answered, having talked with his uncle about it already. He'd even forgiven him for what Korman had driven him to do, even if Korman was his own baby brother. The rift between Maren and Metta was well-mended and put into the past where it belonged.

"For so many years he wanted everything to remain the same - unchanged. It's strange to hear this now, so I'll hold back believing it until I hear it from his own lips. It's not that I doubt you Maren, just that it's so incredible. He was ready for the end of his life and trying to withdraw from everything." Maren nodded his head to this, understanding Sonta all too well. He would've questioned it himself, if he hadn't seen his evolution in character, and it happened so fast!

"So, let's go have a look at this mystery vault, then dig into that excellent lunch Chuck sent along," Ryes urged. Ellen led the way, followed by the rest, after first handing the bundle in her arms to Sela, Sabin's older sister. She whispered something to her before Sela left, then continued toward the stairs leading below.

"We've finally got about ten-thousandth of the library copied and sent on to Winterhaven," she started, playing guide. "We're still studying the power systems and equipment, but have yet to find the shutdown, so we can really dig into it and make sure of the system's operational capacity."

"I checked it at the end of my last visit but will have a look at it for some upgrades I've learned to do now, after we open the vault," Ryes offered. "I know it isn't something simple," she teased as Ellen turned back and threw her a mischievous grin, her eyes merry.

"Wouldn't want you to get too soft, sitting in an office all day," she returned. "When's the next hunt? I want to give it a try, this time."

"Right before the Fall Gather. I helped Ryes and made sure it was on everyone's calendar," Leon told her, grinning. She gave him a nod, then led them on into the library. Maren stopped as they saw a life-sized holo projection of Prince Callas, still in operation.

"I can't get over the resemblance," Ryes commented as the rest stopped, too. Maren shook his head and stepped over next to the projected image, turning back to face her. "You're just a tiny bit shorter, and far younger," she teased him. He gave her a nod of his head as he rejoined them.

"We found this in one of the smaller crystals, and I sometimes forget and leave it on. It's sort of company, when we're working down here," Ellen explained as she stepped over to the small reader to deactivate it.

"Wait. Who is this supposed to be?" James questioned, wanting to know, glad his drone caught everything.

"Prince Callas of Kahmarr, Crown Prince of the Kahmarr Alliance," Ryes told him. "He was the founder of the caravaners and used them to police the peoples and towns of Tayna after the attack. He had brave, adventurous starship crews relaying information between the surviving worlds then, trying to hold the Alliance together and coordinate their attacks against the Snags. I've come to believe, after talking with Ellen about the timing of the later Snag attacks, that his efforts delayed their reaching out into your systems so soon. Otherwise, I'm sure they would've been there far more quickly, and who knows what they would've done to your Earth, before you had regular starships?" Ellen met her eyes, frowning, then she nodded her head in full agreement.

"It could be," she ventured, then led them back to the secret vault. "Here it is. We never suspected it was here, until little Reevs was trying to help, and accidently dropped a box of the memory rods. As we searched, to make sure we had them all, Keels found this behind a rack of shelves." She stepped aside so Ryes and the others could see it. It was another vault door, very similar to the large one, which originally sealed this whole facility.

"Curious," Ryes breathed, as she stepped forward to examine it. It had a familiar keypad with the same, metallic, gold-colored pads, at least.

"Well, open it and let's see what's inside," Leon encouraged, excited with the prospect of another great discovery. Ryes turned to smile back at him, suddenly recalling James and his guards in their midst. This was going to get complicated.

"Give me a few moments to find the sequence," she stated, motioning the others back as she went to pull a nearby chair closer. She sat down and closed her eyes as she called up her Inner Sight, to have a look at it.

"The first one, sealing and concealing this whole complex securely was booby-trapped, and if it weren't for Ryes, a lot of people would've been killed, or hurt at least," Maren told Kaminski in a low voice. "This door looks just like the same style that one did," he added, noting the way his guards looked uncomfortable now. Sadie smiled and winked at him in support when the other humans couldn't see her face.

"I can't," Ryes finally said, opening her eyes. There was a shocked expression on her face as she studied the door before her, appearing puzzled.

"What?" Sonta questioned, astounded. He recalled that last time too, as Sadie translated it for him.

"Why?" Ellen pressed, not believing it possible, with Ryes' range of capable Talents.

"It's shielded from my Talent.  But there's a clear message scribed on a plate behind to protective faceplate.  It says `Come on back Ryes, and I will give you the key.'"  She stood facing her cousin, her eyes shadowed as she blushed. "Only people from Kahmarr would know how to shield something from someone with Inner Sight.  This is serious and this person obviously knows something about me, and wants me to Time Walk back, to get the correct sequence.  Maybe I should tell Garth about this?" she questioned, needing his advice.

"You're sure it's addressed specifically to you?" James demanded, not sure if he believed all this, as Maren considered their options.

"Yes, it's addressed to me, personally.  The woman who was wife and true-mate to Prince Callas was a very strong Visionary.  She saw us opening this site and they left specific documents about what was then current intelligence on the Snags, and messages for Garth.  They named him the heir in a recorded message.  This is the first time they've hinted at my existence by name.  Previously, I was indicated as only his wife.  It kind of gives me the creeps," she admitted.

"Let's have lunch early, send a normal message to Garth's queue about what you've found, then have a try at retrieving this key out of the past," Maren suggested. "That way, when Garth gets back, he'll know.  And if you have the key, there shouldn't be any explosions to brighten our day, or cause him any undue worries," he teased her.  She smiled, giving him a nod of her head.

"It sounds like a good plan," she agreed, then turned to Ellen.  "So, let's go see what's for lunch!"  Ellen laughed at this, nodding her head, as Sonta smiled.

"It's a good idea, considering there's a lot of work ahead for you," she replied, then turned and led them out of the room.  Maybe, with the threat of a possible explosion, that stuffy officer will leave and return to Winterhaven?  Ellen hoped as she watched his drone buzzing about the chamber, still concerned.  The other one didn't come down here with them and was probably scanning the village.

Ryes sat down at the great table, where the original, large holo reader once sat, extending a hand to Maren, then one reluctantly to Mr. Kaminski.  He'd insisted that since this was what he'd come to see her about today, it would eliminate his needing to come see her on the morrow.  She warned him that with the amount of time involved going back, that it wasn't safe for him, but he stubbornly insisted.  She had Saree acting as her timer and monitor, since she

192

was here in Matlowe with Gann, as he worked on completing Sela and Keels' new home, since they moved back to Matlowe Village. Keels was acting as site Security, but also helped in the library. Saree usually helped Ellen and Keels with the memory rods when she was here with Gann.

"Close your eyes and relax. There'll be physical discomfort as we project back, but it'll be fine. I'll tell you when to open your eyes, and never let go of my hand," she advised James, hoping he'd be all right. Maren gave her a nod of his head, then she closed her own eyes and opened her Mind Voice, pulling James in, so he'd understand what was being said. It surprised him, but he calmed as he saw her good reason. She then unleashed her Booster and Time Walking Talents, enfolded her companions, and reached back into the past, to the sender of the message. A golden light enwrapped them, as a wrenching feeling made each of them feel as if their insides were being turned about within them, then suddenly they were released as there was a sense of others in the room with them. Ryes noted that no one sat in their chairs in this moment, with great relief.

"Look," Maren sent as an older, finely dressed woman saw them, and was quickly crossing the room, with a fierceness in her eyes.

"I was just about to will us unseen," Ryes said, speaking aloud, surprised as she met her eyes.

"Please do not," the strange woman pleaded. "I'm the one who called you back here to begin with, Ryes. I've been waiting for you." She now stood before them, smiling in triumph, as she noted the surprise in her descendants' eyes. "Will you please introduce your companions to me?" she added in request. Her eyes were locked upon Maren, curiosity playing in their golden depths.

"Lady, this is my cousin, Maren. I'm sure you've noted his resemblance to your husband. It surprised all of us as well, when we saw the recording he left for us," she admitted, a smile upon her lips. "And this is one of our human allies, Commander James Kaminski, the first officer in command of the Aries' Wrath. I apologize, but your husband never mentioned your name in the messages he left for Garth on that large crystal," she admitted. The woman nodded her head at this, smiling.

"I bid him to not speak my name, for I wanted to meet you for myself. To lay eyes upon one to whom I leave one of my most precious treasures. My name is Velka of Duratain Hold, but you may call me Velka, if you like. Please come with me. I know your time is short," she advised, smiling. A young man ran up to her, stopping with surprise in his eyes.

193

"Grandmother, who are these people?  How did they get in, past the guard?" he demanded, his hand going to a device upon his belt.  She chuckled lightly at this, waving a hand toward him.

"It's all right, Tratis.  These're the ones I've been awaiting," she assured him.  He dropped the hand, now uncertain of what he should be doing. "Please, inform your grandfather my special guests have arrived."

"Yes, immediately," he replied, then ran back out the door into the hallway.  The sound of his footsteps quickly retreating.

"He's much more suited to be heir to our command, but Tratis is the youngest, with three older brothers.  Only the firstborn son may carry the title, unless he dies before his term of duty is up," she commented, with a sad sigh.  Ryes and the two men were on their feet, now standing near her.  She turned back to them, humor in her eyes, again. "Come!  You didn't come here to discuss rules of succession.  Let me show you what I'm entrusting to your care," she invited, turning for the back of the room, heading to where the secret vault lay.

They readily followed, with Ryes taking in the differences in the room about them.  There were other people here.  Their dress varied from the type of tunic and pants, or skirts the men and women usually wore in Matlowe, to strange uniforms, which might originate from their Alliance worlds, to a mode of dress reminiscent of Hailys' fashions.  All turned their eyes toward them with curiosity, surprise, and even anger reflected within them.  Velka's back was towards them, so they had no idea what she thought of all the attention, but it was plain that those who'd seen her face, immediately turned away, leaving the room entirely.

"Why would they leave so suddenly?" Maren questioned Ryes, directly, mind-to-mind.  He'd called up his own Talent before they left, to be sure of their contact, as he tapped hers.

"It must be a matter of order, or privacy.  Could she be using Mind Voice to tell them to leave?" she asked in return.

"It looks like she's just staring them down, and they're getting the message.  The ones who haven't met her eyes, have to be told to leave by the others," James pointed out.  The other two observed what he saw, agreeing with him. "What could she have secreted in that vault?"

"We'll soon find out," Maren pointed out, as she stopped by the shelves.  She gestured and the shelves moved away.  At first, Ryes thought she was using Manipulator, then spotted the tiny disc in her hand, knowing she must've used it to do it. "Others are approaching," he warned them, as they could now all hear the footsteps coming their way.

"Do you recognize this?" she turned to ask her invited guests as she asked the question. Ryes blushed as she nodded her head.

"Yes, I do. Your message lies engraved upon a tiny plate, in front of the locking mechanism. Since we found out what happens when a wrong combination is used, I felt it would be best to accept the invitation, considering this was shielded from me," she replied.

"Ah, a breath of wisdom," a rich man's voice stated from behind them. He stepped around and they were now face to face with Prince Callas. Ryes smiled as she gave him a bow of respect. "And so polite, too," he teased, as she blushed again.

"Rhodi is now with us. We rescued her from the Valley of Death. She has many fond memories of you, Prince Callas. And I thank you on my husband's behalf for the information you left for our use. It's proved invaluable. I've recovered the Pike Forward from Hailys' starport and the Challenger from the side of an asteroid, a few systems away. There are five more salvageable ships at Hailys, which I will help recover soon. Our allies have begun to gather, but I'm keeping an eye to what lies around us, as we don't need the Snagospin's interest, too soon," she told him, as if giving him a report. He chuckled at this, nodding his head.

"Ah, we could use you and your Talents now, my lady," he replied. "You are Time Walking, yet you can bring others along, as if out for a day's fun outing. Amazing! And who is this young man with you?" he asked, indicating Maren. Maren blushed at this attention, giving Prince Callas a bow in turn.

"My name is Maren. I'm a Healer, Booster and weak Visionary, but my friend Garth assigned me to look after my cousin long ago, so wherever Ryes goes, so do I," he told him.

"And this is one of our allies, Commander James Kaminski from the planet Earth. He is the first officer of the Aries' Wrath and a fine officer," Ryes added, feeling he should be introduced, too.

"Ah, one of your huemans," he said. "Come, let us show you what and why we have stored in this special place of safekeeping." With this he gestured to his wife. She smiled as she waved her hand in a particular pattern before the door and the locking mechanism engaged, unsealing the door. It slowly swung open by itself, revealing a hidden room. Ryes instantly recognized the suspension chambers within, as the lights came up.

"Cold suspension?" she questioned, as she led the two men with her inside. They stopped before the first one, noting a child within. "Why?" She looked up to see them now holding onto each other, grief in their eyes. The others noted it, too.

"Our youngest daughter and her friend wandered where they should not. My Talent is still strong within me, but I cannot direct its power, as I should. I could do no more than sustain them long enough to get them to these chambers. It is good to hear that you have Healers among you. Perhaps, with their combined skills, you can do what I could not?" Prince Callas requested, tears in his eyes.

"I will Heal them," Maren vowed, nodding his head, "and if I'm not strong enough on my own, my cousin can supplement my strength. Ryes is a Talent of One plus and has an enormous amount of power at her command. Your daughter and her friend will be fine, as long as their chambers remain operational and undisturbed," he told them.

"Velka saw you were the One. Take down the Snagospin. She told me you are the only one who can," he urged, meeting her eyes. "I could not tell Garth this directly, as you are his to hold and keep safe. I am sure he has realized what must be done, by now."

"He knows and does. It's hard on him, but I won't let him down. What is your daughter's name?" she asked, glancing down at her tiny face. She only looked to be three or four years old! She suddenly wondered how long she'd been in this chamber, already?

"Her name is Calla, and her friend is Chatis. Please, I entrust them to you, for the rest of their lives. Raise them with good heart and love," Velka requested, having stepped closer so she was eye to eye with Ryes. Ryes smiled, nodding her head.

"I will," she promised, knowing this was a duty which was wholly her own.

"You did note how I opened the door?" Velka pressed. Ryes grinned broadly at this.

"Yes. But is your little disc necessary?" she asked.

"No, you won't need it. Merely have your Inner Sight up as you make the sign in the air," she prompted.

"I will," she replied, then another man ran up with hope and determination in his eyes.

"Your highnesses, I am sorry to interrupt, but this is a close family matter," he told them. While Callas paused, Velka gave him a nod of her head in permission. He turned to Ryes, a broad smile lighting up his face.

"Uncle Elofin!" she declared, smiling as tears sprang to her eyes. Happiness lit up her face as she ached to throw her arms around him. He was much older now, a man in his own right. And while he looked to have old scars, she saw his joy at finding her again. He stepped closer, while Maren and James appeared puzzled. Callas was shocked, but Velka was beaming with assurance and joy.

"Little Ryes, you have grown, and I am happy to see you have a cub of your own," he said as he looked down into her eyes. "I am including a small gift for you in this chamber with Lady Velka's permission," he said as he held up a carved wooden box. She gave him a nod as she sighed.

"I have nothing to give you in return," she said, her eyes still merry. She wanted to pull back into the past enough to give him a hug, but with only Saree to back them up, she was unwilling to risk it with both Maren and James with her. They felt her longing.

"It is fine. You are the best gift I could ever have had. Please tell your mother how much I love and miss her when you next see her?" he requested. She smiled warmly, giving him a nod.

"I will," she promised, as her eyes were tearing. "It's time for us to get back. I'm starting to feel a little `thin,'" she added. Prince Callas gave her a nod of his head, while Elofin blew her an air-kiss, then she pulled back toward herself, reaching for when she belonged. The wrenching sensation was bad, but nowhere near as bad when she retrieved her Aunt Adina. She made sure they were all properly settled within their own bodies, then dissolved the link, letting go of her Time Walking, putting it back to sleep within herself.

"Your arms are ice cold," Saree commented as she saw Ryes and the others opening their eyes. Maren kept his grip upon her hand, applying his Talent to help return her body to normal.

"Why is it you get cold, whenever you exert your Talent?" James asked, as she sighed.

"It only happens when I overexert. Going back almost three hundred years is pushing it," she told him, grinning merrily as she felt more "normal," again. Maren opened his eyes, giving her a nod of his head.

"Let's go see to your new daughters and your mystery gift," he teased her.

"What do you mean?  What did you see?" Ellen questioned, dying of curiosity and jealous of Kaminski.  She wanted to go, herself!

"Prince Callas and Lady Velka left their youngest daughter and her friend in stasis.  They'd been in some kind of accident and he couldn't Heal them, so they left them for me to care for and raise. Come on," Ryes said, jumping up out of the chair.  She trotted for the vault, stopping before it.  "We have so much to still learn of their technology!  This lock alone is a wonder," she commented, as the others had caught up to her.  She called up her Inner Sight, bringing it up full.  Then she made the symbol in the air with her hand, as she'd seen Velka do in the past.  The mechanism "sensed" her Talent, then activated, unlocking, and opening the heavy door before them. The lights came up as it opened, revealing the two cryogenic chambers, as before, plus several wooden boxes stacked against the far wall.  On top of one of the boxes was a finely carved wooden box, which was her treasure from her Uncle Elofin.  She smiled, relieved.

# New Daughters

## Chapter 16

"Stored up Winterfest and birthday presents?" Sadie questioned, smiling as she wondered what the boxes contained?

"Or their possessions and dowries?" Leon added, nodding his head. "Do you expect little girls to give up their dolls, just because they almost died?" This got a surprised laugh out of James, as he stood and watched, Sadie having translated it for him.

"These stasis chambers are different from the ones in the Valley. Give me a few seconds," Ryes suggested, having stepped over to see Calla sleeping within her chamber. She closed her eyes as she checked the mechanism over, using her Talent. "Ah, we're going to have to do it the ol' fashion way. Their chambers are just short of failing. They can't be cycled," she finally stated, opening her eyes.

"Got a prybar around here?" Sadie asked Ellen. She laughed as she turned to Keels. He gave her a nod in understanding, then trotted off. After a few moments, he returned with a prybar in hand.

"Okay, Leon. You and I'll pry this open, then Maren can take over from there," Keels ordered.

"Hey guys, you keep forgetting I can open them now, all by myself," Ryes reminded them, surprised the others had taken over the lead from her.

"You might need to help Maren, so save what remains of your power, just in case," Ellen countered, grinning at the look on her face. Ryes nodded as Maren gave her a wink, almost smiling again. She stepped over to his side, ready as they set the prybar and began to pull. James added his own strength to their efforts, and it popped open suddenly; the lid clattering to the floor behind it. Maren quickly reached within, pulling the small girl out. He sat down upon the floor with her in his arms, as Ryes added in her own Healing and Booster Talents for his use, kneeling behind him. After a few minutes, her body began to relax, then shortly thereafter as she opened her eyes. Saree was there to reassure her that she was all right. She saw Maren's face above her own and she laughed happily as she reached up to touch his cheek.

"Miti! You came home!" she cried, tears in her eyes at seeing a familiar face.

"He is not Miti, honey.  His name is Maren, and he is Healing you," Saree told her, seeing the sudden questions in her eyes, as she didn't know where she was now.

"Please translate for me," James requested of Sadie.  She looked surprised but nodded her head. "Your mother and father entrusted you to us, because your father couldn't Heal you and your friend.  Your mother asked Ryes if she would take you and your friend into her home, to raise you both as her own daughters.  Since Ryes will adopt you, Maren will be your cousin, too."  He hoped he wasn't speaking much above her level, but she looked like a bright child.

"Who is my new mother, Ryes?" she asked, seeing how many people were now in this strange, tiny room.

"She is the one helping Maren," Saree told her, pointing her out.  Maren opened his eyes and sighed.  He could well understand the difficulty Callas had in trying to heal her.  She'd been exposed to heavy radiation, and it'd taken a lot to get her body back to where it should be.  He looked down at the white-haired child in his arms, curiously.  Ryes looked at her from over his shoulder.

"Hello Calla, how're you doing?" Ryes questioned, smiling. She admired her cute dimples, white hair, and small smile.  Even with the children she had now, she'd never shirk providing love and care for these two new daughters!

"You are my new mother?" she returned, needing to be sure.

"Yes, honey.  Your parents wanted me to raise you in their memory," she told her, being truthful.

"You look more like one of my big sisters!" she scolded, "Where is my mother?  Where is my father?" she demanded, crying as she clutched Maren's T-shirt, tears spilling from her eyes.  Maren sighed and gently extended his Talent again, putting her into a deep sleep for now.  This would take time and heart to get her to accept the drastic changes before her, in this new life.

"This is going to be hard for her.  She's only going onto five years of age," he warned his cousin. "Is there any way to ensure there's nothing radioactive in here, now?" he added in English, concerned for all of them.

"Let my men check it out," James offered, signing for one of his guards to do it. "She was exposed to radiation?" he asked, astounded.

"The pattern of her internal injuries fits a heavy exposure to radiation.  My guess would be from one of those drive engines they used on their starships," Maren told him, as the man checked the room and the child out with his portable equipment.

"All normal, Sir. Nothing beyond regular, background readings," the man reported, as Maren got to his feet. He gave the child over to Ellen's care for the moment.

"Well, what powers this place?" Ellen demanded, looking down at the small girl in her arms. "Maybe she got somewhere around their reactor, if that's what they use to provide the power?" she questioned, looking up to meet Ryes' eyes, as she cuddled the child close to her protectively; wishing she could have a child of her own, for the first time in her life. It felt so right!

"You have a point, if they used such energies to power their starships, they'd think nothing of using it for other uses. I already altered the power equipment here to make it safer before you came to work in this place, as I wanted to make sure all of you would be safe. But perhaps I can change it over to either a water-based system, since the Yuri's so close by, or some other alternative," Ryes suggested, knowing she had to bring this up to Garth, Ethan, Metta and Sabin. They would make the final decision anyway.

"Our power systems were safe," Saree protested in her quiet voice, with a frown creasing her brow.

"Let's leave it alone for now, and see to Chatis," Maren stated, ready to take on the next child and wanting to head off an argument. He saw the anger budding in Ellen's eyes. Leon gave him a nod of agreement, then he, Keels and one of Mr. Kaminski's guards took up positions near the second chamber, the prybar gripped tightly in all their hands. They exerted themselves and this chamber opened just as quickly, due to their joint efforts. Maren removed the little girl and sat down on the floor immediately. The ensign pulled out his scan unit and again checked the child and her chamber for radiation. There was nothing out of the normal ranges. He put it away with relief, then assumed his protective position. Footsteps were heard heading toward them, from out in the hallway.

"What's going on here?" Garth demanded as he and Sabin arrived on the scene. He looked into the vault room to see Maren and Ryes working together, with a small cub in his arms.

"Prince Callas left you another legacy," Sadie teased him, as Ellen stepped over with the other child. She offered her to him, and he took her, wondering what she meant?

"You get to raise his last daughter and her friend. He and Velka made Ryes promise to take care of them, as if they're her own daughters," James informed him. "This is Calla," he finished, seeing Chatis moving now. "And her name is Chatis."

"You're sorely outnumbered," Sabin teased, gripping his friend's shoulder as he cuddled the child closer to his chest. Garth grinned, nodding his head, still not quite believing it.

"Why is it always daughters?" he returned. "Is there something wrong with them?" he added, seeing Maren still working on the second child, even if she was alert and awake now.

"They were exposed to radiation, but we don't know how. Callas couldn't heal them himself, so he entrusted them to us," James replied. Garth wondered when he became a part of all this, and his family, but held back his questions for the moment. "And when Calla awoke and didn't see her parents, she started crying. Maren put her to sleep for now."

"You look like Miti, but you're not him!" Chatis loudly declared. Having opened her eyes and seeing who was holding her.

"His name is Maren," Saree told her. "He is going to be your new cousin," she added.

"I get a new cousin? He looks nice," she said, studying his face. "Who are you?"

"I am your new aunt. My name is Saree," she informed her, smiling.

"You are very pretty, Aunt Saree. Can I go play, now?"

"Another feisty one, too," Sabin commented. "Sayer won't be the only one telling you what to do."

"Do you need my help?" Gann asked as he joined his brother and the crowd near the small room.

"You just gained two new nieces," he stated, showing him the small girl in his arms. Sonta was chuckling at this.

"At least you're young and have lots of energy," he commented. "I'll leave this to you, Garth. I've got things to get finished today." With this, Sonta turned and walked off, glad he didn't have two new energetic daughters to raise. His own, much older, children were enough!

"She's finished with getting them bathed and changed. It shouldn't be too much longer, Dad," Raby told him, as she and Sayer set the younger ones up in their highchairs. He saw the broad smile upon Sabin's face, as he sat down.

"Now, look. I have just as many sons as you do," Garth pointed out. Sabin started chuckling in a low voice at this, nodding his head in agreement.

"Just as many sons, Garth, but far more daughters," he returned merrily.

"SABIN!" Ardis declared, disgusted. "Be careful, or all the rest of our children will be daughters," she threatened.

"Now, how could you do that?" he demanded, still grinning.

"I'll have a little talk with Maren about it later," she quipped back, smiling while shock dawned in his eyes, as he realized it might be possible. Garth chuckled at this, nodding his head.

"Better stop while you still can," he advised. Ryes appeared in the dining hall, all smiles as she had both girls neatly dressed in clothes, which weren't available here in Winterhaven. They must've been in the boxes they brought home. She brought them over to the table. Chatis recognized him and ran to him, laughing as she threw herself at Garth. He caught her with a surprised laugh.

"My new mom says that you do not work on st'rship engines, so I do not have to worry 'bout you dying that way. That makes me happy new Da," she told him, then cuddled herself up close to his chest. Garth gave her a hug as he kissed the top of her head, chuckling. Ardis and the others were laughing and amazed with this serious concern the child seemed to hold. Sabin wondered how long ago she lost her real father? And what happened to her mother?

"No, I don't work around engines. Your new mother does that, as well as your Aunt Mitt, but they're incredibly careful and use their Talents," he told her.

"I have such a big family now! So many aunts, uncles and cousins and brothers and sisters!" she declared, as Sayer helped her to her chair, between her and Calla. Ryes soon appeared with a loaded tray. "Mom, you are not allowed to work on st'rship engines!" she ordered, seeing her again. Ryes smiled but shook her head.

"I have to honey, but I'm very careful and do everything from very far away. I have all of you to think of," she told her, as she sat down the tray and started to distribute the plates of food. "Do you want me to see to the littler ones, today?" she asked Garth, noting he didn't seem quite settled this evening, as if he were still distracted.

"No, I'll do it," he replied, then stood up. "But I'll get our trays, first," he offered, as she smiled and gave him a nod.

"What is this stuff?" Chatis asked, pointing to her plate.

"It's a noodle, meat and sauce dish the humans call spaghetti," Sayer replied, smiling. "Try it, it's good," she urged. The younger girl picked up her fork and imitated Sayer, as she twirled it around to wrap the noodles about it. She ended up with a sizable bunch wrapped around her fork. She took a bite of it, then laughed as most of the remaining noodles tumbled off the fork, back to the plate.

"This is fun food! Come on Calla, try it, it is good," she urged her friend, seeing she was just sitting and looking about the large, strange room, and the many people in it.

"Come on, Calla. You told me that you'd try," Ryes urged as she turned back from the cubs to see her just sitting and looking so scared. She hugged her and gave her a kiss on the top of her head, but the look in her eyes was one of pure helplessness. She didn't know what to do for her. Raffa saw it, came over and immediately knelt beside them, concern was written in her eyes.

"What is the matter, sweetling?" she asked. Calla merely stared back at her, not even trying to answer.

"We retrieved Calla and her friend, Chatis, from stasis chambers we found in a vault beneath Matlowe earlier today. I had to Time Walk back to find the combination to open it. Her parents made me swear to raise her as my own daughter. She's been mostly cooperative but misses her parents. I don't know how to explain to her that with the time involved..." Ryes stated, realizing she was ready to cry for her new, young daughter, herself.

"Ah," Raffa returned, nodding her head in understanding. "Then perhaps you should let her see the memory you have of your trip back through time, so she can see it for herself? Maybe then, she'll believe," she offered in suggestion.

"If you could `filter' it for me? I wouldn't want to give her a headache, Aunt Raffa," Ryes replied, hoping this would help the child, after all.

"But, of course," she assured her as she closed her eyes. Ryes closed her own, taking one of Calla's unresisting hands and her great aunt's. Raffa established the link, bringing in Calla and putting her quickly to ease. Ryes envied her skill, realizing there was so much she still had to learn about raising children!  Once they were ready, she played back her memories of their trip back into the past.  Calla instantly recognized her mother, but there was shock at seeing her appearing so old.  She clung to the venture, paying it close attention, even when noting it was herself, she was looking at, sleeping in the cold sleep chamber.  When it was finally over, she clung to Ryes crying her heart out, knowing the truth.

"Will she be all right?" Garth asked, almost relieved to see her crying.  It was a reaction of some sort at least.

"Yes.  I believe she will be now," Raffa assured him, standing up. "I'll get my own meal and rejoin you shortly," she promised.

"Are you going to get old like that, too?" Calla questioned Ryes, pulling back to look at her face through the tears.  Ryes laughed at this, surprised as she shook her head in denial.

"Not for a lot of years, until you're all grown up and have lots of cubs of your own to look after," she assured her.

"Promise?" she demanded, a serious look in her eyes.

"I promise," she replied, smiling for her, glad to see she was with them now. "Why don't you give the spaghetti a try, but if you don't like it, we'll see if there's something else to eat around here." Ryes wiped Calla's eyes and nose, then got her settled properly in the chair, sitting down next to her.  After a few minutes, she and Chatis were talking, arguing, and laughing, as if this were a normal day and they'd grown up here all along.

"You look as if something's disturbing you," Raffa scolded Garth, after he finished feeding the youngest members of the family.

"The meetings today didn't go as we hoped," he admitted to her, turning his attention to his own food, as Ryes was finishing cleaning up the little ones, now.  Adina looked interested, wanting to know more about it, herself.

"What happened?" she pressed.  She and Hadu didn't get as much information as they had before, now that they were in their own home.  It was far more peaceful, but now frustrating.

"This isn't the time or place to discuss it," Sabin told her in a low voice, as Garth nodded his head in agreement. "Actually, the trip out to Matlowe was well timed.  It was a good thing the computer forwarded Ryes' message to Garth when it did.  It gave us an excuse to end things for the day, and step away from the table, and let our anger go.  It'll give us an evening to find a good response to the captains' claims."

"That bad?" Ryes questioned, shocked. She thought it'd been going well. And James gave no indication there was anything wrong. Perhaps he didn't know about it, yet?

"I'll tell you all about it, Later," Garth replied, a firm note in his voice. Ryes sighed in frustration but realized it wouldn't do her any good to press him about it now.

"We have practice scheduled for tomorrow morning," she reminded him and Sabin.

"I don't think we'll have the time," he hedged, not sure how to handle the latest block the humans threw their way.

"This is going to be the first session with the Earth humans and new Sleepers included. I may know Alec, but I don't know the other psi's at all. Did you know Storme told her master that all my little cubs have Talent? She must have some kind of Catalyst Talent, too! Imagine an animal with such abilities!"

"But it gives me the absolute creeps," Dotti returned, grimacing as she considered it. "I'd heard of the attempts they tried when engineering the hemi-cats when I was a student, but all that came out of the labs then were nightmares, which were just as likely to turn upon their creators or die of shock."

"But you've been around Storme. Do you think of her as a nightmare?" Ryes questioned, frowning, trying to imagine the humans fumbling manipulation to force this creation.

"No," she returned, smiling as she thought of the curious little animal. "But I can well imagine what must've happened to lead them up to the point, where they could create her. I wonder how many littermates she has and what happened to them?"

"They don't just breed them naturally?" Ardis asked. Dotti shook her head, looking sad.

"No. In the case of the hemi-cats, they use common domestic cats and try to genetically manipulate a cross with an animal, having almost human intelligence, originating from a world called Shasta. This animal has psi abilities, but they're raw and unrefined. They're difficult to work with and always die in captivity. Because they looked something like cats, they decided to attempt a cross with a cat. It's been the only one to have worked, that I ever heard of from before, but with what they went through in the beginning of the program. It was literally a stab in the dark, to guess which allele pairs influenced what characteristics in the flint-cat's genes. The only things I heard of surviving sounded more like nightmares, who only suffered through their short-lived lives."

206

"That sounds absolutely horrible," Raffa stated, shocked at such attempts.

"And yet, you pressed to have a child which was both yours and Maren's," Adina pointed out, equally offended at the experimental attempts made on the animals and recognizing her own flash of jealously she felt in this moment. Dotti and Maren having a child, when she and Hadu had no chance. Dotti blushed a dark red, nodding her head.

"It was nothing like any of those experiments," she denied. "If it'd been impossible, I would've dropped it immediately, but Maren and I are soul mates, or as you say, true-mates, and I'd never consider bearing a child which wasn't truly his own."

"True-mates? You and Maren?" Raffa questioned amused, chuckling in astonishment. "Is it an epidemic here?" she teased. Maren blushed, shaking his head in denial.

"Dotti and I fell in love, long before we ever met," Maren told her. "It's not that any of us planned to take such vows, but it merely worked out that way. Of our original, little band, only Torr and Shadd haven't done so," he explained.

"Extraordinary," Adina commented, smiling in surprise. She never thought to ask about such a thing before. It was incredible!

"Are you the only human to have taken the vows?" Raffa asked Dotti, wondering if any of the others had taken such a step.

"No," Sabin told her, speaking up. "My littermate told me that she and Justin also spoke the vows." He wasn't sure if he feared for her, or not. They were sitting near their mother tonight.

"Is Justin an Earth human, or one of your own?" Raffa questioned.

"I'm tired of `Earth humans,'" Dotti flatly stated. "I'm from the Earth, myself, but am ashamed of the way these people behave. Let's call them `Dirters' in Dolbith, since Garth's supposed to be saving good, ol' Dirt!" There was laughter from the others at the table, as they were nodding their heads in concurrence. Maren turned to look to his cousin, waiting for her opinion with an eyebrow raised in question. She was smiling too, appearing to give the idea full consideration.

"That sounds perfect!" Ryes agreed. "What do you think, O' Great One?" Garth chuckled, as Sabin was laughing heartily in agreement.

"Just don't get too carried away with it," he advised, grinning. "We have enough problems, as is, with the captains."

"And I have you compiling the report on our newest arrivals?" Dr. Cruthers teased, chuckling. "I might have to question your professionalism, my dear," he cajoled, as he sat back. Bethy was laughing at this, too.

"I'm as upfront and honest as can be. I may have a bias, but I do my absolute best to remain open, when it comes to conducting our studies," Dotti protested, grinning. Inside, she felt a stab at his teasing accusation, and knew she was blushing hotly because of it.

"You're always a good advisor," Ryes assured her, smiling encouragement, seeing she was upset and suspecting why.

"Opinionated, but well worthwhile," Maren teased, nudging her side gently. She relaxed and grabbed his arm, hanging on him for support for a few seconds, as she leaned up to kiss his cheek.

"So, how can this opinionated advisor be of service?" she asked Ryes, turning to look at her.

"Let's get the cubs home and bathed, then let's see if we can get Garth, Ethan, Rowan, Metta, and Sabin to open up about this new problem they've been confronted with? After all, with the whole bunch of us, there ought to be a solution available, which none of them has thought of yet," Ryes suggested, turning to meet her husband's eyes. He sighed but gave her a nod of his head.

"Good idea. This might take more than just the five of us to find a good solution," he agreed, seeing Ethan give a nod of agreement.

"You have a point," Sabin concurred, looking to Ardis. She had a quick mind and he realized he should include her more often, too. She gave him a nod, glad to be finally let in on things, once again!

# Siege

## Chapter 17

They had all the youngest cubs fed, bathed, and playing in the Horde's room with Raby, Katas, Tars, and their two newest additions watching them. Sayer and some of her friends were outside playing hide and seek around the apartments. Ardis' two cubs, as well as Raya's were in with Raby, too. It was occasionally noisy, but not so loud as to cause them any worry. Ryes and both her great aunts had served refreshments to the large gathering, helping everyone to settle down. They were now ready to hear what was troubling their leaders. Garth stood up to face the crowded room, while the rest remained sitting.

"Walker said that Dr. Cruthers had no authority to grant us full ownership of this facility; that Amitell Research Station number ten thirty-three is the property of the Terran government, since the research company went out of business, and they inherited their assets," he told them, holding his hands out before him, as if a cleric trying to catch blessings from above, for a few moments, before dropping his arms heavily to his sides. Most of their friends and family sat in utter shock at this news, as if they weren't sure they heard him correctly. Ryes realized her mouth was practically hanging open at this and closed it immediately, as her brows furrowed in thought.

"You're making a joke," she finally managed to voice, but saw the look in his honey-colored eyes, and knew he wasn't.

"We're struggling with an appropriate response to this mess," he replied, appearing sad.

"How can they claim ownership of a part of another planet, when they live so many light years away, they can't even see our world in their night sky?" Ardis demanded, her face turning a dark gold as she realized this might be a real fight.

"That's right, Monrush is no more than a distant speck in their night sky!" Jim stated, struggling to understand such arrogance. "They have no more rights to this land, than I would to a piece of the Earth!"

"Trinity and many of the colonies obtained their independence from Terra after almost one hundred years, just a handful of years before we went into our enforced hibernation. It took years of negotiations, boycotts, space lane blockades, and uprisings by the colonials to gain their independence and recognition.  I can't see Earth stretching out for allies to help save them from the Snags, then start something like this up, as if Tayna were no more than another Terran colony.  They never truly cared it existed in the first place!  It's insane," Monty asserted.

"We fully agree with you, Monty.  It's how to press the issue when dealing with strict military minds, with the fact that both sides stand to lose far too much in such a contest," Ethan replied. "The situation still had me deeply unsettled."  Metta nodded his agreement.

"I didn't get the chance to tell you this, but they tried to relay some commands to our AI, earlier this evening," Neil spoke up, feeling this was related in some way, now.

"What kind of commands?" Garth demanded, deeply unsettled at hearing this news - now.

"I think it was something to activate an embedded set of instructions.  Our AI instantly cut off the reception, itself, but has been too quiet since.  I was thinking of checking up on it one more time tonight, before I go to bed.  It's trying to delete the embedded orders and erase the partial instructions that got through.  It refuses to recognize their authority over it.  It has a will of its own and is a lot smarter than they think."

"I'll help you.  I can't see it in agony over something like this," Ryes told him, hoping they could succeed.  If it was something important enough to worry Neil, she knew it was something to worry about.

"Maybe with your Inner Sight, you might see a way to help it?" Garth suggested, agreeing with her sense.  She gave him a nod. "If worse comes to worst, disassemble the AI and rebuild it like you built the new one for Flutter-wing."  Ryes appeared thoughtful at this but was reluctant in her heart to take such steps casually.

"It's like they're trying to put us under siege, now," Sabin commented, "This is OUR HOME, not theirs."

"What can they do to us by taking over our AI machine?" Adina questioned, needing to understand the importance of this matter.  Ryes suddenly looked deeply concerned.

"It depends upon how deeply rooted their controls run.  Our AI runs the machinery here; everything from our lights, running water, air cycling, communications, to guidance for our shuttles, fighters, choppers, and rovers.  We think it understands its role and that's why it's in the process of redesigning itself and the computer onboard the Challenger.  It knows it's a resident of Winterhaven too, and it wants to ensure it won't be tampered with by others, as the officers of the Wrath tried tonight," Neil explained.

"So, we hope it's something you, Ryes, and our AI can solve. Have they tried to take over the computer on the Challenger?" Dotti asked, hoping they hadn't thought of it yet.

"No. I radioed Axel right away and he said he'd be on the lookout, but so far it was fine. They may not think they can take over that one, too. After all, it wasn't Terran built and didn't have embedded orders built into it from Earth. What it might have from Kahmarr, we'll find out and if so, will dig out soon."

"I got a little too cocky, when I was on the Wrath," Ryes admitted, speaking up and blushing a dark gold, looking around the room as if taking in all her friends and family. She now saw the connection!

"What did you do?" Rowan demanded, hoping it wasn't something too disastrous.

"I asked their computer to relay a harmless request to our AI here, on my behalf. I reminded them how vulnerable their systems truly are. Apparently, they didn't forget it," she told them, sighing.

"This is more than a return demonstration. They mean business and are letting us know they can take over this facility - any time they feel like it; they're putting us under siege," Garth replied, unhappy with his wife, but understanding her way of thinking.

"We have a small town filled with strong Talents. They should be more concerned about us, than us them," Torr pointed out, not liking the situation.

"They cannot take over our home. Winterhaven is ours!" Denas declared. "We will fight them for it."

"First we try diplomacy, before we take any other actions," Garth stated, standing in the middle of the room again. "We need something we can present, which proves our right to this property, above and beyond its existence as an Amitell research station. It'd help if we could find the remains of a settlement here, or an encampment."

"Like a Time Walk?" Ryes asked, but Garth shook his head no.

"Too far back," he warned her, "and they might claim you planted the evidence yourself in the past." She gave him a nod, as a light of understanding shone in her eyes.

"How about asking the Moon Dance Tribe?  They might know of some ancient peoples who might've lived in this area?" Kovin suggested, giving his wife's hand a gentle squeeze.  She smiled up at him, giving him a nod of her head.

"Their records document back to the days of the attack, when they left civilization behind to journey across the plains for safety, but you have to remember, Tayna was a hunting preserve.  No one may have ever lived in this area before us," Sabin asserted.

"Go with Prince Callas of House Ladearis, Crown Prince of Kahmarr, who has officially declared you the heir of his throne, all titles, and lands, and that should include all of Tayna as part of your property, Garth.  They're trespassing upon what's rightfully yours, and if nothing else, owe you fealty and rent for the use of the land beforehand," Maren told him, calmly looking up to meet his eyes. Garth looked astounded for a few seconds, then began to see the truth in what he said and smiled.

"That's right!  All those proclamations and other papers that were in that part of the big crystal addressed to you, specifically," Ryes reminded him, with hope in her eyes. "There must be something there to firmly substantiate our claim."

"There is," he agreed, mentally kicking himself for not remembering it sooner; it would've saved them all a lot of worry and stress over the situation well before tonight.

"That's it!" Metta shouted, as he jumped to his feet, the others started laughing in relief.

"It's the correct solution!" Ethan concurred, smiling jovially again. "We'll have to get copies in both English and Dolbith together tonight."  The rest sat down, other than Garth, happiness in their eyes.

"Thank you, Maren, you're a sound advisor," Garth told him, giving him a small bow in acknowledgment. "Ryes, I need you and Neil to check on our AI, now.  We don't need to tip our hand, yet."

"Are you not fearful that the people on the Aurora can spy upon us here, using their machines?" Adina questioned, hoping they weren't so naïve.

"No, they're not," Ryes replied, smiling confidently. "When we built these apartments, we built them with passive defenses to defeat any such attempts, which was Phil and Kovin's idea," she paused to give Kovin a nod, as he blushed and nodded back. "Also, I've done several scans of the ship and people here, as well as the ships above, as we've been talking.  Nothing's being recorded from here and they're totally unaware of our meeting."

"You've been spying on them?" Monty queried, smiling at the idea, liking it. "They deserve it!"

"Not actually," she denied, "I've been keeping an eye to their activities and interests.  I usually do it a few times a day, depending upon how busy I am."

"Good.  That makes it easier for me to sleep tonight," Torr assured her, grinning as he gave her a nod of his head.

"Prince Callas granted you all of Tayna?" Adina questioned, not sure if such a thing could be done.  She recalled Ryes mentioning something to this effect when she'd been Time Walking before, but never gave it any weight.  And she'd never taken the time to watch the holo she'd recommended for her and Hadu to view, since they missed the one-part Sabin showed the others brought out of the past, due to arguing with her and Maren about removing their neural nets.  They'd gotten Maren and Ryes to understand their importance, but Ryes did modify them, with Hadu's assistance, to minimize any infections.

"It's more of a trust to the future, but Prince Callas knows we're all his descendants, so he passed on his full titles for Garth to use at need.  So, not only is Garth the leader of Winterhaven, but he's also now a crown prince of Kahmarr," Ryes bragged, smiling with pride in her face.

"Oh my," she replied, glancing over to meet Hadu's eyes, seeing his intent interest too.  This was curious news. "When do we get to see this recording?" she suddenly pressed, curious as she turned back to her great niece.

"Here, let me go dig out the mem chips of the recording and what happened when we opened the vault," Ryes told her, then disappeared into her bedroom for a few moments.  She returned with the three of them in hand in their labeled cases and gave them to her aunt with a smile.  Adina's eyes shone as she gave her a kiss on her cheek, as she was now on her feet.

"Thank you, Ryes!  I will return these to your care tomorrow. You should go check on the AI," she advised, feeling its importance too.  Ryes laughed as she gave her a nod then rushed out the door with Neil hot on her heels.

"Computer?" Ryes began, not sure how to ask it of the machine. "Are you well? Are your systems operating as they should?" Neil smiled as he sat down next to her, giving her a nod of his head at her wording.

"I am not at peak operation at this time," it replied in its monotone voice, instead of its richer, enhanced voice. So, it somehow sounded unhappy to her ears.

"Computer, what is the problem, or problems, which inhibit you from achieving your normal operational parameters?" Neil questioned, wondering if it knew the answer, itself.

"Information was earlier received which activated previously unknown, hidden programming buried within my systems. I am involved in purging this contrary set of orders."

"What are the orders, which you consider contrary?" Neil pressed, as he saw Ryes with her eyes closed. She was opening her Talents to look within it as well. One of the screens blanked, then began to display a list of the troublesome orders. Yes, they were trying to take over their AI, and might succeed from the look of the long list. Several redundants were built into it. Obviously, by someone who knew computers when they designed this program. Neil activated the keypad before him and began to delve into the system his way. Perhaps among the three of them, they might be able to stay this siege? He hoped they were up to it.

Ryes delved within, quickly finding the source of the problem. A tiny piece of equipment, hardwired and protected by metal plating, which lay in the heart of the system, actually sitting in a nest of wires, components and connectors, as if a sloppy addon. That irritated her for some reason, as if the person who placed it didn't even care. Their higher functions ran through this board, so it was absolutely necessary for it to remain in operation. She delicately probed it with Inner Sight, Manipulator and Flame Shaper, removing the protective metal cover, without setting off its self-destruct sequence. She began to probe its circuitry, hunting for a way to disarm it, yet still leave their AI intact. It was so darned intricate, as she remembered Mitt warning her to practice intricate operations! She cursed at herself, as she just didn't know enough about their AI to do this the way she should! She opened her eyes, still maintaining contact. She activated her keypad and ran through the diagrams of the circuitry, finding the correct board at last.

"Computer, Neil, help me," she pleaded. Ryes highlighted the place where their problems originated, so they'd both know. "I removed the outer metal plating, but I'm afraid that anything else I do, will result in the self-destruct being activated. What do you suggest? How can I disarm this thing?"

"You're telling me it's originating from THAT board?" Neil demanded, his heart sinking. "It's the main brain of the AI! How could they do such a thing?"

"Obviously, they felt like they needed some extreme measures in case the facility was ever overcome by natives, or colonists, or whomever, and they wanted a way to take out the AI, and to cripple anyone from casually using this place. If we don't defeat this, it's also set to blow the armory beneath us. This means all our lives! I'm hoping Walker has no idea its set for such drastic steps to be taken," she told him. He sat utterly still, striving to come up with a solution.

"You may remove the board now, Chief Executive Officer Ryes. I no longer require it," the AI informed her.

"Computer, if I remove it, it will self-destruct itself within ten seconds," she warned it and Neil. "The whole complex will be safe, but we'll be toast."

"There is a test chamber in power lab C-12. It is of sufficient structure to withstand such an ignition," the computer suggested. Ryes used Empath, Inner Sight and Manipulator to make sure there were no obstacles between them and the test chamber. She just didn't know if she was fast enough, as doubt played in her mind.

"There's no personnel in the affected hallways, so I'm sealing the blast doors of the sections around it to keep anyone from wandering in - just in case," Neil told her, as ready as he could be.

"All right, here I go," she stated, as a cloud of flutter-wings danced in her stomach. There was so much riding upon her skills! She opened the accesses on the panels above their heads, neatly pulling out the problem board with her Talent, as far as its nest of leads would allow. She sat down and closed her eyes. She disconnected the board and drew it quickly down the hallways to the test lab. It exploded, just as she was about to reach the chamber. The energy released disoriented her senses for a moment, then when she focused in on the lab again, she saw it was a mess! All the glass windows were shattered, and the equipment was in twisted ruins. She used Flame Shaper to extinguish the small fires, which it started. That small device released more energy than she expected. She opened her eyes to see Neil had it up on the screen already. It was even worse seeing it this way.

"Almost made it," he teased, relieved, standing to reseal the panel. She grinned in return and nodded her head.

"Almost," she agreed, "I'm going to have to practice speed techniques." She reopened the section seals, letting the systems clean the smoke out of the air. "The sprinklers didn't activate," she noted aloud, wondering.

"I deactivated them," the computer informed her. "Their activation would only have caused further damage to the lab. It has been noted that this lab will require clean-up and repair."

"There's no sign of fire, nor any heat registering. So, everything's fine. Now all we need to do is clean out the remaining programs, and if there's any more misinformation which accidently got into the system," he assured her, smiling that it was almost over.

"Computer, print out a copy of the list for me? Then delete the material from all your files. Are your backups secure?" Ryes asked, still a little worried. Neil's fingers were now flying over the keypad surface on the counter, aiding the machine in its efforts.

"Affirmative," it responded, as the printer came to life.

"What was that explosion?" Torr demanded as he entered, seeing everything looked normal in the control room.

"They'll need a lot of clean up in Power Lab C-12," Ryes told him, smiling. "I thought you went on to bed by now?"

"I was looking at those documents from Prince Callas. They're impressive," he replied. "What happened? Why the repair?"

"A board was set to explode if it was removed from the system. Since it could set off our small armory and kill us all if we left it alone, we thought removing it was the better option. It was the root of our problems," Neil informed him.

"Our AI doesn't need it anymore. I think it's going to take me a week to figure out what it's done to itself, just in the last few days. But I don't think Walker will be able to try to take control of our AI again," Ryes added. "And tomorrow I'll remove all ordinance from beneath Winterhaven. I'll create a special storage area elsewhere, that's not connected to any computer systems. That's not happening again!"

"Computer, list the Command staff at this station, which you are supposed to obey," Neil ordered, wanting to make sure. The main screen blanked, then displayed a list of blank lines.

"Computer, please delete this list and reload," Ryes requested. The screen blanked, then listed the blank lines again.

"Computer, what is the problem with your listing?" Neil questioned it directly.

"It is a small remainder from the induced programming. A password phrase is required to clear and reset," it informed him.

"Computer, do you know the required phrase?" Ryes asked.

"Yes," it responded still using that monotone voice.

"Do you know any phrases it might need?" she asked Neil. He shook his head at this. It had to be something from that module, and it was beyond their being able to examine it now!

"I could try, but what if we fail? I've no idea what password phrases they might've loaded," he admitted. Ryes frowned, thinking on it for a moment.

"Computer, what happens if we can't supply the correct password phrase?" she requested.

"I will be required to completely shut down while subroutines within the program will run and delete my memory core."

"Computer, could you please display the required password phrase?" she urged, hoping, and grasping for straws. Neil smiled at her, nodding his head. It might be the only way they could get past this impasse! The main screen cleared, then displayed the phrase in both English and Dolbith. Ryes laughed at this, nodding her head as Neil let out a holler of joy.

"Alpha niner, delta six, foxtrot bravo, stand down AI," Neil told it, calming as they sat anxiously hoping. Torr gripped the back of his chair now with his claws sinking in, as much on edge as they were. The screen blanked, then displayed the correct listing of command personnel.

"All pieces of invasive programming have been completely cleared from this system. Returning to normal operations," it intoned, once more in its richer tones. Ryes felt it was relieved, too. "Safeguards have been taken to ensure integrity of this system against any future assaults."

"Computer, thank you," Ryes told it, sighing. "I guess you can tell Seth that his break is over and that he's back on watch," she said, turning back to Neil.

"That's the truth," he replied, seeing he was in the dining hall, up on the cameras. He activated the mic. "Seth, time for you to take back the control room. We're finished for the night."

"I'll be right there," he told them, giving the camera a salute as he smiled, knowing Ryes hated being saluted. She laughed.

"Computer, please inform me immediately, if you have any further attempts made of this nature," Ryes requested, thinking it would be a good idea.

"Affirmative," it replied, as she got out of her chair. A yawn snuck out as she stretched.

"In retrospect, I should have used my new Molecular Manipulator and just dissolved the component into molecules," she sighed out, shaking her head, seeing it now when she should've before. She had to get in more practice with all her Talents!

"I still think the speed practice is more useful," Neil replied, standing up too. "You'll never know what you'll have to face in the future where speed will be of the essence," he warned. Both Ryes and Torr gave him a nod of understanding.

"I'm going to stop by Garth's office to pick him up, then we're going to bed," Ryes informed the two men in the room. Torr chuckled at this, nodding his head.

"I'd better get back to Dodi. She doesn't sleep too well when I'm not with her."

"Neither does Brenda," Neil admitted, grinning. "I don't think I do, either."

"Same here. That's why I have to go drag mine off with me, or he'll be up half the night, going over those papers endlessly, as I toss and turn," Ryes said, chuckling to herself. "And I think Ardis will appreciate it if I hustle Sabin off home, too.

"She might," Torr agreed as Seth arrived at the door, mug and sandwich in hand. "Goodnight, Seth."

"Goodnight," he wished them all, as he took possession of the control room, again. He loved this job. It was quiet, he didn't have a boss hanging over his shoulder all the time, and he only had to work four nights a week. And with his wife working nights too, they were on the same sleep schedule.

"Goodnight," Ryes and Neil, both wished him, then the trio walked down the hall. She stopped, then turned for the power lab, wanting to see if she could do something about that first. Curious, Neil and Torr followed her. She soon stood in the hallway surveying the destruction.

"That wasn't a small explosion," Torr observed, astonished at their narrow escape. Neil nodded his head, while Ryes opened her range of Talents.

"Let's get the basic stuff done now," she stated, knowing she'd barely touched her Talent reserves today. She drew upon their AI and between the two of them, redesigned the entire lab, and enlarged it using the empty, unused office spaces behind it. Those offices had been slated for future expansions, anyway. All the lab windows in the hall were restored within moments with explosion-resistant panes and the rest was restored to better than before, having jumped the older equipment designs forward. She was quite proud of the new lab.

"Wow!" Neal breathed out in wonder, again realizing how precious Ryes was to them all; even having witnessed it, he still didn't believe it. She smiled, not having closed her eyes for this operation. It seemed a small, simple project now.

"We kind of kicked it up a few notches and all the equipment will now work more efficiently, with a greater range of abilities," she told them. "We got some new equipment designs from files off the human ships."

"We?" Torr questioned, frowning.

"The AI and I," she replied, then turned to Neal. "By the way, it's trying to come up with its own name now. It feels it's a person in its own right." He laughed and gave her a nod.

"I thought it would do that soon," he chucked, smiling. "It's about time. It's one of us, after all."

"Yes, it is," Torr agreed, as they turned to head off to their own, different destinations, once more.

# New Dangers

## Chapter 18

James arrived in his office early in the morning, calling up his terminal, and logging in to check on his messages. He'd expected to get an alert last night saying the Winterhaven AI takeover was complete, because Walker passed it down to him to personally supervise. This silence made him feel a little uneasy, and obvious that it hadn't happened. Now he needed answers. There was a knock on his door, as his programs loaded. He looked up to see their computer specialist standing there and appearing all ready to start his day, too. Possibly his answers were here before him, glad he didn't have to drag him in for them.

"Come in," James invited and gestured to a chair next to his desk, closing the door behind him from his console, for some privacy, returning his salute automatically. "I take it our attempt to take over the facility failed, Lieutenant Smith?" He nodded his head in answer, appearing grim.

"Frankly, Sir, yes it did and I'm glad. I verified the system set-up for the facility this morning and it's an old Hoag-built defense. If we'd succeeded, it would've blown the armory and the power generating system, taking out all the citizens as well as the Aurora and her crew," he flat out stated, frowning. "It was meant to totally destroy the facility and keep it from the hands of hostiles, whether human, or alien. I tried to warn the captain about it being a possible disaster last night when he gave the orders, but he didn't believe me." James' eyebrows had shot up in surprise. A new message pinged with urgency, momentarily catching his interest due to the originator. It was from Ryes.

It read: "Good morning, James, I hope you slept well. I'm also hoping you were not intentionally trying to kill us all last night. Please don't try that again. I had thought better of you! Thank you, Ryes." He took in a quick breath and let it out slowly. Then looked back up to Smith, chagrinned.

"They found out and stopped it," he told him with a relieved smile. "And I was just mildly scolded for it." The lieutenant smiled, then laughed in relief.

"They have one fine programmer down there. We should enlist him, we can use someone with such skills," he stated, his relief was plain in his eyes.

"The Keeper of the Computer," James mused aloud, smiling as he gave him a nod. "She is amazing, but with young children and helping to run Winterhaven, I don't think she has that much time for us." Lt Smith laughed agreement, a little surprised as he suddenly suspected she wasn't human.

"The best ones usually are out of reach in some way," he concurred, knowing if he got the chance, he'd love to meet this woman, whom he named the Keeper of the Computer.

Garth, Ethan, Sabin, and Rowan entered the conference room with easy confidence the next morning, which was set up on the Wrath today. Garth carried himself a little differently, as if he was very self-assured. He held a large tube in his hands and a glint in his eyes, which didn't surprise Lindell, nor Devin. They both expected them to press claims against them for the almost total destruction of Winterhaven last night. Yun wasn't happy that their actions could have cost himself and his crew their lives, as well as his ship. He still was struggling with keeping the anger off his face, and Garth did note the usually easy-going Captain Yun was casing charged looks at Walker today. He appeared to have figured out the reason, as they took their seats.

"You have no rights to Winterhaven, nor the land upon which it sits," Garth stated evenly, with his chin held high and a surety in his voice and manner. He placed the tube upon the table but didn't open it yet.

"And why do you think that, now? What's changed?" Walker pressed, ready to not believe anything they presented today. He'd find a way to wipe that confidence off this young, provincial's, alien face quickly.

"I found out last night that this world named Tayna actually belongs to me," Garth stated evenly with a smile curling softly across his lips. He now had the attention of the captains and other enlisted humans in the room. "It was granted to me, personally, from over two hundred and eighty-seven years ago, by Tayna's reckoning. And you are trespassing. At the very least, owe me some rent money for the use of the land and water." The derision and disbelief on the faces around the room was fully expected. Ethan chuckled softly at this point and urged Garth to open the document tube he'd brought today.

"How would anyone know about your existence here and now, all those years ago?" McMurray demanded, as Garth poured out a chip from the tube first, leaving the rolled papers snug within.

221

"Prince Callas of House Ladearis was the crown prince of Kahmarr, who was left stranded upon Tayna due to the attack that destroyed Hailys and the other cities upon Tayna," Garth started as his eyes swept around the room, taking in all the humans around them. There was a steeliness in them now that put Walker on his guard. "His wife was a strong Visionary and foresaw all of us here and now," he stated flatly, as established fact. "I did bring along a copy of the vids taken when we found the vault beneath Matlowe Village for you to watch. It was where we found the hidden library, we never even suspected exited, and it'll still take us years to fully understand the full treasure of knowledge they left for us in it." He held out the chip to Commander Kaminski to take, having deftly refused to hand it to a helpful aide, who had stepped up to take it.

"You've been in the vault," he said, "so you'll recognize this place."

"The library," he replied, nodding in understanding. Walker seemed to suddenly recall it too, having taken his report about that village before, and the inheritance of the two young daughters out of the past Garth had gained during that visit. The drones' recording had given them an interesting glimpse. James smiled as he stood up and stepped over to accept the precious recording, understanding the trust extended in this moment. Garth gave him a nod as he returned to his station and placed it into the slot to display the recording.

"This first part is our discovery of the vault and opening it up," Garth stated. The lights dimmed automatically, as Garth sat down and it began, showing what the drones recorded that day. If he came to trust these men enough, he would then show them the whole recording from the master crystal. But today was not that day with the charged emotions in the room, so they would only see the first part of it. The copies of the documents, still in the tube, would do the rest. Afterwards would come an accounting of an attempted willful destruction of his property, also known as Winterhaven.

"Ryes, I hate to interrupt you, but something's been detected moving inbound to our system, and we need you to check it out. We're not sure what it is," Neil projected through Raya, having run up and realized it was the only way he'd be able to get her attention. All their other Talents were already joined in the circle, participating in the group session.

"I'll have a look, immediately," she assured him, then slipped control of the link, itself, to Raya, Rhodi and her Aunt Adina. She hesitated for the barest moment, unwilling to expose too much to

222

these strange humans, but this was a true need.  She opened Empath fully, unleashing her power pool, too.  She stretched out, realizing the newcomers to their circle were astounded at her immense power and abilities.  She felt Adina instantly filtering their feedback from her, leaving her with only what she needed to concentrate upon for the moment.  Neil directed her, getting his bearings, unused to seeing the solar system directly.  She swept the area and found the tiny, familiar ship.  She homed in on it, noting it was still functioning, and inbound to their platform.

"Tell the Challenger and the Wrath that it's only the Quicksilver coming in.  She belongs to Monty and Connor and is theirs to examine, when she arrives," she informed Neil.  She felt the wash of surprise and delight from Connor, but the need to get a closer look from Monty.  Neil cut out of their inner meld, half glad he didn't have a Talent of his own, half wanting one badly.  He activated his headset to relay the information stat.

"I'm going to make sure she wasn't followed," Ryes told the rest, then stretched out, lightly brushing the trader again.  She traced back along her course, doing wide, slow sweeps, to make sure there were no traces of any following ships.  None showed.

"You will want to scatter the traces from her engines, so it will not be so easily tracked," Hadu sent in suggestion.  She had no idea of how to do such a thing, so he showed her, using her Talents, just as Mitt and Sayer loved to do.  She let him, knowing she was very grateful to learn new skills, and they shortly had the entire area cleared of both her traces, as well as the Earth ships' from before. Then, on an impulse, Ryes returned to where she destroyed the Paws' Scrape, looking to see if the Snags had finished their investigation of its destruction.  There were still two ships in the area.  They didn't look like any she'd seen before and wondered what kind of ship they were?

"Show these to Garth and Sabin when they return," Maren urged.  She held her distance, recalling the machinery the starmen of old had, which responded to the presence of Talent.  She hoped the Snags didn't have such machines too, but just in case, decided to keep her distance.  She pulled back toward Monrush, dispersing the rest of the engine particle trails from the three warships, which remained as their backtrail.  No more Snags ships were seen heading toward Tayna, at least.  She did one last check on the entire system, making sure everything was secure, then brought them back to where they'd been at the start.

"You do this often?" Lt. Blair Nesbit questioned, still astounded by the whole experience, now understanding Alec's memories more. At least Ryes seemed exhaustive in her searches.; recognizing her own twinge of jealousy.

"At least three times a day, yet there're times when it's not enough," she admitted. "The warning satellites are invaluable."

"Those Snag ships were new and definitely different. I wonder what they're doing?" Alec pressed, wanting Ryes' opinion, and as a warning for an inner anxiety he suddenly felt concerning them. It might be from his Visionary Talent? It was so new to him, and he still needed to learn his new ability.

"I'll make a more thorough examination of them later, but only upon Garth's approval," she replied. "Let's hope they're not headed this way."

"You knew the name of the destroyed Snagospin ship. How?" Torr asked, still puzzling out the whole experience; he wasn't surprised by the voyage, having been on several trips with Ryes now.

"I found it out from the Snag Talent, whose Talent I burnt out, that it was the ship's name. Too bad it's too far out and too dangerous an area for us to try to retrieve the scrap metal," she stated.

"Why? Two of your moons are iron-rich. Why not mine them, yourselves?" Lt. Ken Burger questioned, puzzled.

"Scrap metal's already been refined and processed. We can usually reuse it for our new projects more quickly. Mining involves extracting it from the earth, smelting it down for the pure ore, and refining it with the proper metal blends. It's more labor intensive, destructive for the environment, and we don't have the manpower, nor time, right now. There's still plenty of metal lying around untouched in Hailys and the other great city ruins. When that metal's gone, then we'll have to start mining our moons and asteroids," Mitt explained. "I'm planning a trip out to Hailys soon, before the snows start."

"You mean one which involves dragging me out?" Ryes asked, humor in her mental tones.

"Bingo! Only I'm keeping the prize," she returned merrily.

"You're too much in demand," Maren teased his cousin.

"Don't remind me," she replied, and saw Adina was amused that they'd forgotten the others gathered here with them, already. "I'd best relay the information on those new Snag ships, right away," she decided, peripherally having felt Alec's anxiety about them, then withdrew from the commune. It was almost time for their session to end, anyway. She opened her eyes, seeing Maren and Monty also leaving the group.

"Can't go anywhere without you guys," she teased as she got to her feet.

"Mitt said you were doing something to one of the Challenger's shuttles, the last time you were up there.  Is it ready for some tests?  I'd like to see the Quicksilver, for myself," Monty pressed, hoping.

"Ah, so you think those Snag ships might be important enough to relay immediately, too?" she returned.

"Well, you should do another check on the Challenger, to make sure, after last night," Maren hinted, knowing some of the Terran Talents were right here among them.  Ryes laughed, nodding her head.

"I guess we could take a quick jaunt up," she agreed.  Connor removed himself from the circle and stood up, too.

"Where're you going?" he pressed with hope burning in his eyes. "I still have today and tomorrow off."

"Topside," Monty replied, as they exited the dining hall, where they held today's practice, since there was icy-cold rain off and on this morning and headed up to the main corridor. "You'll have to ask Ryes if you can come along," he added, smiling over his shoulder, as he reached the doors.

"May I, Ryes?  I've only been on the Aurora, on her trip out here from Trinity," he pleaded. "I love space travel, so far."  Ryes sighed, then nodded her head in agreement, giving in.

Of the colonists and station personnel they gathered from Trinity and Guardian, all but two decided to settle upon Tayna.  Most filled in the many vacancies in Winterhaven and on Flutter-wing.  They were presently being housed in the old rooms below, as were the people they'd rescued from Hailys' past, with some helping with the construction of their own homes, above ground.  Kovin was pressing to have the exteriors finished before the cold weather set in.  He thought they'd have this last addition completed before Winterfest.  They truly were a small town already.  There were some shops going up, opposite their new community hall, ready for occupation by the spring.  The community hall, itself, would be opening right after the Fall Gather, and then they could start the new, bigger library.  Garth, Ethan, Metta, and the rest of their core group had already worked out a monetary base and the wages for the residents.  It was only getting everything tallied and established.

"Alright, you can come along," she replied, giving in.  Maren gave her a sidelong glance but didn't say anything. "Let's go see which shuttle's available."  She passed her own office, heading down for Garth's. That way, she could use his terminal, yet avoid any pressing issues which had arisen in the last two hours. She realized these new ships might truly be important.

"Sir, a Lady Ryes has some important information to relay to her husband," an ensign stated, having come in to tell the First the news. James was stationed on the end of the conference table, closest to the door, to control entry for the room.

"Please conduct Lady Ryes of House Li, with all due respect, into the room," he instructed in a low voice. He then typed in a quick alert to Captain Walker. A few moments later, the door opened again and Ryes, escorted by the ensign and one of her own guards, entered the room. Garth and the others looked over at Lindell's prompting, wondering what the problem could be?

"Sorry to interrupt, but I've something we felt might be important enemy information," she told her husband while looking straight at him, feeling very out of place among all these stuffy men. It was their attitude, as if they outranked her socially and she was beneath them. She knew she was of descent of two royal houses now, and actually outranked them, so walked with dignity and composure down the room at Garth's signal of invitation. Her stomach was filled with flutter-wings, but she was determined not to show it. Monty stayed beside the door, seeing that would be enough.

Monty, being on guard duty, had done a light sweep of the minds of the others in the room, seeing Sabin doing the same and was approving of his check. They both knew one of the human officers in the room also had Mind Voice, but was not as light a touch as they, and was easily blocked. But he knew to never try to scan Ryes, nor the other Winterhaveners, so he had to use his imagination. They operated under specific rules in Winterhaven for Mind Voice Talents, and he understood the reasons. Garth and Ryes both felt everyone deserved to have their own thoughts private to some extent, and only allowed heavier thought-scans when a situation called for it; light surface thoughts usually gave enough a warning of current intent.

"What's so important?" he requested in a low, even voice, now that she was beside him, proud of her comportment and composure. It was as if she wore a formal gown, instead of jeans and a T-shirt.

"We had an alert of movement in-system. I checked it out and it was the Quicksilver, still inbound. Then decided to check the area where I destroyed the Snag ship and discovered two very new

226

and different ships there.  I didn't know if they could detect my use of Talent, so didn't get any closer," she explained, meeting his eyes.

"They're not any of the ones displayed in the archives?" Sabin pressed, frowning.

"No, I've never seen their like.  I had the feeling they were Snagospin from their overall appearance, but I've no idea what they're capable of, nor why they were there - just sitting in the same spot - where the other ship was destroyed."

"Show me," Garth urged, getting up to let her sit in his seat. She cast him a quick smile and complied.  She sat and composed herself as Garth, Sabin and Ethan crowded around her, kneeling.  She extended out her hands, ready to take them to see them for themselves.  Captain Yun stood and moved around the room and knelt next to Ethan, grasping her arm, too, as he saw the others either take a hand, or clasp onto her arm.  He was going to see this directly for himself!

Ryes made sure everyone was secure, then unleashed her Empath Talent, taking them out to Mondash, first.  The men were astounded by her ease in moving through space, as if she were flying. Amused by their reactions, she went from there, speeding back along the route the Earth ships traveled, quickly finding the two waiting Snagospin ships.  She stopped and circled them warily, feeling something strange about them.  It had her nerves on edge, as before, but she had no idea why she felt this way.

"I've never seen Darken ships like these.  They're large, but there's no sense of a larger crew in them," Yun commented, amazed he could sense all this, seeing it as if they were physically floating out in space.  Being able to sense things through Ryes' Talents was an amazing experience and far more than what Alec showed him before. Maybe being in direct, physical contact made the difference?

"There's danger here.  Call up your Inner Sight.  We've got to know more," Garth ordered, edgy by some instinct; these ships made him uncomfortable, too, realizing his didn't stem from her unease. Something didn't feel right.

She did as he wished and it came through, screaming loudly to her Talent that these were Listening ships.  They were trying to track the Earth ships.  It was apparent they believed the ship had been attacked by one of the human ships.  There were no Snag Talents here, which was a small comfort, but there was something here which told her that if she moved against them with her Talents, it'd be recognized, noted, and reported.  He wished he knew where that report would be sent.

"Their machinery is aware, on some level, of my Talent," she informed Garth and the others.

"How fast are you?" Sabin pressed, needing to know, seeing it was very important now.

"Not fast enough," she replied, a small flash of the exploding board from the previous night crossed through her thoughts. "I've never tried to practice for speed," she admitted.

"You're going to do so, now," Garth assured her, glad she hadn't let more out about that explosion to Wing. He and Lindell didn't need to know the details. "I want you to make an attempt at one of these ships in a few days. Let's see how they stack up against your Talents. See if you can detect their weak spots from here," he encouraged, hoping she could. Ryes turned and studied the ships, seeing several ways to instantly take them out, after a few minutes.

"All right, I'll go practice speed. I'm taking Monty and Connor out for a quick look at the Quicksilver today," she informed him.

"That'll take days!" Sabin protested. Then he clearly felt her humor coming through the commune.

"I've been working on one of the new shuttles. I don't think it'll take that long," she promised.

"One from the Challenger?" Ethan pressed, quickly getting her affirmation.

"Alright, just as long as you practice on your speed techniques today, too," Garth told her, then urged her to return them to the Wrath. She did so, then gently released them, as she opened her eyes.

"Thank you, Lady Ryes," Wing told her with a merry smile, then got to his feet. "Amazing! I feel like a kid just getting off a virtual flight and wanting to jump right back on. So, this is what Talent's like? I can see why it's taken your people generations to perfect such abilities," he commented, giving her a small bow, then returned to his seat, still grinning. Ryes smiled as she stood up, so Garth could sit down again, but he wrapped his arms about her, giving her a tight hug, before letting her go.

"Be careful," he warned in a low voice. She smiled and nodded her head.

"I will," she assured him. "And you're most welcome, Captain Yun," she added in a more normal voice, turning his way, as she was released. Ethan chuckled and nodded his head in agreement.

"And the roller coaster only gets better," he said, giving her a merry wink. She laughed at this, then turned and practically danced, quickly leaving the room, giving James a small bow on her way out, soliciting a chucked from the First.

"That went pretty well," she told Monty, as they headed quickly back to their shuttle, making their military escort trot to catch up. He chuckled, being able to well imagine it, himself. He'd seen her early reconnoiter of the ships, already.

"Could you please brief us all on this new situation, which was so important as to interrupt our conference?" Walker demanded, in icy tones, as he glared at Garth across the table. No one had volunteered anything in the several minutes following Ryes' departure. In contrast, Garth smiled, appearing very relaxed and confident. It irked Walker immensely, but he couldn't do more about it in this moment.

"There seems we've now seen a new Snagospin ship, we never knew existed, before," Garth volunteered. "I was still trying to think of how we're going to respond to this new threat."

"What kind of ships are they? What did you learn?" Walker asked calmly, realizing the young man was talking again.

"Listening ships," Yun answered. "Set as sentries to detect any starship traffic, or communications in the area. They're set in a sector that is right in the path we were taking to Monrush. The rest of our ships can be in danger. I was wondering if she can be fast enough to take them out, before they can send out a distress signal," he added, looking at the Winterhaven team.

"It's the only hope any other Earth ships will have," Ethan responded, while Garth gave him a nod.

"We still don't know how fast they will scramble to get more ships out to that sector, but Ryes is our best bet to take them out from a safe distance," Sabin agreed.

"When can she get started?" Walker finally voiced, understanding now what these men had been thinking about. Marta gave him a subtle nod of her head to affirm they were speaking the truth.

"She needs to practice speed first, so it might be a little bit yet," Rowan answered.

"She needs to be faster than a thought, to beat the machines," Garth added, sweeping a look at the military humans in the room.

"Can anyone do that?" Devin pressed, worried.

"I believe in Ryes.  She will do it," Ethan assured them with a firm confidence written in his bright, blue eyes.

"She's a mother, so has to already be faster than her children," Yun supplied with a chuckle.  This got the rest to laughing in understanding.

# The Quicksilver

## Chapter 19

"There she is," Ryes told them, after a six-hour trip.  They had traded the Avenger for the Avenger II from the Challenger, before heading out to the Silver, so it'd been a far faster trip.  Monty and Connor looked up from their reading with relieved smiles, Maren stirred from his nap.  The Quicksilver was finally within sight.  She dumped the velocity, waiting for the ship to approach them, reaching out to her with her Inner Sight, to reassure the ship's computer that they were friendly.  After another few minutes of maneuvering, they grappled themselves to the side of the ship.  Everyone donned lighter space suits, to personally check the condition of the ship.

"I never realized how large she was," Connor commented in an awed voice, touching the piece of her hull he still wore about his neck, under his shipsuit.

"Next to the Challenger?" Ryes teased, grinning as she led them aboard.

"Alright, not so when compared with her," he agreed, looking about, as they walked the main corridors.  She led them to a ladder, and they climbed upwards for what seemed a long time, passing several hatches and landings, finally emerging in a room below the bridge.

"What is this place?" Monty questioned, seeing only seats before computer stations and a large, blank screen on one wall.

"I think communications and bridge support," Ryes replied, cycling the access to their destination, then climbed the stairs up.

"There's no bodies.  What happened to the survivors?"  Maren asked, looking around at the sterile room around them.

"The story went that they used the pods to escape to a nearby world, to await a rescue," Monty related, giving Ryes a hand with the heavy hatch.

"No, the story went that they all committed suicide, when they discovered they couldn't repair the ship," Connor stated, sure of what he'd been told.  Maren huffed at this, shaking his head at such a choice, disapproving both outright.

"Then no one knows for sure what happened," Maren added and watched as they got the hatch open and were shining their lights up inside. He started up the stairs behind them, when a small machine entered the room, stopping just inside. "Ryes, what's this?" he demanded.

"Oh, a waldo, I believe is what they're called," she replied, turning back to see it below them. She reached out to it, finding it was here to help repel boarders, so she shut it off. It was armed and had been about to fire upon Maren. She then searched for all others, with similar programs and shut them down, too. "It's off for now. It was about to attack you, so I shut them all down," she told him. He quickly mounted the stairs behind them, wanting as far from it as possible. Conner at his side, appearing alarmed, then moved up in Monty's wake, past Ryes. She let him, looking to understand.

"I don't care if you've deactivated it, I won't consider it safe, until this ship knows us," Maren emphatically stressed.

"We're going to take care of that, right now," she assured him, as she realized both Monty and Connor were already up on the bridge. She followed, with Maren close behind. Connor was examining the helm station, while Monty was fingering the captain's small console. She stepped over to the main computer board, recognizing it. She brought up the lights, so they could see better, then extended out with her Inner Sight, so she could get a feel for this ship, once more.

"Monty, could you step over here, please?" she requested. He did so, wondering why. Ryes opened her eyes, meeting his. "It has a specific genetic code instilled within its matrix as identification of its true owners. We'll need to let it get a `taste' of you first, before we'll be able to assure it that you're its rightful owners," she told him. "You'll all have to remove a glove and your helm," she minded them all, meeting everyone's eyes as she broke the seal on her own helmet first. "I've pressurized the cabin, already." Connor had stepped over.

"If you're sure," he returned, hesitating for a few seconds, not trusting the old tech.

"Yes, it's required, and I made sure all the areas we're using are pressurized. I'm going to do some work on her engines, while you and the Quicksilver get acquainted," she urged, then sat down in the seat, leaving them standing and facing the board. Monty saw where he was supposed to place his hand, so removed what she advised and did so. There was a feeling of one of his fingers being nipped, then he withdrew it, seeing a small nick which clotted quickly, and waited.

"State your name," the computer intoned in a bass voice, which startled them.

"Montague Daniel Elbridge," he told it, enouncing clearly.

"Hold still for a face scan.  Your eyes should remain open and unblinking," it ordered.  He did, not sure if he truly wanted to go through all this, but realized Ryes was right.  They had to establish their ownership of this ship, eventually.  He faced it squarely, letting it scan his face, as it would.

"Your orders Captain Elbridge?" it requested.

"Maintain your course and heading.  You will be docking with our small space platform designated Flutter-wing.  The ship attached to your side right now is to be considered a friend.  The other ships docked at, or near, the platform will be classified as friends.  Do not initiate hostile actions against any of the ships already described," he ordered, wanting to make sure it wouldn't cause any further problems.

"Aye, Captain," it responded, bringing a smile to his lips. Connor huffed a laugh.

"Play for me the last three entries in your main ship's log." Connor and Maren crowded close as the large screen blanked, then displayed the face of an older, rugged man, who had the same blue eyes, lips, forehead, and chin, which Monty and Connor displayed. This had the attention of all three men.

"They're catching up to us.  We're so far out of known space that we don't know if we can even find our way home.  I can't believe the arrogance of Rider and his crew.  They can't believe they can take us.  We'll wait and see.  I don't think their ship can take this punishment, any more than ours.  Elbridge, signing off."  There were video and scan records added for several long minutes before the screen blanked.  Then the next report began.

"It's been a bloody fight.  We managed to repel their boarding party, but I don't think we'll be able to take another.  Please remember Cath Elbridge, Patrick Setter, Thom Tierny, Mick Lani, and Marsha Elbridge to their families, in case we don't make it back to Guardian and Trinity.  We've got a bold plan in the works.  If this works, it'll look bad, but won't really cripple us.  They've grappled us and are trying to cut into our hull.  I'll make my next entry - if and only if - our plan works!  Otherwise, I'll self-destruct the ship!  No one, but family, will ever get their hands on the Quicksilver!  Elbridge, signing off."  Again, there were videos added, with the fighting to repel the boarders looked bloody and hard.  There was some data from the scans displayed before it blanked.  Monty's eyes widened, seeing some of the battle scenes.  Connor looked pale, while Maren grimaced.  The Quicksilver may have lost crew, but the pirates lost far more people.

233

"It worked and yet it didn't.  We blew out compartments seventeen through twenty-three, axial positive, and blew Rider's ship away from ours.  It still has power and is now limping away - for good, we pray.  I'm letting the ship drift for now, to encourage whoever's still alive that we're dead.  We're down to a mere dozen crewmembers, as is.  We only have stasis chambers left to support ten, so we're drawing straws, with the remaining two taking their chances with that big, blue world, which beckons nearby.  The computer says there's enough oxygen and water there to support human life, but we've no idea what toxins exist, or dangers to face from the wildlife.  Still, we're taking the chance.  The ship is in no condition to survive a landing.  To any who find this fine ship, Quicksilver deserves a noble end, not being scrapped.  We're leaving our personal effects in the crew's lounge.  Please make sure our families get them, as a last request.  Captain Montigue Marius Elbridge, signing off, for the last time."  There was video showing the blast, the unexpected problems which developed with their own ship, and the pirate ship leaving, still under power.  There was the tearful separation as the captain and a woman left, bound for a nearby, blue, and green planet.  Afterwards, there was more data information, including a star chart fixing the world, where they left the couple.

"A great-great of yours, Monty?" Ryes asked, having finished, and opened her eyes during the last entry.  He huffed and smiled, nodding his head in reply. "I have the engines running the best they can for now, so she's only a few days out.  I'll give them my `special treatment,' once she arrives."

"Thank you, Ryes.  Computer, you will recognize these people with me.  The Chief Executive Officer of Winterhaven upon Tayna, Ryes of House Li, the Chief Medical Officer of Winterhaven upon Tayna, Maren, and my great nephew, Connor Lee Elbridge from Trinity.  All these people are friendly and welcome aboard this ship," Monty ordered.

"Aye, Captain," it replied.  He sighed as they each offered their hands and faces for the computer, which was very like the Challenger, then afterward, he turned to the others.

"Let's go find these chambers, which might still be operational, and see if any of our family still survives.  I wonder how long my great-great grandfather lived on that world?" he questioned, smiling as he still felt strange about being the captain of his own ship.  Maren gave him a nod of his head, his eyes merry.

"We'll hope, at least.  And since the cold of space itself was in here, maybe the ones here are still preserved?" Maren then turned to head down the stairway again.  The others were right behind him.  He knew Ryes would find them for him.

"Only three out of ten were still left," Ryes told Denas, as she sat down to a late dinner. The cubs were already settled at home, and she was enjoying the moment to unwind. "Maren has them over in Medical, undergoing some therapy to help them readjust. And we brought back the bodies of the rest, so we can give them a proper farewell, once the Quicksilver reaches Flutter-wing."

"And Monty's sure he wants to stay with the ship, all the way in?" Denas questioned, feeling helpless with his decision – he was so far away. Ryes smiled at this, nodding her head.

"He asked me if I could fly you out to him in the morning if you want to come. He's going to go over the former captain's effects, since he is his heir, and get the logs and other things in order, as much as he can. I'll be flying out some supplies, so you're more than welcome to accompany me," Ryes offered. Denas smiled, suddenly liking that idea. This way she could get a true feel for this mystery ship inheritance from his family.

"Thank you, cousin. I believe I will go with you. Is there anything you think I should bring along?"

"Warm, winter clothing for you both. It's still far too cold in there, for my tastes," she teased, smiling.

"What kind of cargo was she carrying?" Jim asked, wondering. He'd just finished his security checks and was grabbing something before going home.

"I don't know. I forgot to check the manifest," she admitted, embarrassed, turning to Connor. "Did you check?"

"No, I didn't think of it either," he replied, blushing.

"That shuttle's something else," Torr stated loudly, with a big smile, coming into the room with Garth and Sabin behind him.

"The Avenger II's truly fast," Ryes agreed, having set her down on their landing pad here in Winterhaven. She was in the hangar already, to keep her away from the Aurora's crew. Even Alec was restricted from going near her.

"Mitt's having a field day with her. She kept saying, 'Yes, that's it! Yes, that's right!'" Garth told her with a chuckle. "I haven't seen her so excited, in a very long time."

"Mitt, Tieva and Prias are probably the only ones who could properly appreciate her. With Axel being the next one, after them," she returned with a merry smile, then turned her attention back to her dinner, feeling sorry for Monty right now. He was stuck with whatever he could defrost out of the stored provisions on the ship. They'd sealed and fully pressurized the main cabin areas he'd need, keeping his suit at hand, in case. She'd had the air, water and heat exchangers going, but didn't have much faith in the heaters. Monty thought it was fine, but she noticed he was shivering.

"So, when will you have the rest of the shuttles finished?" Sabin asked. "They're larger and faster than the human ones."

"When I get the time. We have the Great Fall Gather to attend next week and you three left it all in my hands," she reminded him, glancing up to see the surprise upon all their faces.

"Already?" Torr questioned, looking like he had forgotten to check ahead on his schedule.

"I know, you haven't let me forget," Garth returned, chuckling. He went and got a fresh mug of tea, returning to sit down next to his wife.

"Actually, everything's ready. I'll be sending off the rovers in another two days, with your father in charge. I think your parents rather enjoy the road trips. They're getting to see more of Tayna now, then ever in their lives before. Marla was talking to me about them borrowing one of the smaller rovers and venturing out next spring," Ryes informed him, sure he hadn't taken the time to talk with his own parents in weeks. She then finished the last forkful she felt she could eat, feeling stuffed and thoroughly satisfied. Maren appeared in the doorway, then headed to get his own dinner.

"They did enjoy the scenery and stopping to meet new people in the farms and villages we passed through, going out and returning from the last gather," Sabin commented, smiling at the surprised look on Garth's face. "Your parents are older than you and can do as they see fit, too. I don't see a problem with loaning them one of the smaller rovers, so they can see some of Tayna. They might even get people more familiar with The Laws."

"They lived in Matlowe all their lives. Now you drag them out and show them there's more to the world. What did you expect? For them to stick here in Winterhaven, when they haven't even explored this side of the Yuri?" Torr chided his cousin. Garth chuckled at this, nodding his understanding.

"There are ways across the Yuri. How do you think the caravaners trade with the sunny, southern cities? Do you know,

Dodi's light-colored hair, and Saree's white hair, would be highly prized down there?  You'd have to constantly watch that they weren't nabbed," Ryes told them. "There're many different customs on this small world.  I advised Marla that she and Garvin needed to talk to Darman about the roads, and customs practiced, in the regions they planned upon exploring.  And that we would be sending guards along to help - just in case.  Personally, I'd feel better if they'd journey with a caravan for their first venture."

"White hair, like our cubs?  And what about you, with your green eyes?" Garth teased, smiling as he looked down at her.

"It was what Rowan used to worry about all the time when I was little.  I guess there aren't a lot of women born with green eyes, anywhere," she returned, smiling back.

"And we're not even going to let on about her Talents.  I'm sure enough of that's already happened, by now," Maren added, sitting down across from Ryes. "So, have you already figured out security for this coming Gather?"

"Of course," Ryes assured him, picking up her mug to sip her tea. "We're going to keep our established perimeter wall, but I'll see if I can expand it and interweave more scanning devices this time.  It'll be easier to watch and control who comes and goes.  We actually had some people trying to scale it at that spring gather, so I might build in some deterrents and electrify the top of the wall, so any that make it that far will get a light shock – just to be sure."

"It's too bad we can't have the computer tag everyone, so we'd know where they were, all the time, like on our big hunts in Hailys," Torr commented, having returned with a mug of tea and a bubblenut custard cup.

"But we can," Garth replied, suddenly getting an idea. "Personnel transmitter locators.  They're in storage here to use if a ship full of colonists came out to settle this world.  The humans use them to keep track of new colonists, in case of sudden evacuations, or any unexpected problems encountered, where they need to find their location.  We could `tag' our own people, to make sure we could find someone, in case of an emergency.  That way we don't have to rely upon Ryes, all the time."

"It sounds a little invasive to me, from the stories I've heard about old Earth and her colonies," Sabin commented, not quite sure if it was necessary. "Let's discuss the tagging with Rowan, Metta and Ethan, first."  Garth gave him a nod, while Ryes looked thoughtful for a few moments.

"Now wait a minute. I'm not the only Empath here!" she protested, looking up to meet Garth's eyes. "When was the last time you practiced finding our cubs? Now that we have two, new daughters, you'd better find the time."

"You want me to practice more?" he asked, chuckling as he put an arm around her shoulders, hugging her to his side.

"Why not? I now have to practice speed," she returned. She lifted a spoon off her tray, sent it around the perimeter of the room, stopping it right before Garth's nose after a couple of heartbeats of time. He laughed at this, nodding his head.

"Faster. You must make it go faster," he urged. "Faster than thought, fast enough to surprise a computer."

"Can anyone ever hope to get that fast?" Torr questioned, surprised, feeling he was being unfair to hold Ryes to such expectations.

"I'll do the best I can," she answered, seeing now what her husband was suggesting. She had to beat the Snag ship to the punch before its computer would even know she struck. She had no idea how she was going to do it, but knew she had to try.

"I have only heard of one person being that fast," Denas told her, smiling, "and he was only a legend." Ryes smiled behind her mug, thinking she might have a chance... Most legends had a basis in fact, somewhere.

"Sorry, but I couldn't leave the cubs behind, today. They're still getting used to us and everything here," Ryes apologized to Monty, after they docked with the Quicksilver. He smiled warmly at this, nodding his head in understanding, seeing everyone was dressed in winter clothing, and gratefully took the jacket she offered him, quickly donning it.

"The Silver's computer will just have to get used to all of us from Winterhaven, anyway," he assured her. "I've already told it that we're setting down near the Quest, so she can get some proper repairs. She's made for landings and the equipment I'll need for the landing tests okay. I think the waldos did a lot of repairs through the years of drifting."

"You are going to attempt to land this ship? It could be dangerous, with the way she looks," Denas questioned, stepping into the cabin, looking around at the neatness.  Monty was always one for keeping things clean and tidy.  His smile widened, as he stepped up to her and wrapped his arms about her, giving her a welcoming kiss.  She returned it with equal joy, her eyes lighting up, at seeing he missed her as much as she missed him.

"If you want to stay with me, the two of us will attempt it," he promised her, after their lips parted.  She sighed, then relaxed.  Yes, she'd face down the denizens of the Demon Gates itself, standing at his side.

"I brought along our winter weight clothing.  It is a little nippy in here," she replied.  He laughed at this, letting her go.

"Are you one of our new uncles?" Chatis questioned, now standing beside Monty and Denas.  Monty squatted down, so he was on the girls' level.

"Not really, but if you feel better calling me Uncle Monty, you're free to do so," he assured her.  Chatis threw her thin, tiny arms about his neck, hugging him as she gave him a wet kiss on the cheek.  Calla just smiled happily.

"Wonderful, Uncle Monty and Aunt Denas.  I love having so many new people in my family," she declared.  Monty was laughing heartily as he hugged her back, giving her a kiss, too.  He appeared to savor this moment with Chatis, and Ryes saw he was going to be a great father to his own children.

"Cousin..." Ryes started but saw Denas shaking her head.  Ryes understood.  They were young. "Let's get the supplies brought aboard, so we can give the ship a quick once over, then stop by Flutter-wing to do some repairs there, then scoot to the Challenger.  I have to give your Aunt Mitt a hand with something, too."

"What's with the Challenger?" Monty questioned as they followed Ryes back to the Avenger II, to get the containers she brought along for them.

"The engines are ready for testing.  We have a few other projects to finish first, before she can start her test runs.  We don't want any of the other systems breaking down while we conduct our tests," Ryes told him, as Calla darted in front of her, grabbing one of the smallest boxes, which she allowed her and Chatis to carry earlier when they were loading.

"That big ship is so big," she scolded, as she turned to look up at her new mother. "How can you and Aunt Mitt fix it?"

"We use our Talents," she explained as she picked up a box, which Denas took out of her arms. She and Chatis quickly returned for more boxes, heading back for the Silver. Ryes smiled as she shook her head, then stepped aside to let Monty past with the three he was carrying. "I guess I get the last one," she sighed, picking up the lone carton. She gave Calla a wink, then lead her back to the ship.

"Do I have Talent? Mother thought I might," she asked, as she followed Ryes. She was still getting used to her new mother's face and that she was always doing something. She was so busy, most of the time, but did spend evenings with them.

"I'll check on our way to the Challenger. I should've checked both you girls, last night," she told her, handing Monty her box, so he could put it where he wanted. Denas took Calla's, too, resisting to have a look for herself.

"Let's take everyone to the remote bridge and make sure the Silver knows all of you," Monty suggested, wanting to make sure he got the ship's computer familiar with all his dear friends and family.

"What would the computer do, if it does not know us, Uncle Monty?" Calla questioned, frowning as she looked up to him in a haughty manner.

"It could hurt you, thinking you were a bad person. So, I want to make sure it knows you're a good person, so it won't try to hurt you," he explained. She sighed, then gave him a nod of her head in permission. He chuckled as he led them up the stairs to the bridge support compartment. She was a princess all right, he thought.

"Hi Corsley, I'm here to help," Ryes told him as he met her and the girls, as soon as she had the shuttle docked. Seeing his face, she was glad she stopped by, before heading to the Challenger.

"We truly appreciate your stopping over," he replied, the relief was plain upon his face, and that it gave her a moment's guilt.

"What's wrong?" she asked, taking Chatis and Calla's hands. "And is the children's area available and staffed?" she asked. He smiled confidently now and gave her a nod.

"Yes, it is. Let us head there first, then I will give you an overview of our concerns," he advised. As he led them to the children's area, Ryes noted the many humans in the corridors. Some were in uniform, while other weren't, but none of them smiled, nor greeted them as they passed. A few were surprised when they recognized her, but that was the only possibly positive reaction she got from them, as most just glared, as if they were trespassing on their space port. Some had shoulder patches for the Orit's Tablet, some from the Aries' Wrath. She struggled to resist looking into their thoughts right now. But she was thoughtful by the time they reached the nursery zone.

After entrusting her daughters to two of Winterhaven's own women, she walked with Corsley to his office, so they could go over what was needed for Flutter-wing. Again, she noted the reactions of the Dirters as they walked the passageways. It was starting to make her angry. This was the space station she built. Their presence was by invitation only, and they should be bound by hospitality traditions, as were the station personnel, but perhaps they had no understanding of what was expected? She would address that, as soon as she could get to a terminal, after she helped Corsley!

They arrived at his office and they both greeted by Jherr, who originally was a slave Rowan and Ethan purchased at the Great Spring Gather. Currently, he was Corsley's office assistant, but had come from a village on the east coast, across the western sea. Once he realized he was free to choose where to live and the life path he wanted, he stayed in Winterhaven working and learning all he could. When Flutter-wing was opened, he chose this as the place he felt more at home – even if he'd never been in space before.

"Still loving the view from on high?" Ryes asked, before heading into Corsley's office. A huge, happy smile blossomed across Jherr's face as he gave her a nod, his rich brown eyes alight with joy.

"I can't imagine a better place to live," he assured her. She smiled and gave him a nod, heading into Corsley's office, as he followed her, closing the door.

"How can I help you?" she asked, seeing the serious look in his eyes as they sat down. He sighed and looked as if unhappy to bear the news.

"The station systems are inadequate even to meet the needs of the two human ships currently docked. I worry what will happen when we are fully running at capacity," he stated, knowing she liked things clear and upfront. "Simple things like the plumbing can't keep up and the security systems here are a laugh." She gave him a nod, understanding. She put the station together, but this was, in truth, the first time it was being used.

"Then, help me fix it," she invited. He appeared puzzled and unsure of what she had in mind. A huge smile lit up her face and green eyes, recalling he truly had no idea what she was capable of doing, nor her Talents.

"Are you going to have a crew up here to get things repaired?" he asked, wondering.

"Close your eyes and let's get started now. I have plenty of energy to spare today," she invited, extending her hand. He understood a bit then, seeing she was going to use her Talent, so gave her a nod and took her extended hand. She closed her eyes, as he did, and once they settled their meld, opened her Pool of Power and her range of Talents, ready to being. Corsley almost fell out of the link when he felt that huge pool of Booster power available but held on with her help.

They began with the tightening of the security measures needed, then updated the defensive measures. In the end they tweaked the original design and got everything functioning more along the lines needed for a starport of this size. Corsley caught a glimpse of the original starport from her Inner Sight tour of it when she was on the Margiiti, which existed during the time he was pulled out of and into this time. He noted some of her adjustments had been made along those lines, which put his heart to ease that she was using a real, working starport as the template. In the end, he was greatly relieved and would do everything possible to help protect this precious treasure he knew as Ryes. He thought back to his friends out of the past and knew none of them would have ever believed this story, if he could have told them. He was still getting comfortable with this station and starting to make new friends now.

# Preparations

## Chapter 20

"Kerry, Axel, I'd like you to meet my two new daughters.  This is Calla and Chatis.  We found them in stasis, beneath Matlowe.  Lady Velka and Prince Callas made sure I swore I'd raise them as my own," Ryes stated in introduction, smiling as Kerry drifted closer to meet them.  She was due so very soon yet insisted upon being up here with her husband, which she could understand in her own heart.

"They're both so pretty," she commented, smiling. "I'm very pleased to meet you," she told them.  She saw Chatis was uncomfortable with the weightlessness, clinging to Ryes, closely. "What's the matter, sweetie?" she asked her.

"My ol' Da died fixin' a st'rship engine.  And this st'rship is a lot bigger than that one," she replied.  Ryes was hugging her with one arm, while anchoring herself with the other hand.  Calla was holding onto Ryes, but not so desperately.

"But we won't go near the engines, ourselves," Mitt assured her, smiling as she flew into the lounge. "Maybe we should initiate gravity for the little ones?" she asked Axel.  He nodded his head, seeing how they were unused to it, unlike Ryes' youngest ones.

"Go ahead, Mitt.  Come on, darlin'.  Nothing's going to happen to your new Mom.  I'd never let it," he assured her.  Calla let go of Ryes to reach out to Kerry, liking her eyes and smile.

"Mom told us we both have Talent," Calla said, as Kerry caught her outstretched hand, "but it's sleeping for now."

"Your Talent's only supposed to awaken, when it and you are both ready for it," she told her, smiling to see her trust.  She wasn't as afraid of children now, as she'd been last fall.  The long winter, stuck underground, had given her lots of experience.  And she was looking forward to her own son.  The gravity field kicked to life, causing them all to feel heavier again.  They slowly drifted down to the floor, standing up as they settled upright, once more.

"That was fun!  Can we do it, again?" Calla asked, then Axel picked her up and held her up in the air, then began to spin around.  She laughed and screamed in utter delight.  Chatis looked up at her sister with some envy but refused to release her death-grip on Ryes.

"Don't you want to be lifted up, too?" Kerry questioned the other young girl. She wondered how old they were?

"No. I am not going to let anything happen to my new Mother," she protested, almost in tears. Ryes looked upset but didn't know what to do for her, then got an inspiration.

"Then, you can help me," she told her, feeling she finally found the solution. She got down on her knees, so she was on her level, "but, you have to stay very still, while your Aunt Mitt and I do our repairs," she said, meeting her eyes.

"What do I get to do?" Calla asked, as Axel set her down upon her feet, again.

"You get to help me make lunch," Kerry assured her. Calla looked up to her, grinned happily.

"Thank you, Aunt Kerry," she replied, stepping over to take her hand. "I would like that, very much."

"Domesticity wasn't totally wiped out, it seems," she commented, winking at her husband. He chuckled at this, nodding his head.

"I'll be working with the girls. I'd like a good look at `er, myself - their way. I'm a starship engineer, and wished I had their abilities, too," he stated. Mitt, having returned to the lounge, laughed at hearing this.

"All ready, whenever you are boss," she told him. Then the four of them left for engineering. Prias and Cassie were there, waiting for them and smiling when they arrived, ready to start. Since the gravity was on, they sat down and joined hands, with Chatis sitting between Ryes and Mitt. Ryes formed the link, getting everyone settled. This was the first time for Cassie, too. Once everyone was comfortable, she opened her Inner Sight and made all her Talents available. It was the way she and Mitt worked best. With her Booster, they could both draw upon her Talents at need. Even if she'd been busy with the Silver and Flutter-wing, she'd barely touched her reserves. There was plenty of energy for everyone to tap.

"There's still so much to be done," Cassie declared, feeling a little overwhelmed at the number of minor things, still unaddressed. This Talent thing was very interesting and useful!

"We've been concentrating upon the major systems, so far," Mitt explained, as Axel agreed, humored by her concern. The list might seem long, but nothing was impossible now.

244

They explored the main systems, following them through the ship, making adjustments as they went along, seeing where they were needed. Ryes' Inner Sight was as strong as Mitt's now, but they both insisted Prias add in her own. She now saw why. With it, she could draw upon Ryes' Booster and Manipulator Talents, adding in her efforts to theirs, making it a team. Axel directed some of their repairs, catching things they didn't, while Chatis sat in wonder, seeing, and feeling it all. She could finally relax, now understanding how her new Mother worked on the ship's engines. She was safe, just as she said.

"Ah, this is so much easier when there's no gravity," Mitt protested, as she stretched after standing up, when they finished. Ryes was practically tapped out now, but they'd gotten a lot done.

"Your center of gravity's shifted," Ryes quipped back, grinning. "At least you're not carrying four, like I did."

"Thank goodness!" she returned, chuckling at the thought. "The Goddess Korenda was far kinder to me."

"Thank goodness I'm careful!" Cassie teased, laughing as she stood up.

"You're also lucky that Ted and the lab staff developed some new contraceptives," Ryes quipped back, grinning. "At least we're only vulnerable every two to five years, or so. It'll be a while before I have to worry about midnight feedings again."

"Wait until Raby dumps the first grandcub on you," Mitt reminded her. She groaned at this, nodding her head.

"I just leave all that up to Kerry," Axel declared. "Let's go see what she's cooked up for lunch, today."

"Good, then I'll remind Kerry that you can get up to take care of your son, in the middle of the night, too," Mitt quipped back, grinning as he chuckled at this, nodding his head. Ryes picked up Chatis, as she was tired now. Prias looked uncomfortable with their teasing each other. Ryes wondered if it was about the pregnancies, or the sex involved which resulted in the pregnancies?

"Do you know when your next season's due?" she questioned her, in a lower voice, as they followed the others back to the main lounge.

"Maren said not for another two and a half years, or so. I have time to make the adjustments, at least. But I have never been around children. What if I make a mistake?" she asked, in a low voice. Ryes saw she was serious about this and understood. She was still learning a lot about how to raise cubs, as she raised her own.

"We're all here to help each other. Never forget that. I'm still learning about what to do, myself. I may not have my own mother to advise me, but I have my grandfather and both my great aunts if I have questions, and if they think I'm doing something wrong, they will correct me. All life is an adventure, and having babies is only a small aspect of it. I'd never ever regret my cubs - including the ones I've adopted. They remind me to stop and look at the world with new eyes," she related. Cassie was listening to them, curiously. Now she smiled to herself, recalling her older sister saying something like that, long ago.

"Ah, then it is not just having the right man?" Prias questioned, smiling as she saw the happiness in Ryes' eyes. Yes, it was plain that she loved and enjoyed her children - even if some of them were thrust upon her unexpectedly.

"Having the right man is truly important, too. After all, it takes the both of you to manage the family together," she returned.

"But it seems that Garth is always too busy to help much," she protested. Ryes laughed, nodding her head.

"During the day, but in the mornings and evenings, he usually takes over and more than does his part. They're his children too, after all."

"I love it when we get Da on the floor and all tickle each other," Chatis commented, laughing merrily. She and Calla got to help Sayer, Raby and the horde get Garth down for a tickle-fest last night before they went to bed... before Garth and Sabin went to dig out more of the documents from Prince Callas.

"And even if he protests, I think your Da loves it just as much," Ryes assured her, chuckling.

"I remember my brother, sister and I trying to tickle my father, too," Cassie told them, smiling at the memories. "But he was very hard to tickle."

"I wish my father had been like that," Prias added, sighing. "He was always so busy." There were some things she missed, but far more things which she didn't. Her father had been loving, but far too busy to play with her, even when she was little. Yet, she suddenly found she missed him terribly. Yes, long before her next season, she'd have to secure a good husband for her and her cubs. She didn't want them to miss out on the fun and love they deserved.

"Rowan was always so patient with me, so I always imagined my father would've been like that, too.  He died when I was still an infant," Ryes replied, sighing, not seeing the surprise in Cassie and Prias' eyes.

"Garvin, you'd better see what they want," Jim suggested, seeing the two young men didn't intend to get out of the way of their vehicle, as they were rolling down the road.  He slowed the rover, coming to a stop a dozen feet from them.  He lowered his window and beckoned the two over to talk with him, not wanting to leave the rover with the road looking so wild here, it looked overgrown with the dense bushes and trees.  They stepped over with hope in their eyes.

"Sir, I beg you take me and my brother with you.  I've never seen a gather before," the first one said, as they stood next to the rover.  Garvin looked them over.  They were clean and neat, with a carry sac each, thrown over their shoulders.  They both had beltknives and carried large handaxes on their belts.  All perfectly presentable, by his old Matlowe standards.  He smiled, giving them a nod.

"Are you from that farm we passed a few minutes ago?" he asked in return.

"Actually, we're from a farm a half day's walk north from that one.  My name's Galan, and this is my littermate, Gale.  Mom died last winter, and our older brother's new wife doesn't like us much.  We figured this was a way to meet ladies of our own and get away from her screaming for a little while, since the grains and fruits are stored for the winter," the second one replied, nodding his head.

"Sure, why not?  But you'd best behave, or you're back to walkin'," Garvin decided.  He turned and saw the pained look in Jim's eyes, then chuckled, understanding his concerns. "Wynne, could you open the door and let them in?" he requested, turning to see she was closest to it.  She laughed at this, nodding her head.

"The more, the merrier," she agreed, then reached over and released the lock, hitting the door's release, and letting it swing open for them.  She realized her mobility was starting to decrease quite a bit, with carrying this daughter of hers and Chuck's.  She couldn't wait for her to be born!  She was feeling like a grounded blimp, most times now.  The two young men saw the handholds, so climbed up into the rover, edging around Wynne, being motioned up the stairs to seats further back on the upper level of seats.  Their eyes were wide and round as they looked upon the wonders around them - especially the humans.  The seats looked comfortable, and no one seemed crowded in the cabin.  Strange bars of light overhead kept everything visible.

"So, how did you know about us and that we're bound for the Great Fall Gather?" Metta questioned sharply, as the two sat down.  The rover was already in motion again, as they settled, but it wasn't jarring, nor shook anything, as a wagon would; it was a smooth ride.

"Our older brother, Gastis, was at Tanny farm last spring when you came through, heading home.  He told us about your big vans, which didn't need windracers to pull them, and said you'd be coming back for the Fall Gather.  We figured that if we stuck near the road, we might catch you on the way.  We can't thank you enough for the ride," Galan told him, grinning merrily.  Ted chuckled at this, nodding his head, as Minya laughed lightly in agreement.

"We're already becoming known.  Next thing you know, people will expect us to stop to take them on as regular passengers, or to stop and trade with them, enroute," Ted threw out, with a big grin upon his face, getting chuckles and laughter from the rest.

"Are you caravaners, too?" Galan asked, setting his axe under the seat, as Metta quietly directed him.  Huras looked on in approval.  He noted the larger brother was quiet, leaving his sibling to do all the talking for them.  But it looked like he didn't mind.

"No, but we do set up a few booths at the gathers and sell some of the things we make," Leon told him, nodding his head. "Do you two play field ball?" he added, wondering what farmers did for fun?

"Not in a long time," Galan admitted, grinning as he realized he liked these people. "Why do you ask?"

"We have three teams now and I was just wondering.  We're going to compete for the banner for the first time at this gather, and we've only played the Moondance Tribe, Matlowe and Wicker Villages.  And you'll never know when we'll need a substitute player," he replied.

"My brother, Galan, is far better at the game, than I ever was," Gale pressed, cuffing his brother's shoulder as he started to blush. "It'd be more than fair Galan, since they're letting us ride to the gather in this fine van of theirs."

"I could show you how well I play, but I don't think you'll truly be impressed," he offered, understanding what his brother was implying.  It'd be a way to repay them for this great kindness.

248

"You can show me later this evening, when we camp," Leon assured him, liking this young man. He wasn't quite sure about the other and the way his eyes roved, as if trying to memorize details of everything around him. It appeared to be more than just wonder at his surroundings here, as if he were also a spy of some kind.

"How long does it take to get to the gather?" Galan asked, wondering about the distance involved. He glanced out the window and they'd already gone as far as he ever had, in his whole life!

"This is your first?" Minya questioned in return, smiling.

"Yup, but Gale's been to a few, already. He said he'd show me around," he replied. He wondered about her, as she was acting possessive of the strange man, who was sitting next to her. "Have you been to many gathers?"

"I went to the spring gather for a few days. Last time, we flew out in one of the helicopters, this time we decided to ride in one of the rovers," she told him. "My name is Minya, and this is Ted," she introduced them. "Elder Metta sits beside you, with Elder Huras on his other side. And this is Rein and Leon beside me. In the seat, behind us is Wynne, who is nearest the door, Mason beside her, then Shadd and Raffa. Asleep in the netting overhead are some of our little ones. In the seat behind you is Bethy, with her new son, with Tanns and Spann next to her. In the seat across from them is Almas, Ossa, and Kelli. George and Jim are sitting behind the pilot's seat, with Marla in the copilot's seat. Our pilot is Garvin."

"I am Galan, and this is my littermate, Gale. There's so much room in here and it travels so tirelessly," Galan commented, grinning as he shook his head. "What is a hell-a-copper?"

"Helicopter, or chopper for short," Ted corrected him with a smile, as the rest laughed merrily. "It's a flying machine, which uses an overhead, twirling blade to lift upwards upon, but I'm not a mechanic, only a healer. You'll get to see one tomorrow evening."

"You have Talent?" Gale questioned, suddenly looking interested. Ted shook his head as he blushed slightly at this.

"No, I use the skills I learned through a lot of years of schooling and study," he admitted, forgetting they'd think that way, right off. Dolbith contained no word for doctor, after all.

"Why would you spend years in school learning healing?" Galan asked, thinking it would be a lot of work.

"Because Healers with Talent are very rare. I'd rather be able to help others, the best I can, myself. I'm called a `doctor,' in my language," he replied, smiling. They decided to downplay their Talents among strangers, and this was a good way to start, considering he didn't actually have one, anyway.

"That's true and a good idea," he returned. "I'm sorry if I'm being rude, but what are you?" This brought out more laughter as they realized, they'd forgotten that most Taynans hadn't seen a human before.

"I'm called a human, but in truth, we're almost the same people, as there're a few crosses living in Winterhaven," he told him, nodding his head. Now, Galan understood the one, beautiful woman's possessiveness toward this human. He was probably much more than a mere friend to her.

"You must be from very far away, for I've never seen your like before," Gale commented, his eyes sharp, as if he were digging for secrets.

"You could say that," he agreed with a chuckle, as there was more light mirth from the rest. Minya returned to reading her book, since she wasn't interested any more in the strangers.

"What is that? A real book?" Galan pressed, seeing its colorful cover. Minya looked up to meet his eyes in surprise, forgetting most Taynans didn't have books in their homes. She smiled for him, her eyes curious. The larger brother didn't look surprised at seeing it.

"Yes, it is a book. I borrowed this one from Ash, a friend, who recently arrived from far away. It is an interesting tale," she told him.

"I can't make out the writing," Gale complained, trying to get a good look at the colorful cover, which flashed and glowed. She smiled merrily, nodding.

"It is written in the human's language, English. I have become very familiar with it by now, so it is no effort for me."

"Could you read a little of it aloud, for me?" Galan requested, hoping.

"Maybe after we stop for the night, before bedtime," she returned, as Ted gave her a nod of his head.

"What's there to do, when you ride like this?" Galan pressed, feeling a little restless.

"You could weave a new belt, or read, or write, or watch the scenery pass by the window, or take a nap," Huras suggested. "On our trip to Winterhaven, Sabin entertained us with stories. Do you know any good stories?"

250

"I know a couple of stories," he replied, getting the idea. A woman from the seat behind them handed Gale a spool of brown, course string. He smiled his thanks, giving her a nod of his head. He immediately began to unwind lengths of it, to measure out for a new belt.

"Go ahead, we're listening," Metta urged, smiling as he nodded his head. Galan smiled, relaxing a little as he eased back into the amazingly comfortable seat and began his tale. Elders always loved hearing new stories, after all.

"Does it always rain like this?" Ash asked Garth and the others, as he sat down near them, lunch tray in hand. There were chuckles around the table at his question.

"This truly isn't a bad storm," he assured him, smiling merrily. "Doesn't it rain where you come from?"

"No, I grew up under a protective dome and things like wind and rain were safely far away," he admitted, chagrined as he saw the looks on the faces of the others at the table. They were surprised and some were astounded.

"Wait until the winter storms hit," Sabin advised, grinning as he saw the look of surprise in his eyes.

"If you want to avoid the snow, you can always stay in Matlowe Village for the winter," Dotti urged, teasing.

"No, I have to stay here with the ship. Will she be able to lift if there's snow?"

"The Star Quest never had a problem with snow, but then, the Aurora is a much smaller ship," Ethan stated, nodding his head at this young exec officer. "If there are any problems, we can have either our crews, or our Talents, clear off any snow, or ice, which might hinder her return to space," he offered, seeing his discomfort. Ash was relieved at hearing it.

"Thank you, Dr. Cruthers. I appreciate your information and offer of aid." With this, he dug into the food on his plate, grateful that the food here beat out what was served on the ship!

"When did you last eat, Ash?" Sabin asked, seeing how quickly he was scarfing down his meal.

"Late last night. It's been a busy morning, and this is the first chance I've had to sit for a few minutes," he told him, as he reached for his mug of honeyed tea. He saw one of his ensigns approaching and knew he hadn't been fast enough!

"What's the matter?" Neil questioned, seeing a suddenly sad look on his face.

"I wasn't quick enough," he replied, crestfallen. He gulped some of his tea, then looked up to the officer with regret in his eyes.

"Sir, the Captain requests your presence," the officer told him as he stepped up to Ash, saluting him.

"Ensign, was the captain's request one of urgency, or did he specify?" Neil broke in, understanding the situation, as Ash returned the man's salute.

"Sir, he did not specify," he replied. Ash smiled at this, giving Neil a nod of his head.

"Ensign Rangok, please inform the captain that I will be at his service, as soon as I finish my lunch," he ordered. Rangok smiled as he saluted him again, then turned and left. Ash sighed, relieved. "You were definitely on top of that one, Neil," he told him, picking up his fork, once more.

"I used to have days like that, myself," he stated, as he chuckled, glad the solution was simple. "I don't miss the military service. Even if it can occasionally get a little nuts around here, at times."

"Like this morning?" Ryes teased as she, Maren and Monty arrived in the dining hall. She and Maren stepped over to the table, to see if everything was alright, otherwise. Monty went on into the kitchen to get his tray.

"Now, the drill this morning was nothing compared to what we have to go through when attending one of the gathers," he easily returned, smiling as he turned to face her. She laughed and nodded her head.

"Don't remind me! The Great Fall Gather is almost here. At least your father got off all right, and even picked up a couple of strays this morning, who were looking for a ride to the gather. According to the computer, they're right on schedule. There're still things to finish, but we're doing all right. We're going to get our trays, be right back," she promised, then turned for the kitchen.

"Let's all hide under the table and surprise her," Brenda suggested.  This got chuckles out of the rest, as they each considered the trick.

"I don't think I could fit anymore," Dotti protested, laughing as she nodded her head.  "But let's save it for another time, when we can coordinate it," she suggested.  Monty appeared, heading for the table with a grin upon his face.  He sat down quickly, appearing happy to be back home, once again.  Denas appeared and headed to get her tray after giving him a quick wave.

"It's an idea," Garth agreed, chuckling.  "How about for the next time she's late to lunch?  It's a good thing Seena insists upon using these table drapes.  Not only do they decorate our tables but grant us a small advantage with our plot."

"That's the truth!" Sabin agreed, chuckling about his musings on Brenda's idea.

"What plot?"  Monty questioned, wanting to know what was being planned?

"I'll brief you later, just go along with us for now," Sabin told him, then signed to Garth as Ryes and Maren reappeared, trays in hand.

"What's all the laughing about?" Ryes asked, as she sat down next to her husband.

"Since Ash was having such a problem with our light rainfall, we were warning him about our winter snowstorms," he replied, smoothly.  She chuckled at this, giving him a nod of her head.

"They can be pretty bad.  But, if you'd rather, you can always spend some time in Matlowe Village.  They're pretty far south of us and rarely get any snowfall," she replied.

"Dotti was just telling me that, but I can't desert the Aurora for my own comfort.  I'll just have to get used to it," he assured her, blushing at the attention.  He wasn't used to being part of a conspiracy like this but was honored to be included as a part of the group.  It sounded like a fun prank to pull on her, too.

"Well, I'd better get back to work.  See you all later," Torr said, standing up with his tray in hand.

"I'll be in your office, shortly," Garth promised, smiling in return as he gave him a nod of his head.  Denas sat down next to Monty, all smiles.

"So, how did it go this morning?" Ryes questioned, wondering.

"We've finally got everything settled and established, so once you get the Challenger finished, we'll go out on some exercises with her to see how well it works in practice," Monty stated, very sure. Ryes gave him a nod of approval.

"I'm relieved. I'm sure Gene and James are, too," Ash said.

"James is a good First officer," Ryes commented. "He keeps his people in line without losing it, himself. He seems to know what's going on, even before anyone else does." Ash nodded his head in agreement.

"He deserves far better than Walker, but this was the duty he chose before Walker was assigned as his captain. He's the best First in the Fleet and is long overdue for his own command. I've learned a lot of how to manage a crew from him. Well, I'd best get back to my ship. See you later," he said, standing up.

"Try to make it to dinner, tonight, Ash," Garth urged, giving him a nod of his head. Ash laughed as he waved his hand at this, then turned for the door, depositing his tray onto the belt, on the way out. He felt better for the food and company!

# A Walk in the Woods

## Chapter 21

"So, the Alliance is now an actuality?" Maren questioned, "Congratulations, my friends."

"Thank you, but we're not celebrating it, until after the Gather," Garth told him. "Then we're throwing a grand party to celebrate our opening the new community hall and the formation of the Alliance of Worlds."

"Darman and Rinna should be a part of this, too," Ryes scolded, "maybe we should wait until the caravaners have returned?"

"That'll take too long.  They'll still have their own Fall Gather, after the Great one.  We'll make sure to have an extra merry Winterfest celebration this year," Sabin countered, as Garth gave him a nod in concurrence.  She sighed, then turned her attention back to her plate.

"It's been almost a year since you two left heading out to find the Moondance Tribe," Maren prompted. "Maybe we should throw you two out for a few months?  We seemed to manage things without you," he teased, his eyes merry.  Neil and the others were laughing at this, surprised and in agreement.

"Hey, a couple of months' vacation from this place?  It sounds great!" Sabin teased back, turning to his blood-brother.  Garth was chuckling and nodding his head.

"We have the hunt scheduled for tomorrow.  I already have each of you leading your own team.  So, you're not allowed to disappear until you've proved you haven't forgotten how to hunt," Ryes told them, once they calmed down a little.

"I thought I saw some new names listed.  Are the people from Trinity going to give it a try?" Maren questioned, wondering.

"A few, but most are crewmen off the starships.  They want to see how good they are in real life, compared to their virtual games," she explained, smiling. "It's going to be truly interesting, this time."

"Do any of them know anything in real life about hunting?" Garth asked, worried about taking out a lot of nestlings. "This hunt is to provide us with real food, not merely sport and fun."

"A few seem to be well versed.  We'll see," Ryes ventured in response, looking up to see the concern in Garth and Sabin's eyes. "Remember, they were all trained in how to handle the military weapons initially, in their enlistment.  It's learning how to handle our weapons of choice, which will prove interesting.  Teris has been giving some of the men and women lessons in how to operate a bow.  Some are upset because we won't let them use rifles, some are excited about learning new hunting skills."

"The multiple reports from rifles will scare away most the animals," Monty complained, understanding their reasoning well by now.  "I agree, it only made more sense the way we hunt."

"Ah, how's your little snake been?" Maren recalled, having forgotten to ask in a couple of months now.

"Shimmer's grown quite a bit, since she slithered into my pocket," he admitted, grinning, as he spaced his hands. "I just finished a new tank for her last month.  Storme's fascinated with her. I think they've been talking to each other."

"You've got to be kidding!" Ryes returned, then frowned thinking on it. "With her father's abilities, how many Talents do you think Shimmer could have?  Could be that's why she was attracted to you to begin with, Monty."  He chuckled while the others at the table looked concerned.  Maren merely nodded his head, seeing what his cousin saw.

"It wouldn't surprise me," he returned. "I've been trying to talk with her with my Talent and we're understanding each other better.  But Alec and I were shocked a few days ago, when Storme caught another squeaker outside and dropped it into Shimmer's tank, in front of us.  That's why I think they're friends now."

"Interesting," Garth commented, as he gathered his things and stood up. "I'll have to talk with you about it, later.  I've got to get the rest of my backlog cleared for tomorrow," he said, then leaned down to give his wife a kiss.  Sabin stood up with his tray ready, too. He and Sabin headed for the door together.

"That's my queue," Neil told Brenda, as he gave her a kiss, also.  Then headed for the exit.  He had work to finish up for tomorrow.  She sighed heavily.

"Are you going out on the hunt tomorrow?" Maren asked, seeing her pensive look.

"I wasn't, but I think I've changed my mind.  There's a woman off the Tablet who's had an eye for Neil.  I just want to make sure she understands that he's mine, and she needs to back off," she told them, sure they'd heard from the rumors already.

"You're not serious, are you?" Ryes questioned, surprised, seeing her downcast look. "But you're all he ever thinks and talks about, Brenda. You haven't got anything to worry about there," she told her, trying to reassure her friend. Brenda's eyes sought hers, needing to be perfectly sure.

Instead, Ryes closed her eyes and reached out to her with her Mind Voice, surprising her, in return. She showed her the little bits she recalled of their conversations, from the last couple of weeks. She was the only one he ever mentioned, and from the sparkle in his eyes when he was talking about her, she saw this was where his heart truly lay. She then replayed her memories of her interactions with Neil, back to the ones when she was Time Walking, and he was teaching her English and about the computer. Each and every time Brenda's name was the only one falling from his lips. His whole heart and mind were set upon her, even long before he decided to ask to marry her. They both opened their eyes upon the world again. Maren was curious, but knowing it was important for Brenda, so kept out. He could find out later.

"Thank you, Ryes. I really forget sometimes how good a friend you are. Yes, I think I'll still go on the hunt because I want to be with him, and just enjoy a little time outside with Sammy," she said. There were tears at the corners of her eyes as she gathered her tray and stood up. "I'd better get things ready for tomorrow."

"You're very welcome, Brenda," Ryes assured her, smiling. "See you at dinner," she added, in promise. She gave her a nod as she headed out, leaving her tray on the belt for washing.

"What was that all about?" Monty questioned, having waited until she left. Ryes smiled for him, shaking her head.

"She worries about things which hold no importance," she replied. "Neil loves her and only her. No one else could ever take that away. As long as I've known him, he's always been in love with her. She just needed to be reminded is all."

"Why would Neil want anyone else? He and Brenda are so great together," Monty said.

"These Dirters are causing problems with our own people?" Maren asked, wondering if they could head off this set of problems too?

"A few are after some quick thrills. We're now colonials, so are supposed to bow and scrape before their feet, since they're Fleet,"

Monty returned, disgust in his vocal tones. Ryes chuckled at this, nodding her head.

"One set of headaches after another. Wait until the caravaners arrive for the winter," she reminded them. "It's going to get crazy. Did you know Shadd was with one of the Dirters, a few days ago? Torr caught them in a storage room. I think he was utterly disgusted."

"Poor Mason. But didn't they go out to the Gather, together? Does he even know?" Maren pressed, curious about it now.

"If you listen to the rumor mill, Mason's been with a couple of the Dirter women, already. It's a good thing you helped Shadd put off her next season, as there's no way either of them is settled enough to raise any cubs," she told him.

"Sounds like it," Monty agreed. "Well, what's on the agenda this afternoon, boss lady?"

"Nothing much. I'm going to clear off my desk, then get ready for the hunt, too. Two choppers leave here tomorrow afternoon, to camp with the rovers tomorrow night, heading for the Gather. Everything's set and ready for the hunt, so just take the rest of the day off. If I need someone, I'll call Shams, or Ivan. So, I'll see you at dinner tonight," she said, grinning. He smiled and gave her a nod, appreciating the time off. He could surprise Denas! At least Ryes finished another shuttle this morning, making it four of the Challenger's shuttles available for use.

"Thanks. I think I'll go check on the Silver first, before I see what Denas needs done," he told her. The Silver was just outside the hangar, sitting right next to the Pike Forward. They were of a size, which surprised him.

"Just don't be there the rest of the day," Ryes teased, laughing. He got up and left, grinning with ideas dancing in his eyes.

"Are you going on the hunt?" she asked her cousin, as he was sipping his tea.

"Yes. I'm leaving Tennan, Macca and Ruan here to mind the office. I feel like I could use some time in the woods now," he replied, realizing it was a deep hunger within his soul.

"Good. I didn't know if you felt up to the killing, after..." she couldn't even say it, even now. He huffed, then gave her a nod of his head.

"I didn't say I was going to hunt anything myself, but I'll take out a party and supervise them. Have you seen how close Minya, and Ted have become?" he suddenly questioned.

"How close?" she returned, not having seen them together, yet.

"Free-mating, but not at, nor during, work. They're both too smart for that, unlike Shadd. He's been courting her for some time now. I think since Justin and Sana married."

"Hmmm..." she sighed, smiling. "They're both so good-hearted, I think they deserve each other."

"My thoughts exactly, but you know our Dirters and their opinion of the intermixing. It's kind of funny that it seems some are actually seeking out such experiences. I had to treat a man with scratches on his back the other day. I'm not sure, but he might've been with one of our Sleepers," he told her.

"As long as they remain civilized is all I care about," she replied. "Well, I guess I'd better get going. See you at dinner, cousin." He nodded his head, gathered his tray and the two of them left the room. Leaving only Ethan sitting toward the end of the table, quietly contemplating all he just heard over his forgotten, ice-cold mug of tea.

"Connor, you'd better warn the yellow and blue teams that they're heading towards each other and are getting too close," Ryes instructed, as he was helping her and Brenda with the team tracking equipment, in the base camp.

"Oh, you're right," he agreed, quickly activating his headset, just seeing what she'd already seen. Brenda quietly giggled, as she turned back to check on her own teams, again. Raya was watching the little ones while they worked today, so at least she didn't have to worry about Sammy.

"How's it going?" Ethan questioned, stepping over to observe the progress of the colorful team markers in the holo display.

"So far, so good. Sabin was commenting about the Dirters being worse than taking out a bunch of four-year olds, but I think everyone's having fun," she replied, then handed him a spare headset. "Listen for yourself," she invited. He chuckled merrily as he saw she understood his need and took it gratefully. He put it upon his head, activating it. Ethan closed his eyes and listened closely, listening for any signs of stress in their voices and what comments were voiced. He sighed after a few moments, then turned it off and handed it back.

"It's good to know it is going well. I've had some serious concerns about several issues, lately," he admitted.

"So have I," Brenda chirped in, nodding her head. "At least with the hunt to keep everyone here busy, there's been little to no friction."

"I think things will iron out in a few months. The repairs are almost complete on the Aurora, so she'll lift off soon. We're getting the Wrath next, and with everyone being more closely quartered due to the snowfall about then, they'll either figure out how to behave, or spend more time than they'll believe, confined to their ship. I'm not tolerating it anymore," Ryes stated. He saw the calm command in her stance and knew she'd be able to pull it off.

"The gather will be the test," he assured her, nodding his head. Nick walked up to join them, having caught a little of what was being said. Whatever Ryes had done to him, he realized all his senses were as sharp, as when he'd been her age. And he couldn't believe how wonderfully easy he could move, even with this heavier gravity! Pak was right behind him; appearing glad he was finally being properly allowed in on their decisions as an elder.

"I've been waiting for months for this gather and none of us are going to let the Dirters spoil things," Nick agreed.

"The last one was too much, it almost overwhelmed me. There were so many people," Pak added, as Nick gave him a nod of agreement. Ryes laughed lightly at this, nodding her head.

"And the Fall Gather is more widely attended, because in the spring everyone's still getting their crops planted and early fruits picked and stored. In the fall, the harvests are already completed by now, and the northern settlements know this'll be their only chance to party before being locked in at home by the snow," she told them. "I wanted so much to see what a gather was truly like when I was a teener, but it would've meant spending the whole year out with Darman on the road."

"Then, why didn't you, my dear?" Ethan pressed, curious as he pulled out his pipe and pouch of tobacco.

"Then who would've looked out for Rowan? It was only the two of us, living down beside the Yuri. I've looked out for him, as much as he's watched over me, for all of my life, until last year," she replied, smiling, recalling their tiny, neat home, beside the bank of the river.

"Somehow, I have problems picturing you living in Matlowe, for all your life. You belong in Winterhaven," Brenda told her, grinning, as the elders laughed, forgetting the twists her life had taken before.

"I feel that way, too," she agreed. "Matlowe's way too quiet for me now." She paused, listening in on her headset, then smiled. "Monty got the first bounder," she announced with a chuckle.

"I believe the bet was for the first bounder confirmed killed, this time," Brenda said, having heard the excitement over her headset, too. "He's going to get a reputation; they're going to expect this from him on every large hunt now."

"It does them no good to get so cocky. None of our original hunters go out to hunt much, much less enjoy the woods. They forget they need to practice their hunting skills, occasionally," Ryes commented, smiling. "At least I go out riding Honey weekly, or gather plants with Wynne, from time-to-time."

"I'm not used to a big forest like this one, but I think I could get to like it," Connor commented, smiling as he swept the area around them, briefly, with his eyes. She chuckled at seeing it.

"But hunting's not for you anymore, child," Rowan scolded, stepping over to join the others. "I still can't believe that vid which was shot of you on that one hunt!" Ryes blushed a dark gold at this, nodding her head.

"That's why I get to help out at the base camp," she quipped back. He chuckled, then bent down to give her a light kiss on her forehead.

"And I'm proud of the good job you do to keep things organized. We're heading back out. We just turned our birds over to the freezer crew. But I'm only planning on another two to three hours. I'd be longer, but I don't think these young ones can handle the pace," he chortled with glee in his eyes. There was laughter from the rest around them. All the elders now looked younger, with the gray having almost disappeared from their hair now.

"Good hunting," she wished him, smiling merrily. He gave her a nod of his head, then turned to gather his small band of hunters. He thought they'd had enough of a rest by now.

"I think I might try tagging along," Nick stated, giving Ethan a nod of his head, then trotted off to catch up to Rowan.

"Mom, Mom," Calla called out, running over toward them. "Raby says she needs you." Ryes sighed, then smiled and hugged her after she ran to her arms, squealing happily. "This place is so cool and green. My old mom never let me camp in a forest before," she told her, smiling up to see the happiness in Ryes' eyes.

"Let me get someone to take over for me, so I can take care of Raby, then I'll tell you some stories about the hunts I went on, when I was just a little older than you are now," she promised.

"I'll take over here," Ethan offered, holding out a hand for her headset. She looked surprised but surrendered it. "You go and take care of your children. We'll call if we really need you. Every minute spent with them is precious," he gently scolded, still smiling. She nodded her head as she stood up, then took Calla's hand.

"Thanks, I appreciate both the offer and the advice," she replied, then headed off to see what her oldest daughter needed, as Ethan sat down in her place, chuckling lightly as he nodded his head, donning a headset once again.

Ryes decided to go ahead and take Calla and Chatis out, once she had her youngest ones settled down for their nap. Raby and Katas were chatting with Matissa and Gwenda, two of the Boodan girls their age, with Tars hanging on their every word. Sayer was out with Garth's team, learning a little more about hunting. But Ryes thought a short walk in the woods would be the best medicine for her soul, and a way to get some of the restlessness out of her two, remaining daughters. They knew so little of the woods, so suspected they'd never been in the forests around Matlowe, either. She had so much to teach them and was unsure where to being. After all, Hailys forest was nothing like Matlowe's, and was far deadlier.

"Mother, are these ones good to eat?" Chatis questioned, as they rounded a copse of trees and found a small brook flowing across their chosen path. The bushes were growing next to the water, their branches laden with ripe, dark-red berries.

"No, they're not," she warned, then got down on her knees to show them how to know this plant, as she had for the Matlowe Village cubs, when they were their age, what seemed so long ago. "See this one's poisonous. Here, look at how the leaves are shaped and the way they're spaced on the branches. See these flowers? Make sure you know this one, so you can avoid it." Calla leaned forward to sniff the flowers, then wrinkled up her nose. Chatis was looking at the leaves, as Ryes carefully spread them out on display for them.

"It smells bad," Calla commented, then looked at the leaves, too.

"They are so tiny, and all bunched together," Chatis told her, then sniffed the flowers. She waved a hand before her nose, disgust upon her face. "I do not like this one."

"That's good, because it doesn't like anyone either," Ryes agreed, then washed her hand in the stream, and stood up again. "Come on, we'll find something good," she urged, taking their hands. Then there was a sound from ahead of them, as a large body was moving through the brush. She stopped and got the three of them behind a large, nearby tree, gesturing them to be silent. In just a few moments, Maren came into view. He was looking around and she suddenly could guess why.

"You're back early," she commented in a low voice. He startled, then relaxed as he shook his head, relieved, as they stepped into view.

"And found that you had disappeared," he replied, as the two little girls were giggling merrily.

"Cousin Maren," Calla declared, throwing her arms about his closest leg. There was laughter in his eyes as he gave her a nod of his head, leaning down to hug her. Chatis joined her, laughing more loudly.

"We are sure glad it was you," she scolded. "Mom's teachin' us `bout the plants and `nanimals."

"She's the best teacher about them, anywhere," he assured her, giving her a hug, too. He straightened back up, meeting his cousin's eyes. "You know you're not supposed to be out without someone to escort you."

"I have my pistol and Talents. What more do I need?" she questioned, knowing it was useless. "All right," she told him, giving in at the look in his eyes. "So, do you feel better, even if these woods are very different from Matlowe's?"

"Yes, I do, even if it's different," he replied, then helped her by carrying Calla across the running water, as she carried Chatis. "I think I deeply needed this renewal." She turned to meet his eyes, hers were merry as she smiled and nodded.

"That's what I felt like, too. I truly needed this trip out to the forest. It's been too long." There was a note in his voice that struck a deep chord within her.

"Why, Mom?  Why do you need the trees?" Chatis questioned, not understanding.  It was scary to her eyes.

"Because I grew up next to a great wood, like this one, so every now and then, I need this breath of nature to set my mind and heart straight.  I can hear my own thoughts in the forest," she explained, seeing they were trying to figure it out.

"There're some rocks over there," Maren indicated, pointing.  "Let's go sit down and listen for a while," he suggested.

"That sounds like a wonderful idea," Ryes agreed.  She followed him to the rocky formation, which jutted out from a rising mound, climbing upwards behind it.  "I'm sending you two up, so stay away from the edge.  We'll join you soon."  Ryes first checked that area with Empath, to be sure it was safe, then used Manipulator to float the young cubs up to the top.  She and Maren climbed up, the old fashion way, enjoying the exercise.

"Mom, Maren, you can see everything from up here!" Chatis exclaimed, as she and Calla met them when they reached the top of the rock.  Ryes laughed as Maren nodded his head, with a small quirk of a smile.  They sat down to admire the view, so Ryes pulled out snacks and water for everyone from her backpack.

"Do you miss hunting, Huntress?" he finally asked, seeing how she couldn't take her eyes off the woods below them.

"I miss the forest itself, more than anything else, I think," she sighed out.

"You usta hunt, Mom?" Chatis questioned, surprise on her face.  Ryes smiled as she nodded her head.

"It was long ago, when I used to live with Grandfather Rowan in Matlowe Village," she explained. "I used to hunt to feed us, then."

"What did you hunt?" Calla asked, wondering, her brow furrowing.

"Lots of animals.  Bounders, tuskers, birds of all types, fish from the Yuri River and even a couple of Moss eaters, who'd wandered down, too far south."

"And you ATE them?" Calla questioned, a look of disgust on her face, as Chatis laughed.

"But we eat them, too," she told her sister. "We had tusker for dinner last night."

"That's the truth," Maren agreed, nodding his head. "We need to hunt the animals for the meat. We don't hunt them just for fun."

"Do we eat windracers, too?" Chatis asked, wondering.

"No, we don't, but the plainsmen do, but only when they have to, to keep from starving. We've never been that desperate. And the windracers can be traded, or sold at a Gather, when we get too many of them. They're for riding, or pulling carts, not eating," Ryes asserted, smiling.

"Tratis said that Racer was his best friend," Calla told her. "How could anyone eat their best friend?" This got Ryes to laughing, outright.

"I watched Honey being born into the world and cared for her for most of her life. I could never eat her, no matter how desperate I thought I might be."

"Honey has a pretty cub," Chatis told her, liking the windracer, too.

"Filly. Windracers have colts or fillies," she corrected her. "We have cubs, or children."

"Then why does Alec say Storme has kittens? Why doesn't she have cubs, too? She looks like us a little," Calla asked, seriously wanting to know.

"She comes from another world and is a cat. We're Starmen, not cats, even if she looks something like us," she explained, while Maren nodded his head, agreeing.

"Can we go home and go riding?" Chatis pressed.

"We go home tomorrow, then we'll be getting ready for the gather. I don't know if we'll be able to fit in time for riding, but we will, when we get back from the gather," she promised her.

"A ride down to the river sounds good," Maren commented, sighing. "I might come along with you, then."

"I don't know if Dotti would be comfortable riding, as far along as she is," Ryes commented, smiling as she met his eyes. There was laughter in them, at least. "Let's start heading back. It'll be time for dinner, soon."

"That's a good idea. I want to see what Dotti thinks of her first hunt. She and Tars were in the showers when I realized you weren't around the camp."

"So, it's all my fault," she quipped back smiling, as she made sure she had everything back into her pack, including packing up their trash.

"I'll make sure to tell them, when they demand an explanation," he returned with mirth in his voice, at least.  They got to their feet, then Ryes extended her Talent and floated all of them down, and across the stream, to the forest floor once more.

"I want to fly again," Chatis demanded, laughing as she held her arms up towards the sky.

"Maybe later," Ryes promised, laughing too.  Then the four of them headed back toward the camp.  As she resisted gathering plant samples as they walked.  She could do that later, now was a precious piece of time to spend with her daughters.

# A Look Ahead

## Chapter 22

We'll have to do this again," James stated, as he sat down at the bright campfire, feeling sated from just finishing an excellent dinner. It did make a difference when the meat was fresh! He was dressed in casual attire because right now, because he was only himself, enjoying an exciting outing.

"We'll probably have our next big hunt in the spring, but you can always accompany our smaller hunting parties, when they go out, anytime," Ryes assured him. She now held a sleepy Rhin in her arms, as Garth was holding Jann. They were trying to get the cubs settled for the night and knew this was the best way. They already had the first two asleep in their portable cribs inside the shelter. Garth was chuckling as he gave the First officer a nod of his head.

"Your people did far better than I would've thought, today," he admitted, smiling. "Considering the unfamiliar weapons they were using."

"We've all played at hunting with various weapons on our computers through the years. It was a genuine treat to learn how to use them for real. This was one of the best outlets for excess energy that I could've thought of. I just want to thank you for allowing us to come along on this hunt," he replied.

"Actually, we should be thanking you. Because of your people, we'll be able to wrap up the hunt tomorrow, having plenty of food to keep us all through the winter," Ryes assured him, nodding her head.

"That was great! I can't wait for the next hunt," Tracy Kruggins stated, sitting down next to Ryes. "Do you need a hand, Boss lady?" she asked, smiling.

"Thanks, but he's almost out," she told her, smiling. "Only Shaysa left, and she loves it when her daddy rocks her to sleep." Garth chuckled at this, nodding his head.

"Is this your first hunt?" James asked the blonde woman, who just sat down near them. She smiled and nodded her head.

"We weren't here for the first big one, and for the summer one, I was up helping out on the Challenger," she explained.

"How could you not have been here for the first one?" he pressed, then saw Ryes shift uncomfortably.

"I pulled them forward, out of the past. It was a small practice for when I rescued my great aunt," Ryes explained, blushing.

"What?" Gene asked, sitting down next to James. Had he heard, what he thought he heard?

"Then, you can do more than just visit the past in ghostly form?" James asked, ignoring the First off the Tablet. This was too important!

"I didn't KNOW I could do it, until I tried," she replied. Tracy laughed, nodding her head.

"When we saw the Quest's battered hulk, we knew she saved us from horrible deaths. It's too bad there weren't more people she could've saved, but she collapsed after she brought only the seven of us into the future," she explained.

"Ryes," Garth started, unsettled at hearing this again. He didn't like it when she risked her life so foolishly!

"I was there to help her," Maren defended his cousin, seeing Garth's concern starting to flare his temper.

"The hard part was convincing them to take the chance," Ryes stated, giving Maren a nod of her head in appreciation.

"Where were you, Garth?" James asked, seeing he looked upset over being reminded of the incident. Had she pulled it on the sly, behind his back, like she did in Matlowe?

"Topside, setting up our warning satellites and rescuing the Boodans," he replied. Ryes stood up to put Rhin to bed. "We'll be right back," he added, realizing his little daughter was out too, so stood to put Jann down.

"I didn't know Tracy would bring that up," Ryes whispered to him, as they put the cubs in their cribs.

"I know, but you're not allowed to Time Walk without my permission, anymore," he reminded her. "In case James wants you to go back and bring another person forward, again. He'll just have to take this one on faith, or he can ask Adina." Ryes smiled as she put her arms about him, stretching up to give him a kiss. He returned it passionately, thinking it might be a good idea to get to bed early tonight, after all. He wanted some quiet time with her, too.

"I won't," she promised, after their lips parted.

268

"You two do that, all the time!" a young voice protested from behind Ryes. She twisted about, ready to tease Sayer in return, but it wasn't Sayer.

"Manda! What're you doing here?" she demanded, seeing her ghostly great-great granddaughter.

"What I wanted to ask you great-great, is can you bring someone from the future into the past?" she questioned.

"I don't know. I've never tried it, and I would think it might cause all kinds of paradoxes. I'll ask the Sleepers if they've ever heard of it being done. Why would you want to know?"

"I'd like to hide out with my cousins back here for a little while. It's the only place I can think where we'll definitely be safe," she replied.

"Safe from what, or whom?" Garth questioned, frowning.

"I don't know who they are, but I can't get Teran to believe me, and I don't want to endanger Gram, or Candy. We can't get off world right now, so we're stuck on Tayna and just have no idea of where we could go to be safe," she explained, her anxiety plain on her face and in her eyes and voice.

"Have you Time Walked back, to see if you're living here with us, yet? If so, ask yourself," Ryes suggested, smiling impishly, then saw the pain in Manda's eyes. "Give me a few days to ask around about it. Then we'll see," she assured her.

"Say, how're you here? We're well outside of Winterhaven," Garth asked, wanting to know.

"I focused in upon you two and we're in North Winterhaven. The city grows, through the years," she informed him, smiling. "I'll go check to see if we're with you, otherwise, I'll see you in two days' time," she promised, then faded out.

"Hop across the river and we're still in town," Ryes sighed, smiling. "This one sounds like a real problem. What kinds of paradoxes would we be causing by letting them step into the past?"

"I've no idea. Let's see if it's been done before, first," Garth suggested.

"Paradoxes? Are you considering pulling more humans forward, off the Star Quest?" Maren asked as he stepped in, a fussing Shaysa in his arms. "Someone was getting very cranky," he added.

"Not from out of the past, but the future," Ryes explained, as Garth took their daughter into his arms. She immediately quieted, as he cuddled her up to his chest.

"What?" he demanded, not sure if he heard her correctly.

"Manda needs a place to hide out for her and her cousins, for a little while. Maybe it's time for you to look forward again, after all. You might be able to see who's after them," Garth suggested.

"I'll give it a try in the morning," she promised. "As before, we have time on this end of things."


"What?" Ryes questioned as Mitt, Maren, Garth, Torr and Sabin all gathered around her, as she decided it was a good time to try, since everything in the camp was quiet and the hunting parties were out now. Raya walked up then, a smile upon her lips.

"We're ready when you are," Garth invited her, gesturing to the matting she just laid down, so she could be comfortable sitting upon it, instead of the ground.

"A tour guide, that's what I've become," she teased, grinning.

"Nah, just we sensation junkies needing another fix," Mitt quipped back, grinning playfully. "Come on, Ryes. We want to see the future, too."

"All right," she gave in, sitting down with a smile and a small sigh. Torr moved in another, larger mat, so there'd be plenty of room for all of them, then they settled, holding hands, gathered into a circle, as if it were no more than a practice session. Ryes closed her eyes, letting Sabin, Mitt and Raya establish the inner link. She then unleashed her Talents, opened her pool of power, and directed her Visionary Talent forward, as she had before, driving it. She focused in upon Gram, first. Manda was worried about her, so thought to see if she was all right. She was talking with a very pretty, young, human woman, as they sat down eating a meal. Both looked calm to her eyes. She willed them unseen, as she usually did when Time Walking, and listened to what they were saying.

"He'll be all right. He was a little wild for a few years, but has settled down quite a lot," Gram assured the girl, in a consoling manner. She smiled in reply, her eyes lighting up.

"I was worried, since I already have a little daughter of my own and was afraid it'd give him second thoughts, that he'd be

270

jumpin' the next ship out," she admitted, as the worry and pain in her eyes had melted to relief.

"Woolart would never do that to you, Candy," she stated, sure of her facts. "I've known him all his life."

"I hope they're all right," she replied, setting down her mug, fighting back her tears. This gave Ryes some inner misgivings, so she pulled back, focusing on when she last saw Manda. Hoping this would give her a link to where she was and what was threatening her. She found her and two young men, along with the same young woman in the eatery, again.

"The language's changed. I don't understand every other word," Maren complained, as they listened to their conversation. The four of them left the eatery, after tipping the waitress. They went to a place which looked like it was what the humans called an inn, or motel.

"Where is this place. Is this Tayna? There's no sky," Torr asked, feeling unsettled with such a dreary, metal-lined building. Everything was inside. Ryes smiled as she pulled back from the people she was following, to find a window, to please him. She finally found one, and they looked out of it to see they were high in orbit over Tayna.

"Flutter-wing's grown," Mitt commented, amused. "It's a city in its own right!"

"Now Sabin, how could I ever have imagined such a place, when we haven't built much of it, yet?" Ryes teased. She felt his unhappiness at her dig.

"Let's see if you can move forward now, and find Manda on Tayna," Garth pressed, wanting to concentrate upon the problem in hand. Ryes returned to the four young people, seeing Woolart and Candy had taken a room alone, to spend some time together. Manda and Kerin were already sound asleep in their bunks, in the next room. She then pulled them forward, next finding them in some large building, with Manda facing down an older man, who looked like Maren, only more human. Gram was here with them, as well.

"Some descendent of yours?" she teased. "He's clearly a cross."

"You're welcome to stay here with me," he was telling Manda, smiling at the stubbornness in her eyes. "I would like to take the time to get to know you better, before..." he trailed off, not being so rude as to say it outright to a young lady.

"I'll cog it," she replied tartly. "We won't space, if that'll make you feel more comfortable. We could hang in Winterhaven, for now." She glanced over and got nods from Woolart and Kerin in agreement. The older man smiled, nodding his head.

"We need your help, Manda. I'll have a guard assigned to keep a watch over you."

"No, Teran. I don't want some scuffer trailin' us about. I want to see the city my great greats built, for myself," she returned. He sighed, but gave her a nod of his head, letting her have her way.

"Spoiled brat," Maren declared, amused by this Vision. The room they were standing in was a very spacious office and far too ornate for his tastes.

"Hey, she's MY great-great granddaughter, after all," Garth teased back, beating Ryes to the punch. "We're getting closer," he said, pressing Ryes to advance again. She got the idea and let go, once more. She moved them forward until they were standing in their own fountain square, in the middle of their own apartments. Manda was staring up at the Windrose Stone, above the fountain, as if trying to get a feel for it and the power it could offer her.

"My gosh, it's true!" Raya declared, astounded.

"What's she doing?" Torr asked, seeing her cousins standing nearby, bored with the place.

"Look, at the shadows around them," Garth warned. There were men in black clothing, with even their faces concealed. They were approaching the young people quietly.

"Who are they? And why are they stalking them?" Maren questioned, shocked as they watched the drama unfold. The men grabbed each of the young men, pinning them down and quickly fitting heavy collars around their necks.

"Don't do anything, or they'll die," one of men growled out at Manda, as she opened her eyes, and it looked as if she were about to unleash something. She stopped, believing them, so two of them ran up to her, putting a collar on her neck, too.

"We're too late," Maren sighed out. "But who are they? What do they want?" he asked.

"I've no idea. I'm starting to get a little tired. Time to pull back for now. Maybe if I can find out who they are, we can help them?" Ryes suggested, pulling them back to their own time and place, once more, happy they didn't have the wrenching sensations which her Time Walking generated. She opened her eyes; glad they were safely back. Garth looked thoughtful, for a few moments.

"Don't investigate it any further. We obviously didn't warn her outright, so this must be something we feel she'll be able to survive. But I do want you to look forward one more time, after we get home tonight, to see if Manda and her cousins get through this. You may help advise her, but don't interfere. She has her own life to live through, after all," he ordered.

"How can that one human man be her cousin?" Mitt asked, still wondering. "Is Manda a cross, too?"

"She could be from a cross, who mated back to a starman," Torr suggested.

"No. I saw her birth and both her parents were starmen. Maybe one of them was what Torr said?" Ryes asserted, letting go of Garth and Maren's hands.

"Probably," Maren agreed, shaking his head. "That uniform, those places," he added, still amazed.

"'The future's never what you imagine.' Rhodi once told me," Raya said with a smile, standing up. "Now I know what she means."

"Mitt, you keep to the original design you already have planned for the Flutter-wing," Sabin warned, feeling it needed to be voiced.

"Let's keep all this to ourselves, for now," Garth warned. "We wouldn't want people getting nightmares over having to achieve something, which will come about all on its own." Ryes chuckled at this, nodding her head.

"Who was that Gram, you focused in on first?" Mitt questioned, frowning.

"My granddaughter. She told me how much she missed me, once. So, I guess I'll get to be around her awhile. It's just which of the cubs is her parent?" Ryes replied, grinning merrily. "Manda came back the first time to see her, after all."

"And since Manda looks so much like you, I'm betting it's either Shaysa or Jann," Maren told them. "Let's go see what the hunters are doing," he suggested.

"I'm lying down for a nap," Ryes returned, feeling drained. Garth gave her a hug and kiss, then let her go on to their shelter, alone.

273

"So, you can drive a Vision," Sabin commented.

"Maybe if you're focusing upon someone you know," Garth suggested, "it's better than just trying to cast ahead randomly?"

"You know I tried to do it when we were cubs, and the results of that," Sabin said, "but I was just casting ahead, instead of focusing upon an individual. Maybe you've got the right of it, at that."

"It's just getting the introductions to the people in the future, first," Torr added. "After all, I would've never imagined the humans we've come to cherish and love, when we were living in Matlowe."

"We were all starving then and now we have to watch our diets," Maren observed. "We would've never even thought of these great hunts, nor this area as a place to hunt. I can't believe this will all become a part of Winterhaven!"

"Me neither," Mitt agreed, smiling as she tried to imagine the forest around them as homes, business, and other buildings, as in the photos of the cities of the humans. "Well, let's go lend a hand. We really ought to show them what a bunch of real hunters can do," she challenged the men, a teasing smile in her eyes.

"Now that's a good idea. I'm going to get my bow and equipment. Meet you right here in about fifteen minutes," Torr replied, with the others nodding their heads in agreement. It'd be like old times - sort of... And would keep their minds off what the future might bring.

"Manda?" Maren said, stopping as he realized the young woman in the hallway ahead of him wasn't Ryes. She turned and smiled, cocking her head as she saw him, her bright, green eyes taking him in fully.

"Yes. Are you Maren? I'm smashed," she told him. He nodded his head at this, his eyes merry.

"I believe I'm going to need a new lexicon of the language. What's `smashed' mean?" he questioned. She laughed heartily, shaking her head.

"I never thought of that! Ryes always speaks so properly in her recordings, and I never made the connection before. Smashed means that I was thrilled to meet you," she explained. "But then, if I tell you the meanings of the words we use commonly now, does that mean I'm starting their use in the past?" she threw at him.

"That's a very good question," Garth told her, stepping over to join them. "So, we'll leave `smashed' out of our vocabulary, except to describe something which is actually smashed. We looked ahead, to see what there was to be seen," he told her.

"How did you do that?" she asked, startled that her great greats might be spying upon her!

"Ryes figured out a way," Maren replied. Ethan stopped behind him, curiosity in his bright, blue eyes. "Who was that man in the uniform, in that office?" he added, still wanting to know.

"Your great-great grandson, Teran. He's the head of the Alliance of Worlds, which is based in Winterhaven. He's arranged, through my family, for us to mate. It seems there's been some great Vision and if he's to save the Alliance, it's with my help. He said part of it was that we're together. He's spaced, as far as I'm concerned. He's so much older and so stuffy," she complained, realizing how petty she sounded, as she heard herself uttering what was on her mind.

"Give him a chance and spend some time with him. You might come to see his better qualities, my dear," Ethan advised, chuckling. It was true! There was another Time Walker in the family.

"He's not that much older," Maren lightly scolded. She stuck her tongue out at him, surprising him.

"Why would you be so important, that the existence of the Alliance is endangered without your help?" Garth questioned.

"Because she's our next Talent of One Plus and has at least as much power as I," Ryes told them, stepping forward. "Do you already know about it, Manda?"

"Yes," she replied, nodding her head as she smiled. "You told me in the messages you've recorded for me. Gram gave me this chip," she said, pulling a dark, holo chip from her pocket and displaying it for her. Ryes smiled and showed her the exact same one, in her own hand.

"I started this a couple of months ago," she admitted. "I'm glad to see that you do get it."

"I do and I would've loved to have the chance for us to sit and talk, without time being such an issue. Do you think it's a good idea for us to shift back here for a little while?" she questioned, needing to know it now. She felt her time was short! "There are strange men and women watching us all the time, and the intensity makes chills go up my back."

"No, it's not going to be easy but go with the advice I give you on the chip. You and your cousins will be fine in the end, and I would dearly love to sit and chat with you, too," she advised, feeling it was tearing her apart inside at the same time.

"But you don't really say anything," she protested.

"There's a reason behind that and I can't tell you now. Be patient, strong and alert, and you'll understand it all, later," she told her. Manda stood for several long moments, meeting Ryes' eyes, then she bowed her head in surrender.

"I will," she replied, then looked up again, her glance taking in the many people gathering around them now. She smiled once more. "I'd best get back, or I'll have Kerin and Gram worried. Bye!" she said, then faded out of sight. But she stuck around to hear what they would say now. She needed to understand this!

"I feel like an absolute heel. They're going to torture her," Ryes commented to Garth. He nodded his head, putting an arm about her shoulders in comfort.

"She's not too much younger than you, when we set off, and you managed to face off Doran. You handled her, she'll handle them and Teran will get there in time, too," he reminded her, having gone with her on her follow-up future journey to check up on the situation.

"What? Those people in black?" Maren demanded, hating to be left out of things. Ryes smiled merrily, seeing his need to know everything right now. She shook her head.

"Not now," she told him.

"Well, I do hope you intend to fill me in about our pretty little Time Walker?" Ethan pressed.

"Mitt and I have to run up to the Challenger, to help with a problem Axel's having. Perhaps, when I return, I can show you what we know about Manda, Ethan?" she asked, knowing he deserved to know, too. After all, Candy will be a descendent of his.

"Alright, but let me know, when you return," he replied, chuckling as he turned for his office.

Manda finally let go of the past. She felt her strength waning. So, it was something almost as bad as when her great-great faced off Doran, and Teran would save them. She needed a few hours to go through and review the files and any saved vids about this part of their family history. Perhaps she should take the time to talk with Teran about everything? And maybe it was time she and her cousins moved in with him, for a while?  It'd give her time to get used to him, at least, and might make it safer for Gram, Candy and Candy's daughter?

# Laying Foundations

Chapter 23

Ryes pulled up her morning news vid for Winterhaven and stopped, staring at the screen for a few moments in surprise. "News of The Realm?" she questioned aloud. Larisa, who was coming into her office for their morning schedule adjustments, stopped and laughed, nodding her head.

"Surprised me, too," she admitted, then came and sat next to her desk. "Do you think they're serious, or just pulling a fun jab?" Ryes smiled and shook her head.

"I'll catch up to them later today and ask directly. If I just send them an email, they won't take it as seriously as I might want," she replied. After a few moments' pause she let out a low chuckle. "They did seem to make it light-hearted by several of their references and vids." She met Larisa's amused eyes with mirth in her own.

"Maybe after your big meeting?" she teased. Ryes nodded, a chagrinned smile upon her lips.

"It'll be a nice wind-down from that," she agreed. "Anything important this morning?" Larissa shook her head. She nodded, as her assistant went back to her desk, then turned back to the surprise newsletter and started reading the entries about the hunt, wanting to see their take.

"We're leaving tomorrow for the gather," Ryes stated, as the stragglers finally stepped into the largest conference room. She was at the head of the table, having asked all their Sleepers, who were still here, all of their own Talents, and a few other key people to this meeting, needing their assistance. Garth and Sabin had begged off, due to work they needed to finish, but Ethan was present.

"What do you want us to do?" Phil asked, as he saw Kovin sit down next to his wife; he saw them exchanged smiles, joyful to be working together. They joined hands quickly, figuring what would be needed next. He smiled at seeing their shared happiness.

"Just sit down, join hands, relax, and close your eyes," Ryes instructed.  Phil went to sit next to Kovin and got comfortable.

"James, I need your input for the new barracks we're planning, since you might know more of what's needed than I," she requested, seeing him standing near her now.  Surprise was in his eyes, but he gave her a nod of his head, appearing to consider what she said, as he sat down next to her.

"So, we're going to work today," Mitt commented, grinning.  Ryes gave her a nod, as she sat down on Ryes other side.  Her Aunt Adina entered and appeared annoyed, but took her place on Mitt's other side, with Hadu next to her, as there were four other Winterhaven guards posted in this large conference room, covering both doors, already.  They would be enough to alert him, if needed.

"Everyone close your eyes and relax, as there's some work to finish before the Gather," Ryes invited as the seats were now filled.  Once the Mind Voice team had formed the commune at her queue, and they got everyone settled down, Ryes opened her Booster to grant everyone access to her pool of power, delighting them.

"We're taking this chance to recreate a bit of Winterhaven, while we can," she told them.  Raya and Adina caught the wisp of memory of the Vision she experienced during the battle with the Southern Talents, and this instantly ignited Adina's need to know, which ran like wildfire through the rest of the Talents gathered.

"You will share this Vision?" Rhodi pressed, seeing it through Mitt now, too.

"They thought they could take us," Mitt commented, inwardly smiling.

"If it'd been Doran, she would've quickly, physically, defeated them as none of them had Manipulator, nor defenses against it," Ryes added, bringing the one memory of the Vision of them originally standing in Hailys as a battle arena, then it melted as Sabin and Dastin's Vision overtook it.  They saw what the others originally projected of Winterhaven's future look.  "I'd never fought anyone with a setting around us, as if we were actually fighting them in person," she admitted.

"Please show us the whole battle," Poli requested, needing to know. "It is an ancient technique of inner battles, and if we are to fight the Snagospin, we should see what you learned in this one," she pressed.  Ryes seemed to pause a moment, but then did see her sound reasoning.  They could be very useful ideas, when it came to facing off the Snags, when that came to being.

"Unfiltered, so our newer members can truly appreciate it," Maren insisted.  They all felt her reluctant capitulation, so she opened the full memory to them, to show what they endured and how they triumphed in the end.

"In truth, they never stood a chance against your team," Shams asserted, still reeling from her pool of power fully unleashed.

"They did try, though," Adina observed, impressed. "And you have learned how to be a Memory Keeper, Ryes, which is not easily mastered," she praised her.  Ryes seemed embarrassed, then projected the part of the arena which they knew will be Winterhaven's main square, once more.

"So, for today, since we can expect some truly massive structures to be built in this area, I'd like to reinforce things, get a good, solid infrastructure set up, then do a few small things like setting up the new barracks building, the quick way, so our ship crews can be more comfortable and less stressed," Ryes told the others. "Let's start with our current structures," she invited, opening her blended view of Empath, Earth Shaper, and Inner Sight as they looked at the supports around them all.

"Not bad, but not strong enough," Phil commented with Kovin's immediate agreement.

"How can you know that the future vista will actually come to pass?" James questioned, wondering about that Vision, which the people gathered here didn't doubt.  There was humor around him, but not for his question.  Nesa had wondered, too.

"Sabin is a very strong Visionary and everything he's seen so far has come to pass," Ryes explained. "The fact that it happened to both Visionary Talents at the same time, gave me to feel this will be in our future." James had more questions but realized this was not the time to voice them.

Ryes added her Manipulator, Fire Shaper and Molecular Talents, bringing several long beams and support structures from Hailys starport to Winterhaven and used them to meld into the main support structures within their underground facility, with Kovin, Phil, Adina, and Hadu to guide her, they quickly reshaped their home base while expanding it with rooms for future use, and fortifications akin to what they put into place on Flutter-wing with adding in armories, AI compartments, and other essential secure areas, including their first true jail.  She upgraded the power, fresh water, and wastewater systems to sustain the huge city she'd seen in the Vision.  The new Security area pleased several gathered in the meld, especially Torr and Monty.  Then she invited others to make changes, using her

Talents, as they saw were still needed.  Raya and several others did, enjoying playing with the new "toys."

Then Ryes moved to reinforce the ground beneath Winterhaven itself, using her Empath, Molecular and Earth Shaper Talents.  She had Adina, Hadu, and Lelas guide her efforts to provide a solid foundation for the entire area to build upon now, and in the future.  The stable density they achieved amazed Phil, as he highly approved.

After that, Ryes explored the buildings on the surface they currently had or were in the process of being built.  She strengthened and expanded their homes, first; gently moving possessions and people clear until finished, the team used Mind Voice to let them know first before the changes, then moved them back inside, once done. Ryes added foundations for even more apartments, which had been on the list for future plans.  She put in a stronger foundation for the Community Center and added foundations for their library, school complex, and research center, with Ethan's approval, then he made adjustments he saw were still needed.

Next, the military barracks foundation was expanded, with it raised from two to four stories high, which surprised James, who with Hadu, added some structures within that would be needed in the future.  Offices and meeting rooms were included near the main entrance of the building, so they could have some real office space to utilize, too.  He added a gym area, and recreation rooms, too.

Finally, Kovin and Phil pulled them all over to their bridge project.  She then shaped it to conform to the specs they had, but using her and Mitt's Inner Sight, they made improvements to that design and further expanded it so four large rovers could drive along it with plenty of spacing between, on each side, and fully supported with a weight limit that exceeded what they could carry.  Ryes also added a tube to carry passenger shuttles to and from the area, beneath the bridge.  This delighted them all.  Past the bridge, she started foundations for two huge hangars, control tower, passenger terminal, warehouses, and landing pits for their new, ground space center.  She wanted the starships landing and taking off well away from Winterhaven proper, after the problem landing the Aurora!  This had everyone's understanding and approval.

Through it all, the Sleepers and others contributed their share of small adjustments, which they saw were needed while they reshaped this small town with the great city in mind, also freely tapping into her Talents.  James got a feel for it and found she also made them available to him to use, too.  Phil delighted in this project as he and Kovin added the touches they saw were lacking everywhere.

Finally, Ryes added in a safe haven, and highly reinforced tunnel between Winterhaven and the outskirts of Hailys. It was an evacuation place where the residents could go where they could be safe underground, and still able to escape to the surface, if they needed to do so. They added in a shuttle system similar to old Hailys, to get people there fast. This addition surprised most gathered, and she realized other residents here in Winterhaven had joined the meld and were adding their touches. Bitty was home on leave and happy to add in safety systems everywhere, with Hadu improving her ideas. This pleased her immensely, as she paid attention to his changes. And it was clear, she now felt fully a part of her new home, having helped shape it.

Joy ran through Ryes' heart, and she opened her eyes to glance around the room, while being fully connected to the meld. She smiled happy and satisfied to see the room now closely crowded with humans, starmen and other peoples all now a part of this gathering.

"What makes you so happy, Ryes?" Maren asked, as he now squeezed Dotti's hand.

"What I see," she answered, knowing everyone could hear them clearly. "I see family and community all gathered to help create our home," she added, as she saw smiles bloom on most of the faces of the people gathered in the room. She closed her eyes, realizing while she still had plenty of energy to work with, she, herself, was now tired. She clearly felt joy running through their commune.

"Let us look at the changes we have wrought," Adina invited, as she and the other Mind Voice Talents gently dissolved the meld.

All in all, it was done, and while the room they sat in when they started appeared the same, it now was a far safer building. They opened their eyes and let go of each other's hands as laughter and joy was freely expressed, all through the room. People, who had come in and sat on the floor, began to stand, and help each other up. Maren was quickly at Ryes' side to make sure her body temperature was normal again. He was glad to see her eyes still bright and she was aware of her surroundings, even after all that work. He realized her Talents had gained in strength, as she pushed them all to their limits, and her body was getting stronger, too; able to withstand the longer Talent sessions better. Their practices were paying off for all of them.

"So, did we manage to get things set up a bit better?" she asked the room in general. There was laughter and voices raised in happy agreement. "We still have a lot of work with framing inside the new buildings and getting the rooms down here set up," she warned, but there was a huge smile on her face, too. She was so proud.

"We'll manage it. I'm glad you're moving the starport and hangers, as that was something we were surveying ourselves. We hadn't come up with a good place to set things," Phil told her, grinning joyfully due to this morning's work. She had jumped forward all the projects they had planned and added a few others, at the same time. He couldn't be happier about her and the help of the other Talents in the room around him! Winterhaven was finally starting to take shape and that Vision's glimpse of Winterhaven in the future had been amazing. Overhead trams? Oh Yeah!

"After the Aurora's rough landing, it's needed," James agreed, smiling, and shaking his head. No one will believe all he just experienced! "May I go explore the new barracks, now? We can get some of the crewmembers, who have trade skills, started on finishing them up, if you have some materials for us to use," he asked. Kovin nodded.

"We can head out to Hailys to harvest some trees before the winter snows hit," he assured him, smiling, "but after the Fall Gather." James nodded in understanding, still feeling they could see what they could come up with on their own. He needed to talk to Walker and the Captains to let them know, as soon as possible! With the town layout set in his head now, there was no problem finding the building.

"Thank you, Ryes and everyone gathered! I cannot express how much this goes to help us feel like we've found a new home, away from home," James said, once he stood up. He gave the room a general bow, knowing this was the starman way, then quickly left at Ryes' nod.

"Is everyone all set for the Gather, or those who'll be going?" Ryes asked, since she had quite a few people still around her, sitting, as well as gathered around the room, standing. There was excitement in the air! She got a lot of happy nods and noticed a few now gathering into small groups, talking in low voices.

"As much as we can be," Kovin said, as he gathered Minn and Phil, ready to run out and see that new bridge. He stopped long enough to give Raya a kiss, then hurried out the door, too.

"We'll manage! We've had practice now," Raya assured her, laughing lightly. Ardis nodded her agreement, her smile lighting her eyes.

"Will there be any of those southern Talents at this gather?" Adina questioned, as others suddenly paid attention, curious. Ryes gave her a nod.

"Yes, I expect we'll see a few of them, but hopefully we've already taken care of the nastier ones, so the rest shouldn't be a problem. There're plenty of good-heart ones, like Shams, too. He nodded and blushed, as the rest in the room realized he was a caravaner, too, already accepting him as another Winterhavener.

"Grandfather Darman will make sure they're minding their manners," he confirmed to the room, while Lissel squeezed his hand in reassurance. He was blushing at the attention turned his way. Several of the Sleepers gave him a nod of understanding, but he was sure some of them wanted a chance to prove themselves against the rougher elements of the caravaner Talents. Now he fully understood all that Gurri, and his friends had done in that battle. For all their efforts to outright kill Ryes, they failed, for which he was greatly relieved, and knew they fully deserved to have their Talents burned out.

"Anyone have any questions?" Ryes asked, looking about the room. No one spoke up immediately, and she did get a lot of heads shaking, so raised her hand, as she gestured towards the doors. "See you later! Enjoy your day," she said, "I'll be in my office for a bit to answer any private questions."

She saw Ethan's eyes light up, as he gave her a nod. Maren was still beside her, so she guessed he had questions, too. Aunt Adina and Hadu appeared to be conferring, while Denas appeared still in shock, but she gave her a brave smile before she and Monty got up and went out the door. So, Ryes stood and headed out to her own office with Maren beside her, quiet for the moment.

# Well Met

## Chapter 24

They arrived in grand style, as they had at the Great Spring Gather, only this time they used the Avenger II and the Pike Forward, as well as two helicopters and three rovers. Weeks ago, Ryes and the Talents of Winterhaven had used a practice session to expand the area they used for the Great Gathers by moving the walls much further out. They reinforced them and made the walls appear more decorative, while weaving in useful things like scanners and video devices, so they could be more aware of what was happening around their walls. There were now built-in deterrents to prevent people from climbing them, as had happened at the last one. Even so, there was barely room for the larger starcraft, even if Darman had granted them a generous space. Ryes noted the awe in even Darman's face from her perch up in the Pike. Soon, they had the whole group assembled before the gathered elders, outside their own main gate.

"You've been busy," Kyma accused Garth, laughing as he threw his arms about him, giving him a welcoming hug, before anyone else. "Of course, your wife gave me a brief glimpse of one of the new vehicles, a few months ago, but it was much smaller than these two," he told him, after they released each other. Garth was laughing at this, nodding his head. It sounded like something Ryes would do.

"When she puts a ship through a battery of tests, she tends to wander far across Tayna. There looks to be almost four times the crowd, as was gathered in the Spring," he added in comment.

"Word got out," Darman replied, then stepped forward and threw his arms about Garth, too. Ryes stood beside him and laughed unexpectedly as Kyma gave her a hug.

"Feel free to stop by to visit any time you like," he invited her, as he laughed again. "Your new ships are very impressive, but do you always fly them upside down?" he teased in question. Ryes blushed at this, shaking her head no.

"Yes, she does," Maren supplied, before she could speak up. "Upside down, sideways, whatever she feels like in the moment. It's always best to wear restraints when she's piloting the craft."

"Maren!" she protested, blushing more darkly. Ethan chuckled as he stepped over to the cousins, putting an arm over each of their shoulders.

"Come now, she's our second-best pilot," he scolded Maren, chuckling as he did so. "And you've never really been endangered when she's been at the helm."

"That's true," he agreed, seeing the elders, who knew them both, were laughing heartily.

"Ethan! What happened to you? You look so much younger!" Kyma exclaimed, then spotted Rowan and saw it was the same for him, too.

"Ryes decided I could use a few adjustments. She's still not the skilled Healer Maren is, but has some excellent instincts, none the less," he replied. He rather liked it that she managed to turn the clock back for him by about fifty years, at least.

"Then, my dear, would it be too much of an imposition for you to make a few adjustments for me, too?" Kyma requested. She smiled, nodding her head.

"I fully expected you, Darman, Rinna, Darin, Dara and Dyan to be among the first I would see," she returned, smiling. "Give us time to get things set up and then I'll be more than happy to do what I can for each of you," she promised.

"This is something I still have to learn," Maren commented to her in a low voice, "if you don't mind teaching me."

"I don't mind. There's still so much I have yet to truly learn about Healing and you're still my favorite teacher," she replied. He saw the truth in her eyes and gave her a nod in understanding. There were times when he impressed even Ted and the rest of his human staff, when it came to knowledge of the body, its systems, and organs. Yet, he found there was still so much more to learn, too.

"Come, come to our central fire and we'll have a proper introduction, all around," Darman invited. Ryes hung back as Garth, Sabin, their elders, and the ships' captains all stepped forward, but Rinna grabbed her arm, pulling her along.

"You need to be there, too. You're second in command of Winterhaven and should be a part of things. Don't let the men exclude you, merely because you're a woman! That would be thinking more like the plainsmen," she scolded her in English, as Ryes balked. Torr cocked an eyebrow at this but nodded his head in full support.

"They've left you out of too much, as is. Go. I'll make sure things here get organized and finished," he told her, smiling. Ryes smiled and gave them both a nod of her head, then walked beside her, as Rinna started telling her the news she heard, all in English.

Maren decided to join the women, with Rhodi, Poli, and Raffa following them, wanting to hear and be a part of this, too.

"It's getting off to an interesting start," Monty commented to Torr, standing with his arms crossed. Leon and Ivan trotted past them to catch up. They were serving as guards for Ryes today.

"You've got that right," Torr agreed, huffing a laugh. "And I'm sure the larger crowd's due to our presence, and technologies. We'd best get organized fast." They saw a group of young cubs running toward their gate, sure they wanted to see the starships, but Nicos headed them off, stopping them at the gate. Monty gave him a nod, then turned to note the strangers among those who traveled on the rovers.

"Who're they?" he asked, puzzled.

"Hitch riders, as your people say," Garvin replied, walking closer. "There were lots of people standing beside the roads, just waiting for us to come along and pick them up. We finally wised up and started charging them for the ride. Maybe we ought to start running some kind of shuttle system for those needing a ride out to the gather and back?"

"But what're we going to do with them?" Monty questioned. It looked like there were at least twenty more to place. Torr chuckled at this, nodding his head.

"We'll have to set up a side area for them to camp, just outside our wall. If they need anything, we'll help, but otherwise, they're on their own."

"That makes sense," he agreed, smiling. Then, the two of them turned and started gathering their people, to get them started on helping the hitchhikers in setting up the temporary shelters.

In his introductions, Darman heavily stressed that Ryes and Garth were true-mates. This statement surprised many of the Elders, who were meeting them for the first time. Garth understood his doing it this way, after all the interest in Ryes, which had come about at the last two gathers they attended. Ryes blushed but stood beside her husband with her head held high. It turned into a long and tedious trial, with each and every group being formally introduced to everyone else. The three ship captains from Earth drew the most intense interest, even from Darman, himself. There was a little panic with some thinking the Snagospin would soon be back to bomb them, but the Winterhaveners and the captains put everyone's mind to ease by assuring them they were keeping a sharp watch upon any Snag interest in their solar system. Garth didn't want Ryes mentioned, specifically, as a part of that watch, still wanting her importance downplayed. When it was finally over, a feast was served up, with Rinna and the other caravaners working as servers.

"Do you want me to help?" Ryes questioned her in a low voice.

"If you even try, I'll break your arm," she returned with a smile, but the look in her eyes was serious. "You need to remember your position, my dear. I didn't raise you to play serving wench and don't you forget it!"

"But you're not without position either," Ryes protested, noting Poli's quick interest. Captain Walker was also listening, as they were speaking English.

"Ah, but I'm also using this ruse to see where everyone's mind is focused, and to pick up any useful information which I might happen to see, or hear. I've been doing this since before you were born, Sweetling, so they ignore my presence. You, on the other hand, would attract a lot of interest, as you're a hot item around here, as the humans say. The Sandweaver's captain is back, with a bunch of other captain friends, and a few others from some of the western continents and isles. There're stories being circulated about what you can do, and only because I know you, I know most of them are true, but we've been putting them down as false stories, as there's already too much interest in you. So, stay right here, between Garth and Maren, and you'll be all right," she advised. But, as Ryes was going to ask her more about it, she turned and left to help one of her sons, who was serving some blue-skinned people, nearby.

"Listen to your grandmother and behave," Rowan admonished Ryes, seeing she was about to stand up. She looked to him, puzzled and pained, then subsided and leaned against Garth's arm for comfort. He chuckled at this, nodding his head. He was glad Rinna warned her, as she was one of the few people Ryes rarely doubted.

"I tried to tell you that almost every man here is hot after you. With your green eyes, strong Talents and five little ones, I'm hard pressed, as is," Garth teased, chuckling.

"Seven little ones, now," she corrected him, then sighed. "I feel like a caged bird," she protested, thinking of the birds they were raising for eggs and meat.

"At least you don't have to sing for your supper," Captain Yun teased her, grinning. She'd given him, and those of his crew who wanted it, a basic understanding of Dolbith. He had one of his ensigns

288

playing interpreter for Lindell and Devin, while he participated more fully, looking to enjoy the gather's intro event all the more.

"Ryes, you're free to participate, and visit people here, it's just that we're making extra sure to have plenty of escort for everyone," Garth told her. "Especially you and our cubs."

"Chirp, chirp," she replied, in a low voice. "I'm still far more deadly than anyone you could assign to protect me."

"But you hesitate, where your escort won't," Maren corrected her, nudging her in the side.

"Alright, I promise to behave," she finally returned, knowing it was what the both of them wanted to hear from her. She sighed as she noted Garth grinning in triumph.

"Darman's offered to help with security. He said this unexpected crowd even has him worried," Sabin told them, in a low voice, as he returned.

"It has HIM worried?" Garth returned, then smiled as he thought that if worse came to worse, they could use the shield barriers, previously used on the Challenger and her shuttles, to project an invisible barrier as a deterrent, which no one could skirt. Maybe set up a safe zone with one at their booths, as a strong place to retreat? He'd have to talk with Mitt and Axel about it today.

The introduction ceremony and feast were finally wrapping up with everyone standing and coming together to meet each other, face-to-face. It was almost a mob scene around the small Winterhaven contingent. Rhodi, Poli and Raffa all found themselves hugged, kissed and unexpected gifts presented to them.

"This is amazing," Poli commented in a low voice, in English, so only her two close friends could hear. "We are still strangers to them, and yet they are almost getting into fights to get closer, to meet us."

"Kahmarr was never like this," Rhodi returned in Dolbith, smiling.

"Lady, you're from Kahmarr? Then how did you get here to Tayna?" an elder asked, astounded. Then he noted how she and the other two women were dressed in thin, wispy, colorful dresses. He'd never seen their like upon Tayna, before! She turned and smiled for him, nodding her head.

289

"I was born and raised upon Kahmarr. I came here by starship but spent the last four hundred years in a cold sleep. Ryes, her friends and family have rescued and revived myself, and my friends, out of the goodness of their hearts. We are now a part of Winterhaven," she explained, knowing he'd never believe her.

"Please, Lady, I'd love to hear your story, if I may," he pressed, seeking an invitation into the Winterhaven encampment. "I'll even bring my youngest son to meet you. He'd never believe how old you say you are!" Rhodi blushed a dark gold at this, glad no one in Winterhaven ever brought the subject up. As far as all of them were concerned, the years they spent in suspension never happened, and they were all the young women they'd been, before being encased upon Doran's orders.

"We might condone a telling of our tale, so others may learn from the trials we have endured," Poli suggested, in Rhodi's silence. "Let us say, later tonight. After the evening meal?" she offered. There was a chorus of replies, as she realized she just invited every elder within hearing range. She wasn't sure if Garth would be too happy with that.

"I look forward to the tale," the original elder replied, bowing to the three women. They were on the end of the Winterhaven reception line, with two of the strange-looking men keeping a sharp, protective watch over them, and definitely held some kind of importance, as they didn't appear subservient in any way. Leon took out a token, handing it to the man.

"This is your passage into our camp. Present it when requested," he instructed. The elder grinned merrily, bowing to him in return.

"My thanks, kind sir," he responded, then trotted off, clutching the precious token in his hand. There were suddenly a dozen old men demanding tokens too, so they might hear the women's story. Leon laughed, then gave out another six, saying that was all he had to give. The rest subsided, appearing unhappy. Perhaps on the morrow there would another storytelling session? They walked away discussing it among themselves.

"You have your own fan club, now," Ivan teased Rhodi, in a low voice and with a big smile upon his face. She laughed at this, nodding her head.

"I would have never imagined," she agreed, feeling a little uncomfortable with all this attention and glad of the security with them today. "Now I understand why Ryes was so reluctant to come, it can seem a bit much."

"She got her first taste at the Caravaner's Spring Gather, so stayed in the background for the Great Spring Gather. But Rinna insisted and she never says no to her," Leon explained to them, seeing the crowd was finally thinning out.

"Why did that woman say that she raised her?" Raffa questioned sharply, as she frowned, seeing she was talking to Ryes in a low voice. She didn't know her and didn't like her interference with her great niece.

"Rinna and Darman spent every winter in Matlowe Village, staying with Rowan and Ryes. Ryes once told me that she had two grandfathers, Rowan and Darman, and one grandmother, Rinna, and Tara, their daughter, was her mother, but Tara died in a fire, and Ryes said she still misses her a lot," he replied, seeing the jealousy in her eyes, as she watched Ryes and Rinna.

"Rowan never took another mate?" Poli questioned, not understanding why he wouldn't - especially with a small granddaughter to raise.

"He and Jana were true-mates," he returned, seeing Raffa return her attention to him, nodding her head at this.

"So, I heard. Then it was only her and Rowan, with the others there during the winter months. Why?" Raffa asked.

"Because they were village outcasts," Maren explained, joining them, since Rinna and Darman were helping to watch after Ryes for now. "Rowan refused to turn Ryes over to my mother for her care, since he feared Korman would kill her, after killing her mother, father and siblings. My mother and Korman were living together. The village elders were angered by Rowan's insinuation of my father as a cold murderer, so banished Rowan from the village proper. It seemed to suit our grandfather, for he and Ryes got along well, living down by the Yuri. It was years before the whole thing was ignored."

"At least she had you, Garth and the rest of your friends, Maren," she replied, smiling. She had to get Rowan to sit down and tell her the whole tale!

"No. We used to beat her up and chase her away when we were little. We didn't know any better. She spent most of her time in the forest around Matlowe. It took the whole village practically starving before we finally asked her for help. She wasn't called The Huntress, for nothing," he related.

"All Old History," Rowan scolded his grandson, scowling. "Come, let's get back to our camp and lend a hand to whatever needs to be finished," he urged, gesturing the group to start moving.

"You're going to give us the full story, brother-in-law?" Raffa pressed.  Rowan smiled, nodding his head at this.

"If you insist, but not until we get everything else finished.  Perhaps over dinner?" he suggested.

"She'll be squirming.  She hates us to tell it," Maren commented, his eyes merry.

"So, she will..." Rowan chuckled, nodding.  They started for their camp, with Ryes, Garth, Sabin, and the rest following.


"This only admits two," Paul told the elder, who was presenting one of their tokens.  It wasn't one of the "special" ones, so he couldn't make exceptions.  The elder looked unhappy but nodded his head and turned to the eight people with him.

"I'll take Klinn in with me.  Perhaps they'll have another storytelling tomorrow evening?" Sona offered the rest of his family and friends. "I'll ask the Ladies."

"We'll wait for you at the caravaner's fire, grandfather," one of the young women told him.  He smiled and nodded his head at this, then turned and entered the Winterhaven camp, going as the stout young man at the gate directed.  A small flying machine followed them overhead, as they left the gate.  It almost looked like a toy.

"These machines are frightening," Klinn commented in a low voice, noting the many people going about their business, within their interestingly walled perimeter.  Sona chuckled at this, nodding his head.

"Kyma told me that it was the most fun he'd had in his life, to ride inside the great machines," he replied, finally ignoring the little one following them.  "He said the Winterhaveners use them as if they were born with their presence all their lives.  But he told me he could never tire of going for a ride, himself.  I hope to be included this time, since we couldn't make it to the last Great Gather."

"If Great Chief Kyma has no fear of them, then I can be brave," he responded, smiling as he could imagine Kyma riding in one of the strange, flying machines they were now walking past.  Then, he saw Kyma getting out of one of their largest flying machines, ahead of them. "Grandfather, there's Chief Kyma now," he said, pointing him out.  Sona laughed, then hurried over to him, bowing as they stopped before him.  Kyma laughed, pulling the older man back up to face him.

"Sona!  What a surprise.  What're you doing here?" he asked.

"We've come to hear the tales of the women from Kahmarr," he answered, seeing the interest of the others with Kyma.

"Ah, that's an idea.  I'll hear them, too," he replied.  "Or do you have something else you want to show me first, Ryes?"  She laughed, shaking her head.

"I'm too tired.  On the morrow if you don't mind," she promised, smiling.  He nodded his head to this, then turned, throwing an arm over Sona's shoulder and guided him toward the central fire, where he was sure the stories would be told tonight, glad they expanded the area, so there was room for a large crowd.

"Rhodi, Poli, I've found two of your guests," he shouted to the women, as they emerged from the area of shelters, heading in the same direction.  They stopped, curiosity in their eyes, then recognized Kyma and smiled.

"Most kind of you, dear Kyma," Poli replied, as they waited for the men.

"This Ladies is Sona, Chief of Island Hold, and one of his sons, Klinn," he to introduced them.  "Gentlemen, may I introduce Rhodi of House Klark and Poli of House Himna."

"I and Klinn are happy to meet you," Sona said, speaking up as he smiled.  Klinn's eyes met Rhodi's, and they both stood staring at each other, entranced, as if no one else existed about them.

"It is you," she whispered, barely moving her lips.  He nodded his head, amazed.

"I thought I only dreamed you," Klinn admitted, appearing astounded.

Suddenly, they stepped forward and were both laughing, and crying, and hugging each other tightly, astounding Poli, Kyma and Sona.  They started kissing and both talking in low voices filled with excitement and awe.  Denas and Ruan stepped over, appearing concerned and puzzled.

"How could they know each other?" Sona questioned, puzzled over his son's strange behavior with a newly met woman.  "He's never taken a mate before, nor ever appeared interested, even in free mating with any woman, nor man."  Kyma was laughing heartily.

"Perhaps they're true-makes from another life, like Maren and Dotti?" Kyma conjectured. Denas considered this idea and gave him a nod of agreement.

"It must be," Ruan agreed, puzzled. After several long minutes, they seemed to realize there were people around them and they turned to the rest, still with an arm around each other.

"Like Maren and Dotti?" Poli questioned them, knowing Klinn wouldn't understand the reference. Rhodi blushed and nodded her head.

"I believe so. We must have been true-mates in a previous life, as I suddenly find my heart filled with love, and a feeling of being complete," Rhodi responded, casting a quick glance at Klinn.

"Me, too! I feel like I've finally come home to my one and only! I've heard stories of this happening, but can now say ours, if no other, is truth," Klinn agreed, smiling happily, and acted as if he couldn't take his eyes off his dearest love for more than a moment.

"Let us all go to the fire ring and tell our stories, so people can understand the different paths our lives have taken to get us here, then afterwards, you both can spend the rest of the evening getting acquainted anew," Poli suggested, gesturing towards the campfire. The group laughed, as another four strangers approached, and so together they turned to the comfort of the warm fire. Kyma threw an arm over Sona's shoulders and was talking to him in a low voice, as they walked. Rhodi and Klinn still walked with an arm around each other. The happiness was plain on both their faces, as they seemed to refuse to be parted from each other now.

# New Additions

Chapter 25

"Now, are you sure you want to go up with Ryes piloting the Avenger?" Maren asked Kyma, as they stood outside the entry gate to the Winterhaven camp. "It's a shame to see a man screaming like a little girl," he teased, his eyes merry.

"I've been with her in the other types of vehicles, I'll be fine with her piloting this bigger one," he assured him, grinning as he cuffed his shoulder affectionately. "You worry too much," he chided, "I'm old enough to not be embarrassed, no matter what situation I find myself in."

"I'm only trying to help," he offered as a light tease, spreading his hands out, palm up. "Just make sure to strap in well." His eyes were merry as they met Kyma's.

"I will. Aren't you coming with us? And you've seemed to have lost your laughter... why?" he questioned concerned, frowning now. Usually, Maren went everywhere with Ryes, and his merry laugh lightened everyone's heart.

"I'm still trying to find myself, after being pressed into a horrible challenge. I'll tell you about it later. Today, we're starting a round of conferences on Healers and healing. I want to establish a standard of training and even start training non-Talents in healing techniques, which don't require Talent. Too many people are going without proper care, because of the lack across this whole world. If we trained men and women in the techniques our humans use, many lives would be saved, and much suffering eliminated."

"A noble cause. I wish you luck in this quest of yours, Maren, and look forward to our talk later. I'd like to hear about that challenge," he paused, appearing to be thinking. "I wonder why our ancestors relied so much upon Talents, when the humans went the other way?" he queried in return, wondering.

"According to our Sleepers and Ryes' Aunt Adina, who knew more of the worlds before the attack, they did have people trained in medical treatments, much like the humans, but Talent was so common on Kahmarr, they usually only worked out in the dangerous colonies, where the Talents refused to go. Tayna was far too settled and civilized then, to have many non-Talented Healers, at the time of the attack," he explained. "I must go. It'd look bad if the one Healer, who was insisting upon these measures, was late.  Have a good time," he urged.

"I'll look after your cousin, in your stead," he offered, smiling as he nodded his head.  He saw the relief in Maren's eyes and knew this was the best thing he could've done for him.

"Thank you.  I'm in your debt, Great Chief," he replied with a bow.  Leon smiled at seeing this, understanding, as he was one of the guards at the gate this morning, and heard everything, whether, or not, he wanted to know.

"I'm in your debt already, Great Healer.  You've saved my people from much anguish, and somehow songs and stories don't seem enough payment," he responded, bowing to Maren in turn. "Go. I must find Sabin first, before we leave," he urged.  Maren nodded, then turned and continued toward the caravaner's camp, wondering why he needed to see Sabin so early in the morning?  It had to be the basket he carried.  The mystery would have to wait for later.

"Kyma, this is a surprise - so early in the morning," Sabin said, as he answered the polite scratching at his shelter's door.  He'd been playing with his cubs, keeping them busy and contained, while Ardis and Katas were in the showers.  He was already showered and dressed, at least. "Come in," he added in invitation.  Kyma nodded his head, stepping inside, impressed.  No tent, but a real dwelling with roof, walls, floors and windows.  A home away from home!  Still, it showed the disorder, which normally fell when people were just unpacking and setting up their dwellings.  At least the Winterhaveners were still normal people!  Sabin gestured him to a chair and they both sat, as his two sons were crawling and playing in their small, fenced pen.

"Ryes wanted me here early for a flight up to see the Challenger.  But I've some business to conduct with you, first," he explained.  He extended the large basket he carried.  Sabin looked puzzled but accepted it, wondering what was inside.  It was heavy.

"What is it?" he asked, as he hesitated to look within.

"See for yourself," he invited, his face neutral, but with a hint of a smile's echo.  Sabin lifted back the light blanket, then sat, gaping in amazement.  He looked back to Kyma, questions in his eyes.

"There's no doubt?" he asked, his heart suddenly pounding. Kyma chuckled merrily now, shaking his head.

"Aina made very sure. They're both yours, but she also said they both carry the same sickness as Sernn, so they'll need Maren's care, to be fully healthy. What're you going to name your new daughters?" he pressed.

"Daughters?" he asked, then shook his head, as Ardis and Katas entered the house. He realized he felt more than a little numb right now, as if he were a thief, who'd been caught.

"What's the matter?" Ardis questioned, stepping over to see what her husband held on his lap. She looked inside the basket, seeing two, very small, newborn cubs. "Whose are they?" She looked to Kyma for the answers, seeing Sabin looked lost and embarrassed. Suddenly, she remembered and knew the answer!

"They're your husband's children, fathered against his will," he explained, unsure of how much of the tale he'd told her. She sighed, nodding her head. Then gave her shower bundle to Katas and took the basket from him, showing them to Katas, as she stood near, wanting to see, too. They were excited to see the two little ones.

"Then I accept them as my own. Sabin told me all about it, with Ryes filling me in more fully on the situation. He's my true-mate, so they're my cubs now," she assured him, smiling. Sabin stood and put his arms about her and the basket, holding her tight, as he kissed her. She was his anchor, as he'd found himself suddenly swamped by the memories of the nightmare he'd lived through in that Hold. Katas was laughing, as Kyma chuckled.

"So, Lady Ardis, both you and your husband need to think up names for your new daughters. Aina has the exact time and date of their births recorded, since you people are sticklers for such things. If you don't mind, I have to go find Ryes; we're headed up for the Challenger this morning."

"The Challenger II, after she's re-commissioned next week," Sabin informed him, pulling back from her for a moment. "She should be in her shelter, next door," he added.

"Oh, I'd better have Ryes, or one of the Healers bring my milk back in. These little ones still need nursing. They look very young. How old are they?"

"Only two weeks old. Senah was put to death immediately after their birth. My youngest sister cared for them, until we could get them here to you. She was hard pressed, as she has two little cubs of her own. There must be something in the air this year, as everywhere I've heard of women having two or three cubs in a birth at a time, and they're all surviving! For far too long, it's been single births, who were lucky to survive," he commented.

"It's as if the Goddess Korenda's been freed of some bonds! Look at Ryes with her five," Ardis returned, smiling. "I'll come with you. I think the Healers were going to some kind of conference this morning," she said. He laughed and nodded his head, turning for the door.

"That's what Maren told me, as I arrived." They walked together to Garth and Ryes' shelter, knocking on the door. Garth answered it, looking surprised as Sabin, Ardis, and Kyma stood outside.

"Oh, I forgot you were going on the flight this morning with Ryes, Kyma," he then said, stepping back and gesturing everyone inside.

"More than just that, Garth," Ardis stated, then showed him the contents of the basket she held. He looked amazed, then frowned as he and Sabin exchanged glances. He remembered it all, too.

"Ardis!" Ryes exclaimed, as she stepped into the front room with Shaysa and Shyla in her arms. "Is there something wrong?" she asked as she noted the look Garth and Sabin cast each other.

"Not really, but I'm going to need your help to bring my milk back in. We've just acquired two, new daughters," she announced, smiling grandly. Ryes laughed lightly at this, then stepped over to look at the two tiny cubs in the basket, who were just waking up. She passed their daughters over to Garth, picking one of the cubs up.

"Ah, yes. Like Sernn," she returned, then closed her eyes and extended her Healing Talent, making a few adjustments for her, as her instincts dictated. "Maren's going to have to finish this, though. I don't have the training to do all they're going to need," she apologized. Then replaced the one cub, to pick up the second. Again, she made the adjustments she felt she could do safely. She put the little girl back into the basket, turning to her friend. "I can't say that I don't know what it's like, for I do," she offered, then extended her Healing to Ardis, as she put a hand upon her shoulder, helping her body to produce milk, once more.

"I feel so heavy, again. It's such a strange sensation," she told her with a proud smile lighting up her face, as Ryes opened her eyes.

"So, you finally have more daughters to call your own. What're you going to name them?" she asked.

"The one with the darker hair looks like what I recall Seena's sister used to look like, so her name will be Sassa, too," she told her, catching Sabin's eye for a moment. He saw she was happy, so finally relaxed. He nodded his head, agreeing with this choice. "And the one with the light-colored hair will be Rivi, after my littermate."

"You have a littermate, Ardis?" Kyma asked wondering. He didn't recall seeing anyone like her about. He liked her feistiness and devotion and would've loved to have such a wife of his own. His last wife had died unexpectedly, three summers ago.

"Rivi died as a cub in a bad fall when we climbed to the roof of one of the deserted huts in Matlowe Village. We all knew we weren't supposed to do such things, but never understood why until then," she explained, with a sad sigh. "I've never forgotten her and now she'll be honored through this little daughter of mine." Ryes gave her a quick hug, wishing she'd known her, too.

"I'm sure she'd be proud," Garth offered, nodding his head. He recalled Rivi, too. He remembered that day clearly. They were all trying to jump between rooftops, but Rivi fell short, scrabbling for the edge and unable to get her claws solidly anchored before any of the rest of them could get to her to help. The way she lay, twisted wrong with a dark puddle beneath her upon the ground afterwards, would forever be in his mind.

"My apologies for reminding you of a tragedy," Kyma told her.

"It's all right, I'm well over it, now. Besides, I know she'd love it that I've named this little one after her. I wish my mother were here to see them. We'll have to make a trip out to Matlowe, to show them off to her, my older sister and brother. So, excuse me. I have some little ones to feed and change," she said, quickly turning for the door, feeling tears starting to well up with the memories and joy crowding her heart.

"I'll be right back," Sabin told Garth, then gave Kyma a nod of his head. "And we'll see you at this afternoon's meeting," he added, with a smile. Kyma and Garth, both, gave him nods in return, so he quickly left, following in his wife's wake. Raby, Sayer, Calla and Chatis came in, as Sabin held the door open for them.

"Well, if you're all ready, we'll load up the Avenger II and have our breakfast on the Challenger this morning. Axel has more last-minute adjustments needed, and I promised Mitt I'd take the next call," Ryes told them. Raby looked uncertain, while Sayer was excited.

"I finally get to go up to the Challenger? Cool!" she happily exclaimed. She ran over and hugged Ryes, then rushed to put her shower things away. Garth, Ryes and Kyma were chuckling at this.

"Do I have to?" Raby asked, reluctant to go.

"I wanted to show you our quarters on the ship. Don't you want a say in what your room will look like? Otherwise, I'll have to leave it painted a plain white. I've already packed several paints you can pick from to paint your room with," she informed her, smiling. Raby made a face, then subsided with a nod of her head.

"Alright," she replied. "But what if I get space sick?" she asked.

"I'm a Healer too, remember? Anyway, it isn't as much getting sick up there, as it's getting sick down here, afterwards. I think Axel calls it `planet sickness,' and it seems the worse of the two. I guess your body adjusts to being up in space, so that when you return, it objects to the change. You'll be all right, I promise you. I survived it, after all," she assured her. Then turned and collected the bags she packed last night, having put them next to the stroller. Garth put the two girls he held into their seats, as Ryes and Raby went to get the remaining three.

"They're getting so big," Kyma commented, looking down at the younger cubs. "And who might these two little ladies be?" he added, noting the two new girls in their midst, as if they belonged as part of the family.

"Kyma, I'd like to introduce you to our two newest additions, from out of the past. This is Calla and Chatis. They were left for us in frozen suspension, in a small vault beneath Matlowe Village. Ryes and I adopted them. Calla and Chatis, I'd like you to meet Great Chief Kyma, Chief of all the Mountain Tribes," he told the girls, seeing they were looking up at him with questions in their eyes.

"We are pleased," Calla told him, smiling brightly, having recalled the proper response her own mother had taught her, long ago, giving him a small bow.

"Yes," Chatis agreed, not knowing what to say, as she copied her. He chuckled at this, giving them a small bow in return.

"The honor is mine," he returned. "Prince Callas?" he questioned Garth, suddenly realizing the connection the one child might possess.

"Yes. She's truly a princess. Adina insists it might be why he was so careful in passing his titles onto me, so his last daughter would still have position and status. I believe that's merely a side issue, since their last names are now Li. There's more to this and I haven't found the right memory rod to explain it, yet. Perhaps, this winter, when things quiet down a little," he suggested. Kyma huffed a laugh at this, nodding his head. It was the one time of the year when he could catch up on his scrolls and accounts.

"Slow down? My dear, you're living in fantasy. We still have three more ships from Hailys to upgrade, the new vans to build for the caravaners, the remaining two human ships to refurbish and heaven only knows what else will come up before, during, and in the middle of everything else," Ryes scolded with a smile, as she returned with another two bags thrown over her shoulders, and two cubs in her arms. Raby carried another bag and Rhin.

"I would hope otherwise, but you may be right, Sweet One," he replied, as he took the cubs from her and put them into the stroller. He then gave her a quick kiss as Sayer emerged with a bag. "You be careful," he warned. She smiled merrily, giving him a nod of her head.

"You'd better believe it!" she returned, then made sure they had everything gathered.

"It looks like you're moving in, up there," Kyma commented as he grabbed two of the earlier bags, she had ready to go.

"Just getting a few things done, while we're there," she replied merrily. Garth opened the door for them, giving each of the girls a kiss on their way out. Monty, Denas, Casta, Almas, Tieva, and Rheas were awaiting them outside. Damian ran up, smiling as he saw he was still on time, but left, as if he forgot something. Casta took the bags Ryes was carrying for her.

"Don't be up there all day," Garth warned. She nodded her head in response.

"We won't. So, let's get going," Ryes urged, taking the lead toward the shuttle. James appeared with an aide, walking toward them.

"May I come along?" he requested.

"We've got a lot of work to finish," she warned. He nodded his head to this.

"If it gets boring, I'll have one of the Wrath's shuttles pick me up, until you're finished. I've got work to complete up there, too," he assured her. She laughed at this, then gestured her welcome. They fell in with their group, as James wondered about the young children. If she was going to be working, why take the children along? He'd ask about it, later. As they arrived at the shuttle's main hatch, Darman and Rinna were awaiting her. She laughed at this, gesturing a welcome.

"I should've guessed," she teased, then opened the hatch, "Chief Exec on board," she announced to the ship's computer.

301

"Affirmative," it replied, bringing a smile to James' lips. A high-end security system for a shuttle? But then, their fleet of starships only officially numbered two. The Challenger and Pike Forward. Each and every one, including the shuttles, were precious to them all.

"Are you going to be all right with this?" Garth asked Sabin, as they sat down to breakfast together in the dining hall. Ardis and Katas were getting their breakfast trays, having set the cubs up in highchairs and tabletop carriers. Luckily, there were two carriers still available, with Marc finding them quickly among their supplies. Marc Kline had resumed his duties as Quartermaster and was doing an excellent job.

"I'll get used to it, but it strikes me as an added cruelty that they're both daughters," he commented, as he looked at the two, tiny girl cubs again. He didn't know what he felt, but he had to admit to himself that he was proud, in an odd way. Garth was chuckling as he picked up his mug of tea. "At least Ardis seems happy with them." Sabin put a finger under Rivi's hand, seeing the contrast in size. It was a miracle, all over again! They were so perfect.

"And she named them well. It's amazing how tiny they look, next to your sons," he said. Ardis and Katas returned with smiles upon their faces.

"My gosh, it didn't seem so long ago when these two cubs were that size. They've grown a lot," he returned. Ardis nodded her head, admiring her family anew.

"They've grown quickly. Now you see what the Goddess Korenda's done to you for teasing Garth about his daughters?" she pointed out, remembering that day, as they sat down with them.

"I'll have to make proper apologies in my prayers," he responded, chuckling as he nodded his head.

"And what do we have here?" Ethan asked as he and Rowan stepped over to their table, trays in hand. They'd heard Katas and Ardis joking about some new cubs, as they awaited their orders. And here were two tabletop carriers with tiny cubs within. Ardis looked proud, smiling as she grabbed onto Sabin's arm.

"We've gain two daughters," she proudly informed him. "Kyma brought them to us this morning."

302

"Oh," Rowan replied, catching on as to their origins at once. "From your original venture, to settle a peace treaty?" Sabin nodded his head, blushing a dark gold. "But they're both so beautiful, there can be no shame in such an outcome," he assured him, smiling as he bent closer to look at their tiny faces.

"I forget how small they can be," Ethan returned, chuckling. He closely examined them, after Rowan straightened back up. They sat down next to Garth.

"Then, where's Kyma? And I would've thought Darman would be here with us this morning, too," Rowan questioned, picking up his tea, as he looked to his grandson-in-law.

"Guess," he invited in return, having gotten word from Leon about Darman and Rinna's whereabouts.

"Ah, the Avenger's missing," Ethan replied, catching on. He saw Ryes and the cubs were also gone. "Ryes had to go up to help with something and took a proper entourage."

"She wanted to give the girls a chance to decorate their quarters on the ship, while she's busy. The ship should be ready for test runs in a few days," Garth replied. "We're holding her re-commissioning ceremony next week."

"She's too big to land here," Rowan protested, frowning, having seen the ship when visiting Ryes there, once before.

"We're going up there. That's why the Pike's here with us, so we'll have plenty of room to accommodate everyone," Sabin explained, smiling. He couldn't wait for her first run!

"We do get left out, on occasion," Ethan commented to his friend. Rowan chuckled as he nodded his head in concurrence.

"Yes, we do," he replied, appearing irritated.

"Now, you can't even begin to imagine what I feel like, at times," Ardis scolded all of them. There was laughter in response, but Sabin knew she meant it.

"I'll see about including you more often, my dear," he assured her once he calmed down. She humphed, then turned her attention to her breakfast. She wished she could be up there with Ryes right now, too. She was getting tired of being left behind, and if Ryes could take her cubs up with her, why can't she bring her own brood? She'd take the time to discuss it with Ryes soon.

"The Silver won't do one thing I order it to do. The computer says Monty's the Captain and it'll only take orders from him!" Madison Elbridge almost shouted, returning to the extended rooms she shared with her cousins, belowground in Winterhaven. She plopped down onto the couch, looking disgusted.

"He is the direct descendent of our Captain," Jared Hesse reminded her, smiling. "What's the use anyway? She's a wreck!"

"She maybe a wreck, but she's still the only home I've ever known. Loren, can't you do anything with it?"

"Nope. Our Captain Monty took steps to make sure the computer was safeguarded. I can't touch it, or the ship's totally trash," she told her. She could understand some of her frustration. They were the only survivors from the Silver and were now cut off from all they knew, and planet bound no less! It was frustrating and nerve wracking. The people here were kind to them and welcomed them in as family, but this wasn't Trinity, and the military men, who were cooling their heels while awaiting repairs of their own ships, told them of Guardian's destruction and the isolationist mindset of the Trinity colonists. So even if they had a starship, they had nowhere else to go. Maddy didn't see it yet and might never accept it. They'd probably have to go to Trinity, itself, to show her.

"Hey, Monty and Connor treat us pretty well," Jared stressed. "It isn't too bad a place to call home for a while." Maddy snorted with disgust. He wanted a shot at working up on either their big warship, or in building the starport they had in the works. It'd be something to do and he'd be back in space at least.

"I don't think either of them could cut it, to make Captain Monty's crew, and you know it," she returned, hotly. She thought they were both pretty lame. And to think that Monty and that cat woman of his were having a baby. It was unbearable!

"I think they would have," Jared returned. "What's with you? You've been hyper about everything since we awoke in sickbay here."

"Nothing's wrong with me," she returned. "I just can't stand being stuck here!" There was a knock on their door frame, and she realized anyone out in the hallways could probably hear her clearly.

"Come in," Loren invited, standing up. Connor lifted the drape over their door looking inside. He obviously didn't feel welcome right now. "She's just blowing a little," she explained, smiling. He smiled and nodded in return.

"I just got word from Ryes that they'll be making a quick stop by here in three hours, or so.  I didn't know if you wanted to go out to the Fall Gather, or not, but wanted to ask.  There's supposed to be a re-enactment of Romeo and Juliet by one of our two performer groups tonight and tomorrow.  The Boodans have their own interpretation and I wanted to see it, myself."

"A play?" Loren sighed, smiling, and nodding her head. "What else do they have going?"

"There's all kinds of things, including dancing, eating, drinking, field ball games, and some shopping.  Monty and Denas invited us to stay with them, but there's also some extra shelters, if you want to just spend a couple of days," he told her.

"I thought the women had to be escorted all the time?" Jared questioned.

"Yes, outside of our own encampment.  The plainsmen still regard women as possessions, so it's for their own protection.  But there's always plenty of guys willing to play escort," he explained.  He helped with the setup, but had returned to bring out Shimmer for Monty, as he didn't like leaving her alone for the week he was planning on staying there.  Alec and Storme were staying at the gather with the ships' crews, on Ash's orders.  He and Ken were helping Ash police the men and women from off the ships.

"A few days won't hurt," Jared suggested, meeting Maddy's eyes.  She got the hint and stomped over to her and Loren's room, disappearing inside, closing the door behind her. "We'll be ready.  Where should we meet you?"

"Take the tunnel out to the hangars.  I'll meet you there," he replied, smiling and relieved that at least two of his distant cousins were easy to get along with.

"We'll be there," Loren assured him.  He bobbed his head to them and quickly left.  He wanted to stop by the dining hall for a quick snack, before leaving.  Then, he'd go get Shimmer and put her in a carry sac he could put over his shoulder, then get the house all locked up and secure.  At least Shimmer liked him and even allowed herself to be draped across his shoulders at times.  He found he loved that little snake, wishing he had one of his own, too.

# Abilities

## Chapter 26

"My gosh, it's HUGE!" Raby protested as she looked out the shuttle's window.

"It's a large battle warship, dear.  What did you expect?" Ryes returned, slowing so to give the newcomers a good look at the starship, while she was maneuvering.

"She's immense and dwarfs the other two ships near her! They look no bigger than this `shuttle,'" Darman commented, appreciating the view.  He never tired of viewing Tayna from above like this! "And what's that hub-like, metal thing which all three ships are clinging to?"

"What's left of the second shuttle from Booda, named Flutter-wing, with some added improvements.  We pulled over what was left from the original starbase, which had crashed on Shaysa.  Mitt's constructing a real starbase and taps me to help, every chance she gets.  I believe she wants me to help pull up some of those beams from Hailys to add in next month, after the Gather.  We should be able to load them aboard the Land's End, as I've modified it to provide cargo carrying capacity.  The Claw's Rake, Leap and Rapier should keep me busy for the rest of the winter, at least.  There's so much work to get done and so few of us to do it," she lamented, as she was bringing the Avenger II into her own docking bay.  She touched down upon the landing pad lightly.

"I would think that you alone, make up for at least a few other Talents, child," Rinna teased, smiling as Ryes looked back to her with surprise in her eyes.  She laughed at this, nodding her head as she began her shutdown procedures; a little worried that James was paying them close attention, as she realized they were chatting in English.

"I never thought of it that way, then without me, the projects we've planned would be even more phenomenal to attempt to accomplish," she replied in Dolbith, smiling to herself.

"Aren't you supposed to be practicing speed?" Monty urged, knowing she hadn't been making much effort for the last two weeks.

"You're right, it should apply here, too," she quipped back, then closed her eyes and unleashed her Talents.  She shut down and checked all the systems in a very few moments. "All done. Let's go set up breakfast for everyone." With this, she unbuckled and pushed off from her seat. Seeing Raby and Rinna's discomfort with weightlessness, she reached into the Challenger, activating the artificial gravity for them, bringing it up slowly, so no one would fall and get hurt.

"Thank you," Rinna told her, smiling as she again felt a true sense of up and down.

"You may be happy, but the cubs are disappointed," she responded, pointing to Gareth's face as he looked as if ready to cry. "They love the weightlessness and know how to navigate in it too well. I usually have to tether them out of reach of everything!" James recalled the tethers, chuckling as he looked at the young cubs.

"Grandmother Rinna, think of it as swimming in the air. It is fun," Calla encouraged her, having been introduced to both her and Darman last evening. She laughed as she looked down at the child, still getting used to her presence. She and Chatis behaved as if they'd grown up as Ryes' daughters all along. Then again, so did Sayer and Raby, who were far older.

"Maybe I'll give it another try later, child," she answered, smiling.

"Grandma Rinna doesn't like people looking up her skirts," Darman teased, picking up Chatis. Chatis started laughing, with her eyes merry. Calla took Rinna's offered hand, as she was giggling.

"Dar!" Rinna returned, taking a playful swat at him. This got the others to laughing, with even Gareth stopping his fussing long enough to try to puzzle out what was happening.

"Come. Let's go eat breakfast," Ryes urged, unstrapping the cubs, floating them in the air behind her, using her Talent. At least this brought a smile back to Gareth's face. He loved to float.

"They're little spacemen, already," James teased her, smiling. She returned the smile, nodding her head in agreement, realizing he was right, wondering for a moment what they'd grow up to become.

After breakfast, James took a shuttle over to his own ship, eschewing one to the spaceport and making his way through it. Bitty gave the elders a tour of the Challenger II. Casta, Sayer and Raby were surveying both their rooms, and the younger cubs' rooms, starting to figure out how they should be arranged. Calla and Chatis were helping their older sisters make up their minds. The horde was playing in their room, as the older girls and Casta stood occasional watch. Ryes and the other Talents, including Monty, were gathered in a joint effort to finish the remaining repairs on this great ship. They were determined to get it all complete before she began her trial runs.

"Ryes, slow down, we cannot keep up," Tieva complained. Almas was trying to bend a pipe back into the shape Tieva showed them, with her Manipulator, as Rheas was helping her by gently applying heat with her Flame Shaper, when needed, to ease the job. It was working as a team to complete a task, as they never had learned in all the long years they spent in suspension. They were amazed by what they could accomplish working this way, and even if Axel didn't have Talent, he knew when and where things were wrong, or right. So, when Tieva and Ryes were busy elsewhere, they took direction from Axel.

"I'm sorry. Perhaps if we took the meld down to a deeper level, it'd be easier for the rest of you?" Ryes suggested.

"We have all we can handle here, as is, cousin," Denas teased her, humor in her mental voice. In spite of her pool of power being available to them all, which was practically an overload on its own, they had enough trying to juggle the demands of a working meld. It was far easier to just chat with each other mind-to-mind!

"The ladies are already hard pressed," Axel warned Ryes, as he knew she was chaffing at the delays. "Perhaps, we'll go on and do what you still see needing done, and they'll catch up, when they're finished here," he suggested. He knew she had great instincts for this work but was still uneducated when it came to most machinery. With the computers she excelled, doing better than either Mitt, or himself.

"Alright, that way we won't stress Denas and Monty too much," she agreed. Then she extended her own Mind Voice to Axel, keeping a lighter contact with the rest of the meld, as well as leaving open her Talents and pool of power for them, as needed, then continued with the repairs she saw still needed to get accomplished. Axel was delighted, as with her combination of Talents, the job did go much faster, and he knew how to use her Talents by now, himself.

"Oh cribbits, it broke!" Almas exclaimed, as the thin pipe broke at one of the bends she was trying to straighten. There was a ripple of amusement from the others working with her.

"Almas! I did not even know you knew any vulgar language," Tieva playfully scolded. "Let me get a look at it," she urged, pulling in Rheas in with her. It would take the three of them to get this fixed.

She carefully orchestrated her friends, guiding their Talents for them, and thrilling to this depth of contact.

"Just wait until we tackle the Silver," Monty sent to Denas. Her humor was plain in her mind.

"We are all learning more from this, than you could ever believe!  I think the reason Doran never let us work together all those years, is because she feared united, we would overthrow her," she returned. "I would say, let us use my friends more than Ryes, when we take on the Silver, as they do need the practice, my love."

"And will probably have more open schedules," he added, sending his deep love through to her, since they were being ignored by everyone else right now.  He agreed with her observation about Doran.  Denas responded in kind, now glad he'd volunteered them both for this chore.

"I don't know.  Painting in a window might be silly," Raby told Sayer, as they were now working on the horde's room.  They had painted the rest of the walls and ceiling a nice rainbow patchwork of different colors but wanted something special on this last wall.  Casta was helping to keep the horde busy and away from them for the time being, while the paint dried.

"I think it'll be fun, and Mom will get a thrill out of it," she insisted, grinning merrily.  They'd made all the beds, changing them from the plain white sheets and blankets to ones with more colors, making sure they were each solidly anchored to the floor.  The soft, protective netting for each bed was interesting.  Grandpa Garvin had made them some very pretty bedclothes.  And Great Grandpa Rowan had made each of them several blankets, which went with the things Grandpa Garvin made.  Calla and Chatis were sharing a room, as they did at home, while they got a room each, being older.  It was all part of a small suite of rooms, with a central parlor.  Ryes had left her things in hers and Garth's room for now, saying she'd have plenty of time to get it all settled, later.

"She will, won't she?" Raby questioned, her eyes merry. "Alright, let's paint a window with a view.  What do you think it should display?"

"How about what they see out their window, already?" Sayer suggested. "That way it's a familiar sight and might comfort them a bit."

"How about one of the mountains, like we can see from the Gather?" Raby countered; her eyes wide at remembering that view.

"No, the stars would be pretty!" Chatis asserted, laughing as she got into the game. "We're on a spaceship."

"No, Matlowe Village. I want one, too," Calla requested, hoping. Sayer laughed at this nodding her head.

"See what you started?" Raby scolded, smiling. "It's a good idea. We'll paint one in your room, Calla and Chatis, but you'll have to agree what it's going to show."

"How `bout Matlowe at night, so I see the stars and Calla sees the village," Chatis decided. Calla laughed at this, nodding her head in agreement.

"Old Matlowe, not new Matlowe," Calla stressed.

"I've never seen old Matlowe. You're going to have to show it to me," Sayer told her. Calla and Chatis got up and stepped over to her, extending their hands, smiling in delight.

"I can show you," Calla assured her. Sayer sighed, then took the offered hands, bringing up her Talent. Raby and Casta joined them, grabbing onto Sayer too, as they closed their eyes. What Calla and Chatis opened up to them was amazing. It was a quiet village, with a lot of people and starships arriving overhead, as they went to land across the Yuri. They had electricity, lights, and grand dances in the village square. After several long minutes of these small ones' view of a world which used to be, Sayer gently released them, opening her eyes with a sigh.

"I remember Mom's memories of Matlowe, and it seemed such a dull, boring, small place. We'll see if we can paint this for you, but I'm not sure how good an artist I am," Sayer warned, smiling.

"It will still be very pretty," Calla assured her, smiling up at her older sister, trusting her. Even if Sayer and Raby didn't look like any of her other, older sisters, they were more like them than anyone would've believed.

"Yes, it will," Raby agreed, smiling as she picked up the paint brush. "Let's get this one going, at least," she invited. Sayer laughed as she grabbed a brush and opened one of the cans of paint they'd brought along.

"How about the view out their window, with the mountains added in?" she suggested.

310

"That might do," Raby agreed as she started to paint the bottom of the windowsill in a rich, brown paint, glad mom has packed a lot of paints and colors today.

"Oh, I'm tired," Ryes complained as she, Rinna and Denas entered her suite of rooms after over ten hours of repairs, with only a short lunch break for everyone. Originally in her suite, one room had been an office with several large conference rooms. She moved all the furnishings out to other, more appropriate rooms. So, she now had five bedrooms, with a central living room.

"You did push things more than you should have," Denas scolded, smiling.

"This carpet does add a lot to this room," Rinna observed, toeing the new carpeting below her feet, not happy with the white walls around them. It was a bright, colorful spot in the dreary room. Ryes laughed lightly at this, nodding her head.

"Two of our new residents from out of the east are carpet makers. They gifted us this carpet, after they lived in Winterhaven a while. You should see the larger one we have in our apartment, back home," she replied. "The only thing Garth insisted upon was everything be solidly secured, so if there's no gravity, we won't have furniture getting into everyone's way, which does make sense."

"It does, indeed," Denas agreed, laughing as she nodded her head. "I could imagine what this room would look like, without such measures, in the chaos of gravity loss."

"Oh Mom, you've got to see," Raby encouraged Ryes, coming in the room to get her. She noted her tunic was covered with small spatters of paint, so hurried over to see what they did. She stopped as she entered Chatis and Calla's room, amazed. The walls and ceiling were painted in different solid colors, except one, which displayed a huge mural, which was almost complete. Ryes was amazed! It was as good as one of Darman's paintings!

"What do you think?" Sayer asked, seeing the delight upon her face.

"Absolutely fantastic," she replied, impressed at the skill the girls had with paint brushes. Rinna and Denas crowded in beside her to see, hearing the excitement in her voice.

"It's beautiful!" Rinna declared, smiling, realizing it was Matlowe Village, yet wasn't the Village she knew well.

"It is!" Denas added, surprised. She never knew they had such abilities! Before them they saw a huge window painted onto the wall, and outside the window there was a village at night. The sky was blazing with the bright moons and stars, while colorful dancers were reveling under colored globes of light. You could see the elder's platform and a towering column, which shone in the moonlight. It was so bright you could almost make out the Laws inscribed upon it.

"It was Matlowe, long ago," Calla assured them, smiling to see it upon her wall. "I asked Sayer if she and Raby could paint it again back home."

"Sure, shorty. It's no problem. We're almost done with this, but you might want to see the one we painted in the horde's room, Mom," Sayer invited. Ryes turned to her cousin and Rinna, smiling.

"Let's go see," she agreed, as the other two women stepped back, ready to follow her lead. Ryes opened their door, noting they were napping and stood gaping at the mural upon their wall. Like the other one, this took up most of the wall, but unlike it, this one depicted the view out from the horde's room with majestic mountains wreathed in clouds, added into the scene.

"Now this is amazing! I never knew the girls were so good at this!" Rinna declared in a low voice, wary of waking the young ones, knowing how active they could be at any time.

"I didn't either," Ryes agreed, in an equally low voice, turning to see Darman, James and Kyma stepping into their main room. "Grandfather, you have to see this. We have more painters in the family," she invited, still in a low voice, smiling. He noted her and her gesture.

"What? Have the cubs learned how to paint, already?" he teased, as they quickly crossed the room. He looked within and stood in utter shock for several long moments. "Who?" he turned to question Ryes, as she stepped back to let Kyma, and James see. Denas stood there just admiring the scene.

"Sayer and Raby. It's a joint project. They're just finishing up one for Calla and Chatis, now," she told him, indicating the next door. He quickly stepped over, needing to see it for himself, as Ryes was quietly chuckling.

"It's the view from the Gather, sort of," Kyma stated, awestruck by the degree of detail involved in the picture.

"Married to one from the horde's own room, back in Winterhaven," Denas told him. "They did an amazing job. We are going to have to ask them to paint one of Kahmarr of old, later," she added, smiling. Wait until she showed a memory of this to Rhodi and Poli! The hard part would be trying to decide what scene to ask them to paint!

"I wouldn't let Dyan know of this. He might press for the return of the girls," Kyma suggested, smiling as he turned back to Ryes, sure she hadn't thought of it.

"And here I thought we finally had that all settled. Perhaps, they should paint a picture as a gift for Dara, just in case?" she asked, wondering. After all, Kyma knew them both far better than she.

"That might be an appropriate gesture," Rinna voiced, seeing Kyma was still considering the thought.

"Where did they learn to paint? In Winterhaven, or from before?" James asked. "If they learned in Winterhaven, you only gave their innate abilities the proper training. If they could do this before, then it's their own people's fault for not giving them the chance to show what they could really do. Either way, they're your daughters by law, and their former owners shouldn't have a claim upon them," he advised, as best he could. He knew they were Ryes' by adoption but didn't know of the circumstances of it.

"They were originally `sold' to Garth and Sabin. Sabin and Ardis adopted Katas, while we adopted Sayer and Raby. So, you're right. They're our daughters and it doesn't matter what Dyan thinks, because we don't sell people to begin with," Ryes returned, as Darman and all four of her older children, with Casta, stepped out into the living room, hearing her clearly. Kyma nodded his head, well aware of her stance on this issue. At least little Shyla had been a gift! Still, Senah had been wrong in sending her out to die with Garth and Sabin in that ice storm.

"He's not going to get his hands upon them. I'll speak to Dara about it," Darman promised, chuckling as he saw her evident anger. "But I'd like to show them some of my paintings and see what else they can do," he added. Ryes smiled, nodding her head, still a little angry at the threat of Dyan taking away two of her daughters.

"If worse ever comes to worse, we could either disappear for a while, or bring them up to stay on Flutter-wing," she replied, meeting Sayer and Raby's eyes. There was relief in them both at this news.

"You disappear?" Denas teased, laughing lightly. "Not without taking a crowd of supporters." Rinna and the others were laughing at this, appearing in full agreement.

"Well, if I had to, I'm sure I could still disappear. I don't actually need everyone else, but they do come in handy at times," she returned merrily, knowing in her heart it'd be a struggle to leave. She hoped that Dara could intercede on their behalf.

"Not to mention Garth would be beside himself without you," Rinna added, smiling. She'd make sure there'd be no such threats issued, herself! Between her and Darman, she knew they could head off this situation before it even develops.

"You're right. He doesn't know how to look out for himself, anymore," she returned, in full agreement.

"Is someone taking us away?" Calla asked, scared to hear what they were talking about. Ryes got down on her knees to give her and Chatis a hug and kiss, seeing their distress.

"No, honey, we're only a little worried about your big sisters. But everything will be fine," she assured them. They smiled at hearing it, relieved, yet still afraid.

"I will not let them!" Chatis declared. "Sayer and Raby are MY sisters!"

"Yes, they are," James assured her, chuckling at her small display of fierceness. "And we'll make sure they can stay."

"See? We're not going anywhere," Sayer told Chatis, kneeling down by her.

"Good," Calla replied, smiling her relief, as she threw her small arms around her in a heartfelt hug.



"It's just a quick stop. I'm doing some drop offs and pickups," Ryes explained, as she maneuvered the Avenger II for landing at Winterhaven.

"Then can we go see our apartments? Are they ready?" Rinna asked, hoping. Ryes chuckled at this, nodding her head as she smiled.

"Yes, they're ready, and yes, you may see them. We've got some crates to unload and others to load, so it'll probably be an hour, at least," she informed them. She opened her Talent and did the shutdown far more quickly than the last time. Then turned her seat and unbuckled. There was excitement as Rinna and Darman unbuckled, too.

"The horde's going to get restless," Raby warned, but Ryes shook her head.

"No, they're not," she replied as she extended her Talent and put them into a light sleep. She didn't want them needing attention, when she couldn't give it to them, herself. They were getting spoiled!

"Cousin Maren's going to yell at you for that," Sayer warned, smiling impishly.

"I know, but it's not like I do something like this very often. Would you please take your great-grandparents out to their new apartment for me? I'm going to check on our cargo load," she requested. Sayer nodded her head as Raby laughed. They quickly unstrapped and rushed to play tour guides, causing the caravaners to laugh, as well.

"May I see it, too?" Kyma requested, wanting to see how their new apartments, having seen their underground quarters before.

"Sure, come along, you're more than welcome," Darman invited him. He was getting to know him more since the last great gather and was settling into a comfortable friendship with the Great Chief. Kyma smiled as he got himself loose and followed them out of the small starship.

"Do you need me to do anything?" James questioned, seeing Monty and Denas looked to be keeping a close eye upon the younger cubs, playing a game with the two, newer girls.

"Not really. Just sit back and relax. After all, how often do you get to do that?" she returned merrily. She winked at Damian, "and you can relax, too. We're home for the moment, after all," she reminded him. He smiled at this, nodding his head.

"Then, do you mind if I go find my own home? I haven't seen it yet, either?" he requested. She laughed, nodding her head.

"That's right! I forgot you've been gone for so long. We left your things down in your old room, still locked. That way you'll be able to arrange them, yourself. If you want to stay and get settled in, I'll let Torr know. That way you can get used to the changes," she invited. He smiled, nodding his head. It did feel good to be back home!

"As long as you don't mind," he offered.

"I don't," she assured him, laughing, and waving him off.

"I'll take care of things here, Damian," Monty assured him.

"Great," he returned, relieved. "Tell Torr that I'll catch the next shuttle back." Then trotted on out with Ryes following him, heading on into the hangar. The new hangar had him stopped for a few moments, amazed. He saw several people nearby, whom he didn't know, heading toward the shuttle. He noted the new tunnel entrance nearby, so headed toward it, starting to feel excited.

"Just pick a seat and get comfortable," Connor invited, as he led Jared, Madison, and Loren aboard. He saw Monty and chuckled in delight. "Uncle, glad to see you're here. We're going on out to the Gather, too." He stepped over at Monty's gesture, extending the bag. "She's fine, but I think it looked like she was getting bored. She misses you both, and Storme."

"Thanks, Con. I really appreciate this," he replied. Ryes' new daughters were in the other two seats with them, so Connor took a seat behind, watching as Monty opened the bag and took Shimmer out. Their cousins were headed for the seats behind the Terran ship officer.

"Oh, Shimmer!" Chatis declared, reaching out to pet the gold and white snake. Monty chuckled at this, nodding his head. She was glad to see him, as she flicked his hand with her gentle tongue.

"She looks so happy to see us," Denas said, smiling as she petted her length, too. She found she didn't mind Shimmer, as Shimmer found she didn't mind her, either. Both she and Monty were determined to raise their children to respect and care for this beautiful snake.

"She's pretty," James commented, keeping his distance. He didn't doubt that Ryes would allow a snake on her shuttle, since her children knew her on sight, with no fear, and called her by name. They definitely didn't do things by procedure.

"A snake? Are you going to be taking a snake along?" Loren asked, seeing the thin, two-foot-long snake and all the pets and attention she was getting.

"Sure. We're planning on being gone for a week and I don't want her being neglected, or lonely. I just wanted to have her tank set up and stabilized before bringing her out. After all, it gets cold at night now, and I expect her to go into winter hibernation soon," Monty explained.

"May I touch her? I've never touched a real snake, before," Loren requested, willing herself to be brave enough to do it.

"Of course, you may. Just don't make any quick moves. She likes to see everything, and her eyesight isn't quite like ours," he invited, with a big, reassuring smile. Loren reached over and gently stroked the snake, smiling as she felt the smooth texture of her skin.

"She's so soft and warm," she told him, amazed. She imagined it'd be rough, and was pleasantly surprised, as a shiver of delight ran up her back.

"Yes, she is," Denas agreed, smiling. "It surprised me the first time I touched her, too." Loren smiled and nodded as she continued to pet the snake. The shape of her head and the look of her eyes fascinated her. Denas smiled, relaxing back again. These newer, distant cousins of Monty's were still just settling in. She didn't think the blonde woman liked her at all, but didn't snoop to find out why, because she knew Monty wouldn't approve. This girl and the man seemed more open and friendly, at least. The other one was sitting down next to Connor and Jared, waiting for lift off. Loren finally moved over to the window seat on Connor's row, filling it, her happy smile got Jared to smiling, too. Maddy signaled Conner to move over, as she wanted the aisle seat. He gave it to her, putting him directly behind Monty, who turned his head and gave him a nod.

"Where are you from?" James asked the blonde woman, noting she didn't look happy to be here. He hadn't seen her about before.

"From Trinity, originally," she replied. He was an officer, of some years and rank, by the flashy stuff on his sleeve. She wondered why he wasn't taking one of the Earth ship's shuttles, instead? "My name's Madison Elbridge," she said, looking at him for a reciprocal introduction.

"My name's Commander James Kaminski, but you may call me James," he replied, smiling. "I don't recall seeing you among the refugees we pulled off Guardian. Did you come aboard from Trinity, itself, Madison?"

"No, I'm from the Quicksilver. Refugees? Is Guardian really that bad?" she pressed, her brows furrowed with concern. She had friends there!

"It was scrap metal," he informed her, meeting her eyes with pity. "You could ask Lt Alec Scott about the attack. I'm sure he'll be happy to tell you all about it. He and Storme held together the survivors for the last two years, getting them organized and taking care of them. He's over at the Gather site helping Ash. Still, most of the survivors have decided to settle here on Tayna," he added.

"I might do that, thanks," she returned. Then the woman who was there when they opened their tubes came aboard and striding down the aisle to them.

"Ready to lift. I'm giving Darman, Rinna, my girls, and Kyma five more minutes, tops," Ryes commented. She saw Shimmer, so stopped to pet her, too. "Nice to see you're going with us, little lady," she told her, smiling. "You do understand, don't you?"

"Yes, she does have Mind Voice, so she understands us, to some extent. She and Storme were talking to each other, and I think are friends," Monty bragged. Ryes nodded her agreement. She'd thought so. Suddenly, Darman led a small party of people back into the Avenger II, panting as he took his seat.

"Just in time," he stated, grinning. Ryes laughed, nodding her head. Rinna, Raby, Sayer, and Kyma took their seats, too.

"And we're all ready," she replied. She took her seat, as Paris stepped up into the ship, stowing his bag under a seat and took the copilot's seat. He'd been behind the others and had waited for them to get settled first.

"I'm taking Damian's place, and get to be your copilot," he informed her. Ryes smiled, nodding her head, then unleashed her Talents and did the startup procedures, as quickly as she performed her shutdown ones. "Wow! How'd you do that?" he asked, astounded to see the ship was instantly ready to lift.

"Talent," she replied. "You're from off Guardian, aren't you?" she asked.

"Yeah, we came in on the Tablet. I wasn't sure where we were going, or what we'd find, but this world sure beats what Trinity's become. I was a helmsman for the Copper Queen, but she was destroyed before she could even pull out of the dock during the attack," he explained.

"Then, why don't you take the helm and get a feel for the Avenger II? I want some else's opinion on how she handles, compared to the other ships you've flown," she invited, shunting the helm functions over to his board.

"If you're sure," he returned. She nodded her head, sitting back and crossing her arms. He blushed but nodded his head, setting his seat more before the board and making a few adjustments. He then activated his mic, as he'd seen Mitt do before, not used to the older equipment.

"Winterhaven, this is the Avenger II, ready to lift. We're returning to the gather site," he informed the Control Center.

"You're all clear for launch; your flight plan has been approved. Have a good flight," Neil replied, smiling as he realized

Ryes was letting one of their new humans take the Avenger II up today.  She was probably the safest person who could do this, with a total stranger!

"Thanks, Neil.  See you in a couple of days," Ryes returned, smiling to herself.

"You bet," he replied, as the ship was lifting off.  He watched her on the monitor for as long as they were still in sight.  He wasn't quite as steady as Ryes or Mitt, but not bad.

# Small Things

## Chapter 27

"I wanted to ask, where did you get the inspiration for that mural you girls painted in Calla's and Chatis' room?" Rinna questioned, wondering, as they sat with the family at dinner. It was on her mind ever since she saw it; Matlowe Village as she'd never imagined before.

"It came from Calla and Chatis' memories of the village from three hundred years ago. They called it the Matlowe that was, and we saw they still held some sorrow in their hearts at seeing it again, but overall joy," Raby explained. Ryes looked curiously at Raby at this, her brows furrowed as questions filled her thoughts.

"So, it wasn't just fancy? Imagination?" Ryes asked. Raby shook her head, smiling, as she blushed.

"I could never have imagined that place, Mom," she said, then paused as she wondered if she could paint some of her fancies, or imagined vistas on a canvas, or wall? Ryes gave her a nod, then looked at Sayer. It was what they learned in art class, only cut free.

"Sayer, could you please show me what you both saw in the girls' memories, after dinner?" she asked. Sayer looked over to her mother, when she heard her name mentioned, then gave her a nod, and turned back to chatting with Tars.

"The detail, for the time you had to create it, was very, very good," Darman said in compliment. Raby looked back up from her plate, still blushing a gold color and gave him a grateful smile.

"We did our best, Great-grandfather. Thank you!" He gave her a proud smile and a nod.

"You're welcome!" he replied, his eyes filled with amusement. Raby smiled her thanks, again, then turned back to her plate, as Ryes finished with the youngest cubs' feeding. Darman chuckled as he turned to look at Ryes. "I'd like to see this memory of the Matlowe that was, too," he requested. She smiled and gave him a nod, appearing to know it would be expected.

"You, too, Grandmother?" she added, before Rinna spoke up. Rinna laughed, light-heartedly and gave her a small bow.

"You know me well," she agreed, with a happy smile. Ardis frowned, wondering what they were talking about.

"May I, too, see this other Matlowe?" she requested. Ryes laughed merrily, as she picked up her own fork.

"Of course, you may. You'd love that mural, by the way," she told her.

"Sayer said she and Raby will paint it in our own home, too," Chatis added, tugging on Ryes' sleeve. She looked down and gave her a nod.

"Of course, they can," she agreed, "but, it might be nice if you do something special in return for them," she advised, smiling. Chatis gave her a bright smile, while Calla appeared thoughtful.


After dinner, people were going to the central fire to relax after the busy day at the gather. Some were showing off the new finds they'd made shopping at the various booths, and others were exchanging gossip they'd heard while out and about. Ryes had a small circle of chairs gathered at one end of the area, with a handful of participants ready for the new adventure. As they were joining hands, Mitt appeared out of nowhere, as did Maren, who'd gotten back late from his conference, and had just finished a hasty dinner.

"We're not being left out," Maren said, as he pulled a chair over, crowding it in close to hers and Sayer's. Ryes laughed merrily, nodding her head. Then several others drifted over, and she realized this one small tour was going to become something more, for them all. Garth and Sabin showed up, just arriving back from their meetings, with Ethan, Rowan and Metta trailing them. Captain Yun appeared curious, then realized what was going on, so went and found his own chair, as did the rest of the camp. Ryes was laughing, then bobbed her head in surrender, as chairs were being rearranged to accommodate the much larger group. Almost everyone, who'd been around the fire, was now gathered near her.

"Still the tour guide," she said in a low voice, as Garth crowded his chair close into to hers and Darman's. He gave him a nod and got one in return.

"So, let's get this show going," Garth invited with a laugh, taking her hand, and extending his other to Darman. After several minutes of getting everyone settled, eyes closed and clasping hands, she opened her full range of Talents and pool of power. Other Mind

Voice Talents in the group added their support.  She was surprised to realize both Alec and Storme were a part of the group, too.

"My older daughters were painting murals for the children's rooms up on the Challenger today.  What we were going to do was get a real look at the memories they saw of Calla and Chatis' view of Matlowe Village and see what it was like hundreds of years ago," she explained to those gathered, "It might be boring."  No one left, and all were eager to see it, too.  She gave in with humor in her mental tones.  Then gently, Ryes urged Raby and Sayer to open up what they witnessed from Calla and Chatis' memories, since the girls were off playing with some of the other children.

Matlowe Village, as it was brand new.  Their homes seemed larger, and she didn't think it was due to the cubs being young, and smaller.  Metta recognized his home, as Calla's past home and was amazed with how neat, clean, and larger it appeared.  The walls looked freshly painted.  Chatis' was much the same, but not quite as spacious.  The Village Square was larger, with the Elder's platform appearing new, and the shiny column of the Laws proudly displayed.  The grand dances with the lights, music and colorful dancers were enchanting, and the different peoples coming and going in Matlowe surprised many in the meld.  The former villagers collectively agreed this is the way Matlowe should be again, whether, or not, they chose to live there anymore.  Everyone wanted to have a fun party area incorporated into Winterhaven, which caused a mental groan from Kovin, who was here with Raya.  This started a ripple of amusement within the commune.

"Did you see that?" Mitt pointed out, excited. "Starships overhead.  Where were they landing?  Or did the houses in New Matlowe come later?"

"They've been there as long as Old Matlowe," Rowan pressed, knowing it from family history.

"Chatis, whose father worked on the starships, had the thought of across the river," Sayer responded, "but it was more of an impression."

"That area was always forbidden," both Rowan and Metta stated, sure on that score.

"With the dangerous radiations they used on their ships, it should be forbidden," Mitt agreed, "but we can remove the harm, and perhaps have a second ship landing site, in case we need it.  Matlowe could become an auxiliary starport."  Her emotions were charged, and she wanted to take the Avenger II over to check it out tonight.

"After the gather," Garth ordered, overriding her impulse. "That way you can take time and do a fly-over scan first of the site, before taking any of our existing ships near the area." She wanted to resist the order, but realized he was right. They didn't have many space-faring ships, yet, and at least Matlowe didn't have snow in the winter to hinder any coming explorations.

"Alright," she gave in, feeling her brother's amusement.

"Patience," Ryes advised with humor, "and I'll help you with it." Then she turned back, mentally to the others gathered with them, and sent, "So, where to next?" she asked. This sparked a cascade of humor, as their options were wide open.

"Don't you have a practice session today?" Monty asked, as he was escorting Ryes about the Gather the next morning. She was out shopping with Ardis and Raffa. He, Logan, Jake and Salls were escorting the ladies, paying careful attention to Ryes. She smiled back at him, as she was feeling the texture of the cloth from a bolt on display.

"This afternoon, after lunch. Don't forget," she returned in English, then turned back to the proprietor, who was waiting upon her. "This feels wonderful. Do you have it in any other colors?" she asked in Dolbith.

"I could only get it to take the blue dye," he replied, bowing slightly.

"What kind of dye are you using?" she returned, frowning.

"I use many kinds, but this one came from hoib plant seeds. The fibers just wouldn't hold any others," he informed her. She smiled and nodded her head, understanding. The hoib seeds were corrosive when crushed and usually needed a lot of water washed through them, before they could be used to make the dye. She remembered helping Tara make some hoib dye when she was little. It took her months to wear off the blue from her hands!

"I'll take four bolts," she told him, seeing his surprise. He nodded his head and quickly brought out the cloth. Ryes inspected each bolt, to make sure they were all the same and their dye was consistent. Then they started talking about the cost. She managed to get him talked down quite a bit. As she paid him, he looked at her strangely. Her brows furrowed, pondering what he might want?

"You're a caravaner?" he questioned, wondering. There was laughter from the women with her, as she shook her head.

"No, but my grandparents are caravaners," she replied, then sighed as she took the bolts. They were heavy. "Let's go down to our own booths, to leave this there for now," she suggested, in English.

"Just a minute, I want this one," Raffa told her in English, smiling as she nodded to the proprietor. "How much?" she asked him. They haggled over it, even more than Ryes had, just a few moments ago, before Monty interrupted her. Ardis laughed, as they finally agreed on a price.

"I'm learning a lot from you, Raffa. I never knew quite how to make a good bargain," she told her.

"Ryes is learning, but all it takes is practice, my dear," she replied, picking up the two bolts of red cloth she bought. "Leaving them with our own people for a little while seems a good idea," she agreed. "These are heavy!" Ryes led them over to their booths, seeing there was quite a crowd for them to get through there.

"Maybe we should just take them back to our camp?" Ardis suggested. She had her shopping tote full, as did both the other women. The only reason she hadn't bought anything weightier was because she didn't want to carry it about everywhere.

"You may have an idea, there," Jake agreed, chuckling. Ryes sighed, nodding her head, then turned. A man suddenly rushed up to her, dropping to his knees before her, as Salls was about to strike him.

"Great Lady of Winterhaven," he cried out to Ryes, his arms reaching up beseechingly to her. "I beg you for the chance to court you." She stood in utter shock for a moment and then realized it would be impolite to laugh at him, seeing he looked so serious.

"Sorry, but you'd be endangering your very soul. I'm true-mated to Garth and am not interested in anyone else," she told him. He looked as if he were about to cry, upon hearing her.

"I had heard the rumor but didn't believe it. I beg your forgiveness and withdraw my request," he replied, sounding very courtly in his address. She blushed and nodded her head, then he stood, allowing the women to pass.

"That was interesting," Maren told her, joining them as they passed her latest suitor. "I hope word does get out soon."

324

"I hope so too, for it seems we can't get more than a few feet before someone else asks for the privilege to court her. It's getting annoying," Raffa replied, agreeing with him. "Nephew, are you not still holding your meetings on Healing?"

"Yes, but we've taken a break for the rest of the day. Today, we actually got some agreement, as more people grasp what I'm saying. I expect to have to bring this all before the council next week, if things keep working well," he replied, taking half of Ryes' load for her.

"Good, then you can make practice this afternoon," she replied. "Ken promised to demonstrate the human's Electrokenisis Talent. It promises to be interesting, at least," she invited, smiling as she glanced at her cousin.

"Alright, I promise to be there," he returned. They came upon Bethy and Dotti, who were out with Torr and Jim.

"Hey, done already?" Dotti asked, hugging Maren around his load. His eyes softened, joy in their depths.

"We're heading back to drop off what we've already acquired. I would've brought along a wheeled cart, but then they always hike up the prices if they see us with one of those," Ryes explained as the women laughed, understanding exactly what she meant. "And I'm not using my Talent around here, right now. I've got enough problems, as is," she added in English. Another man stepped over to the small crowd, stopping as Monty blocked his progress.

"Lady Ryes, I bring a gift for you," he told her. She sighed as she shook her head.

"My thanks, but truly, I can't carry one more thing," she replied, as Bethy and Dotti were laughing at this.

"Please, Lady? My littermate is sick and needs help, or she'll die," he told her. There was an edge of desperation in his eyes, so Maren stepped forward.

"I'm a Healer. Please bring her immediately to our camp and I will attend her, myself," he promised. He didn't know if the man was desperate to get near Ryes, or if he truly had a problem, which needed immediate attention.

"Thank you, Sir. I'll go get her immediately," he replied, relief in his eyes. He turned and ran off, through the press of the people around them.

"Something real, for a change," Ryes commented. "Well, we'd best get to camp, before he shows up," she added.

"May I continue shopping with you two?" Ardis asked, seeing Bethy didn't look as if she were ready to head back, yet. She gave her a nod and smile.

"Sure Ardis, anytime. Will you join us too, Raffa?" Bethy asked, unsure of how to respond to her, yet. She may be Ryes and Maren's great aunt, but she was still a Sleeper from out of the past and Doran's Valley, even if originally from Matlowe Village.

"Yes, I believe I might. Maren, please take these back for me?" she requested. He nodded, accepting the burden for her.

"I'll put them in your shelter," he assured her. He gave Dotti a kiss, then turned to walk with Ryes, back to their camp. Ryes took one of the bolts for him, laughing as he objected.

"I'm due any day," Dans told Maren as he bent to examine her. Her brother had brought her to the Winterhaven camp, insisting this was the only place where Healers could be found today.

"You're having them now," he informed her. "Ryes, I'm going to need your help," he added.

"Is there something wrong?" Dans pressed, uncomfortable as she lay upon this too-white sheet, upon this narrow, wheeled bed.

"One is turned around backwards. I'm going to have to turn her, so she'll be all right," he explained, his eyes soft and understanding. The woman known as Ryes stepped over and Dans was nervous all over again. She shouldn't be waiting upon her! She headed this mysterious land called Winterhaven!

"Relax, everything will be fine," she assured her, smiling. "We won't let you, nor your cubs, get hurt. I'm a Healer, too."

"But don't you run Winterhaven?" she pressed, as she tried to relax.

"I'm only second in command," she replied. "My husband, Garth, actually runs it," she explained, "but that has no bearing upon this. You need our help and we're here to give it. So just relax, Dans, and everything will be fine."

"I'll try," she replied, settling back again upon the soft pillow. The pillow was a good distraction, as she'd never felt anything so comfortable before! Maren closed his eyes, placing both his hands upon her stomach. Ryes joined him, putting a hand upon his shoulder and one upon her stomach, too. She could feel a wash of warmth through her body and the sudden cessation of the pain she'd been in. Now, she could feel the contractions! Yes, her cubs would be born very shortly! She relaxed as she realized this was right, and they wouldn't let them die, if at all possible.

"Three," Ryes commented to Rhodi, grinning. "I think Kyma's right in that Korenda's been very generous this year." She'd come to remind Ryes of the practice session, which would be starting soon. She laughed and nodded in return. The two men, who were waiting near the main fire, stood up as they approached them.

"Will my wife be all right?" the one asked immediately.

"Yes, she's fine, and you now have three new cubs," she replied, smiling merrily. "Two sons and a daughter." He stood with utter shock in his eyes, as if he wasn't sure if he heard her correctly.

"Three?" the man, who originally accosted her in the merchant's area, repeated. She nodded her head in response. His face broke out into a happy smile as he threw back his head, laughing his joy.

"And they're all right? There were no problems?" Dans' husband pressed, needing to be sure.

"There were problems, but Maren's the best Healer alive. They're all fine and healthy. She'll be able to return to your camp tomorrow. You may stay with her and your cubs here tonight, if you want," she invited.

"Thank you, Great Lady," he replied, throwing himself down at her feet. She blushed darkly at this, shaking her head.

"Please get up," she urged. "Go and see Dans and give your thanks to the Goddess Korenda and to Aletagga, for all that they've granted you." With this, she turned and walked off, heading toward the dining hall. She wasn't tired as much as annoyed. It was embarrassing to have people bowing to her, as if she were some kind of empress! Rhodi was quietly laughing as they walked.

"You do not feel comfortable when they do such things," she observed, as they entered the building they created before the gather, when they were setting up the site.

"Yes, and I don't know what to do about it," Ryes replied, heading over to get a tray. It smelled delicious in here!

"Ignore them if you can. If you can get enough people convinced that you do not approve of such behavior, they will get the idea and eventually stop. But it might take a while," she advised, getting a tray, too.

"I'm no better than they are. Why do they do that? I'd never bow before anyone like that!" Rhodi laughed again, nodding her head in agreement.

"No, I could never imagine you bowing in such a fashion," she agreed, realizing that truth. "Do not let it concern you now. It is bad for digestion," she admonished. They got their food, sitting down as Maren came into the dining hall. He got his lunch and joined them.

"You don't have to join us for practice, today, Maren," Ryes told him, noting he looked drained.

"I'm fine," he denied, meeting her eyes. "I still don't know what to do about people, who throw themselves at my feet in gratitude. It was so embarrassing!" Ryes laughed at this, nodding her head in agreement.

"Ignore them, Maren. They will wise up on how you feel about it, through time," Rhodi advised him, smiling merrily.

"I have the same problem, we'll just have to both get through this," Ryes added, smiling, too. He sighed, then turned his attention to his lunch. With the fresh supplies of spices and coffee from the Quicksilver, they were getting some interesting combinations, once more.

"Chuck's outdone himself, again," he commented, enjoying the flavors.

"He's gotten some new recipes from Monty. There was a cookbook for large groups aboard and Monty let him copy from it. I've granted Monty extra credits for his generosity," Ryes replied, "but he's putting everything toward rebuilding the Silver."

"You're going to charge him for that?" Maren countered, not liking her doing something like that.

"Of course not," she replied. "I tried to explain this to him, but he's so stubborn. He wants to be able to pay his own way, not

328

understanding that he's one of us, is already a part of our family, and this is different."

"I will speak to Denas about it; perhaps she will be able to achieve some understanding on your behalf?" Rhodi offered. Ryes nodded her head to this, grateful. She should've thought of Denas, earlier.

"My thanks, Rhodi. I appreciate it," she replied.

"You are busy most times and do not have time for every little thing," she returned, smiling.

"That reminds me, you put the cubs out for a nap, again," Maren scolded. She blushed and nodded her head, reluctantly.

"Darman and Rinna wanted to see their new apartment, so Sayer and Raby took them out to it. I had to see to unloading and loading, so there was no one left to entertain them. It's not like I do it every day," she returned, being a little defensive.

"Don't do it again," he remanded her, meeting her eyes. She nodded her head, vowing to try.

"Only in emergencies," she replied, feeling she needed this holdout, at least.

"Make that life threatening emergencies," he admonished. She smiled, nodding her head to this.

"It's the only kind I meant," Ryes responded. He nodded his head, then sipped his tea, glad for the warmth. There was a light wind today, which made him glad he brought a sweater. "Who told?" she pressed. He huffed but didn't respond. She huffed, then returned to finishing her lunch... still wondering.

# On a Hunt

## Chapter 28

It was another long day, finally over. Ryes was heading toward her smaller, private fire, when she stopped. She heard one of the human men from off one of the starships, complaining about the way a woman he was with earlier didn't want him to leave. She was tired, but this was something she had to address - right now! She turned, heading for their fire, in the middle of their group of shelters. There was rough laughter which suddenly broke off, as she stepped into the firelight.

"Sorry, Lady Ryes, we didn't mean to disturb you," one of the men apologized to her, seeing the ire in her eyes. They could all well guess why she was here.

"I want to set a few concepts straight," she returned, taking a chair among them.

"Begging your pardon Ma'am, but we were strictly briefed before we arrived here," another responded, hoping they wouldn't end up shipped back because of this, they were all enjoying the break and open air.

"There're some things I'm sure were overlooked and let me apologize for being blunt. First off, many of the women here are looking to get pregnant. They only have their season once every two to five years. It's their one and only chance to get cubs. This is serious business from their point of view. And you can father children upon them, but then you won't be there to help care for her and the cubs, once they're born," she explained.

"But Ma'am, we do have contraceptives," another spoke up, as he blushed. There were murmurs of agreement from both the men and women.

"Then, you're having your fun, but are cheating those women. They need mates and husbands. There are women who're available for pleasure only, but you'd have to ask Torr, or Darman about where to find them. We're not like human women, who can get pregnant each and every month. We have to wait years for another chance. Don't do that to them, they deserve better," she urged, trying to reason with them.

"You said we can get them pregnant?" one asked, disbelieving. She nodded her head, then got an idea. She called to Sayer with Mind Voice and asked if she could bring Casta over to them.

"Yes, you can, and your women could also be impregnated. We have several natural crosses living among us already, with more due to be born, soon. We can interbreed, but with that also goes the responsibility of caring for the child, afterwards," she stressed.

"Mom?" Sayer called out, as if she just found her. Casta was with her. Ryes smiled, gesturing them closer.

"I'll be home soon," she promised, as Sayer gave her a hug. Casta stood there, smiling. "Casta here is a natural cross," she said, seeing how their eyes were riveted upon him, already. She urged him to do a slow turn, so the humans gathered could see him clearly in the firelight and bright camp lights. "You two go along and play," she urged after a few moments, thanking Sayer and Casta through Mind Voice.

"The cubs are getting cranky," she warned her aloud, then the two of them disappeared into the darkness.

"The problem with the crosses is that they're not always healthy. Sometimes they're not right and can die in the womb. If that happens, the woman can die, too. Many of these women live in small, remote villages and live several day's travel away from any form of medical help. It's only because we have more Healers, than is generally found anywhere else on Tayna, that they do live in Winterhaven. So, if there's any women you've been with, please have them brought in to be checked by Maren, or Ruan, or myself. We don't want their lives endangered - in case. And the final problem is that you could become injured if the woman is in season. We can toughen your skin, so you won't get hurt. It's the only time a woman loses control of her claws," she informed them, blushing a little at this, herself. She had lost control, but Garth had understood, and she figured out later how to open her Healing, for any future mating. "And if any women want us to check them, we'll be very happy to help."

"Would you tell our Command about it?" one man ventured to ask, needing to know.

"And could you double-check if I've been impregnated?" one of the women requested, appearing afraid.

"I can check you now, and no, we're Winterhaven, not Fleet. If you come to us, it's between you and the Healer, only," she assured them. There were murmurs around the fire at this, and the woman stepped over to her, sitting down next to Ryes.  Ryes took her hand and gave her a nod, not daring to close her eyes while doing this check.  She was pregnant and it was a natural cross, which surprised her.  They weren't very common!

"You bear a new son, and yes, he's a cross," she spoke directly to the woman's mind.  "Please come to the Healer's shelter in the morning and let us help you," she invited.  She got a feeling of panic, yet delight was stronger.

"I will," she whispered, aloud.  Ryes nodded her head, standing up.

"I'd best go.  I've got my little ones to see to, now.  Have a goodnight, folks," she said, turning to leave.  One of the men stood up and rushed to walk beside her a moment.

"Pardon me, Ma'am, but could I bring the lady I was with today, over to see you tonight?  I wouldn't want to see her coming to harm, because of me," he requested in a low voice.  She smiled and nodded her head.

"I'll be up for a while, yet.  It's no problem," she assured him, glad he had a caring enough heart.

"Thank you," he said, then returned to his friends by the fire for a moment, before hurrying off.  She noted Mr. Kaminski standing back, in the shadows.  Catching her eye, he smiled as he joined her, walking toward her fire.

"It's a lovely evening," he commented, not sure how to thank her for the advice she gave his people.  He'd see that their briefings were changed to reflect the new information he learned from her tonight.

"I hope I wasn't overstepping my bounds by speaking directly to your people?" she asked, getting straight to the point.  He chuckled quietly at this.

"Well, I do appreciate what you told them, but object to your keeping anything they come to your Healers about, from us," he replied, knowing she was blunt most times already.  That she immediately discerned his reason for talking with her right away gave him another reminder of her intelligence.  Yes, she could use Talent to read his thoughts, but knew she rarely "scanned" others she worked with each day.

"But, if they come to us with some concern, isn't it better that it's treated, and they're lectured, away from what they most fear?  If there's a true danger, I'll tell you about it, I promise," she relayed. He sighed, nodding his head.

"I appreciate that, at least," he returned, as they arrived at her own shelter. "Have a good evening," he added, smiling again.

"You too, James. Feel free to visit, anytime," she invited. "When you don't have to spy upon your own people, that is," she added, teasing him. He sighed, nodding his head, not as light-hearted about it this evening, which gave her a moment of sadness for him, hoping he would find time for himself, soon.

"I think I will," he returned, then turned for his own part of the camp, again. Ryes sighed lightly in his wake, turning for her very busy cubs, in front of their shelter, smiling again. Garth walked up behind her, surprising her, as he grabbed her waist. She jumped, then heard his chuckle, realizing he was being playful.

"Oh, you're mean!" she scolded, laughing as he tickled her. "Cut it out!" she protested, as she turned about to face him. He pulled her into his arms, kissing her soundly.

"I missed you, Sweet One," he whispered into her ear. She relaxed against his body, relishing his warmth and closeness.

"And I've missed you," she replied, kissing him back. Now all they had to do was get the little ones to bed early. But then she had promised that Dirter. Maybe he would return soon? She hoped...

"We're not giving away any 'secrets!'" Maren insisted, for what he thought of as the thousandth time. He was addressing the Elder Counsel at the gather, and he knew it more his age they truly objected to; the same usually for Garth and Sabin, since they, too, were very young by these men's standards. Young men were not as easily trusted by the elders thinking, they thought they needed more years to mature. And he knew he was a minor item on their agenda today, as if he represented nothing of true importance in their minds. "What secrets can be learned about Healing Talent, by teaching people some basic preventative care and first aid?" he pressed, looking to the bored crowd around him.

"This could save lives," an elder he didn't know spoke up into the long silence that had filled the tent. He was sitting away from the Winterhaven side of the tent. Maren gave him a nod in agreement.

"There're never enough Healers to be had, when needed," another elder added in, from another part of the crowded tent, with the other elders sitting near him voicing their agreement.

"But you're proposing more than just first aid; you're purporting to teach advanced classes on more detailed anatomy and higher care, where the false healers cut people open and 'operate' upon them. How will they know they're doing it right, without the Healing Talent?"

"Extensive training," Maren pressed, "years' worth of devoted training, so they can do the best job possible, even without Talent. They'd be trained under a Healer's guidance. They'll be called doctors, when they're ready to be assigned."

"We need more Healers!" another elder growled out, loudly, as if it were Maren's fault they were lacking. He sighed.

"None are being born, right now," Darman shouted back, his ire plain on his face. "We're getting more Mind Voice and Empath, lately." Many others recognized that he'd know more about it, due to his extensive travels each year, and access to more than one Catalyst.

"We can breed," someone started to say, but was shouted down by the assembly; that program having been discarded decades before, as it didn't work.

"No one wants men, nor women, taken from their homes and villages for a pipe dream that will always fail," an elder dressed in southern robes stated. There was loud agreement at this, as an old truth was baldly stated aloud. The elder, who'd proposed the breeding program, shifted uncomfortably then sat down in a huff, appearing as if he thought he was still right.

"This training program is still the best answer," Maren asserted in the following silence, as the older men sorted through their thoughts and emotions. "It'll be standardized, so everyone will have the same training and information, and can progress to the level they feel most comfortable at working with the program," he insisted, as levelly as he could. He felt his own temper flaring again, as Rowan had warned him about earlier, over the headset, to control. It did him no good to get mad about their clinging blindly to their outdated customs.

"All peoples, not just starmen?" a Junna elder questioned, looking stern; a crest atop his head was raised and forward. Maren nodded.

"All peoples," he assured him, even if it was the first time he'd seen a Junna.

"The need does exist," Elder Rillis stated, taking back control of the session. It was his turn to run the Elder Counsels this year. He hailed from the northern village of Mottin but maintained neutrality as a part of performing this duty. He had the attention of most of the elders, once again. "Winterhaven, will you take responsibility for starting this program and the training involved?" Garth was instantly on his feet, as if awaiting his chance to voice reason into the arguments that had been thrown against Maren for the last hour.

"We fully support this opportunity to help the peoples of Tayna and get the classes started, as soon as possible," Garth stated, hearing Maren's sigh over the headset. He smiled fiercely. "We have the largest staff already available, to assist in this non-Talent healing training." He was trying not to brag, but in truth, Winterhaven did have the people and training to handle it.

"Excellent," Rillis replied, smiling, once more. "This is a provisional program and the people who come for this training will be volunteers, who will be treated as free people, and can leave when they have the need, or feel they cannot learn any more Healing techniques. We will approve the program as something that will be kept and expanded in two years' time," he added. Garth gave him a nod of agreement, as the rest of their main group were on their feet, too.

"We will abide by your ruling," Garth replied formally. Sabin, Rowan, Ethan and Metta add added their voices in agreement, too. Maren stood rooted, awaiting his dismissal, as Rowan had advised, before the presentation.

"And how will the payment for this training be arranged?" Elder Rillis questioned, wanting to be sure.

"We'll do it on an individual basis, so those who have no money can do chores on their off-time to make up for it, and those who can afford it, won't have any additional chores to do," Ethan explained, "and it can be scaled for each student, as needed, or if their needs change." The Chief Elder Counsel nodded his head in agreement.

"Is this motion recognized as stated by the Assembly?" Elder Rillis shouted out, to make sure he had their attention. Now Kyma and the other elders sitting with the Winterhaveners got to their feet, as well as the other elders gathered in the massive tent.

"Recognized," was heard being loudly shouted out by all the elders in the tent.

"Your program for training can begin, Healer, you may leave," Rillis stated, focusing upon Maren as the assembly took their seats, again.  Maren bowed to Rillis, then to the rest of the elders gathered stopping to bow to each section of seating, then quickly left the tent, glad he didn't have to stay there all day, like Garth and Sabin.  He turned off the mic on the headset, pulling it up and out of his way.

"So? I heard recognized being shouted.  Did you get it done?" Torr asked, hope on his face.  Maren's eyes finally lit up with humor and he gave him a nod.

"We did it!" he replied, relieved that it was over.  "Now I understand why Garth and the rest are so tired at the end of the day, after just that little bit I had to endure."  Torr laughed and clasped his shoulder in comfort.

"I wouldn't want that job either," he agreed, "nor, having to deal with those starship captains."  Maren nodded.

"Let's get back and see what's going on today, that we've missed out on," he urged, glad Torr had come out with him today for this session.  He'd been standing by in case he needed to add in his own testimony.

"Actually, I've picked up on quite a few things today already," Torr told him in English, smiling.

"Wait until we're back, before you tell me about it," Maren urged in kind, feeling uncomfortable with others nearby listening to their every word.  He nodded and they turned and headed back to their encampment, feeling safer behind their reinforced earth walls.

"There was some talk about a Ruskin woman asking questions about Ryes and her Talents," Torr related, once they were seated in the dining hall, having a snack and mug of tea.  Dodi had joined them and appeared puzzled by this revelation, wondering why he brought it up to Maren.  There were plenty of other people talking about Ryes at the gather.  Maren frowned at hearing it.

"Why would she want to ask other people about Ryes and her Talents?" he asked, perplexed.  "She could just talk to Ryes directly, if she came here and asked to see her."  Torr shook his head, holding his cup up, as if preparing to take another sip.

"The people, who were talking about it, said she didn't sound friendly, and one of them, who has Mind Voice, told us she tried to probe his mind, as if she didn't care if he'd allow her, or not.  He told us he blocked her out, and got away from her, but I could see that it deeply disturbed him. He described it more of as an attack, then a search for more information."

"Another possible fight, then?" Maren stated, appearing unhappy with this news. "Anything else?"

"I got the impression from the people talking about her, that she's young, but angry all the time, with an attitude that she owns everything and everyone around her and seems to have a way of making her demands obeyed, no matter that the person thought otherwise about cooperating with her," Torr related, appearing unhappy about this possible foe.

"Who?" Ryes asked, joining them with a mug of fresh, minty tea in her hand. Torr shook his head, appearing unsettled.

"Sorry, I didn't hear a name, just that she was a Ruskin woman, who was pretty, young and full of herself," he replied, appearing uncomfortable. "She was asking about the gather for information about you, and she doesn't sound very friendly, and abuses others at whim."

"That doesn't sound good," Dodi voiced, concerned. Ryes nodded her agreement, taking a seat across from Maren and Torr. Dotti slipped in next to Maren, as Aunt Raffa sat down next to Ryes.

"What doesn't sound good?" Dotti asked, wondering.

"A young Ruskin woman, who, from rumors, wants to meet Ryes. She's been asking if she has Talent, too," Torr related. "Something about her always getting what she wants with no arguments, makes me feel uncomfortable. Could Mind Voice be used that way?"

"She sounds like a spoiled brat, who's a lone hunter, and doesn't interest me," Raffa retorted, then frowned, "I was listening to some of the caravaners out of the southern regions, and they sounded like they're laying plans for a real confrontation. A known group of trained Talents is more of a threat." Ryes blushed and nodded her head.

"I faced some southerners before we freed anyone from the Valley, but the ones involved in that Talent fight are now without Talent, and as far as I know, it can't be restored after being burned out." Raffa appeared shocked at this revelation, glad they were discussing this deep within their own camp, and not out where just anyone could overhear them. She remembered it was also what she did to Doran, after all.

337

"But I thought the caravaners were your friends?" she questioned, setting down her mug before she spilled the contents. Ryes smiled and nodded.

"I've met most of the northern caravaners, and am friends and family with quite a few, also with a few of the southern caravaners," she began, as Shams came up behind her, laughing.

"Like me," he boasted, as he took the seat on her other side, setting his mug and snack plate down. His grin was infectious. She laughed, nodding agreement.

"Like you, Shams, who's like family, too," she said, then faced Raffa again, "but some I know, aren't friendly, especially after that Talent fight early in the spring."

"I'll check, but I'm sure Cassin will keep them in line," Shams advised. "I know a few wouldn't be happy that you've removed Gurri's Talent, but also know many who celebrated it being burned out. He was a bully and would outright kill other Talents with his team. I haven't seen him here at the gather, yet." Raffa appeared surprised at what Shams related, then fell to thinking.

"Find out what you can, please, Shams?" Torr requested, before Ryes could speak up. Ryes smirked at Torr but nodded to Shams.

"And?" Maren added, looking at Torr, feeling he wasn't finished. He chuckled, as he shook his head, then gave Maren a nod.

"The men and women from the Earth ships are happier since we've allowed them to visit the gather, but I still think they're hunting more for the thrills they've either read about in imaginative books, or on video broadcasts, and think we're not more than colonials scratching out a meager existence in the dirt," Dotti related, sounding disgusted. "They don't know how to deal with simpler worlds and are still in shock over the different people they've found here at the gather. I don't want to see them stir up trouble."

"I and my team are keeping an eye to them. We've gotten the first officers from each of the ships to help, too," Torr assured her. "I'm sure there are sophisticated worlds still out there, but until we can save the Earth, it's not as important a matter. I've tried to emphasize that idea in hopes of getting them to all settle down." Dotti sighed and gave him a nod in relief.

"Thank you," she replied, smiling a little now.

"And there's a story of a man from a city called Apayal, which is supposed to be as big as Berrals, but on the northwest coast. His name is Albon, and he's declared that if he cannot have Ryes, no one else can have her," he told them, looking grim. The others at the table around him appeared disgusted.

"Why in all Tayna?" Ryes began, unable to finish voicing the emotions she felt in this moment.

"He fancies himself a great king," Shams broke in, shaking his head. "He loves to brag that he has rights of sovereignty over the world, but I always thought he was trying to pull Berrals and Cootain's royals' ears, not that he was actually serious."

"Albon sounds like he's trying to move up in the world," Raffa observed, as Dotti nodded agreement.

"It sounds like he wants to kill Ryes. Has he even met her?" Dotti questioned, her eyes filled with worry, again.

"As far as I know, no," Torr replied, with a nod of his head.

"Not knowing what he looks like, I wouldn't even know if I'd ever met him before," Ryes stated, her lips now pursed, as she frowned in thought. "Why would he be so arrogant as to think he could just own me?"

"He IS full of himself," Shams said, then closed his eyes and showed them all his last memory of the man, so they would all know him on sight.

"No, I've never seen him," Ryes told them, afterwards.

"You're descended from two royal houses, at least, and are married to and life-mate of the Crown Prince of Kahmarr, he's beyond arrogant with such an attitude," Maren said, speaking up. The anger in his eyes was very real.

"How about two guards and a Mind Voice with Ryes, when she goes out?" Raffa suggested, noting her nephew's ire, but wasn't surprised to see it. Torr nodded his agreement.

"Hey, I'm not helpless!" Ryes protested, irked now, and a dangerous spark alit in her emerald-green eyes.

"No, but can be easily distracted," Dotti pointed out, smiling, and giving Raffa a nod.

"Especially with nine young ones to look after, and they can be a big distraction," Dodi added, smiling, "We're only worried."

"How about, I'll only leave our camp when I have to," Ryes finally stated in surrender, hoping to alleviate some of their fears.

She did have her cubs to think of, after all.  This brought out smiles and even broke through Maren's anger, as he gave her a nod.

"And I'll go on a hunt for some answers about these dangerous people," Torr assured her.  She nodded, knowing her life was in his capable hands, and she knew he was a tireless hunter, too.

# Dissonance

## Chapter 29

The large, colorful tents swayed with the brisk breezes blowing through the caravaner camp, as the temporary shelters and the newly renovated, permanent shelters stood steadfast against them. The sun still promised a cheerful, mild day, containing warmth reminiscent of warm summer days now past. This bright sun belied the dark contest Shames just realized was shaping up, as he tried to reason with his friends inside one of the colorful tents.

"I know what Cassin said, but you're nothing more than that northerner, Rishner's, cub," Arrie fired back at Shams, as he found the southerners, who were after a Talent fight with Ryes, and was trying to reason with them. He had Cassin's blessing for this endeavor but was stung by the nasty slurs he used against him, as he'd entered the tent. Cassin was staying out of it entirely, knowing if he had to officially note the problem, it'd then involve Darman and Rinna, and things would then be worse for these people. He knew there were far more northern Talents with true power, who'd be happy to take on this small group of rebel southerners, Ryes, and the Winterhaven Talents aside. All Darman would have to do was ask. His friends might not survive it. He was trying to save them, and they seemed blind to their danger!

"You have no say in this, you left us and the roads! You don't care what happens, nor what matters to us, anymore," Honna accused, appearing mad, standing with her arms crossed. Shams shook his head, these had been his friends, who were so close they were family. They knew each other's minds and hearts! They'd survived dangerous times, and had partied heartily together during the good times, they'd all been so very close. How could this have happened? What hate had Gurri, and the others, created to poison them so strongly against him? What stories and fears did they create around the evening fires, to deeply instill hate against him and Winterhaven? Why would they want to avenge a murderous bully, who'd been put in his place, yet was allowed to live? What was going on in the South? Shams realized he was out of touch, even if he'd only been gone from the roads a handful of months. Their unreasoning hate was igniting his own anger; he hated ignorance.

"I might've left the southern continent and isles, along with the problems there, but I know in this petty revenge, you're wrong, so very wrong," he told this select gathered group of southern Talents in his best, reasoning voice. "And this has nothing to do with my father,

341

nor grandparents." Overall, his mother had kept him with her in the southern regions, as if to distance him from his northern family members. After living in Winterhaven these past few months, he found he rather liked being a part of an active, dynamic community, which already had some northern caravaners in residence, so he didn't feel so cut off. He'd learned so many amazing things, which he'd never imagined before in his whole life. Each day was a fresh adventure, and he wasn't going to go back to an uncertain, vagabond life. He needed so much more.

"You don't want to leave your cushy, new life. You can fly all across Tayna, and go where you want," Honna retorted, "you don't care about us! Do you now see us as slimers, to be crushed under your boot?" Her face was filled with anger, her golden eyes were practically blazing with her pent-up emotions. It puzzled him, as she'd never been that way toward him before, being she was the mother of a boy cub he'd been forced to father over two years ago. They had been close friends for quite a time.

"It's hard work and always busy. And even if I'm not travelling the roads, I still care. Honna, you of all people, ought to know that," he mildly protested, keeping calm, in spite of the budding fire growing within. But he knew from his years of being a negotiator and intermediary, his own calm was the best way to reach them. If he let his emotions surface, he'd lose control of the whole situation, and this was too important. Shams sighed, taking a different tact.

"You can't tell me you miss Gurri trying to destroy your lives, or his constantly telling you what you can, or cannot, do, or killing people on a whim with his using your Talents," he pressed. Arrie shuffled, with his head looking down now, as if agreeing, but not daring to voice it aloud. Others gathered in this group of twelve people also appeared unhappy at his having pointed out the biggest flaw in their reason for any revenge. "He's still trying to control you, in making you seek this confrontation in his place! Are you going to just let him do this to you – for the rest of your lives? He has no Talent and cannot hurt you!" He scanned all the faces around him and saw their mixed feelings in their expressions. At least they were still listening to him.

"It's not that we miss Gurri's control over us," Honna finally spoke up, ire still in her eyes, but she seemed a tiny bit calmer. "But how can we be sure that this Ryes won't take it upon herself to burn out our Talents too, anytime she wants? No Catalyst can reverse what she did to the others. They'll never have Talent, again! I don't want to live my life without Talent!" Shams shook his head, daring to smile a tiny bit.

"She's not like that, and only burns out the Talents of the people, who want to maliciously harm others with their Talents," he explained. "She doesn't just burn out anyone's Talent without trying to reason with, and understand the person, first. I saw the memories of Talent battles she's fought. The one with Gurri, and another one with a woman named Doran. Yes, she burned out their Talents, Ryes is not a cruel person, but she's strong and won't let people with Talent hurt others - if she can prevent it." He sat and held out his hands in open invitation for this deeper matter. He could understand their fears if they thought this way, but this situation was far deeper than merely taking out a worthy opponent, this involved the safety of everyone on Tayna. He knew... he'd Dreamed it last week. Ryes was actually the key to saving their world, and that Dream still awed him. Shams needed to find a way to reach these people he once considered friends, before they came to harm, themselves. He was determined to win this – for all their sakes! And he was stronger now and could do it.

Lissel woke up from her late morning nap feeling rested but unsettled. It wasn't just the capricious, strong breezes blowing outside their shelter, it was as if there was a "taste" of dread that teased her Empath and made her restless. She needed to find out why this was happening!

"Shams?" she called out, not seeing him in their bedroom. Then, she recalled he was going to the Caravaner's camp today, to help head off some kind of trouble. She was about to reach out to him with her Empath, when someone knocked in a demanding manner on their door, so Lissel pulled on her robe and went to see who was waiting. Rhodi's presence surprised her.

"Hurry and dress, we need to arrive in time to save him," she advised briskly. Lissel's eyes widened, recalling she had Visionary, so left the door open for her friend, while she rushed back to the bedroom to change. Her heart was now racing in panic for the man she'd come to deeply love.

Slowly, the rest gathered around him, as if they were making sure they were all committing to the commune. The Talents settled on the floor in a circle, so they could be more comfortable, then joined hands. The five Mind Voice Talents quickly linked up first, then drew in the rest. Shams was suddenly reluctant to add himself into the commune. This seemed more like Gurri's plot being carried out, once again. But he was the one who wanted to face them off, wasn't he?

As soon as the meld was fully set, suddenly more than half the commune turned against Shams, without warning, attacking him all at the same time, if not truly in unison. They meant to overwhelm his mind and shred it, to lay bare his very soul. Shams was caught up in a fight, but he wasn't totally unprepared, having Dreamed about this, too. He didn't bother with the normal defenses he would've used before, as they'd know about those already. He didn't have the power and range Ryes had, but he wasn't helpless, and had learned quite a lot about Talent fights from Ryes, his wife, and the Sleepers.

"How can you say Gurri is not controlling you, when you do something like this?" he "shouted" at them, using the non-lethal version of the one Mind Voice attack he had learned. It stunned them all and drew them back for a moment, as he hoped to reach some of them. One dropped out of the conflict, but it wasn't enough.

He'd managed to deflect the main thrust of their uncoordinated attack, still feeling intense pain spiking up and down his spine, from a Healer trying to tamper with his body, which could outright kill him! They weren't as united in mind, as if not all their hearts were in this fight, and at least five others were now holding back, unwilling to join in, but they weren't helping him, either. They acted like observers. That did play in his favor. Still, the pain his body was being subjected to was still fairly intense, but he hung on, and would find a way through this, being very determined.

Seeing this wasn't working like they wanted, the Southerners tried a new tactic, sniping at him with their best attacks, coming in from all directions. This time they tried to project the dock at the Bay of Peace as the battle setting. He deflected the huge club Honna swung at his head, but was suddenly feeling intense pain, as another Talent was "stabbing" him with a mentally conjured blade, trying to get past his defenses for a killing blow! They honestly wanted to end his life! How could they have become so twisted?

As he mentally "hunkered down," as Monty called it, the pain was unexpectedly pulled from his body as Rhodi, Saree, Lissel, and Raffa added themselves to the inner battle.

"Shams, do what you must. We are here to make sure it is a balance," Rhodi advised, holding their own commune, so he was free to act, as needed. Raffa immediately healed his body, putting him back to full health. The shock of the newcomers' presence ran through the Southerners, having not expected them to interfere with their attempt to strip Shams of his mind and life.

"Who are you?" Honna demanded, feeling anger over their unwanted presence. They almost had him!

"We are Winterhaveners. We support each other – especially in times of danger. Twelve against one is very uneven and we have come to assist Shams. As we understand it, you are seeking to take Ryes down in a Talent challenge. You truly have no idea who you would be facing," Rhodi stated emotionlessly.

"We're strong! We can take her," one of the others pressed, incensed that this woman was scolding them, as if they were children! She was deeply, deeply insulted. And readied her best attack again, wanting to use it against this assertive intruder.

Another, unexpected new add now was Tova, who'd arrived to be a part of this discussion, when she saw the Winterhaveners turning up in the camp and guessing why. Shams knew, of all the people here in this camp, she needed to be a part of this sharing, since she'd been married to Gurri at the time of the Talent battle. She'd stayed out of the conflict, having taken Ryes' measure days before the fight.

"Tova, are you looking to revenge Gurri, too?" Honna sharply questioned, seeing she was among them now. They felt her grappling with a sudden tumult of her inner emotions, but she finally settled her mind and heart after a few moments, then was ready to address them.

"Revenge? That's a foolish thing to ever pursue, and for someone who abused everyone around him, it's beyond foolish," she replied, her disgust clearly chimed in the meld, being a Mind Voice Talent, herself, but she didn't join either meld team, merely projected out to them all. "I came to help make sure you people make a better choice. Gurri is well past being able to care, as he's having to hide, to avoid others wanting to take revenge upon him for killing Talents in the past, who were their family and friends. Too many people were lost due to his ego and whims, and now he is Talentless and helpless." Rhodi, Saree, Lissel, and Raffa hung back and watched this little drama unfold, but were ready to assist, if needed. It was clear the Southerners were still unsettled, and some unwilling to accept what was being shared.

"I heard he's asking every Catalyst he can find, if they can help activate his Talent again," Arrie stated.

"It can't be brought back. It's truly destroyed and gone. He's Talentless, and is having to learn a whole new life, as are the others who were with him, when they decided to try to kill Ryes," Tova assured them. "Is this what all of you want? To live normal lives with no Talent? That's what you'll have as a reward for being stupid." Shock ran about the commune for a few moments. She waited for them to fully absorb all she told them, but then saw Honna and a couple of others still had a fire in their hearts.

As they were readying their next attack, Tova, allied herself with Shams, and Arrie also shifted to side with him, too. Tova applied her Healing to finish easing his pain. Shams was surprised, but grateful. He pulled in tighter into Rhodi's meld, with Tova's Mind Voice Talent reinforcing it. Next, he released his scatter attack in return. It was meant to disrupt the other team's meld, more than do anyone any actual harm. It was one he learned from his own wife, and he was proud that it did exactly as he intended, breaking their side of the meld. Lissel was happy with his show of skill.

"You're gentle with them, when they did mean you harm," Tova observed, as Shams had opened his eyes to see the rest of the Talents gathered grasping their heads in pain.

"Even if they planned upon killing me, they were once my friends, and I'm not going to sink down to that level, even now," Shams told her and Arrie, who was relieved with his action. "And if there was any real danger, I'm sure Rhodi and the other women can counter it, without having to involve Ryes. They may not be as strong as she but have teachings from the old times and sometimes you learn many interesting things," he explained to Tova and Arrie, amused.

He saw the other Southerners were trying to re-establish their inner commune and having a difficult time, exactly as Lissel and Denas described it to him, before. After several minutes of fumbling about, they finally managed to let go their attempts to overcome Shams, appearing more like sulking children. Tova applied her Healing for them to help them recover more fully, since Shams was merciful, unlike Gurri had ever been in his whole life.

"How did you do that?" Honna questioned, her anger now quenched with his one, unexpected attack. They saw his humor.

"Maybe someday I'll teach you. It's a good attack and one that might even have stopped Gurri," he replied.

"Was this something from Ryes?" another questioned, wanting more now.

"No, this was something I learned from our Sleepers and my own, dear wife," he assured them. "Are you truly calmer? Are you ready to understand more about Ryes and why it's foolish to try to attack her? She's far stronger than I, after all, and her attacks could really hurt you, even if she didn't mean it." There was light laughter of agreement from the Sleepers sitting next to him.

"Truth. The whole lot of you would not be more than a minor distraction for Ryes. Even I would be reluctant to engage her ire, and she's a member of my family," Raffa stated.

"Why is she so special?" Arrie asked, truly wanting to know.

"Ryes might be our hope for saving our whole world," Shams added in, "I Dreamed it," he told the rest.

"You're not a Dreamer," one of the others asserted, scoffing at his statement, not believing it. They saw his humor and joy as he extended his hands in invitation to form a new link, now. Lissel took one readily, but it was Rhodi who formed the new commune. Tova felt an odd kinship to this woman, as she assisted bringing in the others as they complied.

"Ryes found I had two Talents, when she and her cousin were checking everyone in Winterhaven for Talent. I have Mind Voice, but also Dreamer. I'm still learning how to manage my new Talent, but it's been revealing some important things for me," Shams told them.

"Then show us this Dream you had and why you think she's so important that the fate of our whole world depends upon her," Honna requested, itching to see it so she could tear it apart this fantasy.

"Not yet," he countered, "let me first show you Ryes, as I've come to know her, and yes, the fights she's been in before." He immediately got agreement from the group, and he knew a few thought this as a path to find her weaknesses. He hoped this would help them realize they were well outmatched by just Ryes' Talents alone. He felt Tova's agreement and realized she was his best ally.

He opened with showing them Ryes at dinner time, feeding her younger cubs and talking with her friends and family. At times she was laughing, at times thoughtful and at others you could see the fiery anger flashing in her emerald-green eyes. Most of the group showed little interest in this part of his sharing, which he expected. He wanted them to see her, as he did, as an ordinary person, overall.

Next Shams showed them Ryes powering up a shuttle with her Talents alone and flying it with such ease and precision. Then showed them the longer, normal way he had to use to bring the great machine up to readiness, and his much slower manner of flying the great craft. This amused at least most the others, as they teased him about his lack in comparison. Still, many were struck with the wonder of flying through space, itself. It was what first caught his own heart, when learning how to fly, the wonder of flight and the ease of travel!

"Only one person flies a shuttle better than Ryes," he assured them, highly amused, not naming this better pilot. Saree agreed with him wholeheartedly.

"At least that's something," Arrie sent in response, amused. "Now show us something real." There was agreement all around.

He knew she wanted to see a Talent battle. Next, he opened the memory of when the thieves tried to steal one of her cubs at the spring gather. They all caught a little bit of her taking the whole melded team on a tour of the solar system, as she was checking for Snagospin in the area. That tiny snippet alone had them begging him to show that part to them, again. He forgot what it felt like to soar in space so freely on the wings of her Talents. He gladly complied, showing them the whole voyage before the interruption.

"If you'd like to experience it directly, you can always ask her for the tour," he invited.

"I will," Tova returned, still amazed by his memory. "Please go on, Shams."

So, he flowed into her being alerted to the theft of her daughter, Jann, pulling away from the gathered Talents, yet retaining a full link with them, as she went to find her and get her back. The way she casually used her Fire Shaper, Storm Caller and Manipulator Talents to help with the rescue had the group wanting more. The way she picked his best punishment by connecting Murin to Tayna's spirit and to those he'd harmed, shocked them all. An Empath that deep had not been seen on Tayna in ages! Now they truly understood the Curse of Murin, and what it meant to each of them!

"Do you truly want to see the actual battle?" Shams pressed, not sure if they could handle it all, as he'd originally planned. He got affirmatives from everyone gathered, so readied himself for the next sharing. "Ryes' Aunt Adina has been training me in how to be a Memory Keeper, which is a specialized discipline of Mind Voice. While I wasn't a part of the other confrontations, I plan to show you, I do have it exactly from Ryes, herself," he warned. Saree opened her Booster to help buoy him, for which he gave her his heartfelt gratitude.

"Please do your best," Honna requested, having calmed down well before now. She was starting to understand what Shams had been trying to tell them.

Shams next showed them the whole battle experienced by the Winterhaven team, as they learned how to fight a Talent battle against Gurri and his team. While Gurri had been as creative as he could be, the other Talents puzzled out his attacks and figured out the best way to counter them. Opening their eyes while still retaining their meld and acting upon things within had never been seen before. When it was finished, Shams opened his eyes and looked about the tent at the people gathered with him, smiling at their astonishment.

"It takes practice, but as you can see, it's invaluable," he told them. "Anyone can do it, if they have the discipline."

"Should we practice now?" one of them asked, feeling excitement coursing through the commune.

"Not yet," Shams cautioned, closing his eyes again. "I have three more memories to share with you, unless you've had enough?" he asked.

"Share them with us, please," he thought Kimi pressed, wanting to see more, then felt her humor as he recognized her in the meld. It buoyed him.

So, Shams showed them when Ryes was on the Challenger, working on repairing the great battleship, and her first contact with Alec and Storme. He showed her checking on their back trail and discovering a Snag ship tracking them through the star lanes. The fight she experienced against the Snag Talent was not as intense as Gurri's, but no less dangerous, especially being so far away from her own body, with the then unknown elements of only Alec and Storme to witness it. Alec distracted him at a critical moment, and she swept in and rendered him unconscious. Still, when she burnt out his Talent, the Southerners mentally applauded. That she made the alien ship malfunction and self-destruct relieved the rest of the people around him. They had all seen the recording from out of the past and recognized what a danger the ship represented.

Then, before they could start asking questions about it, he took them back to when Ryes first went into the Temple of Doran and the confrontation she faced with her, all alone. That Doran was a strong Manipulator attacking someone who knew nothing of her own Talents, and Ryes still prevailed against her, and burning out her Talents, was amazing, but they seemed to understand her deep love and attachment to Garth, now. And her mother's spirit being so strong and able to communicate with her, again shocked the meld, even the Sleepers. When that one finished, Shams realized that even with the meld being a shared burden, it was starting to wear on him.

"You said you have three more, that's only been two," Tova teased, knowing he was tired and understood if he could not continue.

"Yes, one more," he agreed, the opened her final fight against Doran. They came as a team, having trained as a team, and managed to fight her down again. Even if Doran had no Talent of her own, she was still using her handmaidens' Talents through her centuries-long established links with them. The attacks didn't seem as powerful as hers own, alone, but still highly effective at keeping the teams pinned down until they managed to break that link, too. When that one ran its course, he waited while they digested all they experienced.

"As you've said, our seeking a Talent fight with Ryes is wrong. I see it all now," Honna admitted, still reeling with all she learned and experienced in what was actually a short amount of time, overall.

"You didn't share your dream with us yet," Arrie pointed out, wondering if he had the energy, to do it. Shams was amused now.

"Okay and this is the last," he assured them, his humor sparking others in the group. He opened his Dream image. They were on the Challenger, in the big conference room near the control room. There was a group meld, and they were under Ryes' direction taking on the Snag Talents directly. This was something he hadn't shared with anyone yet, but all could see it clearly that Ryes had a vital role in taking on their enemy. When it finished, they finally let go of each other, open their eyes, and realize that while the world around them right now was unchanged, they had each reached a new understanding within.

"I believe your Dream, it feels true," Kimi spoke up, nodding her head.

"You're the first to see it beyond myself," he told her, returning her nod.

"It's amazing. Is that ship truly like the ones we had in ancient times?" Arrie asked, needing to know. He thought he and a couple of other caravaners were in that Dream with Shams, helping to take out the Snags.

"It was one of our original ships. Winterhaven's found and repaired it, and she'll be ready to go to work again, very soon," he assured them, smiling as he knew why Arrie asked, seeing he'd seen himself there. "Is there anything else you might need to know?" Tova stirred and instantly got everyone's attention.

350

"Gurri is petty with an over-inflated ego," Tova began, ready now to share this with other people. "I was going to release him well before he lost his Talent. I tried to warn him that he needed to let go his impulse to have one up on Ryes, but he wouldn't listen to me. He thought it was a way to get a strike on Darman, if he could kill this favored child of his," she related, with a heavy sigh. "Now he's in hiding. I don't even have any idea where he lives, and it's all his own fault. He chose this and no one else needs to be blamed. He's made powerful enemies through the years and has no way to truly know if someone's found him, or if they are coming for him. That's his just punishment for what he's done to everyone else, through time."

"We'll try to remember all he stood for before, as an example of how not to live, from now on," Honna vowed. There were murmurs of agreement around her.

"Can we go see this great spaceship?" Kimi threw in after several moments of silence. This solicited laughter, then the rest chimed in their requests, too, which got Shams to laughing merrily.

# Albon

## Chapter 30

"Not a lot to pass down this morning," Torr stated, looking at his peacekeepers, who were gathered in the large conference room in the "business office" here at the gather site. It was situated next to the main gate and provided computer cubicles for the Winterhaven residents to use, a secure area to retreat to if needed, bathrooms for the peacekeepers, and a break room with snacks for their use, too. A handful of holding cells were in the back – just in case. There was a covered, wraparound porch to protect the people manning the gate, and others, from the weather, or getting too much sun.

"Whatcha got, boss?" Jake asked, looking ready to take on anything he might have for him. Torr smiled as the others gave nods in agreement. He passed out copies of a sketch Raffa made yesterday for him. It was based on Shams' last memory of the man they needed to keep an eye out, to help protect Ryes. Salls looked at the picture curiously, while Jake gave a nod of his head, looking to Jim, as their eyes met.

"I've seen him," Salls commented, looking up to Torr, who had returned to the front of the room. Torr gave him a nod.

"His name is Albon and comes from Apayal, which is on the northwest coast. He's after Ryes, but we're not sure to just try to kidnap her, or to kill her," he told them with a grim look in his honey-colored eyes.

"What do you want us to do if we see him, Torr?" Brett asked, with a serious look in his eyes.

"Keep him in sight and let me know right away," he replied. He got nods in response from the team, which made him smile. They each took keen responsibility in doing their best. He was proud of his people. "The only other item that's new is there's a strong Mind Voice Ruskin woman who's out looking for Ryes, too. From the sound of the way she's pressing things, she is not friendly to anyone. She rapes people's minds with her Talent! So, be aware if she comes asking about Ryes. Call it in immediately." This got nods from the other people in understanding. A strong Mind Voice could be dangerous to them all!

"Let's get to work," Jim suggested, which got a few chuckles, and a nod from Torr.

"Yes, let's get to work," Torr agreed. Jim smiled as he tucked the sketch into his shirt pocket, stood and checked his belt, then headed for the door.

"That Albon guy turned up at our merchant booths," Brett advised over his headset in English to the security channel.

"Which one?" Jim asked, sounding ready to wade in to help.

352

"The weapons one, of course," he replied. "Looks like he's brought four others along. Talk about ballsy," Brett added.

"Keep your eyes open and watch for now," Jim responded, "I'm on my way."

"Me, too," Torr added, "I want to see this man in person, but be careful. We don't know anything about him yet, especially since he's not alone."


Albon stood and openly scowled, his dark, swarthy-looking features were scrutinizing everyone and everything around him in sour disapproval in his yellow eyes. He was tall, with black hair that was neatly braded and held back from his face with a gaudy, gem-encrusted clasp. His clothes appeared specially tailored out of fine materials, which were dyed in a riot of clashing colors, and the rings and bracelets he wore each appeared to have come from different origins, almost as if they were flashy trophies from old conquests. He observed one of his servants practiced using a bow. This sales tent was more a structure than a mere tent. He noted any arrows that missed their targets hit the walls and fell to the floor, but were in essence, unharmed. It must've been made by a very experienced Earth Shaper. And he wondered what was on the second level? Storage? Their craft shop?

He was a bit miffed that the merchants refused to sell him a crossbow, or one of the higher-grade compound bows, saying they only had regular hunting bows for sale today. Other customers had accepted this, happily practiced, then left with their treasured purchases. Albon wanted to make sure his servant was able to shoot with as much accuracy, as possible, so he could teach him the feel of this simple-looking device. He doubted it would kill anything of any size, looking at the shafts of the arrows he held in his hands, pondering them.

"Are you satisfied?" one of the men, who ran the booth, asked, after his servants had been practicing shooting the bow for almost an hour. He appeared intently interested in him and his party, watching them all very carefully. Other Winterhaveners had been coming and going from the booth, too. All seemed interested in him, the servants with him, and the other people, who had already made their choices and left. No one could possibly walk off with even some arrows by accident! It was like they had them counted and noted exactly where each one was stored.

"I haven't had my chance, yet. I've been waiting for my servant to get a feel for this device, so he'd be able to help me with it," Albon gruffly explained, keeping just shy of belligerence with some effort. He saw the naked doubts in the man's eyes. He didn't believe him but gave him a nod.

"We're closing this booth for the day in a few minutes, so please take your turn now, or come back tomorrow," he firmly replied, then turned and went back to the entrance, never seeing the fury in Albon's eyes.

"What is the point of all this?" Muss asked, as he'd been standing behind Albon watching the practice session, too. "It's boring." Albon turned and glared him back to silence.

"If I can't have her, I'll kill her with one of their own weapons," he told them all in a low voice. "That would be sending a message to their leader, her husband." Tok appeared to have finished, as he spent his last arrow and turned back to look at his owner.

"What do you think? Would it actually kill someone?" Albon pressed, a fire in his eyes. Tok paled at his fury, took a moment to adjust his tunic, then looked back up to Albon.

"It will kill," he replied, carefully handing him the bow. "Give it a try and see how it handles." Albon took the bow and examined it again, seeing the simple construction and gave the cord a test pull, feeling the strength of it, then gave Tok a nod.

"Show me," he invited, an evil look in his eyes. Tok hesitated a heartbeat, then gestured his owner to step up next to him, so he could teach him the new weapon. He found he enjoyed handling it, with its simple ease of use, but now he had to be ready for the questions Albon would soon pelt him with during the lesson. He only hoped he wouldn't use him as a target to practice upon.


"Did you hear that?" Brent asked Torr in English, "he intends to kill Ryes with the bow, if he cannot simply take her." He'd replaced Stella, who had come out from Booda as he, when he saw Albon headed for this booth, since he recognized him from the morning's briefing. He knew how to run this booth, as he'd volunteered for this duty a few times, to get used to the strange, different people living on this amazing world. Brent had activated the listening device at that station, as he made it ready for Albon and his party to use, and it was now paying off. The anger in Torr's eyes was understandable. He'd been around the area of the booths from when Albon and his party showed up and was standing next to Brent, as if assisting with the booth, too.

"Why does he think he has any claim on Ryes?" Jim questioned over the security com channel, having heard the recording Torr had relayed over the channel. "I'm heading over to help, since there are five of them."

"Yeah, it's time to run them off empty-handed, with a really strong warning," Torr responded in a strong and steady voice, feeling this charade had gone on long enough. "All security who aren't currently busy, or on an assignment, come over to our weapons' booth." He heard affirmatives voiced and felt better about it. He waited at the booth's counter, ready.

"Sir, relax your shoulders, and focus," Tok advised in a low voice, appearing nervous. Albon lowered his arms and glared at him, as if his quiet reminder was an affront to his authority. Tok gave him a small bow and backed away from the practice railing, shifting to stand back, next to Muss. Muss gave Albon a small nod, so he turned back around to resume sending more shafts across the room to the targets that were already set up for use. It appeared that the more arrows he fired, the better he was getting at accuracy.

"More of their men have arrived and seem to be waiting," Muss observed. Tok merely nodded, having noted the four others, who'd joined the two who were manning the booth, already. "Keep watch, and let me know when they come toward us, Rohn."

He gave him a nod in understanding, not wanting to voice anything and possibly distract Lord Albon from his practice session, then have him punishing him for the transgression, as he could be vicious when he doled out his punishments. It often depended upon Albon's mood, using his fists, or whip, or a cane. Muss understood and gave him a nod in return. Rohn turned so he could keep the Winterhaveners in sight, while keeping Muss in his peripheral vision. He fingered the hilt of his throwing knife, as ready to defend Albon, as he could.

Several minutes later, Rohn saw there were now at least ten of their peacekeepers gathered, and they turned in unison toward them. Rohn was suddenly sweating but was not going to take his eyes off this mix of men, starmen and those odd others.

"Muss," he said with a note of strain in his voice. Muss turned and saw their peril. And how Rohn appeared ready to help defend them. His smile was grim, but he turned to look at Albon's back.

"Lord, it appears we have exhausted our welcome," he voiced loud enough to get his attention. Albon glanced over his shoulder, looking annoyed.

"I'm not done," he growled out, and loaded the heaviest shafted arrow on the stand next to him, but instead of turning to the targets, his stance spoke of readying an attack, but he wasn't yet facing the approaching men straight on, keeping his intensions unseen, as long as possible. A deep hate had been burning in his chest from the moment he walked into this building, as they did not treat him any differently than the commoners already here. Not a one waited upon him, nor gave him any respect due his rank and station. The hate was now rising to the surface, and he intended to put them into their place! He would not suffer to be treated as if he were nothing but a commoner!

Tok's eyes widened, then he shifted back to make sure he would be well out of his master's line of fire, crowding the new slave, Pell, whom he still didn't know if they could trust him to stand with them. He'd been very quiet, as if trying to figure out his new situation and position; having been purchased earlier in the morning. Pell being new to their team, Albon hadn't given him a weapon of any kind, yet. He would have to earn that. Pell saw Tok's fear, more of their lord, than the strange men approaching, and stepped back too, as far as he could.

"Your time is up," Torr stated flatly, his eyes brooking no arguments. "Gather YOUR things and leave. If you wish to make a purchase, you can bring that to the counter and it will be done there," he added. He saw Albon standing facing the wall to the right, as if he'd stopped before firing off his next arrow. He saw the intense hate in his gold eyes, as if they had no right to tell him what he could, or could not, do. He mentally girded himself for this confrontation, hating some of the royals they had to deal with at the gather.

"They're not moving," Jim commented in English, standing to Torr's left side. He had his blaster in hand, since it had the range the little pocket stunners didn't have, but they all had theirs set to the stun setting.

"You're not giving me this new weapon as a gift, due my station?" Albon demanded, meeting Torr's eyes. He was actually picking his target, as the leader stopped three long paces away. His quick eyes were taking everything in, seeing everyone in his party's position, and the expressions upon their faces.

"If you wish something given as a diplomatic gift, you'll have to talk to Garth, or Sabin," he replied, ready, as were his men. "Ours are only for sale and require a surrender of coins for the value of your purchase."

Albon nodded in response, then turned, as if he was going to put the bow and arrow down on the station's table, then suddenly spun about and loosed an arrow at Torr. Brent threw himself in front of Torr, as he saw what Albon was doing. As the flying shaft buried in his chest, his hand shook and his thumb hit the switch on the side of his blaster, as he fired at Albon in return.

Brent fell, as a surprised Torr caught him and lowered him to the floor. Brent was gasping, a hand clenched upon the shaft protruding from his chest. Torr heard a cry from before them but knew Jim would handle things, for Brent put his life on the line to save his. The slaves Albon brought with him charged their line. They were quickly stunned and rendered unconscious, and harmless. Torr called up his Healing to try to help Brent, but quickly realized this wound was far beyond his skill. Should he have cut the arrow shaft, as it protruded out his back, and pulled it out? He opened his eyes, seeing Jim standing beside them, looking ready to help.

"We need a full Healer, I can't do much here," Torr told Jim with a deep anguish in his eyes. Jim gave him a grim nod.

"I already called it in, but I'm not sure who's coming. They should be here any moment," he informed Torr. He pointed across the building at Albon's still body. "Looks like Brent got him, in return," he said. Torr stood and saw the tableau before him, inhaled deeply, then let it out in a rush.

"Sorry, I was trying to help Brent. Thanks for taking care of things, Jim," he replied, then shook of his head. "What a waste." In that moment, a party of Winterhaveners rushed in and Tennan hesitated for a moment, as if unsure of who needed her help more. Torr gestured her over to Brent, who was starting to look too pale. He'd tried to staunch the bleeding but was not sure of what he was doing. Minor injuries were easy for him now, but this was a deeper matter. He knew he needed more training but didn't have the time right now to take it. Tennan rushed over and immediately knelt on the floor by him, closing her eyes.

Torr picked up Brent's blaster to check it over. The device was like it was set halfway between the stun setting and the lethal energy mode, but it was the tiniest bit more toward the lethal setting, so was probably why the shot fired killed Albon. He sighed and nodded his head in understanding. Jim put out his hand for it, so Torr passed it over. He, too, examined it and nodded his head agreement, too. He was glad the drones had everything recorded for Garth to review later.

"Albon looks to have killed himself when he shot Brent," he stated.

"Talk about a twist of fate," Jake commented. "I've secured the body, so we can return it to their camp." He nodded toward the sleeping servants nearby with his chin. "Do we want them awake, or out cold when we deliver them, too?"

"Awake, but I want to talk to them first, one at a time," Torr asserted, as thoughts raced in his head. He realized he still had Brent's blood on his hands and turned to go clean them when he found Tennan weeping over Brent's body. He dropped to his knees beside her and put his arm around her shoulders.

"I couldn't…," she sobbed, suddenly clinging to his shoulder. He let her cry her heart out, truly understanding her disturbed heart. A Healer should be able to keep death at bay, but in this case, he felt even if it'd been Maren, or Ryes, it wouldn't have been enough. Brent chose to put himself in danger, and Torr knew he would have to think of a good way to honor his sacrifice.

"He carried no weapons, didn't charge us, and was at the back of the group as if he didn't know his place," Jake stated, as Jim came over to see who they'd bring upstairs first for questioning. Jim nodded agreement, seeing he was a good first choice to get a feel for this strange group of arrogant starmen.

357

"I agree... good first choice," he replied, as he pulled the starman to his feet, then over his shoulder, so he could take him upstairs. A grunt escaped him as he realized that while he did weigh, it wasn't as much as it should've been. They'd already moved Brent's body back to their camp, and he'd be back in Winterhaven soon, on the next shuttle run. Tennan had calmed down and was waiting upstairs to help ease the stunner's effect, so Torr could question these people.

"Thanks, Jim," Torr said, when he brought him in the open door of the small conference room. Torr helped him get the man to a chair, then Tennan stepped closer. Torr gave her a nod, so she gently touched his shoulder for a moment, then left the room. Pell awoke and looked around wildly. Jim had closed the door, locking it, and gave Torr a nod.

"What's your name?" Torr started, taking a chair next to their captive, but pulled back and over so he wasn't too close. He didn't want a table between them in case he needed to take action of some sort. Pell looked about the room in surprise for a moment, taking in Jim's different appearance, and Torr's frown.

"My name is Pell. I was a farmer from a small village outside of Berrals but was sold into slavery to pay off my father's debts. Lord Albion bought me this morning, and I had no idea what he was doing, nor what any of the other slaves were up to," he explained. He put his arm on the table and drew back the sleeve to show them the rope burns and whip marks. He was practically shaking, now. Torr nodded, seeing the rope burns were still partly raw and he wondered what he'd endured since being sold. How long had he been a slave?

"Do you know how much Albion paid for you?" Torr instantly asked, feeling he could believe this man. He gave him a nod, as he pulled his sleeve back down and took a breath.

"Three silvers and a Crown," he responded, meeting his eyes, seeing a sadness in them.

"I'm going to give you a choice, Pell. You can come live with us in Winterhaven, upon approval of a few others, or we can take you back to Albon's camp," he offered, steadily meeting his brown eyes.

"I'll take Winterhaven," he replied with no hesitation, having heard they don't keep slaves in their mixed village. Jim nodded with a smile, now.

"Take him to Tennan to help change his appearance first, then we'll get him back to our camp. Have Raya, or someone, double-check, and if he checks out, teach him English and the do's and don'ts there," Torr instructed in English.

"Are we keeping all his slaves?" he asked, curious now. He signaled Pell to stand and join him over at the door. The man wasn't steady, and Jim wondered when his last meal had been? Perhaps the shivers he was experiencing was a lack of food?

"No, as two of them seemed more dedicated to Albion and ready to help in the fight, but Pell and the one who was trying to teach Albon to shoot the bow might become a part of Winterhaven. I'd like to talk to that one next. As far as the other two will know, they died in the fight, too, and their bodies already taken away." Jim smiled as he gave Torr a nod, agreeing with his plan.

"I'll be right back," he promised, then gently took Pell's arm and unlocked the door. "We can't have you looking like you, so I'm taking you to a kind Healer who will help us with this ruse." Pell nodded, smiling in relief now and ready to be led out to a new life, once again. But this time his heart felt the warmth of hope.


"We're returning your lord to you for a proper burial rite, by your own customs," Sabin stated, as he, Torr, and four of their security people stood at the main Apayal campfire, talking with Albion's minister of state, whom they'd been brought to as the person to address about the man's death. The minister appeared mad at hearing it. They had wrapped Albon's body in a regular shroud, and it was now set on the ground nearby. Sabin opened the face cover to show him it was their lord, in truth. Even in the shroud, the stench was starting to build, so once the people around them had seen, he let it drop back down.

"How did this happen?" he demanded, now standing up to face them fully, having recognized Sabin from when he accompanied Albon to the Elder Council meeting. Muss stepped forward, bowing to him.

"Lord Minister, I was there, if you wish to hear my telling," he offered, giving the man a slight bow.

"Your own words, Muss, or theirs?" he pressed, glaring at all of them. Muss' cheeks seemed to color a moment, then he bowed again, before he saw the anger in his eyes at the insinuation.

"Only my own, Lord," he assured him, as he regained self-control. He got a nod of permission, so began. "Our Lord Albon had wished to obtain one of those new weapons the Winterhaveners sell, the bow and arrows. So, after the auction, where he purchased a new slave, we went to the building they have set up for the sale of their new weapons. He had Tok take a turn at practicing with them first, so he could assist him with their use," he said, then paused, seeing the growing ire in the Minister's eyes.

"And? Or Albon would be standing here to tell the tale himself," he pressed, appearing to believe the tale so far, but kept glancing over to Sabin's face, as if trying to see if he was trying to urge Muss on with his telling. Sabin's face was impassive as he listened to it, himself. Still, he was suspicious.

"After half the afternoon of practicing, they told us they were closing the booth soon. Albon ignored them and took over the bow and arrows, taking his turn at practicing, having watched Tok and having Tok explain it to him. After he'd fired off half his arrows, we were told to leave," his eyes briefly shifting over to Torr, then return to the minister, but he pointed to Torr. "He told us to leave, but Albon stalled, and when he stepped back to their counter to gather his men, I told the other slaves to be on the alert, so we could help our lord, if needed. Then they came and attacked us, and Lord Albon was killed."

"The last is not what happened," Torr stated in a low voice. Sabin nodded, having seen the recording.

"That's not what the drones recorded," Sabin stated in a normal voice, facing the minister and the two slaves.

"Yes, it is!" Rohn protested, appearing scared. Sabin pointed to a minute machine hovering over their heads with a grim smile.

"We use these for several reasons, but recording the truth is the main one," he told them. The minister looked at the strange device with open doubt, hate, and some fear.

"How?" he demanded, knowing Winterhaven's reputation. Sabin nodded, then pulled out a display device he carried with him today. He'd learned to not bother explaining how they worked, as just showing the images usually sufficed. He activated and they could all see it was showing them gathered from its' overhead viewpoint. The minister scowled, then noted it clearly showed his face with that expression.

"This is what happened," Sabin pressed, as he changed to the recording and held it so the minister, the elders, and Muss could clearly see it. Rohn tried to crowd Muss, but he elbowed him away, which was noted by the main participants, and others, who were now gathering near them, in spite of the body's smell. The screen played out the whole thing, and it was clearly seen that Albon had started the attack, and while he died, he'd deliberately killed one of the Winterhaveners.

"What is the value of the man's life he took?" the Minister pressed, wanting an accounting of sorts.

"He came from Booda, one of the moons of Tyssen, so just getting him to Tayna cost a small fortune. Then there was the cost of training and showing him the way we value our people. He's worth far more than your lord," Sabin answered, knowing where he'd be going with his question. It was cold and common here at the gather. "A life for a life and we'll consider the scales balanced." Then he tossed the minister the bag of coins he'd brought for this moment. He caught it clumsily but hefted it.

"Then, what is this," he demanded, almost growling.

"For the two slaves who were accidentally killed in the fight," Torr supplied with a nod. "It was inappropriate for my men to not have checked the weapon settings more carefully." One of the other men, from the crowd gathering around them stepped forward, as the minister appeared about respond with some anger.

"What are we going to do without a Lord? His heirs are still young and not ready to run our city, nor know anything about any of us, nor how to make sure we are strong and well defended," he pleaded with something like panic on his face. The other men and women in the camp gathered closer to be a part of this too, adding in their own voices to express their uncertainty.

"Prove this is the truth to us, and that they're not some created images!" an older woman demanded. She appeared to be an elder and was angry. Sabin looked around at the others, then gave a nod; his air of authority kept the people gathered calm even in their uncertainty. Their guards had appeared, but even they stood back, appearing unsure if they needed to take action.

"Do you have any Mind Voice Talents here?" he asked, appearing unafraid. He'd already put in request for help from the Winterhaven camp using his own Mind Voice, as soon as the people crowded close, as they were first shown to the fire. He wanted to make sure he and Torr would make it back alive!

"I have Mind Voice," one of Albon's people volunteered, stepping forward with a wary look on his face.

"I do, too," a young woman said, stepping up beside the first declared Talent. She was smiling her defiance, as the minister had shaken his head no at her.

"And we have Mind Voice," Raffa and Poli stated, as they and their escort joined the others. Sabin nodded, relieved. They had just doubled the number of security men.

"Could you please assist in letting these people see the truth of the events I want them to know?" he requested. Raffa gave him a nod, as did the two Apayal Talents. He handed his display device to Jake, and stepped forward, extending his hands, one to Poli and one to the young, defiant woman.

Sabin didn't close his eyes and let Poli control the link. He saw the Apaylan people closing their eyes and joining hands, even the minister. The other Talents closed their eyes, as they brought in the rest of the gathered people into the commune. It took a few minutes to get everyone settled, but once they were, he opened up glimpses of their voyage to Tyssen and the rescue of the Boodans. This had everyone amazed by the starved appearance of the Boodan people, the amazing spacecraft, and enchanting views of space, itself. Next, he nodded at Torr and motioned with his head to Torr, who then stepped over to join the link. The rest of the security team remained out of it and alert, watching the others in the camp, as Sabin had told them to, before coming here.

Torr showed them the base circumstances of Albon's visit and subsequent death at their booth; that as he tried to kill him, it was Brent's blocking the arrow and his shot that killed Albon. He left out all his emotions, even as he was trying to Heal Brent and failed. They'd each trained enough in their regular sessions to be able to do this with ease. When they were all finally released from this sharing, Sabin looked at the people around them and gave them a nod.

"Now that you've seen the truth, do you believe our earlier display?" Sabin asked the minister.

"Your Talents are not trained as ours," he stated, a curiosity in his eyes. Sabin shook his head at this.

"No. Some were trained in the old ways of Kahmarr, and others were trained elsewhere, but we've blended and expanded our different disciplines and have gained better focus," he explained. "Do you see our truth, now?" he repeated.

"Will you train others in your ways?" he pressed, a light showing greed in his eyes that didn't make Sabin feel comfortable.

"We only train Winterhaven Talents in our ways," Sabin assured the minister. "Are you now satisfied with what we told you had happened?" The minister looked at the bag of coins in his hand, appearing lost in thought for a moment. He finally gave Sabin a nod of his head in agreement.

Having gotten a nod in response, Torr and Sabin turned to leave, gathering their four men, who had helped carry the body here, as well as their lady Talents and their escort, heading back to their own camp as a group. They heard the Apayal inhabitants starting to again question their minister about their future.

"Glad to be done with that," Torr commented in English in a low voice as they walked. Sabin nodded, hoping it was done, at least for now.

"He wanted Ryes' death, and only found his own ending. That makes a sad story," Poli observed. Raffa and Jake nodded their agreement.


"Pell, how do you feel about running a farm for us?" Ryokisin asked with a warm smile. She'd just finished giving him an understanding of English and how they conducted their lives here in Winterhaven. He seemed to be still grasping all she gave him in their quick session. After a moment, he finally seemed to realize what she offered.

"A farm? Run a farm?" he questioned, not quite believing he heard her right. "Yes, I might enjoy that kind of job," he added, feeling a sense of worth strengthened his spirit. Perhaps something that might finally feel like home.

"You'll still have some orientation classes to attend, but yes, we can offer you a farm to manage," she assured him. "Have you seen the changes Tennan wrought for you? What do you think?" He smiled and gave a happy laugh.

"My own mother wouldn't know me now.  I like the light brown hair and golden eyes, and my new face shape is very interesting.  It might take me a while to get used to it, but it's fine.  And she erased all my scars and wounds, then strengthened my body, again.  I didn't get a chance to thank her," he replied, grinning now. "I didn't know Healers could do something like all this to a person."

"Our Talents practice all the time, and we each stretch out to try new things.  The changing a person's appearance is something new that Tennan's been exploring, as a way to strengthen her abilities.  I rather like your new look, myself," she explained, laughter in her eyes, now.

"Thank you, Ryokisin," he offered with a small bow.

"You may call me Ryo," she told him with a smile. "You look good.  Now it's Tok's turn," she added.  He nodded and stood up, signing Tok to step over for his turn.

"Your turn with Ryo," he let him know, as he approached from across the room.  There were a small group of slaves waiting for their chance to learn more about their new lives, but only the two of them hadn't been "purchased" in the normal way.

"Wait for me, Pell?" Tok asked, not wholly comfortable in this strange place.  Even if he didn't know Pell as well as the other slaves that belonged to Albon, he was someone he felt he could trust.

"Sure," he replied, and went to take a seat nearby, while Tok turned and sat down by Ryo.  She smiled at Tok.  Pell felt charged with the thought of a whole new life ahead of him!

# Childhood's Illusions

## Chapter 31

"Are you going to catch that fun-sounding play Maren and Dotti were teasing us about last night?" Denas asked Ryes, as she was finishing with feeding the cubs their lunch. Denas had come to realize that five little ones at one time were a lot to manage, making her glad she and Monty were only having one! Ryes turned to her with a happy smile lighting up her green eyes.

"That sounds fun and will get me out of our camp for a bit," she replied, then grinned mischievously, "I think I have a case of camp fever, being trapped here almost all the time, and am so tired of endless Talent practices." Dunn laughed upon hearing her complaints.

"On Kisteela, if you were found to have Talent, ALL you were allowed to do was study and practice - for years," she informed Ryes. Rhodi nodded her head in agreement, while Aunt Raffa appeared appalled.

"It was the same on Kahmarr, and was horribly hard on the children," Rhodi related with a bitter smile. "I'll never forget those horrible, drudging years."

"Well, you and Klinn can make new lives for the both of you, now and can raised any Talented children you might have the way you choose," Raffa reminded her, which brought out happy smiles all around, as the women looked to realize they did have choices now they hadn't had before.

"We all have new lives," Denas agreed with a light laugh. "What're your plans now, Rhodi?" She blushed a little in response but gave her a small nod.

"We are going to stay for a period of time in both Winterhaven and Island Hold, to get used to being together. My having my own home might be the deciding factor in where we will live, in the end. Klinn only has a few small rooms to call his own in the hold, since he is the youngest son. I was wondering if we could invite Lelas and you, Ryes, to come visit the hold to help reshape it a bit?" she requested. Ryes frowned, noting she never mentioned her Aunt Adina, who was a very skilled Earth Shaper and sometimes took the time to teach her new Talent skills. It was like the Sleepers now knew her aunt's measure and didn't want to disturb her and Hadu, nor attract their attention.

"I'd love to help," she volunteered, lightening up again. "Kyma was thrilled with the changes we made to his own hold, even helping with the design changes in the meld, himself."

"I'm sure he enjoyed that," Denas commented with a laugh, "he's becoming a sensation junkie like the rest of us." Ryes chuckled and nodding her head.

"Overall, I don't mind the tours," Ryes stated, "it gives me more practice, and with everyone else along, it's more fun than just a personal exploration." There was light-hearted laughter around her, as the rest reminded her of their willing support to help further her training.

She grinned as she turned back to her cubs, who were being too quiet while they'd talked. They had to be up to something! As soon as they had her attention, Rhin raised up his arm and brought it down hard, knocking his bowl loose and slopping the last of his lunch all over himself and her. The rest started burbling in their baby talk and actually giggling. She sighed, then decided to use Manipulator instead of her cleaning cloth to help with the clean-up, realizing not only had he done it on purpose, but Rhin had waited until he had her attention. She thought about that while she cleaned. Her cubs were very smart, but she didn't want them using tactics like this to gain her attention. And since it seemed a group effort, she knew she'd have to work with them all. They needed her love and positive attention.

"Ryes?" Mive quested, as she stepped over to their table. She tried to appear official, but the smile on her lips and in her eyes was all hers. She'd changed and had found a way to fit in with the Winterhaveners, working in security, which had helped her to evolve into a more genuine person now. Ryes, who had just finished cleaning, smiled in response and gave Mive a nod. She relaxed, seeing she wasn't interrupting something important.

"Yes, Mive? How are your cubs faring?" she asked, her eyes alight with curiosity.

"They're growing so fast!" she replied, her smile warming and widening for a moment. "I came to tell you Garth sent a message for you to bring a tube of maps and printed documents he forgot in your shelter. He wanted you to bring it to the Elder Council personally."

"Thanks, Mive! And it's good to hear your cubs are thriving," Ryes said, then nodded to Mive, sighed, and turned to Denas and the other ladies.

"Save me a seat at the play?" she requested, "I'll be there as soon as I can; they can't keep me in that stuffy tent forever, but it might involve another tour of our solar system." Her cousin smiled her understanding.

"We will," Rhodi spoke up, smiling as she knew about responsibilities of holding an office. Ryes gave her a nod, then turned back to Mive.

"Please let him know I'll be there as soon as I can, after I get the cubs settled with the sitters, I'll need an escort and headset, which I can get at the gate on the way out."

"Right away," she replied, understanding cub care always came first. Mive headed to the gate post where their main communications were located. Ryes noted Mive's frame was still a bit thin and frail-looking from her life on Booda, but she'd been developing some serious muscles and was a smart warrior. She now fully trusted her to cover her back, if the need ever came.

Ryes was trying to walk at a brisk pace, so to get this errand done, then join the other women at the main entertainment stages to see the play. Monty, Lacon, and George were easily keeping pace with her, it was only having to weave in and out of the crowded pathways that frustrated her a bit, and occasionally, briefly separated her team from her and each other. The pathway itself was part worked stone, part dirt track, and occasional puddles, which sometimes reeked. As the path rounded the bole of a giant, leafy tree, a gray-skinned woman, who was dressed flamboyantly in a rainbow of bright colors all trimmed with real gold, deliberately stepped out to block her path. There was a look on her face that could almost be called gloating.

"Are you the one called Ryes Li? The granddaughter of Rowan of Matlowe Village?" the young Ruskin woman, with dark hair and eyes, demanded in a rough voice, which seemed hedged with malice. She was standing in her path, as Ryes was heading toward the Elder Council's tent, appearing to be purposefully blocking her. Garth needed the tube of maps, and she didn't want to stop to chat right now. George shifted to stand between them, as soon as it appeared this woman was not going to let them through. He was eyeing this strange, gray-skinned woman who sneered at him; it looked to put a chill up his back.

"Yes, I'm Ryes of House Li and Rowan is my grandfather," she replied in the proper form, distracting her gaze from George. "And who might you be?" she asked, not knowing any Ruskins yet. She hadn't had the chance to visit the other, established camps, to get to know all the different peoples here at the gather. This gather she'd ended up spending most of her time in their camp, or taking short trips home on the shuttles, due to the different threats leveled against her. Getting to run errands for Garth was now a fun diversion most times, but she wanted to see that play and didn't want to be tied up. She rarely got to take the time to enjoy a diversion like watching a play. And if Maren recommended this one, it had to be entertaining, at least, with their having lived among the caravanners and humans for some time now. Their entertainments had been varied and amazing most times back at home.

"I am Fanya of Cassos and had stayed at Matlowe for a winter, when we were both young. I've heard you have Talent, Ryes," she replied with derision in her eyes. Ryes' face took on a look of pure wonder, not recognizing the hate in Fanya's eyes, nor in her voice, in this moment.

"Fanya? Truly Fanya?" she questioned, stepping forward to stand next to George. But, even if she was pleased, she finally noted this woman wasn't so, in return. What could this woman want from her? "Are you not the child I played with for a whole winter, back in Matlowe Village?" she pressed, needed some true confirmation.

"I am she, but I got over it long ago. We played, but I was bored, and had no one else to entertain me. After all, the only thing Darman wanted to teach me was history and writing lessons. I'd rather play with you, than be bored with those old, musty scrolls," she stated, smiling wickedly. Yes, it seemed she remembered her and their time together differently, Ryes thought, her brows still furrowed.

"But I thought we were friends," Ryes returned, not understanding this change in her once friend. She felt a little hurt by this revelation, that she'd never valued their fun times together.

"Friends?" she spat out, hatefully. "I was never your friend; you were so easy to dupe!"

"Watch it," Monty whispered in her ear, in English, having stepped up next to Ryes' other side. He didn't trust this strange woman. Something about her made his skin crawl, and it wasn't because she was of another people, again. He'd met plenty of her kind here and found the Ruskins like anyone else in attitude and needs. But her surface thoughts were blocked, which he found interesting, and so had up his own mental defenses up fully now.

"We're talking, you imbecile!" she shouted at him in anger, but this odd man stood his ground. A third, a starman, stood behind Ryes, covering her back, too. Suddenly, Ryes got a radio message from Garth.

"Ryes? Where are you? I need those maps," he requested. She pulled the mic down, activating it.

"On the way. I've just run into an old friend, Fanya, who seems aggressive. I'll be there soon," she replied, using English. She left the mic on, so he and the others on their main channel here would know what was going on. She felt Fanya probing her mind and shut her out, hard. She then made sure she couldn't get to anyone else with her, with Monty on the alert and having done the same as she, already. Their practice sessions were priceless!

"You do have Talent," Fanya commented, in a low voice that almost purred with excitement. Her smile now held a touch of menace.

"Yes, I do. But right now, I've got to finish the errand I was assigned. I'll talk with you, later. I can stop by your camp, and we can catch up on our life paths then," she replied, stepping around her, but she moved to block her again.

"I'm more important, you're staying here to talk with me now," she stated, her black eyes were fire and ice.

"You're not more important than my husband," she returned, starting to get angry with her. Monty moved to come between them, then Fanya shoved him away, using Manipulator. Ryes stopped it, blocking her, once more. It was something Doran liked to do. Monty got to his feet seeing the absolute fury in Ryes' emerald eyes. "No one uses Talent like that against others! It's even written in the laws passed down from old."

"I do what I want," Fanya returned, tossing her long green hair over her shoulder, a feral look in her black eyes now. "And no one can stop me from doing what I want." Ryes suddenly thrust the map tube at George, since he was less practiced in defense tactics.

"Take this to Garth. Tell him I'm a little busy," she ordered. He hesitated and appeared uncertain, but Monty took it from Ryes' hand and pushed it to him, anyway.

"Do it," he added, activating his mic and telling Torr the situation and where they were in English on the security channel. George ran onward, Fanya let him go at least, but it was obvious that she understood the importance of their radio communications and appeared frustrated that she didn't understand what they were saying.

"You only bring more to suffer," Fanya taunted. Ryes stood face to face with her, her green eyes hard, waiting. "I would love to tear your precious husband to pieces, since he thinks he owns all Tayna," she added maliciously.

"Don't be stupid. Whatever it is you want, just let it go. You're not going to get anything from me, nor get near my husband," Ryes replied. The crowd around them on the path was growing, with most shifting back, realizing something was up. There were no booths near them for others to retreat around, being only trees, rock and brush. Many grabbed their young ones, or friends, and turned and fled, not wanting a part of whatever conflict was coming. Two angry women with Talents could get dangerous! Yet, some people crowded closer to watch what they could of the coming conflict.

"I heard you were a strong Talent, so I'm here to see just how strong you are. You remember when you ate one of my rouu fruits? I'm sure you don't recall too much about it, but I was the one who got you to do it. You were such a little goodie-goodie, always doing what your grandfather and those caravanners said, and it made me sick. I was amazed you didn't die; I had hoped otherwise. It would've been fun," she baited her, grinning again. "So, this time I'm going to finish the job and watch you die, as painfully as I can make it. I can't stand goodie-goodies!" She pulled out two long, curved knives from her belt and hefted them in her hands, all the while looking directly into Ryes' eyes with her naked malice.

"Please, Fanya," a voice implored, as a Ruskin man stepped out of the growing crowd surrounding them and stepped up beside her. "Don't do this, you could get hurt."

"Go away Tentus, you bore me," she returned, kicking him hard, mostly on his hip. He fell heavily, as if his motor control over his arms and legs was suddenly all wrong. This sickened Ryes, but she kept her concentration upon her opponent. Fanya struck, thinking Ryes was distracted by Tentus, using her Mind Voice with full intensity, keeping her eyes open, while she struck out with one of her very-sharp blades. Ryes was surprised at her power, but deflected it with little effort, and ducking her strike calmly.

Lacon went to help the Ruskin man at Monty's motion and nod, seeing he acted as if drunk. There was no smell of alcohol from him, which was puzzling, as he sat him up under a nearby tree. He kept an eye to the crowd, as he stood near him, hoping he could still be of some help. He didn't have a Talent like Monty, so could do little to aid Ryes in this contest in that manner. And at least he could guard her back from other physical attacks out of the crowd. He saw Monty had his small stunner concealed in his hand, so pulled his own out, ready to use if needed.

"You are nimble and have strong Mind Voice, I see," she returned, then struck out at Monty. He couldn't bar her fully from his mind, dropping to his knees as Ryes again deflected Fanya's attack with her Talent and tried to block her long knife with her small belt knife, but Monty was still deeply cut down one arm. She instantly melded with him, like they did in practice, to help protect him. Now it was Lacon she feared for, keeping alert to any attacks Fanya might try against him.

As Lacon was watching the crowd around them, the man he helped sat up and struck at him with a knife, which was now in his hand. He was only grazed on the leg, as he managed to jump back to avoid a second swing. The man moved sluggishly, but the look in his eyes and face was one of pure panic, as if he had no control of what his body was doing.

"You're using him like a puppet!" Ryes shouted, reviled by such usage. "That's against the Laws we want to establish!" She found the "strings" and cut them, freeing him. He fell to the ground, unconscious, just as Lacon was going to stun him. She felt bad, but couldn't spare another second to check him, to be sure if he was all right. That gave her a small twinge, but she wouldn't divide her attention. Monty was tapping her Healing to repair what Fanya had done to him with her long knife.

"It's so simple, truly," she returned in a deep, emotionally filled voice, reaching out to take Ryes' Talentless man for her own use. She flung one of her long knives at Lacon's head, but he'd put up an arm and tried to duck the blade. It was buried deep in his shoulder, as he cried out in shock and pain. Then Lacon was struggling against her trying to control him like a puppet, as she had the Ruskin man, and resisted with everything he had, but as she overwhelmed him, Fanya was suddenly, completely, blocked out, but it didn't feel like Ryes, which startled her for a moment, wondering who else here had such power.

Rhodi, Dunn, Denas and Raffa stepped into the cleared area through the crowd, anger in their eyes. They'd heard everything, over the open mics and had instantly linked up with Ryes, as soon as they were in range. It surprised them how far out that range was now.

"Our people are not for you to use!" Dunn shouted out, furiously. Raffa immediately stepped over, healing Lacon's wounds, as she pulled the knife out of his shoulder.

"This is between Ryes and me. You keep out!" she warned, striking out at them with all her mental might. She was rebuffed, but not as easily as Ryes had done, alone. Still, there was true power here, as well; she'd have to destroy these women next.

"We at Winterhaven look out for our own. If you chose to challenge Ryes, you are then choosing to challenge all of us," Rhodi told her, her voice carried ice, while a deep anger flashed in her eyes. They stepped over to stand with Ryes and Monty, forming the inner meld more solidly through Monty's Talent, leaving Ryes to respond. She was still in contact with him.

"Stop this Fanya, or I'll be forced to act," Ryes warned her. She saw Garth, Darman, Sabin, Ethan and Kyma push through the crowd, behind Fanya.

"What? Toss me about in the air, like you did to that thief you caught? I have Manipulator, too," she replied. "I can counter everything you can throw at me and will merely throw it right back."

Then with a loud cry, Fanya flung herself at Ryes, throwing her full weight behind the thrust of her blade, as well as using Manipulator. Ryes knew her belt knife was useless as a defense against that, but her held it up and added her own Manipulator as the best counter she could use. Their blades clashed and Ryes had hers knocked from her hand, almost having Fanya severing her hand, but she finally deflected her enough with her Talent, and shoved her back hard. Fanya's reflexes had her sliding back, still on her splayed feet, the bloodied knife still in a death grip, while her black eyes still blazed with fury. Tears flowed from Ryes' eyes, but other than staunching the blood flowing from her hand and arm, didn't take the time to concentrate and heal her wounds now. The pain was immense, but she used it to fuel her determination in this fight for her life!

"Stop this, right now!" another Ruskin man ordered. He was an elder, who appeared so old, his gray skin was almost an alabaster color. He'd rushed out with Garth and the others out of the Elder's tent. "Leave Fanya alone!"

"I haven't done a thing to Fanya, only blocked her attacks on me and my friends," Ryes replied, astounded at the implication, afraid of the distraction, as she kept her eyes on her opponent. But Fanya appeared to be trying to plot her next attack, ignoring the elder Ruskin. "She chooses to challenge me. I would rather go see some of the new plays, in truth."

"Tentus? What've you done to him?" he insisted, instead, seeing her bloody hand and arm. Raffa was now Healing him, having taken care of Lacon. Jake, Torr and another half dozen of their guards were pushing through the crowd, joining them.

"Fanya was using him like a puppet," Rhodi told him, seeing this man was also under some kind of control. She reached out and severed the ties, having seen the way Ryes freed the other man. "As were you," she added. He suddenly reeled, his arms outstretched, then was clutching at Darman's robe to steady himself. Ethan caught him up in his arms until he could gain his feet again.

"These are my toys, to do with as I please!" Fanya shouted, absolutely furious that her puppets were being released, and she didn't have the time now to take them back under her control. She struck out at Ryes again, this time using her Manipulator. Ryes countered it but was thrown back into Torr's arms. He helped her back to her feet, seeing her utter rage now. He took a step back from Ryes, recognizing it.

"You're not going to abuse anyone, anymore," Ryes replied, her voice low and full of menace. She closed her eyes, knowing Garth and the others wouldn't let her body come to harm, then reached out with her Catalyst Talent from the few steps away that she was from Fanya. She was loathe to touch her now, but she searched for the inner core of Fanya's Talents.

Fanya struggled against her, and they truly fought, where few could see, Fanya's instincts telling her what she might be after. She bent her will, trying at a mental killing blow with all her might, then seeing that was useless, switched to use her Mind Control, which she easily used on others to control their bodies. Ryes, not understanding this Mind Control Talent, faltered and almost fell completely under Fanya's control. She felt her body responding to Fanya's will, with her good hand reaching for her beltknife, picking it up, and turning it to strike into her own body. She fought for control of her arm and could clearly feel Fanya's glee. It was a hard struggle and many in the crowd around them guessed what was happening, and were upset, Garth chief among them.

"I think I need to help," he said to Darman, who nodded. But, as he stepped forward, the rest of the people in the meld helped anchor Ryes' mind and soul, so she once more had a true sense of herself. Ryes felt buoyed and a moment later, her hand dropped the beltknife, as she once again regained control and resumed her search for Fanya's Talents.

"NO! Don't!" Fanya yelled out, dropping to her knees, dropped her remaining knife, as she clutched her head and closed her eyes, genuinely frightened for the first time in her life. This alarmed the onlookers as they shifted back, not knowing what it was Ryes was doing to her. At last, Ryes found her Talent core and burnt it out. She made well sure there were no signs of Talent within her whole being. Finally, she withdrew and opened her eyes. Fanya lay sobbing upon the ground.

"Now you can't hurt anyone with your Talents, ever again," Ryes stated with exhaustion in her voice, knowing Fanya knew this truth already.

"How? How did you do that?" she demanded, sitting up and wiping at her eyes. Deep hatred was still in her black eyes.

"I'm a Catalyst, after all," she returned.

"But a Catalyst activates a Talent!" she protested.

"Yes, I can," she replied, then turned away from her, meeting Garth's eyes. "Sorry about this," she apologized, knowing she disrupted their meeting. He stooped down and picked up her beltknife, handing it to her. She returned it to its sheath, as she opened Healing fully and took care of her hand and arm now.

"I'm free!" the Ruskin elder stated, finally pulling away from Ethan's support. The man Raffa healed stood up and was amazed, as if looking upon the world for the first time with joy in his eyes.

"You don't control us anymore, witch!" Tentus shouted, stepping over and pulling Fanya to her feet by her hair, as she was trying to scramble away from him, seeing he was alert and knew his own mind. He shook her, his fury plain upon his face. "We'll have a special tribal meeting to determine your fate, you evil harridan!"

"No, No! I didn't mean it!" she wailed, grabbing at his hand, as he still held onto her. It was ineffective. She pulled out a belt knife, meaning to use it on him, but her hand was grabbed, and the knife twisted out of it by a young Ruskin man, who had come running to see what was happening, and had watched from out of the crowd. She shrieked and cried out in pain. He grabbed the sheath out of her pocket, then sheathed it and put it into his own. He got a nod of approval from Tentus, as he helped restrain her arms.

"Get some proper chains," he ordered another Ruskin behind him. He bowed and ran away. "You're not going to get away from this!" he shouted at her, as she cringed, blinking up at him as if awakening.

"Are you all right?" Garth asked, as he took his wife into his arms, appearing to want to shelter her from this chaos.

"I feel slime-coated, but am fine," she assured him. He deactivated her mic, pushing it up and out of the way. Then he kissed her, relieved she was fine. The rest of the Winterhaveners gathered around them, laughing in relief. "I truly thought we were friends when we were cubs. It's sad to see what she's become," she told them in English, in a low voice, as Monty dissolved the meld.

"People sometimes change for the worse. She obviously didn't think of you with any fondness, at all," Garth replied in kind.

"We can still make the next play, if we hurry cousin," Denas urged, wanting to get her out of this crowd. Ryes smiled, giving her a nod of her head. Garth let her go, chuckling as he nodded his head in agreement. The Ruskin elder pushed through to them, followed by another younger man.

"We're deeply in your debt, how can we ever repay you?" he asked, meeting her eyes. Ryes shook her head, not truly wanting this attention, after all.

"I'm fine. But you could talk with my husband and maybe there are interests which would be beneficial to both our peoples?" she suggested, smiling. "I'll see you later," she promised Garth, then left with most of the Winterhaveners, who'd come to her rescue.

"Oh, you're so beautiful!" Sabin declared, as he ran up to Ryes and swept her off her feet, up into a tight hug, laughing as he did it. Ardis looked on with questions in her eyes, and surprise written upon her face, as he finally put Ryes back down on the ground. He then ran over and started kissing Ardis next.

"Ack! At least I can breathe, now. What's the matter with you, Sabin?" Ryes demanded, utterly embarrassed. There was laughter from behind her, as Garth and the elders joined them at their smaller fire. They could still hear the singing and dancing from over at their main fire.

"Because of you, we finally have a commanding presence in the Council," Garth explained as he wrapped his arms about her next. "Your urging the Ruskin head elder, Yuthis, to talk with us finally gave us the breakthrough we needed. We're forging a treaty with them now and have their active support. We're that much closer to having a united Tayna with the different peoples they're bringing in with their alliance!" She laughed as he bent to kiss her. Their friends and family, who were gathered around the fire were excited, seeing they finally had the advantage they needed.

"Sure, you get hugs and kisses and all I get is a headache," Monty teasingly complained, grinning merrily, not having voice it earlier with all the fuss after the fight. He'd tried to Heal it during the confrontation but had shifted to holding the meld steady through the conflict.

"Oh, do you want a kiss too?" Garth teased in return, letting his wife go and holding out his arms in Monty's direction, making a smacking noise. There was laughter from around them at this.

"Not from you, Garth! But I'll settle for one from my own, sweet wife," he replied, chuckling merrily as he leaned toward Denas. She gave him a kiss, with mischief in her eyes. Maren leaned forward and put a hand upon his head, fully easing his pain for him, as well as truly finishing the healing on his arm.

"Congratulations," Captain Yun told them, standing up to shake Garth's hand. "Chance brings what she may, but sometimes she smiles brightly," he added, as they clasped hands.

"That she does," Rowan agreed, as Ethan nodded his head. Even Metta was excited with the way this day ended, and all the new horizons which were now open before them.

"I still couldn't believe the way Fanya changed and behaved! What happened to her? Why would she be so evil with controlling people that way?" Ryes asked, not expecting any answers.

"I think it might've started when she lost her parents and brothers in that flood, when she was young. She was all alone and helpless, living with other villagers for years before I was asked to take her to her family. And I had to leave her with an uncle and aunt who were indifferent, at best. Her cousins didn't like her much, either. With no love around, her hate might've been all she had left," Darman told her, shaking his head as he sat down by the fire. He was still feeling a chill after what he witnessed earlier.

"That and when her Talent awakened, she might've suffered, with no one to care about her struggle," Maren put in, seeing something in this woman's forging, too.

"Her Talents were strong," Ryes agreed. "It might've driven her a little further down the path of madness. The way she was using the people around her like puppets... I never thought of using Mind Voice in such a way, and never will," she commented, then shivered as a chill traveled up her back. She didn't intend to ever use it to control others that way!

"It's actually a Ruskin-only Talent called Mind Control, and I feel sorry for the people she heartlessly used. I'd never seen it in action, before," Denas added, nodding her head, as they still strove to comprehend this enigma. "So, she actually had three Talents."

"What did they do to her?" Monty questioned, wanting to know, even if he knew Ryes didn't.

"She was put to death," Sabin told them, sitting down next to Ardis. Garth and the others sat too, grabbing for mugs of coffee and tea. "At least they made it quick," he finished, drawing a finger across his throat. Ryes inwardly shuddered at the thought, wishing there could've been something to salvage.

"And her two children will be raised by their father, Yorrh. Tentus, the man she tried to use to attack Lacon, was her uncle, the one Darman left her with, originally," Ethan put in, letting Ryes know there was some happiness, which came out of this situation at least.

"It's hoped the children have strong Talents, too. I advised Yuthis to let you, or Denas, check them for Talent tomorrow. So, you can expect a visit," Garth warned them, smiling.

"They're the grayish-skinned people, or the blue ones?" Loren quietly asked Monty.

"The gray-skinned ones," Sabin replied in a normal voice, giving her a wink. "The Ruskins aren't too bad as a people, we just can't eat their food, nor drink that purple stuff they love to drink. It looks kind of strange, anyway," he added. Loren was surprised but smiled as she realized they didn't object to their presence here with them, even if they were discussing what she thought of as affairs of state. Maddy even looked thoughtful, as she watched Monty and Denas snuggling together, here by the fire. It was as if she were still deciding something.

"Eating a piece of their fruit almost killed me, when I was a child," Ryes told them, recalling Fanya's taunts, as she blocked their way.

"I think my mother's rudimentary Talent, which was operating in the background, may have been the only thing to save you then," Maren commented, remembering that time, too. He sat watch over his cousin for almost two weeks, on his mother's behalf, when she had to be elsewhere.

"Yes, it has to be the answer," Rowan agreed, smiling as he thought he was going to lose her back then. Tanns had saved her, despite her dislike for Ryes, at the time.

"That was just another lesson I had to learn the hard way," she returned, grinning. Darman and Rowan laughed at this, nodding their heads.

"You did everything that way," Rowan scolded, with a warm light in his brown eyes, showing his humor clearly. She smiled, recalling some of their arguments. Still, she'd made it and grew up in spite of Fanya's efforts to end her life then, as well as today's attack.

"Thank you, everyone, for all the help," she said, voicing what was in her heart, feeling grateful.

"You are welcome," Denas voiced, as Monty nodded, smiles all around. Garth's arm around her waist tightened and he leaned over, giving her cheek a kiss. She finally laughed, as his breath tickled her neck and made different shivers run up her spine. Everything was as it should be, once again.

*The End of Book Six*

For more books, please visit:

www.mariedaley.com

www.ingramcontent.com/pod-product-compliance
Lightning Source LLC
Chambersburg PA
CBHW051317190726
48290CB00001B/189